Love is
a time of enchantment:
in it all days are fair and all fields
green. Youth is blest by it,
old age made benign:
the eyes of love see
roses blooming in December,
and sunshine through rain. Verily
is the time of true-love
a time of enchantment — and
Oh! how eager is woman
to be bewitched!

THE FLAME AND THE FROST

Following GOLD FOR THE GAY MASTERS and BRIDE OF DOOM, this story recounts the fortunes of the third-generation orphan, Charlotte Goff. Adopted by the noble widow Lady Chase, Charlotte is seduced by Lady Chase's handsome but heartless son, Vivian. In the enforced marriage that follows, in Charlotte's desperate attempts to give her husband a son and heir, in her intense passion for another man, Dominic, the dark strain in the ill-fated family blood once again shows itself.

DENISE ROBINS

◆

THE FLAME AND THE FROST

Complete and Unabridged

ULVERSCROFT
Leicester

First published in Great Britain

First Large Print Edition
published 1998

British Library CIP Data

Robins, Denise, *1897 – 1985*
    The flame and the frost.—Large print ed.—
Ulverscroft large print series: romance
1. Love stories
2. Large type books
I. Title II. Gray, Harriet *1897 – 1985*
823.9'12 [F]

ISBN 0–7089–3909–0

Published by
F. A. Thorpe (Publishing) Ltd.
Anstey, Leicestershire
Set by Words & Graphics Ltd.
Anstey, Leicestershire
Printed and bound in Great Britain by
T. J. International Ltd., Padstow, Cornwall

This book is printed on acid-free paper

Part One

1

ON that bitterly cold afternoon of January, in the year 1870, London was enveloped in a thick yellow fog.

Sounds were muffled. Boys holding flares ran ahead of slow moving vehicles. The drivers tried to lead their bewildered horses.

Figures emerged suddenly out of the blanketing vapours, bumped into each other and moved back muttering apologies. By four o'clock, darkness had fallen. Few were out. Sensible folk stayed by their firesides. It was raw and uncomfortable out of doors.

A girl, aged about twelve, moved slowly and uncertainly along the Thomas Embankment not far from Battersea Bridge. She was lost. She had gone out an hour ago while there was still light, to buy a reel of cotton for her aunt who took in dressmaking. They occupied the ground floor of a shabby

3

house in the Pimlico Road.

Charlotte had not yet bought the cotton. Having a penny in the pocket of her pinafore which she still wore under a hastily donned coat — she had gone further afield, lured by the anticipation of filling a somewhat empty little stomach with a few sweets. Mr. Ingleby's confectionery shop was only two blocks away. But Charlotte, surprised and somewhat frightened by the swirling fog, missed the turning and now found herself actually alongside the river. The dim lamplights made no impression in such thick darkness. Charlotte tried several times to recross the main road, but each time she stepped off the kerb, she was forced back by the sound of clip-clopping horses' hooves, as some vehicle loomed out of the shadows.

She had a little hood over her head but no gloves. She was rapidly growing colder. The poisonous gases of the 'peasouper' made her eyes smart. She coughed and gasped and the tears were not far away. She wondered what Aunt Jem would say. Poor Aunt Jem — she would be waiting for the red cotton and unable to proceed with the new merino dress for Miss Potter. It had been promised for tomorrow morning because Miss Potter was off to Brighton to visit her newly-married sister. She would be so disappointed if Aunt Jem failed her. But Aunt Jem would sit up all night, sewing and pressing and finishing the dress with those fine, tiny stitches which Charlotte thought so wonderful.

The child knew that the effort would be bad for her aunt whose eyesight was rapidly deteriorating. Miss Darnley suffered from dreadful headaches. Sometimes she could hardly go on with all that endless sewing. Poor Aunt! She was the sole support of the little household which consisted of herself, and Charlotte who was her orphaned niece. Then there was Aunt Jem's only brother, Albert, who had lately come to live with them. He was a widower. At one time he had been comfortably off with a little business in Shepherd's Bush. But the business failed after Uncle Albert's wife died. In her lifetime she had stood between him and his weakness for drink. After her death, he went downhill, got into debt and had to sell up in order to appease his creditors. He had only enough money left to pay his sister, Jemima, ten shillings a week for board and lodging, which barely kept him. But he was a kindly, harmless man when sober. As far back as Charlotte could remember, Uncle Albert had been especially kind to her; reading story books or taking her out for walks while Miss Darnley plied her trade as a dressmaker. Charlotte, in fact, loved Uncle Albert except when he had a drop too much and his breath smelt of beer when he kissed her, or tickled her cheek with his long drooping moustaches.

Charlotte wished heartily that she had waited till Uncle Albert got home and let him go and buy the red cotton. How could she be so foolish as to miss her way like this within a few hundred yards of home? Neither she nor Aunt had dreamed the fog was so thick.

If only she could meet a policeman who would help her to find her way back. She was afraid of strange men. Aunt Jem had so often cautioned her never to speak to one. She sometimes hinted at the Fearful Things that might happen to a young, unattended girl. When Charlotte asked for an explanation it was never given. Aunt Jem just pursed her pale sad lips and said tartly:

"Never mind, miss. One day you will understand."

Charlotte was always being told that 'one day she would understand'. She lived in a constant state of being mystified. Grown-ups were forever hinting at Fearful Things in front of her. Beginning to say something and stopping, glancing slyly in her direction. Once Uncle Albert had come home rather merry, and started to tell his sister about a 'young lady who had been taking a glass of port and lemon with him at The Three Bells'. What a fine bustle she had, and violet kid boots and gloves. Aunt had interrupted, her cheeks red, and said:

"Be quiet, Albert. In front of the *child*. You ought to be ashamed."

But what he ought to be ashamed of was never made clear to Charlotte. By nature she was intelligent and inquisitive. But when she appealed for explanation as to why she could not hear more about the young lady in The Three Bells,

Aunt clicked her teeth and muttered: "Young *lady*, indeed! I know better!" Uncle Albert laughed and winked at Charlotte who was promptly sent to bed because she innocently winked back.

Charlotte, however, was deeply attached to her aunt. And Aunt Jem loved her in her way, quite fondly, considering her cynical mistrust of human affection.

Life had not been kind to Jemima Darnley. First of all, the only man she had ever cared for jilted her cruelly, after which she had lost both her parents and had to take in dress-making for a living. Then Lottie, her only sister (Charlotte's mother), a beautiful girl, happily married to Oliver Goff, a valet in the service of a duke, died tragically when Charlotte was three. Oliver had been taken ill in Paris where he was with his master at the time. Mrs. Goff rushed across the Channel to see her beloved husband but he died without recognizing her. He had typhoid fever. Charlotte's young mother contracted it and within a couple of weeks, she, too, was dead, and lay beside her husband in the cemetery in Paris.

Jemima, who had adored her sister,

never recovered from this blow. Poor Lottie had been so gay and sparkling. A trifle too sparkling, at times, to suit Jemima. Charlotte closely resembled her mother. Her good-looking father, Oliver Goff, had been decently educated, and Charlotte inherited his quick grasp of things, his thirst for knowledge. From her mother, those long slender limbs and charming contrast of colouring. Eyes, the colour of dark honey, and tawny curling hair. At the moment she was over-thin and pale. Her high cheekbones jutted out. Her long fine fingers were always red — half frozen with cold from which she suffered intensely. There was no margin for rich food or piled-up fires in Aunt Jem's household; every shilling had to be watched, every penny saved.

Charlotte received no education beyond that which her aunt and uncle gave her, but, once able to read, she read hungrily. She continued to do so and to improve her mind when her aunt was not calling upon her to help with the housework. The cooking was done by an elderly respectable woman living in this same house, who volunteered to come for a few hours daily in order that Miss Darnley should be free to ply her trade. For this assistance, Miss Darnley parted with the ten shillings a week given to her by her brother. It was a hard struggle. And, alas, Charlotte had no aptitude for sewing. Aunt Jem had hoped to train her as a dressmaker, but Charlotte could not sit still for long, and if and when she sewed, her stitches were big and her little fingers would grow hot and greasy. Aunt Jem could not risk her wrecking the delicate fabrics which belonged to her customers.

Charlotte's footsteps quickened. She began to run through the fog. She *must* get home. She panted and the tears chased down her cheeks. Turning left, she stumbled off the kerb. Her terror drove her on, despite the fact that she heard the warning clatter of horses' hooves on the roadway and caught the glow from the flare held by a lad who was leading a smart landau, pulled by two handsome greys. But suddenly she stopped, hesitated and was lost. For the horses seemed to bear down upon her with terrifying suddenness. Like spectral shapes they materialized, tossing their heads, whinnying as the coachman pulled hard on the reins. Charlotte heard the shouting of men and her own thin scream. Then she was knocked down and she lost consciousness.

2

CHARLOTTE recovered to find herself in the comparative warmth and shelter of a well-padded carriage. She was lying on the seat, her head pillowed in the lap of a woman richly dressed in black velvet, with sable-lined cloak. A sable-trimmed bonnet framed a noble and beautiful face which Charlotte was never throughout her life to forget. It was that of Eleanora, Lady Chase, the subject of several of Sir John Millais' most famous portraits. In the same year that Millais was elected a Royal Academician, Eleanora Chase's portrait with her small son, Vivian, standing by her side, became the rage of London. It now hung over the fireplace in the dining-room of Clunes, — the Chase family seat in Hertfordshire.

But for the last six years Lady Chase had been living in retirement from which she emerged only occasionally, mainly from a sense of duty to her son, Vivian.

Vivian's father, Lord Chase, had been attached to the 13th Light Dragoons and mortally wounded in the Crimea. Since then, Lady Chase had devoted herself entirely to the boy. Vivian was now seated beside her. The landau had just brought them from a luncheon party. They were returning to their house in Eaton Square, trying to fight the regrettable fog. When the coachman pulled in the horses and the landau stopped, it pitched Lady Chase into her son's arms. Startled, she leaned out of the window, and saw to her consternation that one of the horses had knocked down a little girl. She at once ordered that the child be lifted into the carriage, although Vivian protested.

"Really, Mama, she may be verminous! No gently-nurtured child would be walking alone on the Embankment."

His mother chided him.

"Pray remember, Vivian, my darling boy, the quality of mercy."

Young Lord Chase shrugged his shoulders, crossed his arms and sat watching gloomily while his mother's orders were carried out. Charlotte's insensible form was lifted on to the cushioned seat.

"Home, Perkins," commanded Lady Chase.

Vivian pulled a handkerchief from the pocket of the dove-grey coat which he was wearing, and interested himself in smoothing the curled brim of his fine top hat.

Then Charlotte opened her eyes. She stared up at the face of the woman who bent so solicitously over her.

"Aunt Jem," she whispered.

The landau moved on. Lady Chase, with her own lace-edged handkerchief dabbed gently at a cut on the child's left cheek. It was bleeding. A nasty bruise was already swelling on the white forehead. The shabby cloak was streaked with mud but Lady Chase spoke to Charlotte as tenderly as she would have done to any child of her own.

"There, poor little creature, do not be alarmed. You are safe now, and in my care."

Charlotte sat up. Her head was swimming but she had the youthful faculty of being able with rapidity to throw off the effects of such an accident as this. In the gloom of the landau she could barely see the occupants, but she noted the saint-like loveliness of the face which bent down to hers. Charlotte blinked and gasped. Such a fine lady! — and this splendid carriage — how came she to be in it?

Lady Chase explained to her.

"Do you feel better, my little one?" she murmured,

"Much better," whispered Charlotte and stared through her lashes at the youth on the opposite seat. With a child's natural curiosity she admired his finery, and thought how handsome he was. But Vivian glanced out of the window as the coach moved slowly through the thickening fog, towards Eaton Square.

Lady Chase pulled a little gold-stoppered bottle from her pocket, uncorked it, and shook a few drops of scent on to Charlotte's forehead. This she smoothed with her long delicate fingers.

"Lie still, child, you must be in a daze. Why are you out in such bitter weather and unattended?"

Charlotte suddenly gasped:

"Oh, lawks-a-mercy, Aunt Jem will be waiting for her red cotton. She has to finish Miss Potter's dress tonight. Oh, I must go home immediately."

Lady Chase, only vaguely comprehending, shook her head.

"You are not fit to walk yet awhile. I shall see that you have dry clothes and a cordial before you are taken home. But how is it possible that your Mama ever let you venture forth in such a fog?"

"I have no mother," said Charlotte. "No father either," she added sorrowfully.

Eleanor Chase touched her son on the shoulders.

"Do you hear that, Vivian? This poor little girl is an orphan. How very sad!"

It did not seem sad to Lord Chase who had gone into a reverie and was considering the beauties of a certain young woman of quality who had excited his fancy during the luncheon.

Soon after Vivian's sixteenth birthday, less than a year ago, he had been initiated into the mysteries of sex by a pretty servant girl at Eton College where his lordship was receiving his education. Today he had been greatly smitten by the charms of the young lady seated next to him. It annoyed him that he was forced to live under the roof of so saintly and righteous a being as his widowed mother. All the world adored Eleanor Chase. But her only child was a supreme egotist; he was fast growing out of control. He had a callous and deceitful streak which made him unpopular once people became familiar with him. But his mother was blind to his true disposition. It was his boast to the 'young bloods' who were his friends that he could 'twist dear Mama round his little finger'.

He enjoyed these jaunts to London when for his sake alone, Mama emerged from her retirement. He enjoyed life at Clunes only when the great house was filled with friends. Much to his mother's regret, he inherited none of his father's fondness for country pursuits. He rode well but was neither a good shot nor a keen fisherman.

As he followed his mother into the well-lighted hall where two powdered footmen waited upon them, Vivian wondered how he could persuade Mama to take up permanent residence in Eaton Square.

17

The red-haired young miss who had excited his fancy at the luncheon was, he knew, resident in town.

Vivian handed hat, cloak and gloves to one of the footmen and simulated an interest in the little girl who was now able to walk beside her ladyship into the library.

"I trust you are none the worse," he said in his haughty voice.

Charlotte bobbed a curtsy. She looked up at the tall young gentleman, her lashes fluttering. Vivian's imperiousness overwhelmed her. She thought that he looked as splendid as a prince in one of the fairy books read to her by Uncle Albert. Yes, he was princely with his well-pomaded golden waves of hair, his heavy-lidded eyes, blue as turquoises — and the flashing ring on the hand which rested on his waist. A hand as slender and white and womanish as his mother's.

Lady Chase unclasped her sable-trimmed cloak and handed it to her maid.

"We must find something to fit this child, or wrap her in one of my shawls, and then send her home in the carriage. Her dress is soaked through. She fell in the gutter," Lady Chase told the maid.

"My lady, she shouldn't be standing in her muddy boots on your carpet — " began the grey-haired Hannah who was privileged, having been long in the service of the Chase family. Hannah was fond of his young lordship but had never been quite taken in by his facile charm. But my lady admonished her servant.

"Tush, Hannah, the child is God's creature, as are you or myself. She shall not be denied the comfort of our fireside. See — the rent in her stockings — the blood. She is so small and so brave. She neither cries nor complains."

"I could take her down to the servants' hall — " began Hannah with a severe look at the bedraggled Charlotte.

"She shall stay here. I, myself, will bandage her," said Lady Chase coldly. "Be so good as to fetch hot water, towels, and my medicine-chest."

Hannah curtsied and departed, muttering.

"Pray pull the bell, Vivian, and order the fire to be made up. It is chilly in here," added Lady Chase.

Charlotte did not think it cold. She found herself in a warm and wonderful world. A world of magnificence hitherto unknown to her. Despite bruises and cuts and the shock of the accident, she had hardly suffered. She was entranced by the marvels that she now gazed upon. The heavy satin curtains shutting out the fog. The hothouse flowers. The thick rugs on the polished floor. The splendid pictures against dark crimson-papered walls. Over the mantelpiece hung a great French gilt mirror with candelabra in which six tall candles were burning like golden spears of light. There were handsomely shaded lamps elsewhere. The perfume of smouldering pine logs was pleasant to her nostrils, as was the lingering scent of violets from Lady Chase's hair. Fascinated, the child regarded the wondrous rings sparkling on my lady's hands. Her smart bustle, the silky-brown curls only just threaded with silver, falling on either side of her face. Such a wonderful face, like a sad cameo. Charlotte was intrigued by it. Indeed, she was dazed by all that she saw and most of all by the thousands of books. Handsome leather-bound volumes reaching as high as the ceiling. This was the library. Charlotte could not resist uttering an excited exclamation.

"Oh, my lady, what splendiferous books and so many of them!"

Lady Chase smiled down at her.

"Do you like books, then, my little one?"

Charlotte bobbed and blushed and nodded. Lady Chase felt it was strange that a small creature of this class should be so interested in reading-matter. She remarked upon it to her son. He, spreading his hands to the blaze from the logs, yawned a little.

"I suppose some of these paupers have brains," he drawled.

"Vivian!" admonished his mother and shook her head as though at a naughty child.

Vivian strolled out of the library and into the dining-room to pour himself out a glass of wine, because he dared not order it to be brought to him at this hour in front of his mother. He fell to thinking about his red-haired young lady and the exciting curve of her bosom under her sky-blue taffeta dress. He flung himself into a chair, stretched his long legs and wondered how he could get out of this house without being discovered, once Mama was abed, and go on a spree with another young gentleman who was equally thirsty for adventure.

When he returned to the library, however, he received quite a shock. For he saw a new Charlotte. She had had her cuts dressed and Hannah had found an old cashmere shawl of an Indian red which suited the child's lovely skin. They had wrapped it around the slender figure and pinned it over one small shoulder as though it were a sari. My lady intended to put another woollen shawl over her, and thus send her home. They had taken off her wet buttoned boots and torn stockings. Her feet were bare and, so Vivian noted, like alabaster, with high arches.

She was scrupulously clean despite her poverty. And now with her face and hands washed and her long bronzed curls brushed and shining, she presented a very different picture from the mud-stained waif upon whom Vivian had first gazed.

'By gad,' he thought, 'she is quite pretty.'

He drew nearer her. Amused, he let his naturally lascivious gaze wander over the girl whom he judged to be older than she was. She held promise, he could tell, of exceptional looks. She was exceedingly graceful. And never before had he seen such a pair of eyes.

"By gad," he said again aloud, and chuckled at his hot boy's thoughts.

Lady Chase, innocent and gentle, smiled at her son.

"Is she not sweetly pretty, dear Vivian?"

"She certainly looks better than she did," he admitted.

Charlotte tried to thank them both and curtsy. Her bare toes caught in the fringe of the shawl which was much too long for her. She stumbled. The young man reached out and caught her. For a moment he held her up in his arms, grinning down into her rosy charming little face. She had a wonderful curve to her lips, he thought; a pity that *she* was not being trained as a servant girl at Clunes.

"Shall I myself take you home, little

one?" he said lazily.

Charlotte, frozen with nerves, over-awed by the young gentleman who was holding her aloft, now gave a little cry.

"Pray set me down, sir."

"Yes, put her down, Vivian. She is terrified of you," smiled his mother, and added: "Perkins will drive her home. There is no need for you to venture out again."

His young lordship shrugged his shoulders, set Charlotte on her feet and moved away from her. Already he had ceased to be intrigued by her childish beauty. He gloomed at the prospect of an evening playing piquet with Mama. Tomorrow term would begin. He would be quite amused to return to school and indulge in a few daring escapades in the village with his companions.

Snugly wrapped in thick wool, Charlotte was at length carried by a coachman out to the carriage. She was wildly excited. What a lot she would have to tell Aunt Jem. In her hand she clutched a box of bonbons given to her by Lady Chase. A beautiful big round box tied with rose-pink ribbon. It had a glorious rose painted upon the lid. It was the sort of box that Charlotte had seen in the windows of fine shops but never dreamed she would ever possess. As for the beautiful kind lady, she had actually kissed Charlotte on the brow and pressed a sovereign into her hand as well as the bonbons. She said that she would call upon Miss Darnley tomorrow to discuss what might be done for her niece.

"If you so love books, it would seem a pity not to help you to receive some education," my lady said.

So, tomorrow, before her ladyship returned to the country she was going to talk to Aunt Jem. Oh, thought Charlotte, if she could but be *educated*. If she could but read some of those splendid books in that library; what utter bliss!

Charlotte was still in a transport, far removed from earthly things, and having almost forgotten the red cotton which poor Miss Darnley so sorely needed. The reluctant coachman set forth again in the fog which was just beginning to lift a little. As they moved towards Pimlico, the child dreamed again of all that she had just seen and of these exalted personages who had befriended her. It was well worth a few painful cuts and bruises.

The young gentleman — she thought more of Vivian than of Lady Chase, being true female — how handsome he was! The figure of the young lordship had impressed itself upon her mind. In her romantic childish way she had quite fallen in love with Vivian Chase. She was the beggar maid of the story books. He was the prince who lifted her up in his arms, laughed down at her with his light blue eyes, and turned her into a princess. Oh, if she could but return, and become not a princess but his slave. Oh, would she *ever* see him again?

3

ALL too soon, Charlotte found herself back in the depressing ill-lit draughty rooms which constituted her home. She was received by Aunt Jem with floods of tears and loud lamentations in which a semi-inebriated Uncle Albert joined, loudly blowing his nose.

"Dear heavens, I thought you were lost to us, stolen by some Terrible Man. I never should have let you go forth in that fog," sobbed Miss Darnley.

The good soul was genuinely relieved to see her little niece again. She plied the child with questions, all of which Charlotte answered to her satisfaction. It was obvious that except for that cut on her forehead, a scratched cheek, and the grazed leg, she was little the worse for being knocked down. And Aunt Jem grew almost as excited as Charlotte as she drank in every detail of the child's description of the fine carriage and the house in Eaton Square.

"Imagine!" exclaimed Miss Darnley turning to her brother, "*Lady Chase* and her son. They are wealthy and famous. And her ladyship means to call here to see me tomorrow. Albert, I am all of a-flutter."

"We must polish the linoleum and the furniture," said Mr. Darnley mournfully.

Mr. Darnley had just come from The Three Bells. His breath exuded the bitter tang of the ale he had just consumed. But nobody noticed. Miss Darnley was far too excited in what her niece was telling her.

"Oh, fancy! Albert, listen to the child's description of the house in Eaton Square. Look — she owns a sovereign. Our Charl is rich!"

"And what about the handsome young gentleman who tossed her in the air, eh?" chuckled Mr. Darnley winking at Charlotte.

She winked back with youthful devilment, risking a reprimand from her aunt. She and her uncle had an understanding and if he was in liquor she did not realize it. Yes, she had plenty to say about young Lord Chase. She grimaced at the threadbare carpet. Her toes sunk into the deep soft pile of the rugs in Lady Chase's library, she said. Holding up the trailing shawl, she pirouetted, giving a performance as a fine lady.

"Hannah," she mimicked Lady Chase's aristocratic voice, "pray fetch the little creature a cordial — "

And she put a hand on her waist, looked through her lashes and gave a fair imitation of Vivian Chase, whereupon both aunt and uncle laughed until they wept. After which they all tasted a chocolate from the big round box, although Charlotte hated to untie the bow. She cherished the pink rose in her hands and kissed it.

"Oh, my lovely rose! Aunt Jem — it was all like one of uncle's fairy tales. I wish — I *wish* I had not to come home!"

At that, silence fell. Miss Darnley looked down her long thin nose and bridled, but with sadness in her eyes. Uncle Albert sighed and turned away. Charlotte, with her natural love of beauty had been dazzled by the luxury of the great house belonging to the Chases and now saw clearly the poverty of this place. Oh, how untidy and ugly it was with the poor furniture — the bits of material, threads and pins all over the floor. The darned, coarse lace curtains looped on either side of the dusty window which looked upon the roof tops of the poor street in which they lived.

But this was the home in which Charlotte had been brought up. Here, she had received all that she had known of love and care, for she remembered neither of her parents. Charlotte was too sweet-natured to allow the feelings of Aunt Jem to be hurt. She rushed at her and flung her arms round the angular form.

"Dear, dear Aunt Jem, forgive me. I did not mean what I said, I like it here best. I would not exchange our little home for the glories of Eaton Square."

At this, the good woman burst into tears. Uncle Albert became maudlin. They all had a good cry together. Finally Charlotte was given a bowl of bread and milk and sent to her bed. First of all Aunt Jem rubbed her chest with camphorated oil in case she had caught a cold out there in the fog. Before the candle was blown out in the icy cold bedroom, Charlotte knelt beside her aunt to thank God for her merciful escape from death under the horses' hooves.

Charlotte lay wakeful for some time. Her injured leg and cheek felt sore. Her little mind teemed with excited memories which kept her from her usual healthy sleep. She kept seeing the beautiful grave face of Eleanor Chase; then the bold blue eyes of Vivian, Lord Chase, as he had picked her up in his arms. Would she ever, *ever* see him again? Blissfully she hugged the dream of enchantment to herself. Terrified lest it should for ever escape her, she lay wondering whether her ladyship would keep her word to call upon Aunt Jem tomorrow. At last Charlotte fell asleep. But her uncle and aunt talked well into the night.

Miss Jemima, whose fingers were never idle, continued to ply her needle. At last her eyes were so sore, she had to stop and lower the lamp. Fearing to wake the little girl next door, the two whispered together about Charlotte's accident. Sadly Aunt

Jem reviewed the potentialities in her sister's child.

"Alas, Bertie, our little Charl is a great beauty and has a talent to amuse. She could be a fine lady, herself. Did you not see how she looked when she acted for us this evening? It was indelicate, perhaps, with that shawl draped over her naked shoulder as though she were a heathen princess. But quite charming. And she is so tall, she will all too soon be a little woman. If only we had the means to educate her properly. To give her the chance of life she ought to have!"

"Agreed, agreed," mumbled Albert. He sat rocking in his chair, toying with his watch chain, hankering after the warmth and pleasure of The Three Bells. But he dared not go back there. Jemima kept the purse and doled money out to him only in small quantities. Miss Darnley returned to the subject of Lady Chase's visit.

When Mrs. Skipper came up in the morning, she said, to cook the midday meal, there would be no time for cleaning. She, Jemima, and Albert must try to get a little law and order into their apartment tonight. Much against Uncle Albert's will, he rose and lent his sister a hand. Miss Darnley, half dropping with weariness, nobly exerted herself. By midnight the sitting-room had been transformed. Tomorrow morning, Miss Darnley announced, she would move the sewing machine into the bedroom, and there continue with her work so that this room would remain garnished for her ladyship's visit.

Mr. Darnley then bade his sister good night and betook himself to the attic in which he slept. Miss Darnley crept to her own bed feeling every bone in her body aching, and a strange pain in her breast. Yes, she had felt very ill for some long time. She wondered how to carry on and what would happen to Charlotte if anything happened to *her*.

She stood a moment beside the truckle bed in which her niece was lying. Shading the candle with one hand, she peered down at Charlotte's recumbent form. The tawny curls were tossed upon the pillow, the pale young face was flushed in sleep and the lips parted to show a dazzle of pearly teeth. It was a remarkable face and Miss Darnley knew it. In a vague way she felt bitterly afraid for Charlotte. As she had once been afraid for her lovely Lottie, her sister. Lottie had been just such a one for luxury and gaiety, and just as generous in spirit. She had loved Oliver Goff passionately, given her whole heart to Charlotte's father. What would happen to little Charlotte who, like her mother, had so few leanings toward quiet domesticity. What work could she do and still keep her refined ways? What chance had she in such quarters as these to meet or marry a gentleman?

"I must speak to her ladyship, if indeed she comes tomorrow," Miss Darnley thought feverishly, "Perhaps she will patronize our Charlotte. And now I must try to get some sleep and be at my best to receive our distinguished visitor."

But Jemima Darnley was never to look upon the beautiful face of Eleanora Chase; nor to know the excitement of welcoming a lady of the nobility to this modest home. The long drawn-out torture of sewing and pressing all through the tedious hours of day, and half the night, was ended for Miss Darnley. Ended, the bitter struggle for existence, with no one beside her save a useless inebriate of a brother. Long years of semi-starvation, trying to save a little money for the child, added to a congenital weakness of the heart, cut short Miss Darnley's life. Tonight's particular effort to clean and tidy the room had been too much for her. She had time only to blow out the candle and stretch herself upon her bed — and it was the end. A gasp for breath — a convulsion — and her courageous spirit fled.

It was Charlotte who discovered the awful tragedy — the first real tragedy in her life — when she awakened next morning. She yawned and stretched, then by the light that filtered through the yellow blind, saw Aunt Jem lying in a peculiar way, staring at the ceiling as though her gaze was transfixed. She was so ghastly a hue that even the child's heart plunged with horror. She screamed for her uncle. Mr. Darnley, wearing his night-shirt, and with a cap askew on his head, accompanied by another lady in the building, came running in answer to that piercing cry. But it was too late. It was only a cold corpse that they found. The frozen smile of the dead lay upon Miss Darnley's lips.

A neighbour took the horrified, sobbing child into her own quarters. Later, Mr. Darnley answered the questions put to him by a hastily summoned doctor, and while he wept into a handkerchief, wondered slyly how soon he could extract a shilling or two from his dead sister's purse, and take himself off to The Three Bells.

And this was the scene that Lady Chase found when, true to her word, and accompanied by Hannah, her maid, she arrived at the Darnleys' dwelling.

4

FOUR years later.
Clunes, at any time of the year, was a magnificent place. It had been built three hundred years ago by the first Lord Chase who had married a French Countess. To please his bride, this nobleman had designed what might be taken as a small French chateau, with a marble terrace overlooking superb grounds. The dove-grey of fretted stonework was glorious against the sombre green of the trees. The last Lord Chase had spent a great deal of money upon the grounds. A small army of gardeners toiled daily, cutting the velvet lawns, clipping the hedges into the strange shapes of birds beloved by the French. And then there was the famous fountain, a miniature lake, the rose arbours, the herb walks, and the orchards.

Clunes lay like a jewel on the borders of Hertfordshire and Essex, and one mile from the sleepy little village of Harling, with its fine Norman church. The late Lord Chase had been revered by all its inhabitants as was his beautiful and saintly widow who regularly visited the sick and suffering. There were rumours that the young Lord Vivian was not quite so noble as his sire. Gossip from the servants' hall at Clunes suggested that the handsome and charming young man could, when he chose, be a young devil. But on the whole the Chase family was popular and the villagers looked with awe towards the great lodge gates.

In winter, when the grounds were deep in snow and the turrets of Clunes gleamed as though with crusted diamonds, the place looked like an illustration from a story book. And it was in winter that Charlotte Goff had first come to live in the Lodge — a little grey stone house with diamond-paned windows, standing sentinel by the gates. It was spring when she had first grown to love Clunes with passion and think of it henceforth as the most gorgeous house in the world.

On this particular day in April, Charlotte walked down the famous elm drive, and enjoyed the warmth of the spring sunlight on her upturned face. After the years spent in the grime and soot of London, cooped in Aunt Jem's room, country life never failed to appeal to Charlotte.

This carriage drive was nearly a quarter of a mile in length, flanked by tall trees and great rhododendron bushes soon to burst into crimson bloom. Up on the tall trees the rooks cawed and circled around their nests.

Under her arm, Charlotte carried two books — one on French history, and one of Keats' poems. It was half past two. This was the hour that she usually spent with her benefactor, Lady Chase. For the last four years her school had been the library which was twice as large and filled with twice as many rare books as the one in Eaton Square.

Thanks to Lady Chase, the little girl of twelve had developed into an erudite young lady who would soon celebrate her seventeenth birthday, who was proficient in French and English subjects, able to play the piano, to dance and to paint. But still the same Charlotte who could not sew. Lady Chase had given up trying to interest her protégée in the embroideries and tapestry work which she herself executed so well.

As Charlotte neared the broad marble terrace of the house, she paused a moment to look upon a sight of which she had never grown tired. At this time of year the lawns were like emerald velvet. Every tree was in bud. The beeches a tender green which would eventually mature into tawny gold. On either side of the terrace stood two magnificent tulip trees which were Lady Chase's delight.

For four long years now, Charlotte had lived with Mr. and Mrs. Forbes, the lodgekeepers. She never mixed with any visitors who came to Clunes. Only vaguely now she remembered her old life — and Uncle Albert. He had soon followed his sister to the grave. A drop too much liquor one night, and, outside The Three Bells, the old reprobate had swayed across the road and been knocked down by a passing cab. Charlotte then had no one of her own flesh and blood left in the world.

Since Aunt Jem had passed away,

life had been transformed for Charlotte. Lady Chase, having discovered the state of affairs in the Pimlico dwelling house, had at once approached Uncle Albert and offered to take his niece down to Clunes.

"I would like to see that she is properly educated. She is a charming, beautiful child, and interests me," her ladyship had said. And Mr. Darnley, not knowing what to do with a small girl on his hands, gratefully handed Charlotte over to the great lady's care.

Nan and Joseph Forbes, the lodge-keeper and his wife, were uneducated but respectable folk with no family of their own and only too pleased to adopt her ladyship's protégée. They found Charlotte easy to manage and very affectionate, and she soon won their hearts with her beauty and charm.

During the years that followed, she grew tall and strong. She adored the country and quickly learned the names of all the birds and flowers and trees. Her greatest delight was to learn her lessons at the knee of her benefactor. Her ladyship often said to her: "It is a pleasure to teach you, my little one, for you assimilate knowledge as the sun drinks the dew."

But it was not her ladyship's intention to allow Charlotte to move too freely in a *milieu* which could never be hers. Charlotte shared her foster parents' simple pleasures. Visitors to Clunes rarely saw the beautiful young girl. Vivian was nearly always away. He had left Eton and gone up to Oxford.

When Charlotte saw him — which was rarely — she still looked upon Vivian as the prince of her dreams. Now that he had grown to manhood, he had much to occupy his time. During the holidays he filled Clunes with the young friends in his own set. But there were occasions when he condescended to wander down to the lodge and speak to the pretty girl whom his mother had befriended. At such times Charlotte listened, enthralled, while he boasted of his conquests and confided some of his escapades, just in order to see the rich blood whip her cheeks and hear her gasp: "Oh, my *lord*!"

He teased her, shocked, and delighted her in turn. Occasionally he would tell her that she was growing 'deuced attractive'. Then she grew a little scared. But she did not understand why the Forbes, when listening to her rhapsodies about the golden-haired young gentleman, glanced at each other, then looked down their noses. She could see they did not like his lordship. And once Mrs. Forbes said: "Do not believe all that young man tells you, my little dear. Her ladyship is an angel but there is a devil in his lordship."

Charlotte only laughed merrily. She thought the world and everyone in it wonderful. She could see no real harm in Vivian. Innocence shone out of her golden eyes. But she did realize quite soon, that once *he* returned to Oxford, Clunes seemed empty and a little sad.

When his lordship was home, she sometimes watched him ride through the lodge-gates with his companions and she would envy the beautifully-dressed young ladies who had the right to ride beside him, and call him '*Vivian*'. And she wished passionately that she could go to some of the splendid balls and dinner parties up at the house and share *his* life, *his* pleasures. But such thoughts she kept deep in her heart.

This afternoon as Charlotte came up the marble steps to the terrace, gay with vivid colour from the flowers in the big stone vases, she came upon Vivian. He was dressed casually, wearing a light velvet jacket and flowing tie. He looked, she thought, her heart beating as it always did at the sight of him, like a young god. Her inexperienced eyes did not note the dark smudges under his eyes — the looseness of his mouth — the twitching of his slender fingers, betraying the fact that his lordship's nerves were bad.

He had been leading a secret life of debauchery, undreamed of by his saintly mother. He could still manage to deceive her — if not his tutor at Oxford. Last term he had been in danger of being sent down and only escaped by virtue of the fact that the senior proctor had known and loved his father, and had pity on Vivian's widowed mother. But a grave warning had been issued to him.

For a while Vivian, subdued, had resolved to turn over a new leaf. But he was too great a rogue at heart to stay penitent for long. He had not got it in him to study assiduously, or moderate his habits. Drink and women had already taken a hold of him.

However, today, he felt as he put it 'deuced fatigued'. After his mother had gone to sleep last night, he had strolled through the woods to a certain house presided over by a lady on whom his mother would never call. A divorcée, named Roma Gresham. At one time Mrs. Gresham had been a respected member of London society. After her divorce she had turned to a way of life which to a pure woman like Eleanor Chase would seem appalling. The man for whom Mrs. Gresham had abandoned virtue had died before she could marry him. She was still handsome and vivacious in her early thirties. Her lover had bequeathed to her enough money with which to lead the sort of life that amused her; for she was both sensual and avaricious. She passed from one admirer to another. Her latest lover, a dissolute baronet, had rented this house for her — and himself. The countryside was a good 'cover-up' for his excesses. Mrs. Gresham held wild parties, with gambling, drinking and dancing to amuse him and his friends. They also amused Vivian who was more often to be found in Mrs. Gresham's house than in his own.

He threw away his cigarette as he caught sight of Charlotte. Each time he returned from Oxford, he was struck by her fast-maturing beauty. Spoiled as he was by the world of women in which he moved, and growing a little tired of the painted faces in Mrs. Gresham's set, he was equally bored by the empty-headed, well-brought up young females in his own circle. But Charlotte Goff intrigued him. She had, as he so often told himself, a "*Je ne sais quoi*" that fascinated him. She was a mixture of the artless child and the intelligent student whom his mother was teaching. The sun touched her bright bronzed hair to a deep gold. She moved with unconscious grace. Her pale blue dress was plain homespun and without distinction, but, Vivian, the young sybarite and philanderer, saw in her one of the nymphs of the Greek classics which he had to study — much to his *ennui*. However, he felt little *ennui*

46

as he looked at Charlotte. He stood up and bowed as low as he would do to any fine lady.

He quoted:

"'Had I the heart to slide an arm beneath her,
Press her parting lips as her waist I gather slow,
Waking in amazement she could not but embrace me:
Then would she hold me and never let me go?'"

Charlotte with crimson cheeks and a pounding heart tried to laugh.

"Your lordship should not say such things to me."

Vivian laughed lazily.

"My dear child, it was not I who conceived those romantic lines but the poet, George Meredith."

She nodded.

"Her ladyship has given me many of Mr. Meredith's beautiful poems to read."

Vivian let his gaze, critical and voluptuous, wander over the pearly

47

texture of Charlotte's skin; her rounded arms, her delicate wrists, and ankles, her long tapering fingers. Often he wondered from what stock this lovely girl had sprung. She seemed to him more of an aristocrat than many of the girls in his own set. His mother, too, had remarked on the fact.

But they knew little of Charlotte's ancestry beyond what the old reprobate, Albert Darnley, had told them about her lovely mother and her good-looking father, who had both died so tragically young in France.

Vivian put out a finger and touched one of the silky ringlets that lay upon Charlotte's shoulders.

"Sweet thing," he said. "Mr. Meredith must certainly have been thinking of you when he wrote those words. Tell me — would you 'come with me to a beech tree' and lie like the lady in the poet's verse — 'couch'd with her arms behind her golden head' — He wrote that, too. I care little for poetry but this was brought to my mind as I watched you walk toward me this afternoon."

Charlotte meditated. Except for her

visits to the great house, she led a strictly secluded life. She had no knowledge of the world and could not begin to deal with the flattery of a man like Vivian. But she could not ignore the compliment. It went a little to her head.

Vivian watched how her curving lashes flickered. He was no longer inclined to sulk out here on the terrace. A remorseless wish to teach this pure and unsullied girl the meaning of man's passion gripped him. He was positive that she would respond if he could but woo her into his arms. He could see how deeply even his words affected her.

"What time do you finish your lessons?" he asked suddenly in a low abrupt voice.

She fingered her books nervously.

"At half past three, I think, my lord."

"How many times have I told you not to address me so."

"I cannot call you 'Vivian'."

"You can and shall."

She was rendered speechless, for his look was burning. Suddenly she was afraid.

"Your mother will be waiting for me — *Vivian*," she whispered the name which was so often on her mind, and in her prayers. Yes, she prayed nightly for this golden-haired prince of her dreams and if anybody had spoken ill of him she would not have listened.

"I will be here when you come out," said Vivian, and touched her curls again with a caressing finger.

She hurried away through the long open French windows into the library where Lady Chase was waiting for her. The young man seated himself astride the balustrade again. He took a cigarette from a gold box which he carried, and lit it. His eyes narrowed. His thoughts were lascivious. This was not the first time that he had felt a dangerous desire for Charlotte Goff. So far in his young spoiled life he had denied himself little that he wanted. Looks and money and his title secured what he craved. The cloak of virtue which he wore for his mother's benefit and also for the benefit of Sir Harry Cawder, his guardian, was soon dropped once Vivian was out of their sight. Fortunately for Vivian, Sir Harry had long been ailing and only once in recent years had the young man come under the General's jurisdiction. Then, he had received a strong caution.

Charlotte was not the first innocent girl whom Vivian had desired and seduced. Already one unfortunate of sixteen summers had borne a child to him. The babe had died and the miserable ruined young female was spirited away by her parents, Vivian having paid them a sum of money. The boy was devoid not only of morals but of respect for purity. Nothing barred him from indulgence save his fear of losing the money that came to him through the generosity of his mother.

He knew exactly what his mother had planned for Charlotte. Once she was seventeen, she was to go to France. Eleanor Chase's greatest friend, the Princesse de Larolles, who had a family of small children, wished them to be taught English. It was arranged between the two ladies that the young Charlotte should live for a year or two in the big chateau at Fontainebleau and teach the little Larolles all that she knew.

When Vivian had first heard of these plans he had deplored them. He had grown so accustomed to seeing the bewitching young girl down at the Lodge, and talking to her when he was bored. Besides, he thought of what might happen to her in France. Doubtless some hot-blooded young Frenchman would pay court to her beauty. Vivian wanted to be the first to touch those rose-red lips which were curved so splendidly for kissing. He had a sensual knowledge of women which led him to believe that for all Charlotte's childlike, lily-white innocence, she was by nature passionate. She would have much to give a man. Vivian Chase did not intend to let this prize drift out of his reach to France.

He flung himself into a long basket chair. Quite heartlessly, he planned the seduction of Charlotte.

5

IN the cool library amid the books that she loved so well, Charlotte sat with Eleanor Chase. She read first an English essay on Keats; then a short résumé of the French Revolution. Later she would receive a lesson at that magnificent grand piano in the drawing-room. Charlotte loved her piano-forte lessons, given to her by an elderly lady named Miss de Wynter who resided in Harling.

As a rule, Charlotte gave her whole heart to her lessons. Today, Lady Chase found her young pupil unusually *distraite*. She kept stumbling over her words and looking out of the windows; then, flushed and apologetic, would return to her books.

"Your thoughts are not on your studies, little one," her ladyship remarked gently.

"I beg your pardon, my lady," stammered Charlotte.

"Never mind," said Lady Chase and

smiled in her sweet sympathetic way, "I cannot expect an old head on young shoulders. You are progressing well, but the sunshine must be tempting to you today. Perhaps you wish to be out in the wood gathering primroses? I forget that you are still only a child."

Charlotte bit her lip. *Only a child!* That made her feel guilty. For they were not childish thoughts that distracted her from this afternoon's lessons. They were the exciting, troubling, terrifying reflections of a girl in her seventeenth year; *a girl in love*. And it was the handsome face of Vivian Chase which she kept seeing. The memory of the pretty things he had said to her — especially his announcement that he would be waiting for her when she went out again — haunted her imagination.

How horrified her ladyship would be if she could but guess! *Oh, dear,* thought Charlotte, *I am wicked and ungrateful. It is not fitting that I who am nobody at all, should think so much of him.*

But the thoughts were not to be banished. And at last when she spoke a wrong line as she recited 'The Eve of

St. Agnes', Lady Chase stopped her.

"There, my dear, enough for now; go back into the sunshine. It is better for you than learning the verses even of so divine a poet. I will ask Miss Wynter to excuse you, also, your music lesson. You can take it tomorrow."

Charlotte collected her books; her expression was down-cast.

"Alas — I have disappointed you, my lady."

"Not at all. Do not make so much of it. You are far ahead of most pupils of your age."

"I thank you, my lady," said Charlotte gratefully, and curtsied low.

Eleanor leaned back in the winged armchair which was her favourite. She smiled benevolently at Charlotte. The girl was turning into a real beauty she thought. But what Eleanor liked still more was the fashion in which Charlotte's character had developed. All who knew her spoke well of her. The good couple at the Lodge were never done praising her qualities of piety and obedience, coupled with that charming natural warmth and gaiety which made her such a general favourite.

"I did not make a mistake when I took her out of that sad house in Pimlico," Lady Chase mused. "She has amply repaid me."

Almost Lady Chase loved her young protégée as a daughter — the daughter she had wanted and never had.

As the girl returned her ladyship's glances, she felt, not for the first time, a tinge of anxiety. The years had not sat kindly upon Eleanor Chase. The celebrated beauty of the sad 'Madonna' was still there, but the brown curls had turned to silver grey, the eyes were sunken. She had aged; grown excessively thin. Several times during lessons, Charlotte fancied she saw a look of pain cross that serene and noble countenance. Once, one of the wonderful diamond rings which her ladyship liked to wear, slipped from a finger become too slender.

Charlotte had, on one occasion, questioned the son of the house about his mother's health, but he seemed unconcerned.

"Mama has always been delicate. She

does not complain to me," he had said with a shrug.

But even the inexperienced girl could not fail to note today the sinister marks of some secret malady on my lady's face, revealed by a sudden shaft of sunlight that fell on her.

"What is it, my child?" said Lady Chase as she saw Charlotte's expression.

The girl was too shy to say, but suddenly picked up one of the lovely hands of her benefactor and pressed her lips upon it.

"My lady, I thank you from the bottom of my heart for all that you have done for me," she breathed. "I fear I have been inattentive today. Do, pray, forgive me."

"There — think no more about it," smiled her ladyship. "We all have our moments of day-dreaming. As a rule you are a very diligent pupil. Go out and take the air, my little one."

Charlotte curtsied and bade her farewell. Lady Chase did not move but followed the graceful figure with her brooding gaze. Dear little Charlotte! Not once had she ever shown ingratitude or grown too bold. Indeed Eleanor Chase could have wished that her son possessed many of the girl's excellent qualities. She loved Vivian but could not at times fail to see that he was very egotistical; that there was a certain wildness in his blood. She had always hoped that, with the years, he would gain stability and become more like his splendid Papa. She used to shut her eyes to his shortcomings. But she did at times fear for Vivian's future. The best thing that could happen would be for him to make an early marriage. But not to a silly frivolous child like Harriet Dawnay who occasionally stayed down at Clunes, and hunted with him. Indeed, so far none of the young ladies who partnered Vivian seemed to Lady Chase at all suitable. She wanted him to marry a young woman of sterling qualities, as well as of noble birth.

Ah, well! that day would come, she mused, and it was her dearest wish that it would come soon.

In her innocence, Lady Chase even allowed herself sometimes to think what a pity it was that her protégée was not of good birth and breeding. She would make some man an excellent wife. But

Lady Chase never connected Charlotte and Vivian. So far as she knew they rarely saw each other. If Vivian ever spoke of the girl it was in a patronizing way. He counted her as his social inferior. His mother had never been able to persuade him, even when he was a small boy, to be kind or considerate to those beneath him in station.

So it never entered her ladyship's head that Vivian would be likely to take a serious interest in Charlotte. In any case, Charlotte in her ladyship's opinion was still in the 'school-room'.

Eleanor sat quiet for a moment and let her mind dwell with pride and affection on the thought of her son's good looks and his charm, rather than his faults. Then, suddenly, pain struck at her. It struck so cruelly that for a moment she thought she was going to faint. Gasping, with closed eyes, she sat clutching at her breast. And now, suddenly, she knew that it was the coldness of death itself that chilled her on that sunny afternoon.

Lady Chase had known for a long time that she was going to die soon but she did not know when. So far it had been mere instinct, coupled with long wakeful nights, and days when her courage had faltered because of the pain in her heart. Her mother had died of *angina pectoris*. Maybe this same fate awaited her. Eleanor did not know but accepted the possibility with the same calm stoicism that she had accepted all her sorrows. But she did not want her end to come *too* soon; not until Vivian was more stabilized.

Somehow she managed to get up and stagger to the long tapestry attached to the bell and pull at it. A footman entered. She sent him for Hannah, her maid. When old Hannah came in and saw her beloved mistress's ghastly face, she fell on her knees and burst into tears.

"My lady, my lady, you cannot go on like this. You must let me call your physician."

"I suppose so," whispered Lady Chase.

"Indeed, my lady, I will send one of the men for Dr. Castleby at once. Now you must let me help you up to bed."

The terrible pain had passed. Lady Chase was breathing normally again and even able to smile. She drew a long deep sigh.

"Alas, Hannah, I think my end is approaching."

Hannah, with streaming eyes, said:

"Do not say it, my lady. I could not bear that aught should happen to you."

"My faithful Hannah, death must come to all of us. And I shall see my beloved husband again. Is that not a joyful prospect for me?"

Hannah nodded, wiped her eyes and straightened the little muslin cap on her grey sedate head. But as she helped her mistress up to her bedroom, the old servant could see for herself that her ladyship was mortally ill. Alas that they were not in London, for old Dr. Castleby from Harling, although a godly and righteous man, was not a specialist in diseases of the heart.

Hannah helped her mistress into bed and tried to be comforting.

"This is maybe only one of your attacks, and it will pass, my lady."

"Yes — and it will return," said Lady Chase in a hollow voice. She looked mournfully around her beautiful bedroom.

On the wall before her, hung a huge painting of her husband in uniform, one hand on his hip. So like Vivian in face and form, she thought, as she gazed at the fine figure with her world-weary eyes. Difficult to realize that two men could in character be so different. Alas, that the boy was not more like his father. Alas, too, that his godfather who might have counselled him well, was also stricken down. Soon there would be nobody left to guide the young man's footsteps.

At the doorway, Hannah turned and said:

"I will go and make you a cordial, my lady. Shall I send his lordship to you?"

The colour rose to Lady Chase's pale cheeks.

"Under no circumstances is my son to be told that I am so ill. Inform him, if you must, that I have a migraine and that because of that I have asked Dr. Castleby to come and prescribe for me."

Something urged the old retainer to frown at this.

"Would it not be better that he should

know the truth, my lady?" she muttered.

"No, Hannah. The worry might interfere with his lordship's final studies at Oxford. And God in his mercy may spare me a little longer, so why bring needless worry and grief to those who care for me?"

Hannah sighed. She bobbed a curtsy and departed. On her way downstairs she paused on the landing in front of one of the big windows, in order to pull a fold of curtain into place. She had peculiarly good long sight for one of her years. And as she stood there — peering out of that window — she clicked her tongue against her teeth. For she saw something that was not to her liking. It was the figure of his lordship vanishing through the rosary which led past an ornamental lake into the woods. Nothing unusual about this, except that Hannah had also seen that other figure which preceded Lord Chase. Her ladyship's protégée, Charlotte Goff.

Hannah stood still. Her mind was full of unease. She was an old woman, but not ignorant of life and she knew the young master only too well. Had she not seen him grow up, and witnessed many of the youthful follies which had been kept hidden from her ladyship. The whole staff was for ever covering up for the handsome boy. But Hannah knew perfectly well that he would have little respect for a pretty girl in Charlotte's station.

Hannah did not particularly care for Charlotte; she had always thought it over-charitable of her ladyship to bring the orphan to Clunes. The old servant was jealous, too, of the many hours which the girl spent in the company of her ladyship. But she was a good woman, and would not want any harm to come to Charlotte; especially not through Vivian.

Hannah was quite sure those two young things were up to no good; but, of course, she could not so much as mention the fact to her sick lady. Nor could even she, as a privileged maid, speak to Lord Chase. If she did, she knew that she would receive nothing but a laugh and a denial. Vivian either teased her or was rude to her. There was no love lost between them. The old servant uttered a prayer.

"God grant that her ladyship will never know what I and many others know about her son. Better that she should have a peaceful death now, than live to suffer a terrible awakening."

6

THROUGH the beechwoods, dappled with the bright sunshine that filtered through the young leaves, Charlotte walked beside Lord Chase.

The young girl was unspeakably happy. She felt, too, unspeakably wicked. It was really the first time she had ever done such a thing as this. And she seldom left the Lodge without letting Nan know where she had gone.

"I dare not — " she had said to Vivian when he had begged her to take this stroll.

"Nonsense," he had broken in, "*I* shall be responsible for you."

Vivian felt no sense of responsibility in this hour; only an ever increasing desire to be the first man to take this radiant young creature into an embrace.

He knew that she was, in her innocent way, already his slave. He also knew that he must go warily at first. So as they walked, he spoke not of love, but of life. Into her enchanted ears he poured stories of things he had seen and done. Of ceremonial visits to London and Paris. Of a holiday spent with an Oxford friend in Monte Carlo; of others in Rome and Venice.

"Oh, Lord Ch — I mean Vivian — it all sounds so glorious!" she exclaimed, when he drew breath. "How well you describe it all. Indeed, I think *you* should write my essays for me. You have such imagination."

With a careless smile he accepted her flattery.

"Do not dwell always on the thought of studies, Charlotte," he said. "You are young and beautiful. You should be dreaming of more romantic things. Is it not time that you saw life as other young girls see it? That you went to dances and parties? I think it is all wrong that my mother keeps you so firmly shut away from pleasures indulged in by other young girls."

Charlotte looked quite shocked.

"But I am a *nobody*. Her ladyship has shown me great honour by giving me an education. It would not be fitting for me to go to the fine balls like the young ladies in your set."

They had reached a little clearing in the glade where the mossy ground was tawny with last year's leaves. Vivian caught hold of one of Charlotte's hands. Before she could decline, he pulled her down beside him.

"Come — let us sit together and rest a while," he said.

"Oh, Vivian, I ought not — " she began.

He interrupted:

"I shall be the one to say what Miss Goff ought or ought not to do today."

She continued to protest, her cheeks hot and pink, her eyes dancing. He broke in again:

"Tush! You are only too ready to take instruction from others. Will you not take it from me?"

"You are very masterful," she said in a low voice.

"A maid likes a man to be masterful, does she not, Charlotte?"

"I know nothing of men," she said, her heart beating madly fast.

"How old are you?" he asked abruptly.

"Seventeen in August."

"Still sixteen and so sweet," he said.

Now he fingered a fold of her light dress confined at the narrow waist by a belt with an old buckle. It had been made by Mrs. Forbes. The young man said dreamily:

"I would like to see you wear a bustle."

Charlotte giggled.

"I cannot imagine myself in one. It would be far too fashionable for me."

"And I would also like to see you in a corsage slipping off those creamy shoulders," he said boldly, and touched her warm white neck. Immediately alarm seized her. She moved away; yet not too far, for his touch thrilled her immeasurably.

"Let us walk on," she whispered.

But with a single movement he pulled her down to him and held her against his breast.

"Let us stay here. Charl — little love — you are so sweet. It is delicious to be here alone with you — at last!"

"Vivian, please let me go," she said,

and turned quite pale. She was, he thought, like a bird that found itself in a snare.

"Lie quiet. Let us speak together of love," he said. His face was flushed, his voice husky with the passion that consumed him. "Tell me your dreams, your thoughts, your hopes. Surely they cannot always be connected with dry, dull learning."

She was too scared to answer. But she trembled with delight, lying close to him, while his hands caressed her hair.

Unconsciously she had always wanted him with the natural warmth of her budding womanhood. When suddenly he drew her down to his lips and touched them, his kiss — her first — destroyed the innocence of her childhood.

She struggled, first white then red, torn between tears and laughter, between fear and surrender.

"This is wicked — wrong — you must let me go — dear Vivian, *please*."

"Do you not love me, my little darling?"

"It is not permitted that I should love you," she breathed in terror.

70

"That is for me to say. Forget those others who would control your existence."

Vivian felt her whole body quivering. Anyone but he might have had compassion for her. With rougher passion he began to kiss her mouth and her throat. He tangled his fingers through the thick masses of her chestnut hair. This lovely child was completely in his hands, and if to satisfy his own desire he must break her heart, what matter to Vivian Chase? It amused him to remember more of those verses read by him at Oxford only a few weeks ago. With lips wandering across her face, he came to one small ear. He murmured in it.

"'*You, my wild one, you tell of honied field-rose,*
Violet, blushing eglantine of life . . .'"

A desperate bid for sanity, coupled with her natural modesty, led Charlotte to fight him again. She tried to beat off his kisses. He seized her hands, kissed and imprisoned, and laughing, silenced her lips. He quoted again:

"'Oh, the golden sheaf, the rustling treasure-armful
Oh, the nut-brown tresses . . . oh, the girdle slack about the waist.'"

Then he spoke no more but gathered her closer, his hands exploring her slim waist. He was intoxicated by her unblemished perfection. For him it was another conquest. But for her, farewell forever to the purity of her body, to the tranquillity of her mind. Now — an ecstatic surging of her senses. Afterwards would come the anguish of remorse — the darkness of despair. But not yet, not while she lay in Vivian's arms, possessed and enchanted.

As he grew more daring, alarm shuddered through her. She pressed his hot desirous face back from her, the palms of her hands against his cheeks.

"No, Vivian, no, this is wicked."

"There is no wickedness in love," he said blithely and touched the silk of her lashes with his lips.

"Let me go," she whispered.

"To escape me forever? — no." But she was frightened now and cried out as he none too gently untied the ribbons at her throat and moved his lips across the matchless purity of her shoulders. She trembled, caught between her rapture and her fear. Suddenly the cry that broke from her was of pain as well as ecstasy.

"Ah, no, for God's sake, Vivian. I implore you."

But it was too late. The handsome boy was crazy to possess her; careless of her age — her pitiful innocence.

"You shall belong to me," he said against her bruised lips, "you *shall*, you heavenly child!"

It seemed to Charlotte that all the pathways of her life had led to this one moment — led her to her fate, be it for good or evil. Vivian Chase took her in passion, but she gave in compassionate love, true to her sex. Later, when he lay at her side, content and sleepy-eyed, the tears tumbled through her long lashes but he kissed them away with a careless affection. He laughed at the shame in her eyes. He found her state of mind stupid rather than deserving of compassion. He had long since forgotten what it was to be ashamed in such matters as these.

He lay humming under his breath, his hands laced behind his head. He was satisfied and triumphant. Charlotte re-tied the bows at her throat and looked down at him like a stricken doe. Suddenly she threw herself upon him.

"I never meant that to happen. It was truly wrong. Vivian, Vivian, what shall I do?"

"Stupid — there is nothing you should do," he said. His smile was half scornful, wholly victorious. "You are mine now, and shall be again many times I hope — that is when it is expedient for us to meet."

"No," she said under her breath, and shook her head violently.

"*Yes*," he mocked her and pulled her lazily down upon him.

As his lips met hers, the salt of her tears trickled upon them. He sat up and brushed the leaves from his bright gold hair. He was impatient of her. He had had enough of this love-play. For her it was the beginning and end of a life. To him an interlude.

"Why must women always cry and

spoil things," he grumbled.

"Say that you truly love me, say it, *please*!" she begged.

"Of course I do. I love all pretty girls."

Wounded to the core, Charlotte's great eyes reproached him. She said under her breath:

"Am I one of so many? Merciful heavens, do not let me hear you say that again."

He yawned and stood up, smoothing his crumpled suit.

"What would you have me tell you, foolish girl? That you are the *only* woman in my life? It would be a damnable lie."

She stood before him hurt and dumb. She looked as though she had been shot straight through the heart.

"I do not understand you," she whispered, "there is no sense in what you say. I only ask to be allowed to love you and never any other man. Can you not promise to love only me?"

"Oh, stop trying to pin me down. Be satisfied with what you have had," he said in a hard, mocking voice.

Now her eyes were so piteous that even

Vivian softened. He pulled her into his arms. With a fresh spurt of passion, he kissed her long and hard. He whispered between the kisses. "Never mind, sweet Charlotte. You are very lovely and I do, indeed, love you. I will see you soon again. Now I must take you home or Nan will wonder where you are. Come!"

He held out his hand. Charlotte put hers into it, trying to check the turbulence of the grief which had replaced the ecstasy of an hour ago.

★ ★ ★

The Spring day had lengthened into the violet dusk of evening when at last the young lovers emerged from the wood.

Outside the oak doorway which led into the orchard through which Vivian could reach the big house, the young man stopped and smiled down at the girl.

His face was flushed. His eyes were full of satisfaction, tempered only faintly with guilt. He knew he had committed a monstrous sin which, if his mother were to find out, might bring disaster upon him as well as Charlotte. The only thing that worried him was his own danger. Over this beautiful child, not yet seventeen, whom he had so heartlessly seduced, he had few qualms. All girls were the same, he thought cynically; fools, ready to comply with a man's requests, Charlotte was a little *special* perhaps, and he had enjoyed her beauty. He had been pleasantly surprised, too, by the ardour of her response. He had, of course, always imagined that hers was an ardent nature. Now he knew it.

"We must meet soon again and repeat today's splendid idyll," he said carelessly, and touched her cheek with a careless finger.

She was silent. There was no vestige of colour in her face. Her eyes looked huge and scared. She was looking neat and demure again; she had smoothed her dress and brushed away the leaves and twigs. But she could not brush away the consciousness of her fall from grace. Now that the overwhelming excitement was over, she was horrified at what she had done.

"No — no, never to be repeated," she breathed, and bit hard on lips that were bruised from his mad kissing.

"Stupid child, why not? Did you not return my kisses and love me as I loved you?"

"Love," she stumbled over the word, "yes, but not *that*."

"Nonsense," he laughed, but frowned at her out of the corners of his eyes. *Afterwards* a girl never seemed to him so desirable as before; not even this one.

"I should never have permitted such a thing," she whispered, and tears hung like diamond drops on her lashes.

The sight of those new tears irritated Vivian.

"Come — you are not going to make a scene, I trust," he said.

Her poor heart, her dazed mind were shocked by this display of indifference.

"What would her ladyship say?" she breathed the words, then suddenly put her face in her hands and wept.

"Oh, good heavens," said Vivian angrily, "how perverse you women are. You laugh with desire as you come into a man's arms and then when you leave him, you weep with regret. Why not strive to be more like us male creatures who accept these things as part of Nature's great scheme."

Her tears dried. An arrow seemed to transfix her heart. In that moment — scarcely able to credit the fact that the wooing and tender love could so quickly become harsh and dictatorial — Charlotte's first sweet illusions were shattered.

Very pale and in a quiet voice, she said:

"I do not mean to anger you. But in my own mind I have done something terrible."

"Good heavens, you wanted it just as much as I did — is that not so?" he demanded brutally.

She flung back her head and looked at him unsmiling but proud.

"Yes."

His gaze turned from her. For an instant he felt some contrition. He patted her shoulder.

"There, there, foolish little Charl — let me see you smile again. As I say — I found you deuced attractive and I have every intention of strolling with you through those woods again. I must go back to Oxford tomorrow but I will return home for the summer. A pity," he added, "that I cannot ask you to one of the Commemoration Balls, but your position makes that impossible."

Her position! For the first time, humble though she was, Charlotte was nauseated by his use of that word, particularly in this moment. She realized in that terrifying instant, how utterly mad, as well as bad, she had been to give herself to Vivian Chase.

Uttering a cry, she turned suddenly and ran from him. She ran as fast as she could across the meadow. She would not pass through the grounds. She would find her way back to the lodge by a circuitous route. Vivian called after her a trifle angrily.

"Charl, you little fool, come back!"

But she had vanished — like a wild scared creature into a thicket.

Vivian shrugged his shoulders and walked into the orchard banging the door behind him.

"I hope she is not going to do something senseless, such as throw herself into the village pond," he muttered.

"Perhaps I have been foolish to trust her. If she speaks of this, it will be singularly unpleasant for me."

In the great hall he met Hannah. She gave him a queer look.

"Hullo, Hansie," he said, using a childhood's name for her.

The old woman knew that he only used it when he wanted to curry favour. She sniffed at him. She longed to tell him that his mother, these days, walked hand in hand with death. But her lips were sealed.

"My lady is not well," she snapped. "She has a bad migraine and Dr. Castleby has just been to visit her."

"I will go to her," said Vivian.

"Pray speak gently and try not to disturb her too much," said the privileged old woman.

Vivian first slunk into the dining-room to pour himself out a glass of wine. He needed a stimulant. He felt thoroughly nettled about Charlotte. What business had she to run off like that, crying and carrying on like a servant girl; she was, of course, little more than a servant despite her education. She ought to consider it an honour that her first love should be Lord Chase of Clunes.

And now Mama was ill. How tiresome! He must go and sit with her — hold her hand and dab eau-de-Cologne on her forehead and trust that she would be well enough to pay him that money he needed before returning to Oxford. He had incurred quite a few debts last term.

Complying with Hannah's wishes, he tip-toed into Lady Chase's bedroom where he conducted himself like a model and affectionate son.

★ ★ ★

Down at the Lodge, in Nan Forbes' spotless little sitting-room where the casements were gay with frilled muslin and there were pots of geraniums on every sill, Charlotte faced her foster-mother.

"You are terribly late, Charlotte. Whatever time did you finish your lessons? Why did her ladyship keep you so long today? Where have you been?"

These and many other questions were

put to Charlotte by the anxious woman who had been awaiting her at the door.

Charlotte answered at random. She found it difficult to prevaricate and could not explain that she had left Clunes several hours ago, and had since been in the woods with Lord Chase.

Mrs. Forbes eyed the girl anxiously. How pale she was. She had been crying.

"You have not given her ladyship cause to reprimand you. I hope," the good woman exclaimed, "I have never seen you so tearful."

"Please leave me alone — it is just that my head aches — I have been for a — a long walk," stammered Charlotte. "Her ladyship sent me out to enjoy the sunshine. I — I did not realize it was grown so late."

"Uncle Joseph will be in for his supper in a moment," said Nan. "Better wash, my dear, then come down to eat."

"I want no supper," said Charlotte abruptly.

Nan stared the harder. She had certainly never seen Charlotte in such a state. Why, the girl was trembling, as though she had a fever. Was she ill?

There had been two cases of scarlet fever in the village.

"Perhaps you had best go to bed and let me bring you some hot gruel," said Nan.

Charlotte tried to gain control of herself. She was really very fond of this little woman with whom she had lived for the last four years. Nan was a dear lovable person; round, plump, red-cheeked as an apple. She was a woman without education but spoke well, and at forty-five years old was a respectable and pious matron. Joseph, her husband, was equally religious and a kindly diligent man, devoted to his job, and to the Chase family. Not only he, but his father and grand-father before him had served them. The great regret of the Forbes had been that God had not sent them children. But during the last four years they had been happy in their affection for the beautiful little girl whom Lady Chase had entrusted to their care.

"Truly, I feel that it might be best for me to call Dr. Castleby to see you and send word to her ladyship that you are taken ill," began Nan.

Quickly Charlotte protested, her cheeks a burning red.

"No, Nan dear, do not dream of it, it is just that I do not feel myself. But it is nothing to be agitated about. Tomorrow I will feel quite well again. Now I should like to go to my bed, if you do not mind."

Nan did not mind. She fussed and brooded over her like an anxious hen until Charlotte felt ready to scream.

At last she was tucked up in bed in her small room. Charlotte, feverish, troubled, lay rigid and tormented by her memories. She was no longer a child but a woman. Lord Chase was her lover. She could not bear the heavy sense of shame and guilt. It weighed her down; all the more so because she truly loved her patroness, Lady Chase. She *knew* that Lady Chase would look at her in horror if ever she discovered what had happened. And dear, good honest Nan, and Joseph — 'Uncle Joe' — they, too, would be amazed and scandalized. With all her heart and soul she regretted her weakness.

Turning her face to the pillow, with a

little moan, the young girl fought against her inclination to sob bitterly, lest Nan should hear her and come up and ply her with questions, and once more threaten to send for Dr. Castleby.

7

A HOT July morning at Clunes, with the sun beating down. The flower beds looked parched, despite the efforts of the gardeners; for the last week there had been a drought. The blinds were continually drawn in the big house to keep out the heat.

Lady Chase had never known a warmer summer. Normally she would have enjoyed it. But this year she felt too ill; she could only lie languidly on the *chaise-longue* in her boudoir most of the day.

Hannah fussed and worried over her. Friends who called exclaimed at her pallor and increasing loss of weight.

Dr. Castleby came often and had lately prescribed stronger drops. He also begged her to see a specialist in London, but Lady Chase declined. No doctor, however good, could cure her now, she said; she knew it. It was just a question of time — of how many more of those terrible bouts of agony her poor heart could endure.

Meanwhile, Vivian knew nothing of his mother's condition; she would not have him told. Nor did he bother overmuch about her. He had only returned from Oxford this summer for a brief twenty-four hours, then rushed away to join a friend, the Earl of Marchmond whose parents had a yacht. Vivian had been invited to sail with them to Brindisi.

Greatly though Lady Chase longed for the company of her son, she was almost thankful to let him go. She could no longer bring herself to act a part for Vivian; to pretend to be well and enthusiastic about his pursuits, or bear the noise of the young gay friends he brought to Clunes.

She was dying. She knew it.

The one person whom she continued to see daily and whose presence never irked her, was Charlotte. To a woman as erudite as Eleanor Chase, the high intelligence shown by the young girl, her progress as a pupil, remained a deep satisfaction. But in these days, the lessons more often than not took place up in the boudoir — with my lady resting on her *chaise-longue*.

This afternoon, as Lady Chase waited for Charlotte, her mind was heavy with the burden of trouble. First of all, she was being forced, inch by inch, to tear aside the veil of illusion; to see that her son's character was deteriorating with the passage of time. His laziness, his refusal to accept responsibility or curb his mad extravagance and love of wine, all were growing more apparent. A letter from his tutor, received at the end of the summer, stated in strong terms that Lord Chase needed the firmest discipline; that it was to be hoped that he would mend his ways, especially as he would so soon be coming of age.

Vivian's mother mournfully echoed the tutor's 'hopes'. Secretly she dreaded Vivian's next birthday with all its implications. She had only one lever left that she could use if necessary. Unbeknown to the boy, the late Lord Chase had been wise enough to word his Will so that his son could not assume control of the capital until he was twenty-five. Until then, his allowance would increase but his mother and the General remained his trustees. Thank God, Vivian's father had had this foresight, she thought.

Not only was Lady Chase conscious of disappointment in her son, but also of a strange apprehension about Charlotte. The girl had changed during these last two months. She was growing tall and thin which, perhaps, accounted for her intense pallor. But her pinched face alarmed Lady Chase. The girl looked as though she spent much of her time in weeping. She would come to her lessons with heavy, red-rimmed eyes. When her ladyship asked what was wrong the reply was always the same: "Nothing, my lady — it is only the heat that tries me."

That might be so, but it did not seem right to Lady Chase that Charlotte, at sixteen, should not be able to stand a little extra heat. Besides her whole demeanour had altered. She used to laugh, to dimple, to delight in life, talk gaily to her instructor. Now she was over-serious, even nervous; she would never stay and talk once her lessons were over.

Hannah, reluctant as usual to allow the young girl to enter my lady's sacrosanct boudoir, opened the door and admitted Charlotte.

Lady Chase extended a white hand, which as a rule, the girl kissed before she sat down and opened her books.

But today she did not take the hand. She stood still, trembling in every limb. So ghastly did she look that Lady Chase half rose from her cushions and gave a cry:

"Charlotte, my child, what is it? Are you ill? What has happened to upset you?"

Charlotte did not answer. Her lips moved but no words came. Lady Chase noted that there were marks not only of physical malaise but of a mental disturbance upon the young face. The lashes were sodden with tears that made them seem too heavy, fringing eyes from which all brightness had fled. She did not even look as neat as usual. Her long cotton skirt was crumpled as though she had been lying on it. As Lady Chase stared, Charlotte tried to gather her courage in both hands and speak.

She had been lying on her bed for the last hour or two, sobbing bitterly after the doctor's examination, while the grim facts were disclosed to her.

Every day for the last couple of months, Charlotte had suffered from nausea; from a physical condition which, in her ignorance, she barely understood. The kindly Nan and Uncle Joe had taken it for granted that she was the victim of a bilious attack. At last they had called in Dr. Castleby.

He, of course, soon discovered what was wrong. After he left, the girl passed through a hideous hour of interrogation. Nan, overcome, told her what the doctor had meant when he said that '*Miss Charlotte was in the family way*'. It was beyond all doubting.

"Better find who this cur is, responsible for our poor young maiden's misfortune," he had muttered as he snapped his bag together and went forth to re-mount his horse.

Again and again Nan had hurled questions at the girl, followed by bitter denunciations.

How could she have done such a

dreadful thing? — she must be sly and deceitful — and ungrateful — oh, how badly had she repaid her foster-parents' tender care! And, again and again, Nan flung at the unfortunate girl this question:

"*Who is the man?*"

With whom had she been consorting? A farm labourer? A gardener? One of the young game-keepers? Nan mentioned all the possible names. Never, so it happened, that of Lord Chase.

Finally Charlotte threw herself at Nan's feet and begged for tolerance.

"Do not condemn me so utterly — I know I have done wrong but I did not understand what might happen," she sobbed piteously.

At that, and seeing the young girl's face so woeful and streaming with tears, Nan herself broke down. The woman and the young girl wept together.

"It was only once," Charlotte kept moaning, "I had but a few brief hours with my — my lover. Merciful heavens, what have I ever done to deserve such a cruel fate? Oh, dear good Nan — I am covered with shame. Let me die. Help me to find some means to do away with myself."

At that, Nan had gathered the girl close and forbidden her to repeat such a threat.

"You are not to die. You shall marry the man responsible for your condition. Your uncle and I will see to it," she exclaimed. "Only tell us who it was. We will not blame you. I believe you when you tell me that you did not understand. Some evil man has taken advantage of my poor Charlotte's innocence. *Who is he?*"

But the girl would not utter the name of her seducer. She thought of him, God knew, with bitterness. Love no longer played much part in her memories of Vivian. He had not written one word to her since his return to the University. Nor had he called to see her once he had come home again. So much for *love*, the poor child had thought in anguish.

Now that the facts had been made clear to her, she despised Vivian. *He* must have known the dangers — the possible consequences of that ruthless passion with which he had taken her.

When Charlotte persisted in her refusal, Nan grew antagonistic. Once more she accused Charlotte of being unco-operative as well as wicked.

"Since you refuse to tell us, then we shall go to her ladyship," she threatened.

"Never, never *that*!" cried Charlotte in a wild voice.

It was then that the truth suddenly struck the good woman. She put a finger on her lips.

"Dear God — *the young master* — it is him. Oh, yes, yes, I know it," she went on as Charlotte shook her head, and turned red then white again. "Now I understand. Fool that I am not to have thought of it before. That day that you were so late in coming home, *you were out with his lordship*. Oh, that monstrous young gentleman! It is *he* who got round you with his winning ways and handsome face. He, who has brought about your downfall."

After that it was useless for Charlotte to try and hide the truth. The time for weeping was over. With the coldness of despair, she admitted, at long last, that it was young Lord Chase who had seduced her on that April day.

Another consultation between Nan and her husband, and the pair agreed that her ladyship must be told. Neither of them realized, of course, how ill Lady Chase was nor knew about her heart trouble, or what effect such news might have on her. They were good, pious people. They had never liked the young master and they were of the opinion that her ladyship should be informed.

"If you do not go, I myself shall do it," announced Nan.

But to this Charlotte would not agree.

"I will not be a coward," she said dully. "It is my sin, so I shall confess to it. Even though her ladyship will recoil from me in horror. Never again will she admit me to the house, or allow me to benefit by her teaching. Doubtless she will have me sent away from Clunes altogether; and from you, too, dear Nan, dear Uncle Joe. From this home in which I have been so happy. But that must be my punishment. I shall accept it."

These words reduced Nan to further tears, but she wiped them away.

"Indeed! And where does his lordship

come in?" she snorted. "Shall *he* not be made to account for his crime?"

Charlotte from whom all childishness had fled, suddenly learned to be cynical. She gave a wretched laugh.

"Ah, no! Remember — in his eyes I am just another village girl who has been seduced; a privilege I no doubt share with many other unfortunates."

"Well, we must make certain the babe — and you — are provided for," put in Nan, being a practical woman.

Charlotte kept a bitter silence. She did not want to hurt her benefactor. She would rather have run away and told no one. But the Forbes insisted.

So now here she was in Eleanor Chase's lovely cool boudoir, scented with lilies — facing the most terrible ordeal of her life. This was the last time she would ever look upon Lady Chase's lovely gracious face and form. She dreaded having to say that which would make her ladyship's smile change to a look of horror and scorn.

Lady Chase spoke with great kindness. "Come, Charlotte, my dear, speak! What is so sorely troubling you? I have noted of late you have seemed poorly, unlike yourself. Perhaps it is that you study too hard. You must take a longer holiday from work than the one I gave you in June, I — ”

But she got no further. For with a groan, Charlotte stumbled to the couch and fell beside it. She crouched there, sobbing, her face hidden in her hands.

Lady Chase's tender heart was deeply distressed by this sight. She let the girl cry for a space while she delicately stroked the thick satiny hair. She said:

“Hush, Charlotte. Control yourself, my child. Share with me the grief that troubles you. I am, I assure you, both your mentor and your friend.”

At this Charlotte raised a face disfigured by tears, scarlet with shame.

“Do not touch me, my lady. I am not fit to be touched — least of all by you.”

“Charlotte — what words are these?” exclaimed my lady, growing uneasy.

“Oh, what shall I do, what shall I do?” moaned the young girl.

“Speak, for heaven's sake and explain these wild words.”

"I cannot bring myself to say it, my lady. Oh, believe, before ever you hear my wretched story, that I have loved and revered you most deeply," said poor Charlotte, "and that I never meant to dishonour your house."

A bright flush now stained Eleanor Chase's cheeks.

"*Dishonour my house?*" she repeated. "Come, Charlotte, this is too much; it cannot be as bad as that."

"It is — my lady, it is! Forgive me. I beg you to pardon me!" said Charlotte. Her big golden eyes burned so crazily, her expression was so wild that Lady Chase was frightened. She put her hand to her heart. It was beating too unevenly.

"Charlotte, my dear, you have ever been a passionate little thing, given to exaggeration. Pray, now restrain your emotions and speak quietly to me. Whatever it is that has befallen you, I cannot but swear to befriend you, as I did when first we met. As I shall always do, my gentle, clever child."

Such kindly words did little to comfort the girl. They heaped coals of fire on her head. Now, face hidden in her hands again, she blurted out the dread words.

"My lady — oh, my lady — I have sinned. *I — am going to bear a child.*"

At this, Eleanor Chase felt such astonishment, such a dire sensation of calamity, that she sat bolt upright. Her cheeks turned crimson. For a few moments she could hardly gather together her thoughts or consider the full significance of Charlotte's revelation. It was so utterly unexpected. Charlotte — self-confessed — *enceinte*. Oh, no, it was too dreadful!

Little Charlotte, who was only in her seventeenth year, going to be a mother! *That*, then, accounted for her change of countenance, her strange bouts of sickness this summer, her vanished mirth. And it was her sense of guilt, of shame, that had prevented her from lingering for the old happy, heart-to-heart talks which they used to have, once the reading, the learning, was over. Now Lady Chase recalled how Miss de Wynter, the music mistress, had come in one day and announced that poor little Charlotte had had to go home because she had been taken ill.

Another thing — a mysterious veiled warning given her by old Hannah, only yesterday. At the time Lady Chase had taken little notice — she was used to Hannah's jealousies. The old woman had said:

"I'd like to know what ails Charlotte Goff. Very queer she looks and behaves. Very queer. You mark my words, my lady, our young Charlotte is a dark horse. One day you'll be astonished. You will find out something, sure as eggs is eggs, my lady."

Eleanor had laughed.

"Fie on you for an old misery, Hannah, always speaking in riddles. Why should Charlotte be a dark horse? What next?"

But now the blindness had fallen from Lady Chase's eyes. She could see Charlotte more clearly — understand what Hannah had hinted. But what did *Hannah* know? —

Lady Chase began to tremble. She caught between her long fingers a bunch of the mauve ribbons trimming the muslin tea-gown which she was wearing.

"Charlotte, stop crying! Get up, and tell me at once the name of your seducer!"

she said in a high, authoritative voice.

The girl rose. She dabbed her eyes with a handkerchief and stood there, meekly, trying to control herself.

"Tell me everything. I insist," went on her ladyship in the sternest voice Charlotte had ever heard from her.

Then in a halting voice, Charlotte described the April afternoon when she had accompanied her lover into the woods; and still more falteringly she described her seduction. Sick with shame, she stumbled over the story.

"He was so masterful, so strong, he insisted — and I was in ecstasy. Oh, I know that it was shocking of me, but I loved him. I had loved him for long. It seemed so magical that he who was so far above me should wish to love me. So I surrendered, my lady; but once I understood the full meaning of such passion, I came to my senses. I wished it undone. It no longer seemed like perfect love — but something brutal and destructive. It has destroyed *me*, my lady!"

Charlotte's head sank. The tears started to flow again. She could speak no more.

Lady Chase had kept her glittering gaze upon Charlotte, listened to the whole story with a painful intensity. She, herself, so tender, so loving, could not fail to be moved. It was pitiful — that one so young, so gentle, should have been so cruelly used by a wicked man. For he must be wicked, he who had not hesitated to despoil a young maiden's innocence. According to Charlotte's woeful tale, he had deserted her. Where had he gone? Where was he? *Who*? Charlotte seemed reluctant to betray him. More loyal than her betrayer, thought Lady Chase.

Then going over in her mind, everything that the unhappy girl had said, and considering those words 'so far above me', Lady Chase almost swooned. What could such humility mean but that it was a gentleman of birth and breeding who had seduced her? Pray *what* gentleman? Where had she met any such person?

Lady Chase found herself shivering. She addressed Charlotte.

"Pull the bell immediately," she commanded.

Charlotte did so, one hand shading her

hot and aching eyes. Hannah appeared almost at once.

"Do you want me, my lady?"

When the old servant saw the wild and terrified expression in her mistress's eye she hurried to the *chaise-longue* and bent over her.

"Oh, my lady, I must fetch your smelling salts. You have been taken ill again?"

"Stay, I wish to question you," said Lady Chase. Her fingers gripped Hannah's arm. She looked up into the troubled face of her faithful maid. "Hannah, you are in my confidence and have been ever since his dear lordship died. In you I place my confidence. A dire catastrophe has overtaken little Charlotte. You are not ignorant of this. You *know*. Yes, do not deny it, for only yesterday you muttered a warning that I did not comprehend."

Hannah put a hand to her lips; she felt scared and showed it. She began to whimper.

"I know nothing really, my lady."

"Hannah, you are to speak, or I shall send you from my service this very day," said her ladyship in a stern voice such as the old servant had never before heard.

"Oh, my *lady*!" exclaimed Hannah and sank beside the couch on one knee. Turning her head, she glanced at the young girl. Yes, she knew what had befallen Charlotte Goff. It was written there for Hannah and all the world to see. Hannah whined a fresh denial but Lady Chase had no mercy on her. She was determined to get to the bottom of this thing.

"Charlotte has been betrayed. Which gentleman has she been meeting? Who has dared to lay a hand upon a young girl who has been beneath my roof for so many years?"

"Oh, for dear heaven's sake," broke in Charlotte, "do not ask any more, my lady."

"No, do not ask, and pray, my dear lady, compose yourself or you will have another heart-attack," said old Hannah, her voice breaking.

Lady Chase looked from one face to the other. Then, indeed, it did seem that that heart of hers ceased to beat, so terrible was the pain that gripped it.

For suddenly she knew the truth. Before she fainted dead away, she guessed it. And she wondered with bitter grief why she had not known before. She gasped:

"*My son*! It was — Vivian, *my own son*!"

She fell back on her cushions, so still, so waxen pale, that the others feared that she was dead. All thoughts were now directed to her. Charlotte was forgotten. Hannah flung orders at the girl.

"Send one of the grooms immediately for Dr. Castleby. Call Millie and tell her to bring burnt feathers. Hand me the drops, there, on her ladyship's bed-table."

Charlotte obeyed. As she ran to the door, the old woman maliciously called after her:

"God forgive you. You have killed a great lady."

Those terrible words followed the unfortunate girl as she hastened to do Hannah's bidding. After that, Clunes seemed to be in an uproar. Servants were running from one end to the other in the vast mansion doing this, that and the other. Dr. Castleby was traced to the home of a patient two miles away. He at once spurred his elderly nag to a gallop, in order to reach Lady Chase's bedside. It was rumoured throughout the district that her ladyship was dying, if not already dead.

Hannah was not to be torn from her lady's side until Dr. Castleby, fingering the delicate wrist, assured her that there was still a feeble flicker. Lady Chase had had another of her attacks but not yet, he said, a fatal one.

Meanwhile Charlotte, suicidal with grief, made to feel wholly responsible for all this trouble, crept into the woods and hid herself from the rest of the world. But it was not long before Nan and Joseph, her foster-parents, who knew her habits, came to find her. She lay face downwards on the mossy ground, eyes blind with weeping, body ice-cold. She had passed beyond tears and passion. She was like a dying person — finished with this life.

"Poor crazed creature," muttered Nan as she helped the girl on to her feet. "Dear God, what his lordship has to answer for! Come home, my dearie, come with us. It will not make matters better for you to catch your death of cold, and starve to death.

"Is her ladyship dead?" asked Charlotte in a dull voice.

"No, she lives and has asked to see you."

With glazed eyes, Charlotte regarded Nan's plump and worried face.

"She *cannot* wish to see me. She knows — "

"Yes, she knows," said Nan with a meaning glance at her husband who hardly returned it. The good man was unnerved by these happenings.

"She *cannot* wish to see me," repeated Charlotte.

"But she does," said Nan. "Hannah sent us to search for you."

"If it is to reproach me, I cannot bear any more," said Charlotte. She was shuddering from head to foot.

Now Nan put an arm around her and comforted her.

"She will not reproach you. Hannah says she herself wishes to tell you what decision she has reached."

They had walked out of the woods

now into the clearing. The sun was still shining at the end of this long day — the longest it seemed to Charlotte, that she had ever known. Joseph muttered a few words to his wife and walked off in the direction of the Lodge. Nan guided the girl into the orchard and through the gardens to Clunes. All around Charlotte lay the superb beauty of that familiar garden — she could hear the soft cooing of doves in the dovecote — the evening song of the thrushes. But for her there was no warmth, no beauty, no song, only a deathly sickness and distaste for life; a feeling that she would rather that Nan had left her there to die in those woods. For what could Lady Chase wish to say to her that could bring her anything but fresh guilt and pain?

8

THE Lady of Clunes lay in bed in a room darkened from the sun and smelling of aromatics and the sharp sweetness of the eau-de-Cologne with which Hannah had been bathing her fevered wrists and temples. Dr. Castleby had gone, satisfied that the poor harassed heart was beating once again with more vigour, if not normally. He would have preferred her to have seen nobody, but she insisted that Charlotte be sent for.

While she had waited, Eleanor Chase had reviewed her whole life and wondered what she had ever done to deserve this anguish, this terrible discovery of Vivian's guilt. It was a guilt that she must, she told herself, forever share with her son. She was a most unusual woman; one who entertained the highest ideals and acted only from the highest motives. The very last trait in her character was snobbery. Although so well born, she was without class-consciousness. Unique in her day, she possessed a strong sense of social equality. She did not believe in one law for the rich, and one for the poor. She did not think that a peer should be forgiven a crime for which a labourer would be condemned. She did not, therefore, see why Vivian should be allowed to get off scot free, whilst Charlotte suffered. When she had first recovered her senses, Lady Chase had forced Hannah to admit that Vivian was Charlotte's seducer. The old woman would have denied it, but Lady Chase made her swear upon the Bible. Then Eleanor Chase had said:

"I must not die. I must live to see this wrong righted."

She sent for Nan and talked with her. The lodgekeeper's wife, weeping bitterly, said:

"Pardon poor Charlotte, she did not know. I had never warned her, so maybe it's me you should blame, my lady, not the girl."

"Nobody is to blame save my cruel and heartless son," had been Lady Chase's response. For she knew that had Vivian loved Charlotte, he would never have deserted her. Love, his mother could have forgiven, but lust was ugly and unforgivable in her sight.

Nan could not understand her ladyship's attitude. Any other great lady would have driven the girl from the house, or paid her off. She said so. And it was then that Eleanor Chase felt indignation kindle within her. In a loud clear voice she denounced her own son.

"He is a grown man. He knew better. Charlotte was still a child and in love with him. She is romantic and tender. She was ripe to fall for a handsome boy's flattery. And she, herself, told me that the love she had thought so sweet, destroyed her. My son has brought about that destruction. He shall not be allowed to sneak out like a cur and leave Charlotte to pay the price."

That was the way that Eleanor felt and those were the words she repeated to Charlotte herself, when at length the trembling girl stood beside the big canopied bed and heard the astonishing verdict passed by this humane, extra-ordinary judge.

"I have sent for Lord Chase. He shall return from the Mediterranean and marry you immediately," announced Lady Chase.

"It is not possible — it would not be right!" exclaimed Charlotte in great agitation.

Lady Chase took one of the girl's slender hands.

"Charlotte," she said, "I admit that you have sinned, my poor child. But your sin was less of a crime than the outrage committed by him who understood what evil he perpetrated. You were frail; too loving, too giving. I, who have known you so long, realize that you were always over-generous and hasty. Have I not often chided you for that tempestuous streak? That lack of reserve?"

"Yes, my lady," whispered Charlotte.

"Nevertheless you knew not what you did," murmured Eleanor Chase, "and you must have suffered unbearably all these weeks. I can well believe the extent of your torture, my poor child."

"Yes, oh yes," said Charlotte and buried her face against the counterpane, "but why do you not cast me out?"

"Because I wish to see justice done, and because you will bear my grandchild," said Lady Chase. "I refuse to lose sight of that fact. That child shall be given its proper name. When it comes — if it seems premature in the eyes of the world — a seven-month child, what matter? Those who gossip must hold their tongues. You shall be Lady Chase and you shall bring up your child here in this house, where it belongs."

Charlotte could hardly believe her ears.

"But my lady, it is not fitting that I should become Lord Chase's wife," she said trembling.

"Other ladies of title and good family might agree with you. I do not. You are fundamentally good. You were pure until Vivian's passion sullied that purity. But he, my son, has defiled not only you but his noble name," her ladyship added.

And now she put her delicate hands over her face and her tears began to flow, breaking through the façade of her dignity, her resignation. It had been fearful to her to learn that Vivian, son of that dear and noble husband she had loved, was a common seducer.

"It is a terrible thing to despise the son I have loved," said Lady Chase suddenly, "but he must pay the price of his crime against innocence."

Charlotte, trembling, had a swift vision of Vivian as she had last seen him; bored and haughty and anxious to get away from her.

"For mercy's sake, permit me to leave Clunes," she broke out. "Vivian will hate me now, more especially if you force him into marriage."

"He shall marry you," said Lady Chase inexorably.

"But his proud name — this great house — I could not take my place here in your shoes," said Charlotte wildly.

"You can and shall," said her ladyship. The extent of her disappointment in Vivian impelled her to enforce this justice. In their circle Charlotte would be considered a 'nobody'. Let him raise her up by giving her and his child the name of Chase. If he hated to do it, it was only what he deserved. The knife-edge of her anger was turned towards *him*. Suddenly, with deep bitterness, Lady Chase said:

"You have more intelligence, and more courage than the one who has wronged you. In my opinion it is Lord Chase himself who is not worthy to have *you* as wife, instead of the other way round."

The young girl knelt beside the bed speechless and bemused. She was beyond fighting or arguing. Lady Chase took her hand and pressed it.

"Go back to Nan and Joseph, my dear. Stay with them and do not leave their care again until I send for you, which will be when his lordship returns."

"Yes, my lady," said Charlotte in a very faint voice.

"You will swear," added her ladyship, "to do no harm to yourself. You must remember that the child you bear is of my blood as well as of yours."

"Yes," said the flabbergasted Charlotte, "yes, my lady."

As she moved across the room, Lady Chase's voice followed her.

"Stay a moment. I have something more to ask you."

"Yes, my lady."

"Do you still love my son?"

Silence. Charlotte knew not what to reply. But she felt a sickness come over her and hid her face in her hands.

Lady Chase saw and understood. She gave a deep sigh.

"He has killed your love. It is little wonder. Alas, that this marriage must have its roots in hatred. Charlotte, my child, do not let it be so. It is love that conquers all. Love that casts out all fear. Are we not told so in the Bible?"

"Oh yes, my lady," said Charlotte weeping again. But she added with some of her old spirit: "Nevertheless it is hard to love when one no longer has respect."

Lady Chase nodded. "Yet we must both love and help him for he is in need of love and strength. You must master your own desires and become so strong, spiritually, that you will be able to strengthen *him*."

Charlotte ran back to the bed, took one of Lady Chase's hands and pressed her quivering lips to it.

"Oh, my lady, it is I who need strength. How shall I be able to give it to Vivian?"

"Because I believe you have the courage. You are not a poor witless girl. Develop your fine character. Earn not only his thanks but the regard of all his friends. Then I shall feel that the horror and shame of this thing may pass. You will be a better wife for my son than many others he might have chosen from a higher social circle."

"Oh, my lady, you are an angel," breathed Charlotte, "an angel whom I shall worship all my life."

"Nay, Charlotte, you should worship none but God."

Abashed, Charlotte dropped her ladyship's hand.

"I will try to do, to be, as you wish, my lady, and pray forgive me for the part I have played in your unhappiness," begged Charlotte.

"I do most freely forgive you. Now go and wait quietly, in meditation and prayer, until I send for you again."

Charlotte hesitated. In a pained voice, she whispered:

"If he — if he is very against it, which he will be, do not consider me, only yourself and him. Oh, anything, my lady, rather than that I should be a trouble to *you*."

She saw Lady Chase's pale face flush.

The dark wonderful eyes glowed with fire and pride. In a quiet firm voice, Lady Chase said:

"I have made my decision and I shall not alter one word of it. If you would please me, keep a quiet mind and prepare yourself for what is to come."

Charlotte choked back a sob and walked slowly out of the room. In the corridor she stood a moment leaning with her back against the closed door, trying to regain composure. This decision taken by Lady Chase was so fantastic, so unexpected, she could not even now believe it. In one way she felt a wild relief. She need no longer fear that her babe would be born illegitimate. But she did not want to marry a man who did not love *her*. *And to become Lady Chase* — Perhaps at this very moment beneath her heart she carried the future Lord Chase.

It frightened Charlotte. It set up a kind of paralysis in her mind.

She tried to think of Vivian as she used to do, as the Prince Charming who had first ravished her childish dreams, as the handsome and fascinating young hero who had taught the maiden, Charlotte, all the ecstasy of love. Alas — her mind and her heart had changed, gone beyond that love; grown critical of him. The feet of her idol were turned to clay.

She heard footsteps. She shrank from the doorway as Hannah approached, carrying a copper can of hot water and soft lavender-scented towels for her ladyship's evening ablutions. The old servant and the young girl came face to face. Charlotte's cheeks turned to crimson. Hannah's withered ones were colourless, but from underneath the white brows the sharp eyes peered at Charlotte with fierce hostility.

"How is her ladyship? Have you done more harm?" she asked under her breath.

"Nay, Hannah, I pray not," Charlotte whispered back.

Hannah looked her up and down with such a glance that made Charlotte feel more than ever the burden of her guilt.

"So! In trouble, and with the master of the house. It was only what might be expected of you, Charlotte Goff."

But they were the last words of the kind that Hannah was ever to speak thus insolently to Charlotte. Suddenly all that was dignified and imperious in Charlotte asserted itself under the lash of the old servant's tongue. The look she fixed on Hannah now was full of mingled grief and pride.

"You shall not speak to me so, Hannah. I know that I have sinned but it is to my Maker alone I shall pray for forgiveness. I am forever beholden to her ladyship for all that has been done for me since I came to Clunes. But if you do not already know it, I will enlighten you. I am to be married to his lordship as soon as he returns."

"Merciful heavens!" exclaimed Hannah, and nearly dropped the can and the towels.

With a choking sob Charlotte rushed away and down the wide staircase and out of the house. Hannah hurried in to her mistress. When she asked for confirmation of what Charlotte had said, Lady Chase quietly gave it. She added:

"Do not argue or protest, for it is my wish. Charlotte Goff was my protégée, I am responsible for her. Let everybody think that I am out of my mind, but I am doing what I consider best not only for Charlotte but for *him*."

"For *him*!" repeated Hannah in a quavering voice, "Oh, my lady, but what of her lowly station compared with his?"

Lady Chase gave a curt laugh.

"She is God's creature and far from lowly. Wait and see how she develops. Her brain will go beyond his lordship's. Her character is such that I wish to God that he had one similar. Oh, believe me, Hannah, what I do is for the best."

Hannah made a gesture of despair, and moved to the windows to pull up the blinds and let a little light into the dim room before she washed my lady's face.

Alas, her ladyship looked shockingly ill, Hannah thought, as she returned to the bed and saw more clearly the pinched and grey countenance of her beloved mistress. Surely she would not live long.

Lady Chase read her thoughts.

"My end is coming, but not yet. I shall live to see this wrong righted," she said, "and you, Hannah, who have ever been my loyal servant, must carry out my wishes to the end."

The old servant sniffed. Gently she

began to brush the brown tresses which were now so plentifully streaked with silver. Oh, what a heavy burden of shame and disgrace had fallen on this once proud happy household! How could Hannah do aught but hate the young girl who was responsible? Never could she bring herself to do as her ladyship, and place the blame at the door of his young lordship.

Once again Lady Chase seemed to read Hannah's mind.

"The child did not understand the full significance of loving. *You* know the extent of his lordship's great charm and power over women. All too often I have watched him exert it. Poor Charlotte had no chancc. It was as though he laid a snare for the tender bird, then brutally wounded it."

Hannah muttered:

"You are too kind, my dear lady."

"See to it that you are kind to her, also, once I am gone," said Lady Chase in a warning tone. "Treat her with the respect due to the one who carries his lordship's child."

The old woman fiercely blinked away

tears that she found hard to shed.

"Oh, my lady, what will his lordship say when he comes home?"

"I have sent a message by telegraph, to await him at Monte Carlo which he reaches next Thursday," said Lady Chase looking out of the window with her sunken eyes. "He is ordered to return to Clunes at once. He should reach London three days later, by train and packet. Meanwhile, Hannah, not a word of this to the staff, or to anyone outside this house. You shall swear on my Bible never to betray how this marriage, when it takes place, came about. I count on your integrity."

"You can, my lady, oh, you can!"

Lady Chase leaned back on her pillows. She felt desperately tired. While Hannah continued to smooth and braid her heavy hair, she fell asleep.

9

DURING the next three days, Charlotte stayed in bed and was devotedly nursed by Nan who, with her husband, could not get over the shock of realizing that their charge was to become the future Lady Chase. Nan, however, in her way, was as high-principled and reliable as Hannah, and she kept her mouth shut. She said not one word to anybody else of what had happened. Joseph went to his work in the grounds. Nan stayed indoors. And Charlotte, exhausted and quite overcome, spent most of the time sleeping. Those early days of pregnancy brought her a nausea that she found hard to control. With all the will in the world, too, she could not acclimatize herself to the fact that she must soon face Vivian. She dreaded meeting the young man. She dared not think what *he* would have to say.

When, at length, she was sent for by

Lady Chase, Charlotte was so terrified that Nan had to coax and then scold, in order to get her to go up to the big house.

More dead than alive, she stood, at last, facing her former lover. They stood side by side before Lady Chase who lay on the sofa in her boudoir. Charlotte gave Vivian one swift scared look, then her heart seemed almost to stop beating. Faintness seized her. She sank on to a chair, and laced her nervous fingers together.

"Pray pardon me, your ladyship — " she began.

"That is all right — do not distress yourself," came Eleanor Chase's gentle voice. "All has been made clear to my son and I have announced my intentions. Your engagement will be public news tomorrow. I shall give it out that an immediate marriage between you two will take place because of my grave state of health. It shall be thought that I wish to see my son happily married before I die, the doctors having stated that death for me is not far off."

At this, Charlotte's head shot up. She

looked with deep concern at her beloved patroness. Words failed her.

Lord Chase stood silent, scowling. Under the tan which he had acquired during the cruise, his face was a yellowish grey. There was nothing handsome about him at the moment. He looked sick with fury and chagrin. And it was with this sickness and fury that he returned Charlotte's gaze.

'*Traitress*!' that glance seemed to say.

But he was given no chance to say it. Instead, a pallid kind of smile wreathed his lips and he muttered:

"I hope I find you tolerably well, Charlotte."

She made no answer. She could not. Came a voice from the couch, clear and cool and controlled. Nothing in it to show the agony of Eleanor Chase's true feelings.

"Charlotte is very poorly, Vivian," she said. "It is nothing to be alarmed about. She will soon recover herself. But she commands your pity and concern."

Vivian crossed his arms. He was a very crestfallen young man without his usual *hauteur* or insolence. When in Monte

Carlo he had received the telegram from his mother, he had presumed that it was because of her sudden illness that he was recalled to Clunes. To reach home and be told that Charlotte was *enceinte* by him, also that his mother knew it, had been a hideous shock to Vivian. Still more so her ultimatum. Never had it entered his head that his mother would uphold Charlotte rather than *himself*. Of course, he thought, it was just another of her crazy acts of idealism. He had ranted and raved, argued and protested, for a couple of hours. He would not marry the slut, he said. He would not mess up his social life right from the start. Who would receive Charlotte as his wife? What had he done after all, that a dozen other lusty young men of good families had not done before him?

But always, Lady Chase made an obstinate reply.

"Charlotte was as a daughter to me. You shall make an honest woman of her. If you find things difficult at Clunes, for a time, that will be less punishment than you deserve. But Charlotte will make you a wife of whom you will one day be proud. You have only to give her the opportunity. And I would remind you that *you* were a seven-months' child although born two years after my marriage. Why should Charlotte not emulate my example? People will not find it amiss."

Vivian lost his temper and grew ugly. He said things that made his mother put her hands to her ears and shut her eyes. Now indeed, the velvet gloves were off. This was the Vivian she had suspected but never so far known.

But no bullying or shouting from the enraged young man altered her purpose. It was inflexible. She considered that what she was doing was the right thing. She had to help her, she informed Sir Harry Cawder — Vivian's godfather and co-guardian.

'It's a bit hard on the lad,' the General had written in reply to her letter telling him what she meant to do.

She had written back to him:

What of the young girl who is to bear my grandchild? It would be much harder on her if the father did not see her through.

129

★ ★ ★

The General was old and ill and disinclined to make an issue of it. He had adored Eleanor Chase since she was a young girl and he, her husband's Commanding Officer. He was not certain that she was doing the right thing, but he bowed to her wishes.

So Vivian faced the fact that if he did not go through with this marriage and acknowledge his child, his allowance would be cut. The sum of money which he would inherit when he came of age would barely pay his wine-bill these days. Clunes would be his but it was entailed; he could not sell the place. This meant virtual poverty for him. Until Lady Chase died, she must remain in authority. She could and would, she assured him, make things difficult for him if he refused to right the wrong. But if he married Charlotte, she would sign what cheques he demanded. Later she would leave Clune, go to a small secluded house with Hannah and her staff (if she lived!) and Vivian would be master of his own home.

The young man gnashed his teeth. He was cornered and he knew it, and like a cornered rat he bared his teeth. He even tried to bluster words to the effect that he could not be sure that Charlotte's child was *his*.

"You know you lie! Heaven will strike you dead if you repeat that lie. Can you, my son, repeat that foul implication with your hand upon the Bible?"

Vivian mumbled that he could not swear to anything.

"Because you know that you are responsible for Charlotte's condition," Lady Chase had said quietly.

Now and again Hannah had crept in, terrified that her mistress's heart would not stand up to the strain of this terrible scene. Each time Lady Chase sent her away.

"God will give me the strength to see justice done," she said.

Once during the argument, Vivian stormed at his mother:

"Is the future of this wretched girl more important to you than mine?"

"No more and no less," had come the answer. "I used to love you as a mother

131

loves her son, more deeply and proudly than anybody in the world; but your recent conduct has broken my heart. I die, a sadly disillusioned mother. I can only leave you to the unfortunate girl you make your wife and to your Maker."

Never before had Vivian Chase heard such terrible words from his once gracious and loving mother. He was reduced to silence. Then to a muttered apology.

"Forgive me, dear Mama, I lost my head," he grunted.

"That is no excuse, my son. I would rather you had been a thief than a despoiler of innocence."

Now Charlotte and Vivian stood, side by side, listening to Lady Chase's arrangements for their future. She had everything planned. Dr. Castleby already knew the staggering facts. His assistance and his silence could be relied upon. There would be no attempt at a high society wedding. Distant relatives and friends would be at once informed that a wedding between Vivian and Charlotte was taking place in strict seclusion, in the little chapel at Clunes, which had long been shut up. It could be opened for the ceremony. Afterwards, said Lady Chase, Vivian could take his bride for a brief honeymoon to a quiet watering place in France. Then, she told her son, he must return here to take up his duties as the master of this house. She would hold a reception for the pair on their return. It was a pity, she added, that Vivian could not return to Oxford. He must forgo obtaining his degree. But she doubted, she said with a sarcasm he had never before heard from her, if he would have obtained one anyhow.

Vivian gnawed at his finger-nails. If looks could have killed, both the women in this room would have been dead. He hated Charlotte with all his soul because she was the instrument of what seemed to him a ghastly punishment. He hated his mother for enforcing the penalty. When she mentioned that her health was such that she was not likely to survive the marriage, he secretly wished for one frightful second she would die before it need ever take place.

Lady Chase lay back on her cushions. She closed her eyes. She felt so very tired, but she was still fighting Death the last enemy. She could not, would not go in peace, until she had restored Charlotte's honour to her.

"Now, Vivian, take Charlotte back to the Lodge," she commanded. "Later this afternoon Mr. Meadows, our Vicar, is calling on me and will arrange with me the necessary formalities."

Charlotte moved towards the couch, her handkerchief to her lips.

"What can I say to you, my lady?" she whispered.

"Nothing, Charlotte. You have suffered enough. Now be at peace, and for the infant's sake keep calm. You have a trying time ahead of you."

Downstairs in the library, as the shadows of afternoon lengthened, Vivian and Charlotte faced each other alone. The moment the door closed on them Vivian turned upon the wretched girl.

"I suppose you realize," he said, "that it is the money that impels me to go through with this marriage. I am not prepared to be reduced to poverty and to have to earn my own living because I have made one mistake too many."

"I do not wish to marry you," she said

in an ice-cold voice, and the look in her eyes as they turned towards him now was one of scorn and even loathing. "It is for the sake of my child that I intend to go through with this dreadful marriage."

He sneered again:

"Surely you are glad to have hooked so fine a title and home." He swept his arm arrogantly around the handsome library.

"I will not listen to your insults," she said.

"My dear," he said, "as soon as we are married you will listen to whatever I say and put up with it. As my wife you will have saved your honour in the eyes of the world but to me you will be the lowest of my chattels."

She knew that he had an evil temper but she could scarcely believe that any man could say things so base to a woman who bore his child. Charlotte Goff was no helpless maiden in distress in this moment. She, herself, was reduced to fury. She came at him suddenly, her eyes blazing, her teeth clenched, her long trembling fingers clawing at him.

"You vile wretch. Oh, how I despise you!"

Now Vivian was amused. Weeping and cringing, a woman had no attraction to him. But he decided that Charlotte looked deuced handsome in her fury. He caught at the fingers that would have torn his cheeks, and imprisoned her against him. When she once more gasped out her hatred, he laughed and closed her lips with a kiss that seared and nauseated her.

"No, my beauty, I shall not let you have it all your own way once you are legally mine," he said. "You shall be taught who is the master. You gave yourself willingly enough that day in the woods. Are you too pure now for my kisses?"

But Charlotte Goff had bade a long farewell to meekness, and the shy tenderness of virginity. She kicked at him, and kicked again until she caught him a blow against his shin which made him release her.

"I do not think I shall marry you even for the sake of my child," said Charlotte in a strangled voice. "I cannot bear you to touch me."

"That would suit me," said Vivian,

"but unfortunately my lady mother has other plans for us. She is a great believer and always has been, I seem to remember, in marriage in such a case as ours."

Charlotte tried to smooth back her dishevelled hair. She felt horribly ill. The library was swimming around her. But the young man no longer tried to force his attentions upon her. The brief renewal of his physical interest in her had faded. He walked, hands behind his back, to the window and stared gloomily out at the approaching twilight.

Charlotte, trembling, looked with hot resentful eyes at Vivian's unyielding back. Hatred was festering within her very soul; in her, who had never before in this life disliked any human being. The hatred was so strong that it surpassed her dislike of herself, of the frailty that had led her to this pass. For a few brief seconds in his hateful embrace, she had genuinely considered the idea of running away from Vivian, and from Clunes. Then a new sensation seized her. It was almost as though she felt the urge within her to avenge the babe he had begotten. Let *him* take his punishment. Let him be burdened with her as a wife, since he so disliked the idea. Let him give a name to this poor infant whom, in the fullness of time, she must bring into this unhappy world. She spoke aloud:

"I thank my God that I can look upon you without love, Vivian Chase. If it is hatred that you feel for me, then your feelings are reciprocated."

He did not answer but she heard the snarl of his laughter as she walked out of the library, and out of the house.

At the Lodge Nan met her and began to ply her with anxious questions. What had happened? What had his lordship said? What had been arranged?

Charlotte looked at her stonily. Nan gasped a little as she saw the changed expression in that once tender and innocent face. It was the face of a woman grown hard and bitter.

Then said Charlotte:

"I shall become Lady Chase as soon as arrangements have been made with the Vicar."

The little lodgekeeper clapped her hands. She looked like one crazy with joy and triumph.

"Oh, my dear life, what an honour! You, my little Charlotte, to become a great lady and live at the big house."

"To me it is no honour, but a sign of my degradation," Charlotte said.

"Are you mad?"

"No, I was so, but I have grown sane. I shall marry Vivian Chase only for the sake of my unborn child. He hates me as much as I hate him. It is a fearful humiliation for him. I have tasted the very dregs of suffering these last few weeks. Now it is his turn to suffer."

Nan stared.

"Come, come, dearie, you are the luckiest girl alive. Think what her ladyship has done for you."

"I shall love *her* always, and spend the rest of my life trying to expiate my sin, and any grief that I may have caused her," said Charlotte in a low voice, "but I shall never be happy again."

Nan, following the girl up the narrow staircase into her bedroom, tried to treat this as a joke.

"You are but sixteen, my dear. You will mature and learn to regard your position differently."

"We shall see," said Charlotte. "Now, please dear Nan, leave me alone."

The little woman found the door shut in her face. She shrugged her shoulders and went back to her kitchen, but she paused now and then in her work to remember the look in Charlotte's eye and the sound of her voice when she had said those words: *"I shall never be happy again."*

10

THE sudden and private marriage of Vivian, Lord Chase, to Charlotte Goff, foster-daughter of the lodge-keepers at Clunes, was a nine days' wonder in the district.

People had of course been warned, after the announcement of the betrothal. From that time onwards, gossip seeped through house after house, both down here in Hertfordshire where the Chase family resided, and up in London.

Not one amongst the many distant relatives or friends seemed to know just how or why this engagement had come about, and been sponsored by Lady Chase. No invitations were issued for the wedding. The wildest rumours circulated. The only information that threaded its way through the gossip was what had been given out by Lady Chase, herself. Her secretary sent formal notes to meet the many inquiries, and Vivian confirmed them; to the effect that this was a long-considered love-match. Because of Lady Chase's failing health, it was decided to expedite the ceremony. Also that the London specialist sent for by Dr. Castleby confirmed his opinion that Vivian's mother might die suddenly and without warning. It was her dearest wish to see Vivian and Charlotte joined in marriage. The only people outside the family who knew the whole truth were Vivian's guardian, Sir Harry Cawder, the Forbes, old Hannah, and of course, the doctor.

Over the teacups and dinner-tables tongues wagged and conversation buzzed.

Everybody knew Charlotte by name, and in what high regard Lady Chase held her. Many in the district had caught a glimpse of her, from time to time, and spoken of her beauty — those fabulous golden eyes and curling chestnut locks, that dazzling complexion which many a high-born lady could envy.

A few ladies lowered their lids and whispered suggestively that there could be *other* reasons for the hurried wedding. In the London clubs, young Lord Chase was discussed by the men who had known his father. They also knew his reputation at Oxford. They confessed themselves puzzled.

There were one or two snobs in the district around Clunes who were affronted by the fact that the future Lady Chase had 'sprung from nothing'. But such folk were in the minority. The Chase family were so distinguished and so enormously rich it would not be in the interests of friends or acquaintances to refuse when the time came to call on the bride.

There was perhaps one other person who guessed at the truth even though she did not know for certain. That was Roma Gresham who knew Vivian and his vices so well.

Vivian had scarcely dared to leave the house in that interim between his return from the cruise and his wedding. It had not taken him long to guess that Hannah had been the spy who had betrayed him, rather than Charlotte. The old servant continued to spy for her mistress, and Vivian was kept at the latter's bedside. Eleanor Chase submitted him to long lectures on morals, and appeals to him to alter his ways and make Charlotte a good husband.

Vivian had plenty of private troubles. He had run up debts of honour in the gaming-rooms in Roma Gresham's house. He was forced because of this urgent need for money to knuckle under to his saintly mother's rule. That he had hurt *her* and made her last few days on earth a tragedy, he hardly cared. He was too filled with self-pity, too resentful of her power over him.

On one or two nights, he walked across the fields to Mrs. Gresham's house and held what might be considered a farewell party to his bachelorhood. When Mrs. Gresham politely congratulated him on his forthcoming marriage, he could see that she was surprised that he should marry this country girl. But he did not, for his own sake, tell her the truth. He would have to reside at Clunes. Decorum and etiquette would insist upon his leading a respectable life and ensuring that Charlotte should be given her due as his wife. No, he was not going to give anyone like Mrs. Gresham the sordid facts.

But Roma Gresham was too experienced a woman of the world to believe that Vivian meant to settle down.

"Shall we see you no more, then? And will you spend your evenings sitting virtuously with your little wife rather than come here where you are ever welcome?" Mrs. Gresham asked him, fluttering her lashes.

Those words fired Vivian as they were meant to do. He looked down into her wicked, painted face and laughed arrogantly.

"Do I seem a man to make the kind of husband never to leave his wife's side? No, rest assured, Madam, I shall often come to your enjoyable parties. And I shall *not* encourage my wife to ask questions."

Roma looked relieved. Even more so, when my Lord Chase pulled out a handful of sovereigns to pay bills that had been long outstanding. She had no scruples about ruining young men, nor for that matter, young women.

"I have a new attraction for you tonight, my Lord Chase," Mrs. Gresham murmured. "She is from Paris, a dancer who is to give a performance at the Crystal Palace this Autumn. She is immensely popular in Paris, and in Cairo, from which she originally comes. I have persuaded her to spend a few weeks down here to enjoy the pure country air." And with a tinkle of laughter Mrs. Gresham moved away, fashionably attired in an expensive evening gown with red carnations in her hair and long lace gloves. To look at from a distance Mrs. Gresham might have been a lady of high degree but Vivian knew well that all respectable doors were closed to her. Moodily he considered her divorce and how far she had sunk since she went through the Courts. But he enjoyed her hospitality. As for the young dancer from Paris: — It was not to enjoy pure country air she was here, but to amuse Mrs. Gresham's clients. This house, hidden away in the woods was little more than a high-class brothel.

Divorce in this period was fearful disgrace. It struck Vivian here and now that he was tying himself up in the matrimonial prison for good and all. And in his twenty-first year.

Gone, for ever, all his hopes of enjoying marriage with a rich dazzling young woman chosen from his own set.

But at least Roma Gresham's house remained near Clunes. If and when life became too boring here, he could still pursue his secret sports. Mrs. Gresham was nothing if not discreet.

11

ON the 20th July, five weeks before Charlotte's seventeenth birthday, she was married to Vivian Chase in the chapel at Clunes.

No bride is likely to forget her wedding. For Charlotte it was an affair so fantastic that she was certainly not likely to forget it.

After the events of the preceding week, she had been as one in a daze, acting like an automaton, speaking only when addressed, living in a kind of nightmare world from which she hoped in vain to awaken.

At Lady Chase's command a dressmaker had been sent to measure and make her a few dresses fitting for her station. Charlotte took no interest in clothes as in happier circumstances she might have done. It was Nan who was excited and pleased. Nan, who kept trying to coax the girl to be thrilled with the many lovely things Lady Chase sent her. But she stood like a marble statue while the dressmaker and her assistant fitted her and barely admired the glossy satin of the bridal dress, or the exquisite Limerick lace veil which had belonged to Vivian's own mother. She only knew that she felt ill and tired. But Nan kept telling her that she must rest and try to look beautiful for the marriage ceremony.

"Beautiful for what, for whom?" Charlotte asked herself bitterly. Her whole being cried out against this wedding. She had felt a hypocrite when at length they had attired her in the gleaming dress and veiled her face with the foaming lace. Apathetically she pulled the long white kid gloves over her hands, and took the bridal posy of white roses and stephanotis, grown in one of the Clunes' greenhouses.

She had no right to wear this gown or to go like a virgin to her marriage and she knew it. Eleanor Chase knew it, too, but she had insisted.

"There are moments in life when a lie must be acted for the sake of others. It is for your child's sake that I wish it to appear in the eyes of the witnesses as though there is no babe on the way. I will not have it known that my first grand-child was conceived in sin."

Charlotte had wept bitterly at those words but it was not often now that she cried. Her grief was too deep. She was thankful that she saw little of Vivian. Once or twice only before the ceremony, they met in his mother's boudoir. When he escorted her home they had nothing to say to each other. In silent hatred they separated.

To one of such warm and affectionate nature as Charlotte's, it was a ghastly state of affairs.

Then the wedding itself.

The gardeners had filled the little disused chapel with flowers. There was an overpowering scent of roses that made Charlotte feel sick. But Dr. Castleby had been attending her and made sure that she would stand up to the ordeal of the day. He had scolded her, too, just before she left the Lodge with Nan and Joseph (the good pair both attired in their Sunday best and hugely elated).

"You are a strong young girl," the doctor said, "in perfect health. This *malaise* from which you suffer is a nervous tension. You must be strong-minded for the sake of all."

So it was a white but controlled Charlotte who finally stood beside the young lord of Clunes that sultry summer morning. There was no sunshine. Dark clouds were gathering. A big storm was on the way. It seemed to Charlotte ironic and correct that such a marriage as hers should be solemnized to the accompaniment of thunder and lightning instead of hymns.

Lady Chase, leaning heavily on the arms of the doctor and Hannah, came up the aisle. She sat in the front pew, alone; that was how she wished it. She could scarcely see the proceedings because of the tears that continually blinded her eyes. She thought of Vivian as a curly-headed, small boy, so full of charm and promise; yet even then with the temper and moods that had made him difficult to control. She thought of the gallant soldier-husband who had died in the Crimea, and she thought of the splendid wedding which should have taken place in a far bigger church with all the glitter and pomp befitting the wedding of a Chase.

But there was just this sad ceremony in the little chapel which struck cold even on a summer's morning and was filled with the shadows of the approaching storm. Mr. Meadows, the aged, white-bearded vicar of Harling, officiated alone. He looked ill at ease. He felt that something was wrong even though he was not in her ladyship's confidence. But he presumed with the rest of the district that this curiously hasty marriage was taking place solely on account of Lady Chase's failing health. Indeed, he wondered if she would even survive the day; she looked so ill. Every now and again she raised the veil she wore and lifted a gold-stoppered bottle of smelling salts to her nostrils.

Sir Harry Cawder had not been well enough to leave his home and attend this wedding. The only occupants of the other pews were members of the staff. All were thunderstruck to see his young lordship being joined in holy matrimony to Charlotte Goff.

Whatever they thought, none dared say

it. But there were few smiles; and no air of gaiety. Charlotte trembled violently as she repeated the words dictated to her by the old clergyman. Her voice could scarcely be heard. Vivian's was audible but exceedingly surly and now and again he tossed his golden head, looking to the left and right as though he wished to escape but could not.

Not once did he glance at his bride. But as he slipped the ring on her finger he felt a shudder go through her. Then they turned to one another. Vivian was quite thunderstruck by the beauty of Charlotte in her bridal gown, despite her ill-health. But the huge eyes were cold and hard, they even made him feel uneasy.

Now Lady Chase's head sank into her hands.

"It is done," she thought. "Charlotte has been vindicated. My son has paid the price. As for me, his most wretched mother, *I think he has cost me my life.*"

Mr. Meadows gave the final blessing. The bridal couple, Charlotte's gloved hand through Vivian's curved arm, turned and began to walk slowly down the aisle.

Charlotte was thinking:

"So I have been made an honest woman and I am Lady Chase. I am also the most loveless unhappy being in the world, hated by a husband whom I despise."

And Vivian reflected gloomily:

"So now I have a wife! Ye gods, what a wedding for Vivian Chase! *She shall pay for it* — that I swear!"

A quiet family lunch had been arranged at Clunes after which Vivian and Charlotte were to take the brougham to Harling station. There, a train would carry them to London, and they would stay the night in her ladyship's London residence. Tomorrow it was arranged that they go by steamer and train to Monte Carlo where a villa had been lent to Vivian by one of his mother's friends.

As they moved down the corridor, still in a sullen silence, the first flash of lightning illuminated the darkness. The bride gave a faint cry and raised a hand up to her eyes. There followed a low rumble of thunder.

154

"So the storm is come. A happy augury," said Vivian with a derisive laugh.

Charlotte made no reply. She felt, as she had felt for long, that her heart had turned to stone.

She was silent and unsmiling while the unhappy wedding breakfast took place in the morning room which the staff had dutifully decorated with flowers.

The Dowager Lady Chase maintained her stoic calm and determination throughout the 'celebration'. The Vicar remained with them. Wine was drunk and sandwiches eaten. There was no wedding cake. No friends or relatives to toast the bride and bridegroom, save Vivian's mother supported by Hannah and the somewhat baffled and embarrassed clergyman, who raised a glass and murmured:

"*To the bride and bridegroom.*"

Charlotte merely touched the ice-cool wine with her lips. She nibbled a sandwich when Nan whispered to her that she must do so. The bridegroom drank a great deal and laughed and talked a little too loudly. He mentioned the inclement weather and discussed the most trifling things with Mr. Meadows. He reminded the Vicar that there was to be an amateur race for bicyclists on the new machine.

"I'm told that it has a driving wheel of sixteen inch diameter," Vivian drawled, looking immeasurably bored but feeling his mother's dark and gloomy gaze upon him.

"Ah, yes," murmured the Vicar, "the Honourable Keith Falconer from Trinity College, Cambridge, has been much talked of as a possible winner of the contest."

"I must say bicycling does not interest me. I prefer riding," went on Vivian and walked across and looked out at the teeming rain. "Our drive to the station will be a stormy one," he added.

The bride followed his figure with her gaze. She wished that she could rouse herself from the terrible lethargy into which she had fallen. This ring upon her finger could not be a wedding ring. That tall, handsome, cruel young man *could not* be her husband. She dreaded the thought of going away from Clunes with him. She would rather have stayed with her newly-made mother-in-law. Now she turned her large despairing eyes to the Dowager who gave her an encouraging smile and beckoned to her.

"Come here, my child."

Mr. Meadows moved to the window. He stood there talking to Vivian. Eleanor Chase took one of the bride's ice-cold hands.

"Courage, poor dear little Charlotte," she said in a low tone, "you must pray to Him who resolves all things in order that He may strengthen you. Do not look so tragic. You are now a wife, and will, in the fullness of time, I am sure, become a happy mother."

Charlotte shuddered, but made no response,

"Try," continued the older woman, "to grow well and strong in the sunshine of Monte Carlo. The sea should do you good. You will see much of life beyond Clunes and Harling hitherto unknown to you. Remember your learning, all that I have tried to teach you. Do not forget, if only for *my* sake, to be a good wife and a helpful comrade to *him*," she indicated Vivian.

Now the bride went down on one knee in all her shimmering draperies and with that look of despair still stamped on her young face, picked up one of Eleanor Chase's hands and laid it against her cheek.

"My lady," she began.

"I must now be 'mother' to you."

"Oh, Mother," said Charlotte in a wild voice, "I do most deeply revere you. I am not worthy to call you by that sweet familiar name but I beg for your forgiveness. Whatever I can do to please you in the future, I will do it. Alas, my love for *him* seems to have vanished beyond recall. It is that knowledge which freezes my mind and torments my heart."

The two women were speaking in lowered voices and could not be heard by the others at the far end of the room. Eleanor Chase's features worked. Tears were not far from her eyes but she stroked the bride's chestnut head and rearranged a fold of the lace veil.

"You are my own dear daughter now," she whispered. "I do most freely forgive you for I know that you remain innocent at heart. But try, oh, try, to love my son — no matter how hard or painful it must seem to you in these terrible circumstances. Now Nan must help you to change. Your train is at four-thirty, and I am very tired. I shall not be able to endure much more fatigue."

"Beloved Mother," said Charlotte with fresh agony in her voice, "pray take care and rest, and be here to welcome us when we return. Oh, do not leave Clunes yet awhile. I could not do without you now."

"One day you *must* do without me," said Lady Chase with a wan smile. "Come, rise from your knees, my dear little Charlotte. Be at peace, and send Vivian to me."

When Vivian stood beside his mother, she looked up at him with a long penetrating stare which seemed to search his very soul. He moved uncomfortably.

"In the name of your dead father and for the sake of your mother who may not much longer be with you — be kind to your young wife," she said. "Cast hatred out of your heart. Turn from thoughts of self. Only by love and kindliness can you ever obtain the true peace of mind which we all seek in this world."

Vivian grunted rather than replied.

"Oh, Vivian," added his mother with anguish, "you are my only son. Can you not let me die in peace, believing that you mean to act like a gentleman, and a Chase."

He shrugged but muttered:

"I will do all I can. But remember, Mama, that you have done my reputation no good by enforcing this absurd marriage."

She dropped his hand.

"I regret that the legal union seems to you absurd, whereas you were willing enough to enter upon an illicit one," she said abruptly.

"Well, I am married to Charlotte now," he said sullenly.

"Respect that marriage bond or you will for ever lose my affection," said Eleanor Chase, coldly.

Thus ended the wedding of Vivian and Charlotte. Her ladyship retired to her bedroom. An hour later the newly-married couple left Clunes in the carriage which took them to Harling Station.

Charlotte sat rigid in her corner, staring

out at the rain. It continued to fall heavily although the storm was abating. Only an occasional flash of lightning lit up the grey sky and made the bride shut her eyes tightly. As a small child she had always been frightened of storms and she particularly hated this one. It was, she felt sure, a presentiment of future evil.

Nan had kissed her good-bye tearfully, trying to comfort her by reminding her of the dazzling future awaiting her when she returned from her honeymoon. Charlotte had made no comment. *She* wanted nothing except the peace of mind that she had lost — the essential peace of an innocence which Vivian had destroyed.

Her husband sat at her side as silent as herself. He barely glanced at her. Yet she was beautiful in her fine blue suit with its coquettish bolero jacket, fashionable just now; fine *guipure* lace at the throat. A charming blue straw bonnet, with silk flowers and a little French veil hanging down from the back, was tied with a little bow under her chin. She carried a small folding fan which she used continuously. A pleated taffeta coat lay across her knee. The afternoon was steamy and close after the storm.

On her way to France! Hard for Charlotte to believe it. In the carriage, following, were their servants. Browning, Vivian's valet and Hester, one of Eleanor Chase's servants who had worked under Hannah for some years. She was excellent with her needle, and was now to be Charlotte's personal maid.

Charlotte gazed out of the window as they passed the Lodge. She thought sadly of the happiness she knew there in her childhood. One or two of the estate workers waved and threw flowers to her. They were standing in the rain to see the bridal couple go away.

Charlotte waved back at them, trying to smile and be grateful, but she felt that the whole affair was one long continued farce. What kind of a bride *was* she? What happiness could she hope for? And with Vivian as her lawful husband and master, was she not facing a veritable martyrdom rather than the brilliant future that Nan prophesied? Eleanor Chase had done what she believed to be the right thing. Ethically it might be so, but from every other standpoint Charlotte felt it must be wrong. It was an enforced wedding between two human beings who had passed from mad passion to mutual hatred and contempt.

She thought with melancholy of the bliss she might have experienced today had she felt about him what she used to feel; had *he* loved *her*, had this been a true wedding in every sense; with no disgraceful memories to pursue her, no apprehension of the future.

She felt even worse when at length they entered the great house in Eaton Square where they were to spend the night, for she was pursued by a sharp recollection of the little Charlotte who had been brought here by Lady Chase and her young son on that night of fog. She thought with pain of poor old Aunt Jem and Uncle Albert, of the old life in Pimlico which had been uncomfortable, poverty-stricken, yet in its way happy, with the happiness of ignorance.

Today she entered the big house on the arm of her husband, remembering how Vivian had charmed her in this same house when he was a mere boy.

How fantastic and impossible it would have seemed to her then, had anybody said that one day she would become his wife.

The footmen bowed; the staff had ranged themselves in rows to curtsy and welcome the bride and groom, and stared inquisitively at the beautiful newly-made Lady Chase.

Charlotte bowed and smiled as graciously as she could. Vivian acknowledged the greetings of his servants with the haughty bored smile he assumed for menials.

The valet, Browning, and young Hester attended to the boxes. Charlotte and Vivian passed up the staircase into the rooms that had been prepared for them.

Charlotte looked around the enormous bedroom. It had a floral wallpaper and deep blue satin curtains. It seemed to her unfriendly, chilling. Vivian made things no better by indicating the huge four-postered bed with its brocaded curtains and saying:

"I was born in that bed, so they tell me, my dear. The confinement should have been at Clunes, but I believe my sainted mother came up to London to be with my father for a State occasion and I arrived with deuced lack of consideration, so my Mama had to remain here."

"Indeed," said Charlotte coldly as she unfastened the strings of her bonnet and drew off her gloves.

She had no wish to consider the birth of Vivian or the sufferings of that poor mother whom he might well call 'sainted'. It made her feel queasy. She longed, too, to be alone so that her new maid could come and unfasten her tight stays. She could not breathe. She was unused to tight-lacing. She deplored the necessity of it for fashion's sake. Her bustle felt strange and a little absurd.

It was terribly hot in London. There must have been a storm here, too, she thought. The pavements were wet. The trees in the square looked sodden.

She had not seen London for more than four years. With her memories crowding down upon her, she moved to one of the windows, pushed aside the lace curtains and stared out. She had never felt more lonely. Already she was homesick for Nan and the Lodge, for the great avenue of trees leading to

Clunes. For the daisy-starred meadows, the grazing gentle cows, the peace of the Hertfordshire countryside. For her books, her dear books, and last but not least, her most *dear* teacher who now lay dying, bitterly disillusioned.

Oh, thought poor Charlotte, if one could but turn back the clock! If only she had never met Vivian Chase, never felt the sheer animal magnetism of the handsome young man and listened to his honey-sweet flattery.

She let the curtain fall and turned round, her bonnet still in her hands, her eyes blinded by tears.

She saw her husband lounging against one of the bed-posts, his hands in his pockets. He eyed her almost malevolently, she reflected.

Suddenly she came towards him. It was as though her loneliness, her abject misery on what should have been the happiest day of her life, broke through the surface and overflowed.

"Oh, Vivian," she said, "can we not start afresh? Do not look at me with such hatred. I am, after all, the mother of your child."

"You cannot expect me to be glad of that, especially when your betrayal of me has meant my ruin."

"Oh, Vivian," persisted the poor young bride, "I did not willingly betray you. But consider my years, only sixteen, and I knew nothing of what passion meant until you taught it to me. Surely you do not blame me entirely for what took place?"

"If you had loved me you would have died before you blabbed to my mother," he said with superb egotism.

"And what would have become of me?"

"No doubt I would have paid to see you through your trouble," he drawled.

Charlotte's mind, still so young, so fresh and idealistic, could not fathom the depths of such utter selfishness. It appalled her.

"Then does this new young life for which we are both responsible mean nothing to you?" she asked.

His eyelids drooped. He kicked the point of a boot against the bed-post.

"Pff! You women sicken me with your sentimentality."

Young though she was, Charlotte had character. For a little while her horror and astonishment at the discovery of her own condition, and of Vivian's callous attitude, had subdued her spirit. Now, her courage and determination were returning. She was the old Charlotte again. She felt a rightful indignation against this young man who seemed to have no respect for virtue.

"What kind of man are you?" she demanded with scarlet cheeks and brilliant eyes, "*what kind* — that you can remain so indifferent to human suffering?"

"Are you suffering?" he sneered.

"More than you will ever know. Being made your lawful wedded wife this morning has saved my reputation but it has not eased my conscience. Neither can it wipe out my sorrow that in a moment of madness I helped to wound that mother whom you have rightly called a saint."

"Oh, come, come," he said, "you were not always such a pious little miss. You returned my kisses very prettily in the woods at Clunes that day!"

She flung back her head.

"I do not deny that I loved you. But I was in your hands — your cruel hands — so experienced and remorseless. Yet you have not one spark of conscience. It is that which amazes me."

"Good God," said Vivian in a violent voice, "you are not the first female to be put in the family way by a gentleman."

This coarse and brutal remark sent an even deeper crimson into the girl's pale, tired face. She stepped back a pace.

"How disgusting you are!" she said in a low voice.

He laughed loudly.

"Really, my dear, your refinement of spirit is most touching. A moment ago you asked me if we could not start afresh. Well, *well*, I fear I am in no way paternal, and I have no interest in this babe that we have begotten. Of course I rely upon your giving me a son. I trust, too, that it favours my side rather than yours."

"What is wrong with mine? The Goffs were good decent people," she flashed. "My father would have scorned to treat my mother as you treated me."

"All the same you did not scorn my embrace when you were in my arms that day at Clunes," he reminded her, and with a lecherous expression he advanced and caught her to him. He let his hand slide down her back to her waist that was still so small, so alluring. The exploring fingers went on to crush the rustling taffeta of her bustle, and up again to her warm, white neck. Playfully he began to pull the lobe of her ear and nibble at it.

"Pretty Thing, I am not unwilling to break the ice," he whispered. "For I can see that it will be dashed uncomfortable if we start off this honeymoon like two antagonists. Besides, London is too hot for quarrelling. Sweet, I'd forgotten how long your lashes were, how silky your skin. Ye-es, I fancy I could be kind to you, providing of course, that you rest as willingly in my embrace as any ordinary bride would do on her wedding night."

For a moment Charlotte stayed stiff and unbending in his embrace. She did not like the things he said, nor the way he said them. She felt that there was no real love in his heart — nothing of the tender romance for which she yearned. The Prince Charming whom she had once so blindly loved, seemed more like a satyr, eager to hurt — to ravish. He did not quote poetry to her today. He covered her face with kisses that wounded, instead of comforted. She broke down and wept.

"Oh, Vivian, Vivian!" she sobbed his name.

"No tears," he said, "if you wish us to make something of our marriage, I want neither tears nor recriminations. If I have sinned, you and my mother between you have made me pay for it. Now it is *your* turn to give, rather than take. Cease this nonsense about my cruelty. You are no innocent maid, you know. You are a *wanton*."

"That is a vile lie!" she stammered wildly, and tried to push him from her.

"Oh, do not make any mistake, I like wanton women," he said with a grin.

Tired to death, Charlotte made no further protests but despairingly surrendered. His fingers tore at the little buttons on the back of her dress — at the rich silk and the lace on her petticoats. He seized a handful of her curls, pulled her head up against his and kissed her with violent passion. After a time he picked her right up in his arms and carried her towards the big bed.

"I am behaving like a model bridegroom," he said and laughed. "Is this not as you would wish things to be, my dear?"

She went limp in his arms and hid her face against his shoulder.

All the heartbreak and pain within her were centred in the one sobbing cry that came from her lips.

"It is love that I need from you, Vivian. *Oh, my husband, it is love that I need.*"

But if he heard that cry he did not answer it. He laid her on the pillows, walked to the door, and turned the key.

Any hope that had flickered feebly in her heart that he would give her such love, died during the hour that followed.

12

THE honeymoon was over.

Lord Chase's carriage, drawn by two beautiful greys, rolled down the broad drive that led to the house. The bride and bridegroom were home again. They had left that home in a thunderstorm. They returned on a mild evening, after a golden day of sunshine late in August. Not yet had the beech leaves turned to gold, but the Michaelmas daisies were already colouring the herbaceous borders with royal purple. The Virginia creeper over the west wall of the old house was beginning to turn red.

Once again for Charlotte, the old formula of welcome from the retinue of servants. The curtsies, the deep bows. This time, no stopping at the Lodge. It was Vivian's wish that his wife should not see too much of Nan and Joseph nor remind anyone that she had once lived with them. She was to take her rightful place at Clunes and must develop, he had told her more than once, some degree of snobbery. For he knew that this was missing from her true nature.

With mixed feelings, Charlotte walked into the familiar hall at Clunes, and, followed by Vivian, went straight into the library where they were told that the Dowager awaited them.

Charlotte had felt thankful while she was at Monte Carlo to receive a note from her mother-in-law stating that, after rest and care, she was better. Equally was Charlotte relieved to approach the house this afternoon and find Vivian's mother still alive. She had almost held her breath for fear that she might find the blinds down. Now as she looked upon the beloved figure on her accustomed sofa by the fire, Charlotte hurried across and knelt beside Lady Chase.

"Dearest Mother, we are here at last," she murmured.

"At last," echoed Eleanor Chase and gave a deep sigh of relief as she looked into her daughter-in-law's golden eyes, then up at her son.

Whatever had happened, it seemed

on the surface, anyhow, that they had reached some kind of compromise. Indeed, they looked quite well, the mother thought, gratified. Vivian was bronzed and good humoured and Charlotte did not look nearly so white or strained as she had done when she left here. She had gained in poise and dignity. It was also evident that Vivian had been generous to her in Paris for she was fashionably attired in a new travelling dress, wine-coloured, with a three-quarter-length coat bordered with silk fringe. A little tilted hat of palest green, with a long veil floating down the back, sat on the chestnut head. She looked mature, and of course, Eleanor Chase reflected, her figure was fuller. She looked much less of a child.

Lady Chase whispered to Charlotte:

"Is all well?"

"Yes, dearest Mother, all is well," Charlotte whispered back.

Then Lady Chase held her arms out to her son.

"Embrace me, my dear boy, it is very good to see you," she said in a voice of deep emotion.

Vivian graciously bent and kissed first

his mother's hand then both her cheeks.

"Splendid to see you looking so much better, Mama," he said and coughed.

"Oh, I am not feeling too badly," said her ladyship. "Hannah has taken good care of me and Dr. Castleby comes every day. Hannah," she turned to the old maid who hovered as usual in the background, "do our young couple not look wonderful? Monte Carlo has benefited them."

"Yes, my lady," grunted Hannah.

But there was no pleasure in the look which Hannah directed at the young Lord and Lady Chase. She still felt that Charlotte ought not to be here in this exalted position. She told Vivian bluntly, out in the hall when they were alone, his mother's looks belied her. Dr. Castleby was most concerned about the state of her heart. But she had insisted upon rising from her bed and coming down to welcome them home.

Vivian pretended an anxiety he did not really feel. It was not in his nature to worry over things before they happened.

He felt depressed, mainly because he was back in England. Clunes held no joy for him, and it irked him to have to act the penitent and anxious son. Just as it had irked him to simulate the adoring husband while he honeymooned in the South of France.

He was no more in love with Charlotte than he had ever been. He could be excited by her beauty when in the right mood — but he found her no companion. She had too fine a mind, too deep a nature. He liked women to be light-hearted and frivolous. And he had seen to it while he was in Monte Carlo that he had obtained as much such female society as he wished. There were plenty of gay *demi-mondaines* to be found hanging round the Casino. He also spent much time and money at the Tables. He had come home 'broke' but knew that if he played his cards properly with Mama, he would soon be able to replenish the coffers. In fact he had grown to look upon Charlotte as something of an investment. His mother seemed so attached to her and the idea of the coming child, she would deny *him* nothing so long as he conducted himself well towards his wife.

Meanwhile Charlotte sat beside her

mother-in-law and the two women exchanged news, while they sipped the China tea that had been brought to them. Lady Chase looked at Charlotte with the old tenderness in her dark sunken eyes.

"Is it possible that the Almighty led me to do the right thing and that you and Vivian have found some common interest, a new contentment?" she asked the girl in a yearning voice.

"Yes, yes, we — we get on very well now," said Charlotte lightly. "The villa was enchanting and I was stunned by the beauty of the French Riviera. You see my new clothes — " she laughed and indicated her costume. "Vivian was generous. Little Charlotte Goff has quite vanished."

"I do not want the little Charlotte *I* knew ever to vanish," said the older woman, "I liked her too well."

"Toward you, Mother, she will never change," said the girl with feeling.

"I do not think an exalted position will do much to spoil you," agreed Lady Chase. "And I feel in my bones that you have a good influence over my son. You do not know, Charlotte, how thankful I am for this day."

Charlotte murmured a reply and went on drinking her tea. So great was her desire to spare Eleanor Chase further pain, that she drew a veil over so many bitter memories of that honeymoon just spent in Monte Carlo. Please God, if his mother had only a short time to live, Vivian would be man enough to play *his* part and so make her happy until the end.

But for Charlotte the future stretched bleakly and without hope. After a few weeks of intimacy with Vivian Chase she knew that she could never find happiness with him. She knew just how base he was, how utterly ignoble.

The honeymoon had been a period of bitterness and disgust for man, man as revealed to her by marriage to Vivian Chase. At times, when she came up against his stubborn determination to master her, she had wondered in despair if he had inherited a single one of his parents' qualities. It seemed incredible that two such noble people should have conceived this monster of egotism.

Most evenings she had spent alone, either wandering through the beautiful orange-scented grounds of the villa or sitting in sad solitude on the terrace looking down at a sea that shimmered like blue silk. Hour after hour, she lay lonely and forsaken in the splendid Italian bed in a room of Rococo magnificence. Day after day, accompanied only by her maid, she wandered through the Casino gardens to see the flowers, or sometimes she visited the glittering, expensive shops. More often than not she stayed at home where it was cool and restful and she could read.

Vivian spent the whole of his honeymoon enjoying himself in the way he desired, which was mainly apart from his wife. He lingered at the Casino with his men-friends and played roulette or baccarat. He amused himself with the *demi-monde*. He drank too much champagne. He would return to his villa at dawn to sleep heavily until mid-day. When he was with Charlotte his mood was usually surly. He taunted her and reminded her that he had married her by force and not by inclination.

Her delicate condition awoke no pity

in him. Gradually she stopped hoping for love or tenderness from Vivian. When he demanded what he called his 'marital rights' she accepted his attentions coldly and silently, believing it to be her duty. On her seventeenth birthday, two days before they returned to England, he threw her a jewelled bangle which he had bought in one of the Monte Carlo shops, but he did not dine with her, or show her any special consideration.

"You are not well. You should go to bed," he said.

'Today I am seventeen,' she thought, 'and already an unhappy, disillusioned woman.'

The gay and warm-hearted Charlotte who had once found life an intoxicating mystery, seemed to have died. This Charlotte, Lady Chase, knew only a dreadful loneliness.

While together in public, they had met one or two people who knew the Chase family. Vivian, who could be so utterly charming when he wished, put a hand through his wife's arm and introduced her with a loving expression as, "*My beautiful bride*".

The honeymoon couple returned from Calais on the newest Channel steamship, the *Castalia*. The journey to Dover took one hour and fifty minutes — a tremendous speed, which caused a sensation. But the sea was choppy and Charlotte retired to her cabin with her maid, deathly sick.

Once mistress of herself again, and during the train journey to Harling, she summoned up her courage to discuss their future with Vivian.

"Whatever you feel about me, I beg you to make her ladyship happy whenever we are in her presence," Charlotte said. Vivian scowled.

"How many times must I remind you to call her *Mother* — or Mama. If our friends hear you say, 'her ladyship' they will think I have married a servant girl."

In this vein they returned to Clunes.

But Vivian was making an effort today and it was not an unhappy meal, of which later the three of them partook. The Dowager was quite delighted because her tall son insisted upon carrying her, himself, into the dining-room, and placing her in her usual chair at the head of the table.

"You are still mistress of Clunes. Charlotte and I will sit on either side of you, as your devoted children," he said gaily.

Eleanor Chase was sublimely happy, confident that a miracle had caused this change of heart in Vivian. But Charlotte knew what a hypocrite he was. Earlier, while they were dressing, he had come into her room and grumbled because his poor mother was still at Clunes.

Now her gaze rested for a moment, fascinated, on the big portrait over the fireplace — the Millais masterpiece. Eleanor Chase, youthful, gloriously beautiful, wearing a ruby red crinoline dress; Vivian leaning against her in a velvet suit with lace collar and cuffs; looking angelic with his large blue eyes and golden curls.

Too early in life Charlotte was becoming a cynic, aware of the painful gulf between good and evil. Almost she found it impossible to believe that any child who looked like that one in the portrait could grow up into such a demon.

Tonight she had the right to live here

at Clunes — mistress of this splendid house. When the Dowager was gone, it would be *she*, Charlotte, who would sit in that tall-backed armchair, facing Vivian at one end of the long table.

A perfect meal was served ceremoniously by Williams, the butler, and Lucy, the head parlour maid. Charlotte did not look at them but could feel their inquisitive glances frequently upon her. They, who had known her in the past, must find it strange, she reflected, to wait upon little Charlotte Goff from the Lodge.

At Vivian's request, Charlotte had put on one of her new Paris gowns: dark rose silk with a yoke of black lace, and black lace frills frothing round the bottom of the skirt. She looked much older in such a frock but it seemed to please Eleanor Chase who complimented her daughter-in-law upon her dignified appearance.

Over coffee the Dowager discussed the plans she had made for her son and daughter-in-law. Tomorrow, Sunday, she was holding a small tea party and reception for them in the garden. Invitations had gone out to their closest friends. Alas, she said, Sir Harry was still not well enough to come down to meet the bride, but Eleanor's cousins, the Miss Ida and Miss Mary Foulkes, were presenting themselves. These old spinsters were said to have made their wills in favour of Vivian.

The most important of local guests would be Sir Claude Glover whose house, Hamfield Court, was two miles distant from Clunes. He was still only in the late forties, but had been forced to retire from the diplomatic service owing to ill-health. Alicia, his first wife, had been Eleanor's dearest friend. Two years after her death Sir Claude married again. This time to a woman considerably younger, without interest for Lady Chase. A pretty prattling little thing but Lady Chase, ever gracious and understanding, had invited the new Lady Glover, more for Charlotte's sake than for anyone else's. Gwendolen Glover was not much older than Charlotte and might make of her a friend.

Vivian, listening to the list of guests in a bored way, perked up at the mention of Gwendolen Glover.

"I know that you find Sir Claude a bore but he is a fine man and the type to do you good," his mother reminded him.

It was Vivian's private opinion that the new Lady Glover would do him much more good. He had taken her on at a game of archery last summer and remembered her trim figure, her flaxen curls, and narrow, laughing eyes. He was quite sure she had only married old Glover for the title. She had given him, Vivian, many an inviting smile.

Charlotte also listened and felt her heart sink a little. It was not that she did not want to meet the Chases' friends. She was sociable by nature. But she felt such a hypocrite at the moment with her Deadly Secret which must be hidden from all the ladies. Soon she could no longer wear these elegant gowns and then, *what*? She would have to pretend illness and lie up for a while, and come down in loose tea gowns; négligées which would hide her condition.

After dinner, Vivian carried his mother up to her bedroom. Charlotte sat with her a moment while Hannah fetched hot water and towels. Charlotte thought that Lady Chase looked mortally tired and ill.

"Oh, pray do not do too much, dearest Mother!" she begged. "Do not hold this tea tomorrow just for Vivian and me, if it is beyond your strength."

Gently, Lady Chase chided her daughter-in-law.

"It is not for nothing that I take this course, my love. It is for Vivian's *reputation*. Your marriage was solemnized in secrecy because I feared that I was about to die. But now, while I still live, it is expedient that you should play your part for the visitors with a natural air. Whatever they think now, after tomorrow they will be forced to accept you as Vivian's honoured wife."

"Would that I did not feel such a hypocrite," said Charlotte and put her face in her hands.

"That must be your cross, my poor child. You must bear it with courage. Do not give way to your innermost feelings. Hide them and continue to make my son happy as he now appears to be. That is all I ask."

"Dearest Mother," said Charlotte and kissed the white hand extended to her, hardly able to restrain her tears.

"In my bureau," went on the Dowager, "you will find a bundle of letters which are the answers to my invitations. Nobody has refused. Everyone is anxious to meet you. Take these letters, read them and familiarize yourself with the names and addresses of the writers."

"I shall do so."

"And you will not fail me tomorrow? You will be my old, sparkling Charlotte, without a care in the world?"

"If possible, yes," whispered the girl drying her eyes.

"Lady Glover has asked if she might bring two house guests who are spending the weekend at Hamfield Court which is the Glover residence. They are a Mr. and Mrs. Peveril Marsh. He is a portrait painter of considerable reputation. They live in Essex. She was the daughter of Sir Harry and Lady Roddney, now dead, and was once wife to the Baron of Cadlington who lived in Buckinghamshire. There have been considerable rumours about the romantic nature of the Marshes' meeting and marriage, but I never listen to gossip so cannot repeat it. I have, therefore, informed Gwendolen Glover that she has my permission to bring her friends to our tea party."

Charlotte kissed Lady Chase good night and went to her own room. It was the most elegant of the guest chambers — furnished in palest grey. It had been prepared with magnificent flowers for the bridal couple. Vivian's suite adjoined. Charlotte wondered if he would hold any conversation with her tonight; or if the pleasant mood put on for his mother's benefit would be reversed once he was alone with her.

But he did not come to her room nor did she see him again until morning. After the rest of the inmates of Clunes were abed Vivian had slipped out of a back entrance and made his way to his old haunt — the house of Roma Gresham.

13

SUNDAY was a disappointment as far as weather was concerned. All hopes of a garden party had to be abandoned. At dawn the weather changed, and a rain storm swept across the countryside accompanied by a high wind. By breakfast time the grounds were in a sorry state. The new Michaelmas daisies were flattened and bedraggled. The branches of the tall elms tossed and creaked. The tempest sent a shower of leaves scurrying across the puddled lawns.

Eleanor Chase announced that Vivian and Charlotte must receive in the drawing-room. The whole staff was kept busy helping to prepare for the event. The Crown Derby tea service was laid out. For hours, cook and kitchenmaid cut delicate, fine rolls of brown and white bread-and-butter, and made *pâté* sandwiches. There was a fine array of iced cakes which had been made yesterday, one of which was in the nature of a bridal cake — three tiered — and with the initials 'V' and 'C' entwined in a circle of lovers-knots.

Charlotte would ordinarily have enjoyed it all, even felt the tiniest spurt of pride in her new dignity of position as the young mistress of the house. But Vivian took care to spoil whatever pleasure she might have extracted from the party. They had a bitter dispute before descending from their rooms — on the subject of Nan.

The affectionate and grateful Charlotte had wanted to run and see her foster-parents at the Lodge. Vivian forbade it.

"Now that you are my wife, you will kindly forget that you ever lived in the lodge," he said in his haughtiest voice.

"But Nan and Joseph cared for me for many years. I cannot treat them now as though they are dust just because I have become Lady Chase," said Charlotte indignantly.

Vivian, whose face was puffy after a night of debauchery, flung her an unpleasant look.

"You will do as you are told."

Charlotte's heart began to beat fast.

"But it is my *duty* to pay my respects to the Forbes."

"Your duty is to *me*, alone — " thundered Vivian.

Charlotte, for once, defied him.

"I refuse to hurt my good and kind friends. I shall call upon them and prove that I am still their loving Charlotte."

A moment's silence, then Vivian said with a freezing smile:

"You have forgotten that *I* am the master of Clunes. Whoever my mother sides with over this, you shall do what I wish. If you dare go near the Forbes I shall turn them out and engage new keepers for the Lodge."

"Oh," gasped Charlotte. "I would not have that happen to them for the world. They love their home and they have always done their job conscientiously. Why, *why* should you forbid me to visit them?"

"Because it must be forgotten that you were ever a nobody from Pimlico and brought up here by common employees; that is, if you wish to be held in respect by our friends."

"Would I be respected for turning my

back upon those whose lowly station I once shared?" she persisted.

"Go to the devil," said Vivian, "and do as I command, or the Forbes receive their notice to leave — tonight."

Knowing him so well, she realized that he would carry out his threat. It was a sickening start to her day. She could not even explain matters to Nan without being disloyal to her husband. All the morning she thought of Nan, waiting for her visit; hating the thought that the little woman would be deeply hurt and disappointed when she failed to put in an appearance.

Then came the party.

Charlotte stood at the drawing-room door beside her husband and received the guests who shook hands and filed past her to the couch on which the Dowager sat, covered with a light cashmere shawl.

The inclement weather had brought the temperature down so low that it was decidedly cool in the house today. Log fires had been lit. Autumn seemed already to be here.

As the Dowager had anticipated, the entire neighbourhood buzzed with excitement and curiosity to see the young girl whom Vivian Chase had married. There had, of course, been a veritable flood of rumours.

The more kindly and well-disposed accepted her ladyship's explanation that the wedding had been a sudden and secret one because the doctors feared for her life. The less charitable whispered to each other that there might be *another reason* for so hasty a wedding.

All knew about Lady Chase's protégée, but few had met Charlotte Goff. *Extra-ordinary*, they thought, that the wealthy and highly eligible Lord Chase should wish to marry a girl of lower station than his own. However, it was agreed that Eleanor Chase was devoted to Charlotte and found her intelligence of a high order. Certainly Charlotte *appeared* to be well-bred, even if she was not. She looked every inch a lady, and behaved with the utmost decorum. Her manners were exquisite. It was generally thought that she looked older than her seventeen years, being a little full in the bust. The ladies cast many envious glances at her dress. For this reception (her mother-in-law had made the choice) the bride wore one of her most beautiful yet simple gowns, in the latest mode from Paris. White sprigged muslin, cut rather low in the *corsage*, with bunches of the crisp material flounced back into a bustle. Pale blue bows on the wide bell-shaped sleeves; ruffles of blue on the hem. Little blue satin slippers. White flowers were pinned to her hair which was dressed in a *chignon*, with long glossy curls cascading down the back of her neck. She was pale but her large eyes looked brilliant under their narrow arched brows. She gave an impression of fresh, innocent youth, a semblance of the purity which nothing that Vivian had done could pollute.

"She is uncommonly handsome, is the little bride," the men whispered to each other.

"Not so guileless as she looks," suggested the more shrewd among the women as they gossiped over their tea-cups in the corners of the drawing-room.

One or two matrons, disappointed that they could not now snatch Vivian as a husband for their daughters who were just about to come out, were less charitable.

So much nonsense, they murmured, about *intelligence*. Intelligent females were always under suspicion. A woman's true place was in the house attending to her servants or (discreet cough) in her nursery.

One discerning lady, who deeply respected the Dowager Lady Chase but had never trusted Vivian, came nearer the mark by suggesting to a friend that young Vivian was a 'real rake' and that perhaps his mother had thought this marriage to a pure young girl would steady him.

However, most of those who had come to pick holes in the bride were forced to admit that Charlotte was charming and interesting. She seemed able to talk on most subjects as well as to look beautiful. Congratulations were poured upon the couple.

But the guests were unanimous in their fears for the Dowager. She looked like a wraith, they said. Not long for this world; they could well believe it! This fact did much to foster the one impression Eleanor Chase meant to convey that the quiet, hasty wedding of her son with Charlotte Goff had been on *her* account.

The Misses Ida and Mary Foulkes, both in the early seventies, garbed from head to foot in the black which they had worn after the death of Prince Albert and never abandoned, asked too many awkward questions to please Vivian. He had to wriggle out of one or two decidedly difficult moments. One on either side of him, the old ladies sat upright, as stiff as pokers, on the edge of their chairs. They barked at the handsome boy whom they did, in fact, adore.

Why this sudden marriage to a nobody?

Why hadn't *they* been informed?

What had induced Cousin Eleanor to give her approval, while Vivian was still at Oxford?

Vivian, however, answered the questions lightly and made all his explanations sound feasible. The Misses Foulkes clicked their teeth and tut-tutted, but finally coated the pill of suspicion with the sugar of a grudging admission that they admired his young wife. But they still thought he should have made a better match.

Charlotte was frightened to death of the old ladies. She felt that they saw through her; must *know* of her condition. She went pale when they approached her. But the Dowager saved the day by calling her cousins to her couch. In her serene, tactful fashion, she brushed aside the dagger point of their critical attack upon Vivian.

"My son fell in love," she said calmly. "That is the long and the short of it, dear cousins. I am soon to be called to the Judgment Throne. I wished to see my son wed to the girl of his choice before my departure. Charlotte is a dear girl and will make him very happy."

Half-way through the afternoon, Charlotte began to feel exceedingly fatigued; at times a little giddy. Oh, heavens, she thought, she must not swoon. She must not in any way draw attention to her state of health. Vivian would be furious. Once she drew him aside and whispered:

"Do you think I could find an excuse to withdraw for a short time? It has become so hot in here with the fire on. I am feeling dizzy."

Vivian hissed into her ear:

"Kindly take a hold of yourself. You must remain. Do you want everyone to *guess*, you little idiot?"

She stood where he left her, as near the window as she could get, nervously fingering her dorothy bag which was made of artificial forget-me-nots. She felt stifled. Soon she *must* put an end to this tight lacing, she thought. She ground her teeth trying to control the faintness that threatened to overcome her.

It was then that she felt a gentle hand upon her arm, and, turning, looked into one of the most beautiful faces she had ever seen. The face of an elderly woman in a dove-grey lace dress and coat, and wearing a small plumed hat.

"I note that you feel a little indisposed," said a soft kindly voice, "these receptions are so trying for a bride. I wonder if I might ask you to show me the portraits in your gallery. There, you will doubtless find it a little fresher."

"It is uncommonly kind of you," said Charlotte.

Gratefully, she walked with this discerning lady out of the hot, crowded drawing-room.

In the gallery, there was a gilt and brocade sofa of the *Louis Quinze* period. Charlotte's new friend insisted upon Charlotte sitting down upon it, and offered her a bottle of smelling salts.

"You are too kind," whispered Charlotte, sniffing the salts and closing her eyes. "I do feel poorly, I must admit. Pray tell me your name, I fear I have forgotten."

"I am Mrs. Marsh — Fleur Marsh, I came with our good friends, Sir Claude and Lady Glover. We are staying at Hamfield Court."

"But of course," said Charlotte who was beginning to revive. "Your husband is the great painter."

Mrs. Marsh smiled.

"I do not know about a *great painter* — but he is a very great man — in my estimation at least," she smiled.

How Charlotte envied her the cause of that smile. Easy to see that Mrs. Marsh adored her husband. Love glowed in her eyes; and what magnificent eyes, thought Charlotte. Of the most unusual shade of violet-blue. She must be fifty, at least, for her red-gold hair was lavishly streaked with silver and the delicate face was lined. But she still possessed an almost unearthly beauty and there was something about her sympathetic manner which instantly drew Charlotte to her.

"I know little about paintings save what I have learned from my mother-in-law," said Charlotte shyly, "but I have often heard mention of, and read about, Mr. Marsh and his portraiture."

"My husband, as soon as he saw you, said that he would like to paint *you*," observed Mrs. Marsh. "Could you sit for him? I am sure Lord Chase would be pleased — " Mrs. Marsh indicated the long gallery — "he will want your likeness to hang here with his predecessors."

Charlotte stayed silent. She could not imagine Vivian wishing to have a portrait of her. The older woman stayed silent, too. When she had first set eyes on the young bride she had thought that those big golden eyes held far too melancholy an expression for one so young — and a newly-made wife at that. She had formed an impression — and had passed it on to Peveril — that the new Lady Chase was unhappy. Now she felt sure of it. Fleur Marsh, remembering the anguish of her own first marriage, the terrors that awaited her at Cadlington House when, as the Baron's bride, she had been forced to entertain his friends, felt a deep sympathy for this girl. All marriages were not made in heaven, like *hers* with Peveril. All men were not as fine or gallant. She had been married to Peveril these thirty-five years, and they were still deeply in love.

What was the secret behind young Lady Chase's look of despair? Of all the guests, only Mrs. Marsh, who had herself tasted the pangs of hell, sensed tragedy.

"You must come to Pillars, our home, and see us," she told Charlotte. "We live just across the border, not far from Epping. We would be happy if you and Lord Chase would spend a few days with us. The partridge season has begun. We have some fine shooting."

"I fear my husband is not fond of sport," said Charlotte sadly.

"Nor, in fact, is Peveril, my husband. He is an artist," said Mrs. Marsh with a smile. "It was my father, Sir Harry

Roddney, who liked shooting so well. Pillars was my girlhood's home. It has many lovely memories for me."

Charlotte nodded dumbly. She, too, had her lovely memories. The four years at Clunes as Eleanor Chase's pupil, before her mad passion for Vivian had stormed into her life.

"One day," continued Fleur Marsh, "I would like to tell you the romantic story of my parents, and my old home."

"Perhaps one day I will tell you mine," said Charlotte in a low voice.

"At any rate, pray count me your friend, my dear," said Mrs. Marsh, laying a hand on hers.

The kindness of this charming grey-haired little woman thawed some of the ice around Charlotte's heart. She returned the hand clasp warmly and said:

"You are exceedingly kind, Mrs. Marsh."

Vivian suddenly appeared. Fleur noticed at once how Charlotte sprang to her feet; how the young girl's whole face and figure seemed to stiffen as Lord Chase sauntered up towards her. There was something in the young man's turquoise blue eyes from which Fleur shrank. Despite his looks, she found him repellent. She saw, too, how resentful Charlotte looked when Vivian slid an arm round her waist.

'He is doing it only to impress me,' thought Fleur. 'I do not like him, and the poor child looks as *I* must have looked when that monster to whom I was first married, touched *me*.'

Vivian drawled:

"If you will pardon me, Mrs. Marsh, I must take my sweet Charlotte away. She has to say good-bye to some of our guests who are departing."

Fleur answered politely and turned to Charlotte.

"Do not forget, my husband and I will be most happy for you to visit Pillars," she said.

Fleur stayed alone for a while in the cool picture gallery. She felt no particular desire to join the crowd in the drawing-room. She wanted to think. She had received such a vivid impression that the new Lady Chase was stalked by tragedy.

After a few minutes she was joined by her husband who had been searching for her.

The artist was a slightly built man with grey curls. He had still a boyish look, although his face was much lined when one inspected it at close quarters. He had been for some years now racked with rheumatic pains which caused him great suffering. He stooped a little. But he never complained. He still worked hard at his painting which was his dearest occupation, and the dearest of all people in this world to him was this wife of his. As he reached Fleur's side he picked up one of her hands and kissed it.

"You have been away from my side for nearly an hour. That is exactly one hour too long," he smiled.

"Dear Peveril," she leaned her head on his shoulder.

He looked tenderly down at that beloved head. Once it had been a glorious auburn; he could not count the number of times he had painted it. But he loved her none the less today because she had grown old.

She began to talk to him about young Lady Chase. She spoke of her involuntary dislike of Vivian and the queer psychic intuition that led her to believe that

Charlotte Chase was an unhappy bride.

"Like myself when first you saw me, Peveril," ended Fleur, and her slender fingers closed convulsively around her husband's.

"Hush," he said, "do not let the sadness of the past depress you now, my beloved."

She bit her lip. Peveril Marsh gazed at her anxiously. He knew that there were many moments when his wife did, indeed, brood upon the terrible things that had happened to her, more than thirty years ago. The horror of them had set an indelible stamp upon her. He grieved that this should be. As they stayed there a moment, arm in arm, he could follow her train of thought. It would not be untrue to say that he, too, remembered every detail of the past. It had a way of creeping in to ruffle the surface of their now tranquil and happy life.

Unforgettable for both of them that day, thirty-six years ago, when Fleur, the hapless daughter of Sir Harry and Lady Roddney, had entered Cadlington House as a bride on the arm of Denzil

St. Cheviot, one of the most wicked and notorious noblemen of his day. He, Peveril, then a mere stripling, and protégé of the Baron, had painted the first and most beautiful portrait of his life of the Baroness. This one and many others, were destroyed in maniacal rage by the Baron after the birth and death of his son. The subject of that ghastly tragedy was *taboo* in Peveril's household. For even after this long time Fleur could not bear to speak of it. The poor little infant which she had never seen (for it had died at birth, so she had been told) was unmistakably of black blood. That blood could be traced back to her African great-grandfather, and had been transmitted through the veins of Fleur's mother, Lady Roddney; she, who had once been called *Fauna*, born a quadroon slave, and had later become the Marquise de Chartellet, wife of the French Marquis of that name. After the Marquis's death she had married Sir Harry and Fleur, their only child, had been born to them.

Of Fleur St. Cheviot's martyrdom during the brief period she had lived with the cruel Baron, of the latter's death by the sword at the hand of her father, Sir Harry, of the destruction by fire of Cadlington House, and of her elopement with him, Peveril, there was both good and bad to remember.

Good had triumphed. For thirty-four years these true lovers had lived in happiness at Pillars. And then, ten years ago Harry Roddney died, an old man, adoring his daughter, respecting the son-in-law who had risen to great heights as a painter, and much loved by them. With his dying breath Sir Harry had murmured the name of Fleur's mother.

"I am going to her," he whispered, "my beloved Fauna."

De Chartellet had re-named her, '*La Belle Héléne*.' But Harry had called her 'Fauna' with his final gasp of breath. *Fauna* — the unforgotten name, Fauna, even now remembered by the daughter who had learned about that African strain — too late.

The Marshes were without children. Much as Fleur had longed for a family, she had known after the tragic events of the past that it must never be. Fleur maintained that she wanted none but Peveril. But sometimes the sensitive and affectionate man who loved her so well wondered if their lack of children had not left a hunger and void in her life. For somewhere, he believed, in the deep recess of her memory, there lingered a yearning sorrow because her ill-fated babe had died.

Now Fleur spoke to him imperiously, as though a sudden and psychic knowledge had been imparted to her. Clinging to Peveril's arm, she said:

"*There is to be a child* — yes, Peveril, the stamp of motherhood already sits on the brow of that girl who has just been speaking to me, and all will not be well."

"Oh, come, my angel," said Peveril with a laugh, "you let imagination run away with you. Besides, such an idea casts a slight upon the newly-wedded pair."

"Nevertheless," said Fleur, "it is so. You will see. Meanwhile it is my earnest wish, dear heart, that you ask Lord Chase to stay with us. Yes, I know you do not like him. Neither do I, but I *must* give what I can of friendship to Lady Chase. You will discover how much she needs it."

"Your wish is my command," said Peveril, and touched his wife's cool cheek with his lips.

But just how much Charlotte was to need the Marshes' friendship, and just what true cause Fleur had for her instinctive fears, neither Peveril nor anybody else this afternoon at Clunes could dream.

14

AUGUST was an emotional month for Charlotte.
Then came September.
Fortunately for all concerned the changes wrought by her pregnancy were few. She no longer laced quite so tightly and a clever dressmaker helped to make her new smart dresses looser without losing their essential *chic*. During the fortnight after the tea party at Clunes, any fears that Charlotte might have entertained that she would be cold shouldered by the neighbourhood were laid to rest. Invitations to the newly-married pair poured in from all quarters. A succession of luncheons and dinners were held for them. Charlotte dreaded them but was forced to accompany her husband. They were, of course, rather too conventional to please Vivian's fancy, but they were consoling to his pride. He need no longer feel that his marriage to Charlotte Goff had wrecked his social life.

The beautiful and intelligent girl seemed to have made a hit with everybody.

If Vivian craved amusement after his own fashion there was still Mrs. Gresham's house, so discreetly hidden among the trees. But just now it was the gambling there that interested him rather more than the women. And he had money to burn. By behaving outwardly, anyhow, as his mother desired, he found her generous with her purse.

Charlotte did not feel well and went perpetually in fear that one or other of the ladies would recognize the signs of her condition.

But as that terror lessened, she became absorbed wholly by the darkest dread of all; those wrapped around her mother-in-law. Lady Chase took to her bed and did not leave it again, as though she felt that she had done what had to be done and was now ready to give up the ghost.

Dr. Castleby's visits increased to both night and morning. Two distinguished specialists drove down from London, only to tell Vivian that nothing more could be done for poor Lady Chase. She was growing weaker and it could only be a matter of weeks before the end.

Charlotte hoped secretly that the impending loss of his mother would rouse the best instincts in her young husband. So distressed was Charlotte, herself, by the prospect of losing the great lady she had loved so well, that tears were never far from the surface. But Vivian took it all casually. On several occasions he lectured Charlotte for weeping. "Death must come to all of us and my mother is no longer young," he said loftily. "Her time has come. It cannot improve matters for you to creep around the place snivelling. I find you most unbecoming with your shiny nose and puffy eyelids."

Charlotte had grown used to the callousness of this extraordinary young man.

"But do you not *love* your mother?" she asked, staring at him incredulously. "Do you not *feel* grief?"

"My dear Charlotte, Mamma is not dead yet," he drawled. "I shall save my tears for the event."

"You are monstrous," she said in a whisper.

He laughed.

The Dowager had two trained nurses, one of whom was a good-looking woman with some fame attached to her, for she had nursed in the Crimea with Florence Nightingale. When Miss Parkinson was present, Vivian sat by his mother's side and made himself excessively charming. He would hold one of the invalid's long white hands, sighing deeply, murmuring endearments which would impress anybody, and certainly a female. Miss Parkinson often glanced quite tenderly at the fair debonair young man. She mentioned to her colleague that she had never known a more devoted son than Lord Chase.

"And he is handsome as an angel," Miss Parkinson sighed romantically.

But the dying woman, herself, was not impressed by any of these exhibitions from her son. Alas for her, Eleanor Chase's perceptions seemed to sharpen with her fast-approaching end. The love that she had once borne her only child changed to suspicion and contempt. She listened to him in silence when he spoke to her. Day after day when Charlotte visited her, the older woman saw how pinched and pale the young girl's face had grown. How sad she was, despite all efforts to be bright. Eleanor Chase knew the worst. Vivian's marriage had not changed him, nor ever would. Her deepest grief now was the knowledge that she must leave Charlotte to bear her cross alone. And she even asked herself in the small hours one morning, when she lay sleepless, if she had done right in making Vivian marry Charlotte. She had saved the girl's name. The child would be born in wedlock. *But had it been for the best?*

If only she could die feeling that he would be good to poor little Charlotte. *If only —*

Suddenly Lady Chase heard a cry.

She struggled into a sitting position, her thin sick body breaking into a sweat.

"What was that?" she panted and pulled the little night shawl over her head, and sat taut, shivering, straining her ears. The night nurse had slipped downstairs to fetch herself a plate of biscuits to eat with her morning cup of tea. Hannah was not yet up. It was still only half-past five.

Again that sharp cry. And suddenly Lady Chase recognized it. *It came from Charlotte* — from the direction of the rooms occupied by the newly married couple.

Lady Chase pressed both hands to her rapidly beating heart.

What was wrong? Had Charlotte been taken ill? The girl had looked so ill lately; could it mean that this was the beginning of a miscarriage? If so, one of the nurses must go to her immediately and a footman be roused and sent for Dr. Castleby.

Again that cry and then a laugh, *a horrible maniacal laugh*, that seemed to freeze the Dowager's blood.

"Nurse! *Nurse!*" she called frantically, in a high thin voice.

No answer came. Eleanor Chase was bathed in perspiration, confident now that something terrible was happening at the end of the corridor. Suddenly she flung off her bedclothes and slid her legs over the edge of her bed. Hers was the false final strength of a desperate dying creature, the last terrible effort Eleanor Chase was ever to make. Without slippers, with only a shawl wrapped over her voluminous white nightgown, she tottered out of the bedroom. She swayed as she went. Once in the corridor, she had to put her hands against the wall in order to keep her balance. She uttered little sobs and moans under her breath as she went. Her heart beat so fast and caused her such agony that she could hardly bear the pain. Yet she prevailed. She propelled herself on and on, whilst oblivious of this crisis, the night-nurse lingered downstairs, searching in the pantry for delicacies that she fancied.

Meanwhile, in Charlotte's bedroom, chaos reigned.

A few moments ago, Vivian had returned to Clunes from Roma Gresham's house. He was drunk and in a venomous, belligerent mood.

Charlotte, who had been fast asleep, had wakened to find him standing beside her bed, holding a candelabra at a tilted angle so that the hot wax dripped on to the carpet. The gleaming light showed up the sweat on his pallid face. He no longer looked angelic or handsome, but hideous in her sight, with loose lips, damp dishevelled locks, all the marks of his debauchery. His fine clothes were disarrayed, his shirt stained with wine, his cravat untied. As she sat upright, clutching the bedclothes to her, he laughed down at her.

"Do I disturb your innocent slumbers, my puritanical wife?"

Quickly she slid out of the bed and into a blue velvet gown. She looked young and intensely sad. She was still half-drugged with sleep but she managed to speak calmly.

"Vivian, for mercy's sake, where have you been?"

"That is my affair. I want no questioning."

Wide awake now, she stared up at him with wide-eyed disdain.

"You have been keeping poor company, sir, that is obvious."

"Do not dare to criticize me if I have had some amusement; that is only natural. Do you think I can live and breathe in such a rarefied atmosphere as this," he waved an arm drunkenly around the cool, fragrant bedroom. The curtains billowed in the strong wind.

Charlotte felt cold and began to tremble. He added:

"It is as freezing in here as well might be, since it is *your* bedchamber. I was brought up by a damned saint, and now I find myself married to a bedamned icicle."

Pale and horrified, Charlotte tried again to soothe her husband. Her one concern was lest the invalid at the other end of the passage should hear Vivian's loud hectoring voice.

"I beg of you to control yourself," she said, "and if you do not like my bedroom, you have your own. Pray go to it."

He ignored this dignified appeal and set the candelabra down on her bed table with a clatter. Unsteadily, he walked across the room and pulled at the cord of the open window, making a crash that was enough, thought Charlotte, to waken anybody.

"I like warmth," he said, "warmth and gaiety, and an impassioned invitation from a flesh-and-blood woman."

Charlotte made no answer. Her pulse rate increased. She was nervous of Vivian in this state. She had seen him drunk before, but never quite as bad as this. She knew, of course, that on occasions he left the house and did not return until the early hours. But never before had he come into her room to disturb her rest. She could see that he was half crazy with the strong liquor he had consumed.

'For the life of me I do not know where he goes to get in such a state,' she thought miserably.

She had deemed it fortunate during the time that she had lived at Clunes, that she did not have to endure much of Vivian's company. But she had suffered from an increasing loneliness which had not been lessened by his spiteful refusal to allow her to visit her foster-parents. Twice in secret she had met Nan in the gardens, then only for a few moments, and had tried to give Nan a tactful explanation. But she had seen that the kindly woman was deeply hurt because she went to the Lodge no more. Nothing Charlotte could say could convince Nan that it was not because she had become too high and mighty for them.

She played her new part as well as

she could, as a lady of quality. But she remained at heart the simple child who had given all for love's sake, and to whom all love was now denied.

Vivian staggered back to his wife and stood leering at her a moment, swaying from toe to heel.

"Damned hypocrite. You weren't always an icicle, were you?" he said with a laugh that chilled her.

She wondered in despair if he would ever allow her to forget that tragic passion which had brought her to this pass. She felt now that the very idea of kisses or caresses from him was abhorrent. He had killed romance, desire, and all natural warmth with his fiendish malice.

Glancing at the travelling clock by her bedside she said:

"In half an hour from now the servants will be waking. Will you not go to your bed and sleep, Vivian?"

"So you want to get rid of me, do you?"

She backed away from him.

"I implore you, go to your room!"

"Damn you!" he shouted, "my wife shall be my wife if I so desire it."

"But I do *not*!" she said under her breath.

"Your wishes are not to be considered. You live in my house and I am your lord and master."

"Vivian, your mother will hear," Charlotte began.

"Your mother, *your* mother," he mimicked, "forever throwing my mother at me. While she forever reminds me that I have a dear little wife. I am sick of the pair of you."

He lurched at her and caught her by the arm, wrenching it in the strength of his drunkenness. His mind was inflamed. He wanted only to prove his mastery over this young lovely girl who looked at him with scorn and loathing. How dared she look at him like that?

"We will see who is master! We will thaw the ice!" he said thickly and wrenched her arm again, this time forcing that first cry heard by the Dowager.

Now there followed a shameful struggle which lingered in Charlotte's memory for many a long dark day. Vivian, with ruthless fingers, tore at her dressing gown. As they struggled, he leaned his full weight against her. The side of her face caught the bed-post as she fell, wrenching another scream from her lips. He kissed her brutally. She sobbed and cried:

"For God's sake, Vivian, oh, for God's sake — !"

"I am master of my home and my wife and shall prove it to you!" he said and burst into wild laughter as he flung her across the bed. The laces at her throat were in tatters. She lay panting. One cheek had been lacerated by a sharp edge of carving on the bed-post. She tried to regain her feet but he bore her down. Her fingers clawed at the satin quilt and pulled the frill from one of the linen pillows. It was as though the fiend himself had entered that quiet room, she thought. It was a devil who grinned down at her with Vivian's features, and clawed at her with Vivian's hands.

"You are really mad!" she sobbed.

"Mad or not, this shall teach you not to argue with your husband," he said, and struck her across the face.

She cried out again in hot protest:

"For God's sake, can you not remember

that I am with child — ?"

"*Vivian!*" Now it was another voice that protested. The anguished voice of Eleanor Chase from the doorway, ending in a gurgling moan.

The young man sprang to his feet and stood swaying. He tried to pierce the swirling mists of his inebriation, and saw the spectral shape of his mother wrapped in her white shawl, horror in her accusing eyes. Clinging to the lintel of the door, she stared dreadfully from him to the prone figure of the girl who had turned her face to the pillow and was weeping bitterly.

"So it has come to this," said Lady Chase in a hollow voice, "to *this*. May Almighty God forgive you, my son, for I never shall."

Then the Dowager collapsed in a heap on the floor. She had spoken her last words on earth. Vivian rushed across and knelt beside her. He was sober now. As he turned her over, he saw his mother's blind, staring eyes and he knew that she was dead.

For the first time in his life he knew, too, both fear and remorse. He went cold. His teeth began to chatter. Those had been terrible words to hear from a mother's lips.

"*May Almighty God forgive you, for I never shall.*"

"Mama," Vivian cried hoarsely, "Mama, speak to me again. Mama, I did not know what I was doing. I went to a party. I had too much to drink. I will do everything from now onward to show my contrition, oh, I swear it. Dearest Mama — !" He stopped and in anguish kissed her cold, limp hands.

But no answer came from Eleanor Chase. The light in her eyes was for ever extinguished. She neither saw nor heard her son as he knelt there, sobbing.

Charlotte became aware of what had happened. Aghast, she knelt beside her husband and added her pleas.

"Mother, dearest mother, it is I — your Charlotte — speak to us," she implored.

By this time the whole house was roused. The night nurse came running in, terrified when she had found her patient's bed empty. Hannah, a shawl over her night clothes, ran in too, and waved Charlotte and Vivian aside. She crouched there on the floor, cradling the Dowager's lifeless form in her arms. Already that ivory face had settled into an expression of tragic serenity, her limbs assumed the frozen immobility that belongs to the dead. The faithful old servant, tears streaming down her cheeks, muttered: "My lady, oh, merciful heavens, my lady!"

"Oh, alas, oh mercy me!" whimpered the night-nurse, her fingers uselessly exploring the dead woman's wrist, "What happened? What made her come along here, my lord? I fear it is the exertion which killed her."

"Yes, what happened, my lord?" echoed Hannah, and looked accusingly from Lord Chase to his young wife, the tears streaming down her wrinkled cheeks.

The young pair looked, not at her, but at each other. On Charlotte's left cheek an ugly bruise was swelling. There were drops of blood trickling from the cut. She did not seem to notice it. Vivian, completely sober now, was spokesman. In his cowardly way he cast aspersions on the unfortunate nurse.

"My mother should not have been left.

She must have had a fright and come along here to rouse us. You have failed in your duty, ma'am."

"I left her only for a moment, your lordship," said the nurse, her eyes terrified.

Charlotte said:

"Hannah, send at once for Dr. Castleby."

"It is too late," said Hannah with a deep sob.

"Yes, it is too late, but he must come all the same."

"I will take her back to her bed," said Vivian. And even he, callous though he was, felt shocked as he lifted his dead mother up in his arms. She weighed little more than a child.

Charlotte was left alone. Shuddering in the cold room, she sat down and put her face in her hands. She was so shocked that she was beyond tears. But she whispered:

"Oh dearest Mother, my dearest Lady Chase, would to God that I had died with you in this hour."

But death was not for one so young and strong. Even in that moment — ironic fact — for the first time, Charlotte felt the child quicken and leap within her. Trembling from head to foot, she lay down and covered herself with her quilt, nursing her injured cheek. Her whole body ached. Her mind, even more than her body, was bruised and shamed by what had occurred.

When a few moments later, she felt Vivian touch her on the shoulder and utter her name, she shrank away.

"Go — leave me alone," she whispered.

He spoke quite humbly.

"Charlotte, dearest wife, I am not going to hurt you. I have come to beg your pardon."

She lay still, too unhappy even to feel astonishment at this *volte-face*. Then the tears came, scalding, rushing through her fingers, soaking the pillow case.

His apology came too late, she thought; too late by weeks and months. In a broken voice she said:

"You are the cause of her death. I do not want to see you. Oh, go away and leave me alone."

But he stayed. He sat on the edge of the bed. He was grey in the face and there was a sick look in his eyes. For once in his life, Vivian Chase knew what it was to feel frightened.

"Hush, Charlotte," he said, "a man does not wish to be told that he has killed his own mother."

She turned her head and looked up at him, her eyes flashing through the tears.

"Nevertheless it is true."

"It was accidental," he muttered, "I was mad with drink. I did not realize what I was doing, or that she would hear. I did endeavour to explain, but poor Mama had gone beyond recall."

"Pray do not speak of her," broke in Charlotte. "Or argue with me, Vivian. Tonight at least, while *she* lies dead, let there be peace under this roof, or do you wish your hatred and selfishness to extend into the very tomb?"

He bit his finger-nails.

"I tell you I am sorry," he muttered, "is that not enough?"

"Nothing that you can do will ever be enough. That heart which ceased to beat was the most noble we shall ever know."

"I will make up for it. I will try to be a better husband to you, Charlotte,"

Vivian said, and, completely unnerved, he suddenly began to whimper like a child.

Charlotte drew a long shuddering sigh. She was so stunned that she could feel no pity, and because he had stooped to ask her pardon, he seemed no more acceptable in her sight. Eleanor Chase had departed, and with her all that Charlotte had ever known of the heart's true affection and happiness.

Vivian, however, was as egotistical in his desire to show a contrite heart as in his cruelties. He could not leave well alone. He pulled Charlotte up from her pillows and held her in his arms.

"Tell me that I did not hurt you or our poor child. Tell me that you will forgive me and let us start again," he implored, weeping in a maudlin fashion.

She stayed, reluctantly in his embrace, her eyes shut, her body unyielding.

"You had best tidy yourself and wait downstairs for Dr. Castleby," she said.

He tried to control himself and taking her hands, kissed them.

"Alas, I hurt your cheek. It is bleeding."

"It is nothing, I assure you."

"Say that you will forgive me and do not accuse me of being my mother's murderer. Her heart was weak, it was the effort of getting out of bed, coming down the corridor that killed her, not anything that she saw or heard in this room."

Charlotte had no spirit left to argue. Vivian added:

"Promise that you will never make that accusation against me again. You shall — you *must*."

Too weary, too sick to hold out against him any longer, she promised.

The colour returned to Vivian's cheeks. He began to feel better.

"And we shall try to be better friends, shall we, my own Charlotte?" he said quite tenderly.

Still she found it difficult to surrender. It was too sudden a metamorphosis. But as Vivian stroked her hair and continued to use endearments and show the first affection she had received from him since the hour when their child had been conceived, she gave way. She was still so young, so pitifully in need of tenderness. She flung her arms around his neck.

"Oh, yes, yes, if you really mean it, I do indeed want to be reconciled with you, Vivian," she wept.

"Then it shall be so," he said, kissed her on the forehead, and then laid her gently back on the pillow. "Rest, dear Charlotte, while I go to meet Dr. Castleby. My mother will see from Heaven that I am reformed. She will forgive me, will she not, Charlotte?"

The girl was silent a moment. She was no fool. She could not help but see that Vivian's present surprising mood of kindliness sprang more from a superstitious horror of the last words his mother had spoken, than from genuine concern for her, his wife. He was afraid of the Unknown. With his mother's corpse lying here in the house, he did not wish to feel that her spirit would haunt and condemn him. Like all braggarts and bullies, he was, at heart, a coward. He appealed for his wife's sympathy, her moral support, and hoped for absolution from his sins. He would not leave Charlotte until she actually declared that she was positive Lady Chase would hear and forgive him.

Then Charlotte heard him sigh with relief.

"I must go and bath and change my clothes," he muttered.

Charlotte looked at him with tired eyes.

"Will you really try to love me and the child — *your* child — for I have, for the first time, felt the life stir within me?" she whispered.

He stood up, rubbing his tousled head, yawning. Gentleness and sympathy did not come easily to Vivian Chase and once more he was beginning to feel tired and cross; the effects of last night's orgy in Mrs. Gresham's house. At the same time he also began to realize that he would have complete control here now that his mother was gone. That old fool, Sir Harry, was on his last legs. Physicians did not expect *him* to last the winter. After that, there would be nothing between Vivian and his fortune but the family solicitor, Mr. Trueby, whom he felt sure he could manage easily. William Trueby was not a strong character.

As he walked to the door, Vivian gave another loud yawn and said:

"Pray remember, my dear, if the doctor questions you, that it is that night-nurse who was at fault for letting Mother get out of bed in delirium."

"But Vivian, that would not be fair — " began Charlotte.

He swung round. The turquoise eyes were cold as stones again; his manner regained its arrogance.

"Little fool, do you wish the whole world to be told that it was *I* who killed my mother?" he snarled at her, "or shall I lay the blame at *your* door?"

Her heart sank. A cold hand seemed to clutch that heart again. It had beaten for a few moments with the real hope that she might, after all, find peace and solace with her husband. But she now realized such could never be the case. The leopard could not change his spots. She spoke no more, but turned her face to the pillow again, blinded by her tears.

Vivian marched out of the room, his nostrils distended, his lips curved in a cruel, self-satisfied smile.

15

ON a cold wet night in January — it was the year 1875 — Charlotte's child was born.

Had the child been a son, perhaps Vivian would have been a little proud and pleased, more ready to show his charming side to his poor wife. But alas for Charlotte, it was a daughter.

It was four months since Eleanor Chase had been laid to rest in the family vault at Harling, Vivian soon broke his pledge to renew the old love and tenderness for Charlotte. He seemed to have little respect for her condition and no interest in her as a woman. He was still vain enough, however, to wish to make a good impression on their immediate circle of friends. In their presence he was gay, chivalrous and affectionate toward Charlotte, who had speedily become a favourite.

Less than a month after the Dowager's death, Vivian brutally ejected the Forbes from the Lodge. Nan had been seen too often in the new Lady Chase's company for the liking of his arrogant lordship. He refused to be moved by Charlotte's tears or entreaties.

"I wish it to be forgotten that you ever resided in the Lodge in the care of those simpletons," he said. "They shall go. My bailiff has found me a new lodgekeeper."

It was a bitter day for Charlotte when the Forbes departed. Heavy with child, sad of countenance, she defied Vivian and went down to the cottage to bid farewell to the poor couple. Nan was in tears. Joseph was grey-faced and bitter. He had done his job honestly and efficiently and he, like his father, had been in the service of the Chase family for over forty years. Nan clung to Charlotte.

"Alas, we have no choice but to go away; his lordship refused to give us our money unless we agreed to go far afield."

They had been forced to seek new work in Suffolk, where Joseph's only brother lived and worked.

"I ask your pardon for this indignity

— but it is not my fault," Charlotte wept in Nan's arms.

"We understand. Our chief sorrow is that we shall not see your babe nor be there to comfort you in times of stress," Nan replied.

Long afterwards, Charlotte had thought: "There will *be* no comfort for me in the future — now my mother-in-law and my foster-mother have been taken from me."

She stood alone; lonelier than the meanest servant in the great house wherein she now lived so exalted a life.

Then came the day of her confinement.

She returned to consciousness from a mist of physical agony that she had for a short space found unendurable. It had been a hard, long labour. The first pains, which had sent one of the footmen scurrying to Harling for the physician, had started at three o'clock in the morning. At first, Charlotte had wrestled courageously with the pangs, relieved to know that at last the long waiting was over. It had been a dreadful nine months for her.

The monthly nurse, Miss Dickson, was

a plump cheerful Lancashire woman in her forties, from St. Thomas's Hospital. Fortunately, Charlotte had taken a fancy to her. She was a kindly woman and good at her job. It was kindliness that young Lady Chase most needed in that hour of her trial. She had received none from Vivian who, once awakened by his valet to be told that her ladyship was in labour, turned on his side and sent the message that he was to be called only when the child was born, and that he was not otherwise to be disturbed, unless anything went amiss.

When these words were conveyed to Lady Chase by her personal maid, Charlotte had given a cynical little smile, not unnoticed by Nurse Dickson. The latter had drawn her own conclusions about this wealthy titled pair. Lady Chase was charming, a mere child, not yet eighteen. His lordship was handsome and agreeable when he chose, but a devil at heart; Nurse Dickson had taken note of the young man's villainous temper and his lack of concern for his beautiful young wife. She had, too, heard it rumoured among the gossips in the servants' hall that Lord Chase had married 'beneath him' and that his bride had been only the foster-child of lodgekeepers who had since departed. But Nurse Dickson cared nothing for gossip. She knew goodness when she saw it, and it was her firm conviction that Lady Chase was, or had been, the victim of tragic circumstances. As for the infant — well, it was obvious to the experienced midwife that it was a fine, fully-grown child. It weighed six and a half pounds. But Dr. Castleby had tipped her the wink that she was to answer all inquiries with the information that the infant was a *seven months'* child.

Charlotte leaned heavily on Nurse Dickson during the terrible protracted confinement which lasted a full day and another night. The infant was not born until near midnight on the 16th of January.

By that time Charlotte was in a delirium of pain and totally exhausted. She was narrow in the pelvis and the old doctor was unskilled at the job. He gave the poor young mother no sedative, no help, until it seemed that she could bear it no longer. It was a wonder that he contrived to deliver the babe alive, and the mother had a severe haemorrhage which nearly cost her her life.

Vivian was sent for once or twice and then, resorting to the bottle, retired blind drunk. He excused himself on the grounds that he could not stand the anxiety and did not visit his wife or give her a word of encouragement because he hated the sight of suffering.

Miss Dickson sniffed as she repeated the message. The nurse had come by chance upon the master of the house late last night in the library where she found him, semi-intoxicated, in the embraces of a girl, whom the scandalized nurse recognized as the lady's maid.

It was the last straw for Vivian when he heard that the ill-begotten child was a girl. But he reached his wife's side soon after the infant arrived, looked down at her with a smile put on for Nurse Dickson's benefit, and raised her hand to his lips.

"I am heartily glad it is all over for your sake, my dearest Charlotte. It has been a nightmare," he drawled. "You look very poorly, my love."

'Poorly' would hardly describe Charlotte's state. She was milk-white, devitalized, still harrowed by the memory of her appalling labour. Her great golden eyes, dark with pain, looked at the handsome flushed face of the young husband who should, in this hour, have been her great consoler.

"Forgive me, I apologize that the poor baby is not the heir you hoped for, Vivian," she whispered.

He dropped her languid hand and whispered back:

"What can be expected of our unhappy marriage, madam? I admit to my bitter disappointment."

She bit her lip. The tears rolled down her cheeks. What of *her* feelings. She was disappointed not only for him, but worn out. She had never needed tenderness more, nor so greatly missed the noble lady who had died. *She*, at least, would have taken her granddaughter in her arms and blessed it, and Nan, dear Nan, would have rejoiced.

The late-night hour was bitterly cold outside. In the big, handsome bedroom a huge fire blazed and it was warm.

241

The curtains were cosily drawn. The infant slept in a wicker basinet which was trimmed with fine lace and satin ribbons, blue for a boy. Everything was blue. There lay the poor little girl, a pink and crumpled object, with her father's narrow shaped forehead and a thatch of darkish hair. Not much like him, but like his mother, Charlotte had noted when first she took the infant to her breast.

The tiny creature was hers, her own, and she would love it, she told herself, if nobody else did.

Vivian threw only a cursory glance at his child. He was annoyed to see that in colouring of complexion and hair she resembled his mother and not himself. Miss Dickson said, also, that she would have dark eyes.

"Your mother's eyes," Charlotte told him and expressed the hope that he would allow her to call the infant *Eleanora*.

"Call it what you like. I am not interested," was Vivian's cold reply as he left the room.

Charlotte began to cry wretchedly. Miss Dickson came to her side and exhorted her to keep calm for the baby's sake.

Charlotte nodded. Lifting a weary hand she pushed the heavy waves of hair back from her damp aching forehead. She could foresee nothing ahead save unhappiness with Vivian. This must be accepted as stoically as possible as her punishment for the weakness of her first illicit surrender to him. But at times like this the thought of the future appalled her.

One of her few pleasures lay in her friendship with Mrs. Fleur Marsh. In October, and again in December, Vivian had consented to drive with Charlotte over the border into Essex to pay a visit to Pillars, the loveliest house Charlotte had ever seen; full of charm and happiness. Sitting in front of a big log fire in Peveril's studio, Charlotte felt peace and a true appreciation of all things beautiful.

Nobody was more astonished than Charlotte that Vivian had allowed her the pleasure of this friendship. The Marshes were too simple and artistic, too quiet, to suit Vivian's taste. Fleur's beauty was fading. The two men had nothing in common. But it was Vivian's immense vanity which had actually won the day for Charlotte. He wanted to have his portrait painted. Since the Millais, executed when he was a small boy, no portrait had been done of the master of Clunes. Peveril Marsh was now hailed by the critics among the finest painters in the land, so Vivian condescended to give him the commission.

When Peveril announced that he must do the painting in his own studio, Charlotte guessed that dear Mrs. Marsh had had a hand in this, too, and she was thankful. It meant that she could accompany her husband and spend quite a number of happy and peaceful days with her delightful friends.

The portrait went well. Vivian was painted in Court dress. It was a full-length canvas. This, too, Charlotte learned, had been cunningly contrived by Fleur in order to protract the sittings. It promised to be one of Peveril's finest works. Vivian was certainly an absorbing subject for a painter. As the likeness unfolded — the splendour of his waving golden hair, the proud nostrils, the strange turquoise blue of the cold eyes, in contrast to the sensuality of the full lips impressed themselves upon all who looked at it.

One morning, while the two women had been sitting together, talking, Fleur Marsh for the first time mentioned her past. For, she told Charlotte, Vivian's portrait brought out certain qualities all too reminiscent of Fleur's first husband, the Baron of Cadlington.

By now Fleur knew the exact position between the Chases. Poor Charlotte, agonizingly lonely and longing for someone in whom she could confide had poured out the whole sad story. Whereupon Fleur had at once taken the girl in her arms and when Charlotte begged her not to feel outraged, she had said:

"My poor child, you have little reason to feel so deeply ashamed. You were more sinned against than sinning. In your innocence you were grossly betrayed. Your love has turned to loathing, and little wonder, for Lord Chase behaved in a most heartless manner. I can only say that I revere the late Lady Chase for taking the attitude she did, towards you.

It was most unusual and indicative of a fine, just nature."

"Then you will still be my friend?" Charlotte had asked, with streaming eyes.

"Ever at your side should you need me, dearest Charlotte," was Mrs. Marsh's reply.

Not then, but later on, discussing the portrait, Fleur spoke of her own life with her first husband.

"Lord St. Cheviot's true character was exposed by Peveril's brush. It showed all his worst instincts. I never, *never* mention the Baron now, nor speak of my dreadful experiences at his hands. But since you have confided in me, I will return the compliment."

So Charlotte learned about the ill-fated young girl who had once lived happily in this very house with her beautiful mother, Hélène, and Sir Harry Roddney, the father who had later fought a duel on Fleur's behalf and wiped off the earth one of the most notorious and wicked men in England — Denzil St. Cheviot.

Charlotte learned how the joy had been crushed from Fleur's life, when she was little older than Charlotte. How — still worse — she had never known the joys of her motherhood, only the horrors of the birth, and her punishment, after the infant died, at the hands of the disappointed Baron.

"At least Vivian is human at times, but St. Cheviot never was," Fleur declared, shuddering. "We must hope that your babe will live to be a great comfort to you, dear Charlotte. My happiness with Peveril has been marred only by the fact that I could never bear him a son. I love children."

Charlotte tried to take cheer from that conversation, but it seemed to her shocking that so sweet a lady as Mrs. Marsh should have suffered so cruelly. She had to admit that Vivian Chase was not always brutal. He could, when he chose, be the delightful boy she had first loved with blind passion. The trouble was that his good moments were few and far between. But as she had advanced in her pregnancy Charlotte began to feel a subtle and mysterious bond between her and her unborn babe.

She felt sure that she would, as Mrs.

Marsh prophesied, find her child a real comfort.

Mrs. Marsh encouraged her to think this and it helped Charlotte through many of her difficult moments with Vivian.

Now, as she lay a-bed with her new-born infant, peace gradually stole through the unhappy wife and drew a kindly veil over the memory of her tortures, both mental and physical.

Let Vivian despise his daughter. Let her, Charlotte, for ever have to forswear passionate love. She now had this tiny creature, sweet-smelling and swathed in flannel, lying in the curve of her arm. Suddenly a smile of pure joy overspread Charlotte's face.

"Eleanora," she whispered that sacred name to the slumbering babe, "you are mine and nothing shall ever take you from me."

In the stormy years that followed she was to remember those very words and the critical hour in which she whispered them.

Miss Dickson, tidying up the room, and arranging some flowers which had been sent up by the housekeeper, saw the expression on Charlotte's face and was spellbound by it. Down in the servants' hall that evening she remarked to the staff that young Lady Chase looked extremely beautiful despite the ordeal through which she had passed.

Vivian, always punctilious about such official matters, had ordered that wine should be distributed amongst the staff with which a toast should be drunk to his newly-born daughter.

The toast was drunk with relish, and relief that her ladyship was out of danger. Only one indoor servant of the old staff remained; Perkins, the head coachman, who had served Vivian's father, and blinded his eyes to the young man's failings.

Vivian could rely on Perkins' loyalty. He was not likely to open his mouth on the subject of Charlotte's lowly birth. He was too afraid of incurring Vivian's wrath. With the same callous unconcern for his inferiors that Vivian had shown the Forbes, he had dismissed the rest of the staff after the funeral of the Dowager. It was his wish that not one single servant should know about Charlotte.

Old Hannah, whom he had never forgiven for the part she had played in bringing his mother's notice to his seduction of Charlotte, left the house of her own accord as soon as her lady was laid to rest. She refused to accept Charlotte as her new mistress. Her boxes were packed and the old servant had gone long before Vivian could give her notice, for which he was devoutly thankful. He had always disliked her waspish tongue.

There was a new housekeeper now — a religious and goodly Scotswoman named Mrs. MacDougal, fresh from the service of a widowed Marchioness who had recently died in the district. Mrs. MacDougal brought several of the Marchioness' former staff with her.

Hester who had accompanied her upon her unhappy honeymoon, had been replaced by a girl called Suzanne. She had been brought over from Paris by his lordship. Suzanne was the perfect lady's maid, but Charlotte did not like her — from the start. She suspected that the pretty blonde French maid had been specially selected by Vivian. He forbade her to dismiss Suzanne on any pretext whatsoever.

"You may know your history dates and your Shakespeare, my dear Charlotte," he sneered, "but you are still too much the country bumpkin to suit me. You could assimilate some ideas of *chic* from a Parisienne who was once in the service of a great French lady."

In bitterness Charlotte had to accept this fresh humiliation. That Vivian should expect her to learn from a servant was an insult. However, Suzanne was punctiliously polite and attentive. But Charlotte always fancied there was derision, sometimes even pity, in the sparkling almond eyes of the *Mademoiselle*, when they regarded her.

The rest of the staff consisted of Mrs. Snook, an excellent cook; Williams, who had replaced the family butler, (the old one had followed Hannah), and Lucy, the head parlourmaid. There were a number of underlings, housemaids, tweenies, and others, whom Charlotte saw rarely, if ever. But there was one more whom she disliked as much as Suzanne and that was the valet who had replaced Browning.

This young man was called Volpo. He was of Portuguese extraction but spoke perfect English. He was excellent at his job, had suave manners, and prided himself on his extreme tact. He had a slightly humped back, for which deformity Charlotte did not blame him — she was far too kind-hearted — but somehow she felt it was akin to the twist in his nature. She was positive that he was a sly, deceitful fellow. She disliked his hooded eyelids, and a way he had of creeping around soundlessly and appearing where one least expected him. She half suspected that he spied upon her at Vivian's behest, which was in fact the case. Vivian, in his mean fashion, was always hoping to discover some wrong action of which he could accuse his wife. From this point of view, Volpo was perfect; his loyalty was undoubted and he was ever partial to the bribes flung at him to keep his mouth shut on the subject of his master's nocturnal wanderings. Volpo was a vicious fellow and happy to serve a young gentleman whom he found equally so. No matter at what hour of the morning Vivian returned from his orgies,

Volpo was up waiting, ready to undress his intoxicated master and put him to bed; impervious when Vivian snarled at him in a rage, enormously helpful and bound to secrecy when required. But the Portuguese returned her ladyship's dislike. He was a spiteful man and he was aware that the young Lady Chase would have got rid of him if she could. He was the first to voice an unfavourable comment on the birth of the daughter.

"Pity his lordship did not choose a lady who could bear a son," he said, and described, spitefully to the staff, how ill my lord had taken the news when they had told him the sex of the child.

Suzanne agreed. She had no liking for the humped backed valet, but she was madly infatuated with his lordship.

The others spoke kindly of Lady Chase. They were in full agreement with Miss Dickson and loved my lady. Whenever they saw her she was sweet and gentle and interested in their private lives, which many ladies were not. Only the other day she had given a sovereign to Mrs. MacDougal for a humble tweeny whose family had fallen on bad times.

Besides, nobody in the household was unaware of the fashion in which his lordship privately behaved towards his wife. Among themselves they wondered why, and their sympathies were entirely with my lady.

"God bless her and the wee girl," said Mrs. MacDougal with her rich Scots burr.

★ ★ ★

That same evening, the little Eleanora's father spent in London, whence he had betaken himself on the excuse that his godfather was seriously ill and had sent for him. It did, in fact, happen that Sir Harry Cawder conveniently chose that very night to give up the ghost; — so Vivian had a real cause of celebration — Sir Harry's death had freed him of the last shred of tiresome control.

He used the birth of his unwanted daughter as an excuse for carousing all night with one or two young 'Bloods' who had been his friends at the University. It was one of the wild kind of nights that Vivian enjoyed, starting with champagne in the house of a musical comedy actress, (mistress of a well-known peer), continuing at a music hall, and ending in a private house for a session of gambling and licentiousness which lasted until dawn.

He woke with a thick head and a vile temper. He would have preferred to have stayed in London, for it was a pouring wet day. Clunes, in such weather, bored him to death. But for appearance sake, he must stay near his wife during her lying-in.

An accident befell Vivian on the way home. One accompanied by a strange psychic experience which had some real effect upon him. It was greatly to Charlotte's benefit and lasted for the next two or three months.

He was returning to the country by brougham. He was nodding in a corner, arms folded, snoring a little, exhausted by the night's excesses, when they passed through Harling. The rain had stopped, but there was a high wind and the horses were sliding all over the road. The coachman could hardly hold them. They had just reached the graveyard belonging to the little Norman church. The coachman had to pull hard on the horses to avoid a farm cart. One of the animals slipped and went down. The brougham skidded, rolled on drunkenly and turned over. Vivian was pitched violently out and passed from his inebriated slumber into unconsciousness.

He half recovered to find himself inside the church into which he had been carried by passers-by and the curate. A funeral service was being solemnized. The coffin of the deceased (an old lady of the parish) stood on trestles before the altar, covered with purple velvet. The young gentleman, who was wrapped in a cloak and bleeding from a gash in the forehead, was soon recognized as Lord Chase. One of the female mourners gave little cries of pity and concern as she saw the handsome boy lying there, white and bleeding from his ugly wound. She rushed forward and, kneeling down, lifted his head on to her lap and began staunching the blood with a voluminous handkerchief.

Another offered smelling salts. One of the wardens hastily ran to send an urgent message to Clunes. The coachman had been killed and his body was lying in the porch.

Vivian Chase, semi-concussed, and badly shocked, received in that moment a strange psychic impression. It was not, in his mind, a strange lady who ministered to him, but his mother. He groaned piteously:

"Mama!"

The lady who supported him looked tearfully up at the curate.

"His lordship is wandering; he calls for his mother," she whispered.

An hysterical young girl, peering down at Vivian from one of the pews, cried in a loud voice:

"Oh, alas! he is dying. *Lord Chase is dying*!"

It was those sinister words which penetrated through the mists whirling around Vivian's brain. Struggling to sit up, he now caught sight of the draped coffin in the flickering candlelight. He believed that he was about to die and that this coffin waited for *him*. He could see his mother's face, pale and accusing. He was, he presumed, about to enter the flames of hell; condemned for his sins to eternal damnation. A spectral voice spoke to him in a stern and hollow voice.

"Heir to Clunes, you shall inherit all, and nothing — for you have lost your soul. Die! You are no longer son of mine. You are a monster of iniquity, a vile seducer, a heartless father!"

Vivian gave a gurgle of pure terror, and dropped back into the arms of the strange lady, senseless.

16

CHARLOTTE never rightly understood what happened to Vivian that January day. She only knew that, once she recovered from the shock of hearing that Vivian had been carried senseless into the house, a sudden blessed peace descended upon her and Clunes.

Miss Dickson told her the news, trying not to distress the young nursing mother too greatly.

"His lordship is safely in bed. Volpo appears to have knowledge of nursing. Dr. Castleby has left him in Volpo's care until the specialist arrives. Meanwhile I hear that the injuries are to his head and one leg, which was broken — the femur is fractured. It appears that, as the carriage swayed, the door swung open, being loose in the lock, so his lordship was pitched out. The poor coachman has expired."

Charlotte gave a gasp, her cheeks flushed with emotion.

"Oh, alas, the poor man! We must

compensate his family. And poor Vivian!" she whispered, "ought I not go to him?"

"Certainly not, your ladyship cannot be moved," said the nurse tartly. She added: "There is nothing to fear. His lordship is not as bad as they first thought. He is in no way critically ill, though naturally he suffers some pain. You might like to know, my lady, that he repeatedly calls upon your name as though it were a talisman."

Charlotte, her heart beating faster, was inclined to utter a cynical reply to this, but said:

"Indeed!"

She could hardly think that Vivian would call upon her name — he, who had left the house on the very day that their child had been born. And she was quite unprepared for a note which was brought to her an hour later by Suzanne. The pretty French girl looked sullen, and as though she had been weeping. Bobbing a curtsy, she handed the envelope to Charlotte.

"His lordship has written this to you, my lady."

"Written to me?" repeated Charlotte,

forgetful of her dignity.

"Yes," sniffed Suzanne and, curtsying again, retired. Her nose was out of joint. His lordship had sent for her and when she had begun to commiserate with him in a familiar fashion he had pointed a shaking finger at her, looking, as she thought, wild-eyed and haggard.

"Leave my sight, girl!" he ejaculated. "Go, kneel down by your bed and say your prayers, as I intend to say mine. My mother's ghost has visited me. I have seen my coffin waiting. I am doomed to the eternal flames unless I repent me of my sins. Look you to yours."

Suzanne had stared, goggling, then fled. Meeting Volpo on the landing, she complained to him. He spoke to her with a sardonic grin.

"Tush," he had said, "no need for tears, my girl. His lordship is raving. He does not know what he is saying. He will recover."

But the letter written to Charlotte was clear enough. The writing was uneven and the paper blotched by ink from the quill which he had used. But the contents made sense.

261

My beloved wife,

I have so much reason to ask your pardon that I hardly dare begin. The terrible injuries I have sustained from my accident are nothing compared with the wounds I now realize I have dealt your sensitive soul. As I recovered my senses after my accident, my mother appeared to me in Harling Church. She showed me my own coffin waiting. She renounced me as her son. Oh, Charlotte, help me to escape Almighty God's vengeance, and my mother's scorn. Forgive me my sins. Take me back to your loving arms. Redeem me. Henceforth I will be a model husband to you and a loving father to our little Eleanora. Henceforth this shall become a truly Christian household. You shall have no cause to fear or despise me. As soon as I am well enough to rejoin you, my Love, I shall be the Vivian who once spoke to you with the voice of the poet Meredith, in our enchanted woods.

I cannot rest until I have heard you utter the words of forgiveness. I demanded to be carried to your room, but the old fossil, Castleby, fears for my leg. I am now waiting for Mr. Thistlebirt, the surgeon from London, who is driving down immediately to set the fracture which tortures me. Oh, Charlotte, do not let the flames engulf me. You are my guardian angel. You alone can guide me back to the path of virtue. Then, my mother will see and hear, and add her forgiveness to yours.

This extraordinary epistle was signed with a flourish, '*Your true Husband and Lover, Vivian.*'

Hardly able to credit her sight, Charlotte read all this again then fell back on her pillows, her cheeks red, her mouth open.

What, in Heaven's name, had happened to bring about such a change of front, she wondered? Had the fall affected Vivian's mind? Was he deranged?

Her natural gentleness and generosity of heart, however, led her to send at once the reply he had asked for. The nurse brought her paper and ink. She penned the following:

My poor Vivian,

I grieve that you have had this terrible accident and that I cannot come to console you. I would have nursed you myself so gladly, were it not for my own poor state of health. But pray do not harbour fears of my feelings towards you. I am most ready and willing to forgive and forget. The moment I am permitted, I shall come to your bedside and embrace you.

Believe me, my Husband, I want nothing more than to live in love and peace with you and so wipe out the past. Let us never refer to it, for it has all been too sad and gloomy.

This shall be the beginning of a new, sweet life for us, I do earnestly pray.

Our little daughter smiles in her sleep and I am sure that smile is one of tenderness for her suffering Father.

This note, sent to Lord Chase's suite, brought another outburst from him of a similar nature. This time it was accompanied by a magnificent diamond star pendant hanging on a fine gold chain. Charlotte recognized it instantly. She had

264

seen the Dowager Lady Chase wearing it, and the latter had told her that it was a wedding gift from Vivian's father. Since her death it had been locked among the family jewels in Vivian's sanctum. He allowed her to wear one or two of these only on special occasions when visitors came, and he wished his wife to show herself off, in all her glory.

This star is now for you, Vivian wrote. *Accept it as a token of my sincerity. I, better than any, know the purity of your intent and your innocence, which, alas, I have not until now respected. Wear the star — my mother's favourite — on your matchless bosom, beloved, and let me kiss it there when I see you again.*

The astonished and bewildered Charlotte read this — the first real love-letter she had ever received — and dangled the pendant while Miss Dickson '*Oohed*' and '*Aahed*' as the fire-light caught the fine stones. They glittered like a prism. Charlotte could only think, indeed, that Vivian was not in his right mind. For not so long ago he had told her spitefully that he would never allow her to wear Eleanor Chase's famous diamond star.

"A low-born creature like yourself is not worthy of it," he had said in one of his more insulting moods.

Now he addressed her as '*beloved*' and wrote in these penitent, almost maudlin, terms of affection. The young girl was stupefied.

Before she slept that night, she sent for Dr. Castleby and questioned him. Miss Dickson begged him to calm the young mother who was running a temperature through sheer over-excitement. The old doctor prescribed a sedative and gave Charlotte's various explanations of Vivian's hysteria. It was the wound on the head, he said, coupled with a strange fantasy which Lord Chase had described to the doctor, in a high fever, after Mr. Thistlebirt had set the fractured leg. Groaning with pain, and in tears, the young man had alternated between cowardly moaning to Dr. Castleby over his physical torments, and an apparently sincere repentance for his boyish follies.

"It seems that he saw an apparition

while lying in the church," the doctor told Charlotte. He repeated Vivian's story which she already knew. She sighed and shook her head.

"How long do you think this condition will last?" she asked.

The physician spread out his hands. Who was to know, he said, what Lord Chase would be like as time went on? At the moment he could not be called *mad*, but he was somewhat mentally disturbed by the shock of the accident and this melancholy ghost that he imagined he had seen. Also, the sight of the coffin seemed to have frightened him considerably. Nothing Dr. Castleby said could make Lord Chase believe that it was not waiting for him. He felt he was doomed, unless he changed his way of life.

"But do not disturb yourself unduly, Lady Chase," ended the kindly doctor. "Do not be disturbed," he repeated, "for no matter what has caused his lordship to crave for a more Christian way of life, it is all to the good, if I may humbly say so."

With this Charlotte heartily agreed.

During the month that followed, Lord Chase's passionate wish to make up to his young wife for past wrongs and so save his own soul, persisted.

Charlotte now became the light of his eyes. He wrote notes continually. Each morning he sent special flowers to her from the greenhouses, with tender messages attached. Finally, he convinced her that whatever the cause, some supernatural visitation from his dead mother had brought about the metamorphosis. She even deceived herself into believing that the new Vivian had come to stay.

She wrote a letter to her friend, Mrs. Marsh, first thanking her for the present she had sent to her babe, then commenting upon her present bliss:

> *Nobody, dearest Fleur, can be happier than I am today. I, who, when you saw me last, was so sad and disillusioned. Vivian's accident has reformed him. Peace reigns in my house."*

(Here she told Fleur all about the gifts, the diamonds, the flowers, the letters exchanged.)

Today, St. Valentine's Day, is fine and sunny. The snows are melting. My baby is four weeks old and a most beautiful child. Her hair is beginning to curl. Her eyes are already turning darker and I trust that the little Eleanora will resemble her noble grandmother, whose name she bears. I asked Vivian if he would approve of your becoming her godmother, and to my delight he at once agreed. Anything for my happiness, he said.

Oh, Fleur, you cannot believe how he has changed. He has ordered the roasting of a whole ox which is to be cut up and delivered to all who work upon the estate at Clunes, on the day our daughter is christened, and a gold piece to be given the entire staff, indoors and out. (This will be on the 1st March.) The first day I was permitted to walk on nurse's arm to Vivian's bedside, we had a touching reconciliation. He looks ill and thin and is much wasted by his suffering. The fracture has caused him frequent pain and has sorely tried his patience. Yet never has he appeared more patient, nor looked more handsome, nor been more kind. He held out both arms and said: "Come to my heart, my Charlotte, for you will feel it beating with a new desire to cherish you". He kissed me and took our infant in his arms and added: "Forgive your father for his past sins. He shall become the splendid parent to you that your noble grandfather was to him."

Mrs. Marsh wrote back from Pillars in tender terms, expressing her pleasure that her dearest Charlotte had found this happiness. She would drive with Peveril to see her god-daughter as soon as the snows melted and made the roads passable.

But to Peveril, Fleur spoke less optimistically after reading Charlotte's long letter.

"I do not trust this change. It is too sudden and violent," she said. "I can never forget how closely Lord Chase's character resembles St. Cheviot's. The leopard cannot change his spots. I fear that the greater part of this repentant state is due merely to Vivian's cowardly fear of Hell. Perhaps he *did* receive a visitation from his mother in his delirium, and it has unnerved him. But I mistrust his ability to keep up such a virtuous pose."

The artist nodded thoughtfully.

"Ay, 'when the Devil is sick, the Devil a saint would be!'" he quoted.

"Oh, Peveril, I pray that fresh misery does not face our dear little Charlotte in the future."

Peveril put an arm around his wife and looked with a tender smile into the soft violet eyes which, for him, had never lost their appeal. She was still the idol of his boyhood, the Madonna he had worshipped at Cadlington long, long ago.

"You are too tender-hearted, my love," he said. "Do not let your fears for Charlotte overcloud your spirit, for they may be groundless."

Meanwhile, at Clunes, Charlotte's happiness continued. Vivian even went so far as to say she might dismiss Suzanne from her service and, to her joy, the French girl was sent back to Paris and replaced by an older woman. The new maid was in her thirties, by name Gertrude. She was altogether different from Suzanne, and far more trustworthy, if not smart and calculated to amuse the master of the House. But Vivian meekly observed that if Gertrude suited Charlotte, that was all that he wanted. Charlotte would like to have got rid of the Portuguese valet too, but hesitated to ask this because Vivian had grown to rely on Volpo. She had to admit that he was a splendid nurse and seemed utterly devoted to his master. On the surface, he was deferential to her too. Volpo was a clever fellow. He did not for a moment suppose that Lord Chase's *volte-face* would endure. It was a period which the servant abhorred, and the wily Portuguese could not bear the pious, honest woman who had replaced Suzanne. But he was content to bide his time. He felt that the devil would not remain saint much longer. Meanwhile he did everything that he could to impress on milady, as well as milord, that his sole desire was to be a loyal servant.

Now Charlotte was up and about again, she quickly regained health and strength. Miss Dickson, with whom she was sad to part, was replaced by a woman they called 'Nanna' and a nursery maid, both of whom had been engaged to take over the full care of little Eleanora. The beautiful nurseries in the sunny west wing that had once belonged to Vivian, had been re-papered and painted a soft blue, furnished with pretty white-painted furniture and filled with toys. Eleanora started her new life with these two attendants to see to her daily and nightly needs. Her mother continued to feed her and although Charlotte would like to have seen more of the baby daughter, she was quite glad, in those early days, of the experienced help. The Nanna turned out to be a strict disciplinarian and often made my lady fear to enter the nurseries. But, as Vivian made more and more demands upon Charlotte's time, she *had* to be free for him. She could see little Eleanora only when feeding her, or for a short time while the infant was bathed.

The day of the christening came, Vivian was carried to a couch in the drawing-room for this. He impressed all the guests by his charm and geniality. Nobody seemed to doubt that Lord Chase had matured, and developed into a model husband and father. As for Charlotte, she looked radiant. A fine March day allowed her to wear a new and splendid dress of palest azure blue silk with frothy white lace collar and cuffs, and a handsome bustle. She wore a blue velvet bow in her chestnut hair. Her cheeks had become rounded and pink. Her eyes were brilliant. She sat by the couch, her hand clasped in her husband's, the picture of proud young motherhood, whilst the nurse, in blue linen, with starched cap and apron, walked around, exhibiting the infant, dressed in a magnificent silk and lace christening robe, to a circle of admiring ladies.

Little Eleanora cooed and gurgled her way through the christening at Harling church, held in the arms of her godmother, Mrs. Marsh. Fleur's painter husband had done a lightning sketch of the infant and presented it to the fond parents.

Fleur declared that she had never seen such a lovely child as Eleanora, who had also been given her own name of Fleur.

"Eleanora, the Flower, we will call her," Peveril declared.

But the sensitive Charlotte detected a hint of sadness in Fleur's violet eyes as she looked at the infant during the baptism. She cradled her closely. Her delicate lips quivered, and Charlotte thought, rightly:

"She thinks of the tragedy of her own infant's birth and death. I am lucky."

And for the first time since her association with Vivian, Charlotte knew what it was to feel fortunate. Vivian gave no sign of returning to his former, heartless conduct. Good had certainly come out of evil.

There had been difficulty about the choice of a godfather for little Eleanora. Vivian had admitted that few of his personal friends would rightly fill the position of religious guardian to his daughter. The choice fell finally upon Lord Marchmond in whose yacht Vivian had been cruising just before his marriage.

Marchmond, only son and heir of the Marquess of Englesby, a Gloucestershire nobleman, was a gay youth two years older than Vivian, but of more temperate habits. When he returned to England to find young Chase married to a girl about whom he had never even spoken, after swearing that he would remain a bachelor for as long as he could, Cecil Marchmond had been much surprised. But any curiosity he had shown about Charlotte's origin had received a terse reply, so he had inquired no further. At his first meeting with Charlotte, he thought her remarkably good-looking. Her child-like charm appealed to him. He was willing and happy to accept the honour of being a god-parent for the first time in his life. He came to stay at Clunes and brought for Eleanora an immense silver gilt christening mug. This was displayed with Eleanora's other gifts.

Charlotte liked Lord Marchmond. He was not handsome, but had a roguish twinkle and a shock of red hair which made him look homely, she thought, despite his illustrious birth. Mischievous he might be, and with an eye to a pretty girl, but she did not think he would have a bad influence upon Vivian. His great wealth had been the attraction for Vivian when he first met him at Oxford. Cecil came to the couch and chatted with his friend.

"When shall we see you on your feet again, Viv?" he asked.

"Old Castleby tells me that the specialist will not hear of my walking, even with crutches, until the end of this month," answered Vivian.

"You must be mightily sick of it."

Vivian stretched out a hand to Charlotte and gave her a languishing look.

"I have been sustained throughout by the devotion of my wife," he said, somewhat unctuously.

Lord Marchmond raised his brows. He wondered how long Vivian's pious attitude would last. But as he glanced at the young girl in her blue silk dress, he found her enchanting. He was not surprised that Vivian should be in love with his wife. Then Vivian added:

"On the first day that I am able to use my crutches, I declare that I shall give a grand ball. We have not held a ball at

Clunes for many years."

"But my dearest, you could not dance — " began Charlotte.

"That is of no account," he broke in, "I can watch. And you shall open the ball with Cecil."

Feeling quite light-hearted, full of effervescing spirits, Charlotte responded: *"Oh, that will be wonderful, will it not, Cecil?"*

"Yes, indeed," he nodded.

"Then it is as good as done," said Vivian and leaned back on his satin cushions languidly.

He did not feel quite so benevolent as he appeared.

For the greater part of the day he was exalted by his own excessive show of virtue. When he embraced Charlotte, it was with the old ardour with which he had wooed her nearly a year ago. But under this desire to be a model of righteousness, lay a feeling of irritation. This was becoming irksome — like his injured leg. The memory of his experience in the church had begun to fade. His love-life was not as exciting as his true nature required. He could not long be content with one woman. He found that he had had more than enough of his young wife since their reconciliation. When he saw the maid, Gertrude, these days, he thought how plain she was. He missed Suzanne and was sorry now that he had permitted her to be dismissed.

For the moment, however, he was content to lie low — indeed his injury forced him to do so.

But he must have some fresh amusement, so he set to work that next week or two to plan the grand ball in celebration of his recovery to health. And why not a costume ball, he suddenly suggested to Charlotte? The dresses of the ladies would give him something to look at.

"I will attend as a beggar on crutches, and look villainous, with a black patch over one of my eyes," he said.

Charlotte protested that she did not want her handsome husband to turn himself into a scurvy beggar, but he decided that it would amuse him to do so. She however, he said, must order a fancy dress to suit her present glowing charms. Why not a Pompadour, which would suit her well; the white curls, with those big honey-coloured eyes of hers, and black patches — would be delightful. Cecil also must wear a wig and costume of the eighteenth century. They two should lead the others in an opening minuet.

Charlotte fell in with all Vivian's suggestions and shared his somewhat childish mood, with pleasure. Money was to be no object. There would be a splendid buffet of wine and rich food, and an orchestra sent down from London. They would issue the invitations immediately.

The house would be filled with glorious flowers, and lights would be hung in Japanese lanterns, in the trees if it was a warm night, so that the dancers could stroll out on to the lawns.

"Oh, I am really looking forward to this!" exclaimed Charlotte, "and there can be yet another cause for celebration. Peveril Marsh has finished your portrait, Vivian. It shall be hung in the hall, do you not think, to replace that rather gloomy one of your great-uncle? Then everyone will see and admire it."

"Excellent," said Vivian, with a yawn.

But there were moments during those next few weeks when Vivian began to doubt if he had sufficient will to maintain his pose of saint; and when Charlotte, to her consternation, recognized the fact. The old symptoms were there, creeping back, now and again. Little fits of irritability, moods of depression and sulks caused not only, Charlotte feared, because the leg did not seem to be going on as well as Castleby liked.

It was nearly the end of the ninth week after his accident before Vivian was allowed to use his brand-new crutches. Then, once he began to hop around on the good leg, supported by Volpo and Charlotte, he snarled at them both. Once again he was rude to his wife in front of his valet.

Vivian made various attempts to overcome his rising impatience. Alone with Charlotte again, he kissed her hand and apologized for his boorishness, while she wiped the sweat from his forehead.

"I understand, my dearest, do not worry," she said.

But she could not forget the dreaded expression in the cold turquoise eyes.

This was no longer the Vivian who had become her adoring spouse. She could only pray that once he was able to manage his crutches alone, he would settle down again.

He did so — but only up to a point. A fresh cause for ill-temper manifested itself when he found that the leg injury would leave him with a permanent limp. Castleby had been afraid to tell him until now. The young man, pale and haggard, ranted and raved over this misfortune.

"A limp — Vivian Chase with a limp — it is abominable!" he shouted.

He was with Charlotte in the library and Castleby had beat a hasty retreat. Vivian had just managed to walk, in a rather crab-like fashion, across the room, to a chair by the windows. At one point he nearly slipped on the polished floor. Charlotte took the full weight and supported him, but it strained her back and made her cry out. Whereupon he snapped at her:

"Anyone would think *you* had the injury, not I. Have the goodness to fetch me a glass of sherry, feeble creature that you are!"

Charlotte's heart jolted. Her cheeks burned. With downcast lids she turned to ring for a servant. But Vivian shouted at her: "Fetch the wine yourself, lazy girl. Are you so much the fine Lady Chase these days that you cannot wait on your husband?"

Her spirits sank to zero. She paled. *Oh, dear heaven*, she thought, *do not let this be true, do not let the old Vivian come to life! I could not endure it.*

She had been so happy with the man he had appeared to be since his accident. She had grown to love such a generous, attentive husband. Willingly, she had sat by him, read to him, played her piano for him, done everything to prove herself a loving wife. Was there, in fact, some mental trouble causing his sudden and violent change of mood? She was in tears when she returned to his side with the wine. But *he* sat brooding over the thought of the limp which must henceforth spoil his gait. He used to be proud of the graceful agility with which he moved.

As he saw Charlotte's depression and wet eyelashes, he made an effort to control himself. The time was not yet ripe when he wished to recreate the old atmosphere of hatred and bitterness.

"Come, come, I did not mean to be so nasty. Give me a kiss, foolish child," he said.

At once her face brightened. She lifted her lips to his.

"Dearest Vivian, do not grieve too much over this trouble with your foot. Lord Byron won all feminine hearts and was a splendid success, and he limped far worse than you will ever do, did he not?"

Vivian shrugged. He sipped the wine she gave him. They talked again of the ball. Everybody had accepted. Preparations were nearly completed. All the guest chambers at Clunes would be full. The Marshes were going to stay the night because Peveril must be here to receive his share of praise after the unveiling of Vivian's portrait. One or two other married couples who were driving down with their daughters must also stay a night at Clunes. And now a footman had just brought Vivian a letter from Gloucestershire, bringing a request for rooms, from Cecil.

"Tell Mrs. MacDougal that two bachelor rooms must be prepared for Marchmond and a relative whom he is bringing with him," Vivian told his wife.

Charlotte, trying to tell herself not to worry and that Vivian's ugly mood had been of short duration, sat at his feet and stroked one of his hands.

"Who, then, is Cecil bringing, dear Vivian?"

Vivian tossed her the letter. She read it. Cecil wrote that he would esteem it a favour if Vivian would allow him to include Dominic in the list of guests. Dominic Unwin — was his adopted brother. It would be more pleasant, Cecil wrote, if he might make the long journey from Gloucestershire in Dominic's company.

Mr. Unwin was a man in the middle thirties, and a passionate disciple of Disraeli. A year ago Mr. Gladstone had been defeated and Disraeli had taken office as Prime Minister. Dominic had at that election again been returned as Member for a constituency in Gloucester. He was unmarried and Cecil wrote with his usual humour: *This should be of advantage to the young ladies.*

Charlotte looked up from the letter.

"Did you know Cecil had a brother by adoption? You never told me of him."

"I did not think of it. He has mentioned the fact from time to time," said Vivian carelessly. "But Dominic Unwin is considerably older than Cecil and rarely at Englesby. I remember now the Marchioness, herself, telling me when I was aboard the yacht, some story of how they had adopted this boy because no children had been born to them, and how, five years later, Cecil made his appearance."

"He may be an elderly bore," said Charlotte.

"But if he is talented, no doubt *you* will find him entertaining. Is it not one of your complaints, my love, that so few of my friends care for books or art," said Vivian yawning.

"I have not had much time lately for either books or art," she laughed. "But I admit I always welcome a discursive hour with a man of learning."

Vivian gave another prodigious yawn

and told her to ring for Volpo. He was tired.

Before she went to carry out his wishes, she suddenly put her arms round Vivian's neck and looked up at the handsome sulky face.

"Do you not love your Charlotte today as much as yesterday?" she murmured, smiling at him with charming coquetry.

In better mood, he gave a little laugh and kissed her silken lashes.

"Of course. Little book-worm, you are still damned handsome. No one would think you the mother of that fat baby."

"I do love you, Vivian. Pray go on loving me," she said with deep emotion.

He was about to reply when a shadow fell between them. The shadow of the hump-backed valet in his dark suit. His thin, foxy face looked small and meaner than usual, half sunk in his collar. He bowed low:

"I came, my Lord, to see if you would like me to help you to bed for a rest before the evening meal."

"Clever fellow, you anticipate my wishes," said Vivian.

"Let me help too," began Charlotte.

287

"Volpo can manage alone," said Vivian abruptly. "Go and feed your infant, my dear."

Biting her lower lip a little, she watched the valet assist his master out of the library. She fancied that she saw a pleased expression playing round the lips of the Portuguese. And indeed, the latter was pleased, if not surprised, to find that my lord was once again in heed of *him* rather than my lady. He, too, had noticed unmistakable signs in Vivian of the master who had first engaged him.

Despite the warmth of the sunny day and a big fire burning in the grate, Charlotte felt cold once she was alone.

The chill of doubt was creeping into her mind. She wished somehow that Vivian had not dismissed her so peremptorily. She loathed Volpo; she could not help it. She loathed and mistrusted him.

Slowly she picked up Cecil Marchmond's letter and began to read it again.

The name *Dominic* fell pleasantly on her ears. A man of law and of learning — well, she would look forward to some conversation with him.

"Dominic," she repeated the name aloud again. "It has a grave sound. I have never heard it before, but I like it."

17

IT seemed that, as far as the weather was concerned, fortune smiled on Clunes, for the April evening of the ball followed the warmest day of the season. It developed into a sparkling evening of full moon and glittering stars. In between the dances most of the guests walked in the garden. It was a lovely scene upon which Dominic Unwin looked as he stood on the terrace alone, smoking a cigar after supper.

Behind him, Clunes glittered like the chateau that it resembled — a miniature castle from a French fairy tale. A flag waved from one of the turrets. Japanese lanterns gleamed rosily from the branches of the budding trees. There were lights along the elm avenue and throughout the spacious grounds. The long windows of the ballroom opened to the terrace. Behind Dominic, the glitter and pomp of the flower-filled ballroom, the sigh of violins playing a waltz. In front, a crowd of guests in their fancy costume, wandering in and out of the trees, a motley gathering. Kings and Queens of former centuries, Egyptians, Greeks, dancing girls, nymphs. Each fresh costume made a vivid splash of colour against the dark green of yew hedges and the velvet of the lawns. It was eleven o'clock. It looked as though the ball might go on until the early hours of the morning. Nothing like it had ever been seen before at Clunes.

Dominic Unwin, however, cared little for dancing, drank only sparingly, and enjoyed solitude. He liked to stand back here alone in the shadows, and smoke the excellent cigar which Vivian offered him. All his adult life he had enjoyed contemplation of others. He was very partial to intelligent conversation, but he had little use for the frivolous exchange of words with empty-headed people. Neither did he care about paying compliments to pretty young women. In fact, as he had told his foster-brother on their journey here from Cirencester, he was going to feel the odd man out at this party. He was too old for it, he said. At which

Cecil had laughed.

"My dear fellow, there will be many grey heads at Clunes tonight, and you have not a single grey hair yet, nor will have for several years."

Nevertheless Dominic felt his age as he watched the youthful couples dancing and circling before him, laughing or whispering amorously as they strolled with clasped hands.

Dominic looked up at the moon a trifle cynically. It was a night for love. A night to stir a man's senses. Yet he was a trifle suspicious of the obvious, and all this was so artificial. It could only breed artificial emotion, he thought. He had, of course, been made very welcome at Clunes, but he had not taken to his host. When Dominic had first arrived, Vivian had been charming. He had looked his best, too — dressed impeccably — every inch a gentleman of distinction, yet Dominic had been repelled by that cold blue eye; by the arrogance which lay under the surface charm. He had been still more repelled once they had all gathered in the hall to laugh and criticize each other's costumes. Vivian then wore his sinister disguise of beggar on crutches; a patch over one eye, a stooping back. Somehow, he produced an atmosphere of malevolence which Dominic found strangely abhorrent.

He had not really wanted to pay this visit. He was working hard in the House these days. He needed rest and would much have preferred to stay at Englesby, which was one of the most gracious and peaceful houses in Gloucestershire — nay, in England. But Cecil had begged so hard that at last Dominic had given in. He was very attached to Cecil; as, indeed, he was to the whole Englesby family. He owed everything to them and he never forgot it. So, good humouredly, he agreed to make the journey. But as for fancy dress, Dominic refused to do more than attire himself as a barrister, in a black gown with a wig. Cecil, on the contrary, appeared as his host had wished as a splendid eighteenth-century gallant.

Now, suddenly, Dominic moved a little out of the shadows, pitched the stump of his cigar into some syringa bushes and looked intently at a young girl who was hurrying across the lawn. It was his hostess. Dominic was surprised to see Lady Chase unescorted. Until he came out here he had watched her dancing and found her adorable. In these days, it took a very fascinating woman to appeal to Dominic, who had long since turned his back upon the love of women. Tragedy in love had touched him too closely. But even *he* had to admit that Lady Chase was all and more than Cecil had described her.

"There is a mystery attached to her ladyship," his foster-brother had told him, when describing the family at Clunes. "As you know, Viv and I were friends at Oxford. He was more than a little crazy then, and sometimes unscrupulous, but an entertaining fellow. The trouble was that his father died when Viv was young and he was brought up by his mother, who was a saint. It had the cynical result of turning Viv into a devil. But he and I got on famously. I expected him to make a fine match, not yet, perhaps — later on. Instead of which, I returned from that cruise with Mama and Papa to find him married, to this unknown girl, and before getting his degree."

Cecil then informed Dominic of the many rumours and conjectures concerning Charlotte. All that was known for certain, however, was that she had once been a Miss Goff who lived at the Lodge; and that she was a protégée and pupil of the late Lady Chase. Presumably, Cecil ended, she and Vivian had fallen madly in love and had married hastily — and in private, on account of his mother's fatal malady.

All this, Dominic found of much interest. When he finally met Charlotte he was surprised by her extreme youthfulness, a touch of childish simplicity which greatly appealed to him. Then, when he looked down into the breathtaking beauty of her eyes, he realized that any man might well wish to snatch her for his own, no matter what she was, or whence she came. It was not just a case of mere physical beauty with Charlotte but of singular charm. A promise of passion, of sensuality, coupled with that child-like purity.

He and Charlotte had talked alone before the other guests joined them, and it had not taken Dominic long to understand why old Lady Chase had wanted to educate her. Dominic, too, probed and enjoyed her fine quick mind. He, who was himself a lover of literature, history and music, touched on all these subjects with her and found her learning matched his own. Charlotte could be gay as well as grave, but she did not seem to share with other girls of her age the perpetual thirst for flattery and frivolous entertainment. Of course, she was already a wife and mother; Dominic thought it delightful when she showed her infant to him with fond pride. Everything outwardly seemed to be well at Clunes at first glance. Later, a passage between husband and wife opened Dominic's eyes to the fact that there was decay under the glitter. Charlotte had accidentally brushed into her husband; and his crutch slipped. She caught and steadied him, with a laughing apology, but in that fleeting second, Dominic caught sight of Vivian's face. He was disturbed to see the look of fury that had altered its whole appearance. He heard the whispered oath:

"Damn you, Charlotte!"

It gave Dominic a sense of shock. Neither did Charlotte's reaction to this remain unnoticed by the observant Dominic. Her smile changed to concern. Her cheeks reddened with mortification. Then she passed on to welcome a newly-arrived guest. For the rest of the evening, whenever Dominic saw Vivian he found him a charming host. But the older man was quite unable to forget that naked fury that had, for a moment, been unleashed, and loosed on his young wife.

Now Dominic watched Charlotte approach. Her dress was dazzling; of rich powder-blue brocade, shot with silver. The full skirt was hooped at the sides and showed a cascade of silver lace. The low-cut neck revealed a curve of snow-white bosom. She looked older than she really was, with her hair powdered, dressed high, ornamented with blue and silver flowers; white curls gracefully falling on either side of her long neck around which sparkled a necklace of sapphires and diamonds. Her face was painted for the occasion. It gave her an artificial glow, for she was, in fact, feeling pale and tired.

Even Dominic could see the faint mauve shadows under those huge eyes. But as she tripped on tiny silver shoes up the steps and on to the terrace, he felt a sudden wish to speak to her.

"Lady Chase!" he called.

Charlotte paused, her hand to her bosom. Then as she saw who spoke, her look of tension eased; a smile curved her lips. She came toward Dominic, and curtsied after the fashion of the ladies who used to wear such wide-hooped dresses.

"*Monsieur*," she murmured.

"*Chère Madame*, you should not be without an escort," he smiled, "allow me to afford myself the privilege of taking you into the dance. You look disturbed."

She drew a quick breath.

"I was just — just — running away from somebody," she stammered.

"Then I feel pity for the 'somebody'," he said, with a lightness that he rarely exhibited, but he wanted to see her smile. His wish was granted. She even laughed.

"Oh, do not; he was so — so hateful."

"Then I withdraw my pity and shall hate him," said Dominic.

Charlotte bit her lip. Mr. Unwin was not likely to know that the hateful 'somebody' was her own husband. Vivian had come across his wife standing by an Italian statue with a gay young man who was dressed as a Greek. A boy no older than herself. The two had assumed a dramatic pose and were declaiming together to the moon. For Charlotte it had been a moment of fun, such as she rarely had. Then had fallen the shadow of the beggar in his rags. It had not taken her long to see that Vivian had drunk too much. For the first time since his accident he was so inflamed with wine that he did not mind his guests seeing him thus. Pointing at his wife with his crutch, he snarled:

"No more of this ridiculous play-acting. You forget, Madam, that you are Lady Chase, and the hostess at our party. Kindly return to your guests. And you, sir — " He had addressed the embarrassed Greek, "Choose yourself a young unmarried girl to join you in your idiotic gambolling."

At this, in an agony of shame, Charlotte picked up her skirts and ran back through the garden to the house.

She stayed talking with Cecil's adopted brother. He could see that she was not at ease. She kept throwing darting glances to the right and the left as though she feared the approach of this man whom she had called 'hateful'. No doubt Dominic thought, some not-quite-sober gallant had been paying her overbearing attentions. So the little Lady Chase was a prude, he thought. All to the good. Dominic liked women to be prudish.

"It was good of you to allow me to come to Clunes," he murmured, "I feel an interloper."

She told him with sincerity that she was glad he had accompanied Cecil. She knew herself to be strongly attracted to this man who, in comparison with her seventeen years, might almost be called 'elderly'. But he was charming. He had tremendous personality. To look at he was not, perhaps, a young girl's ideal. He had none of the sparkling golden beauty of Vivian Chase when first she grew to love him. But she was to learn for the first time the subtle power of a strong, fine nature. Dominic Unwin was an *individual*, with strength and fire behind his quiet presence. A hint of sadness, too, which intrigued her.

She examined him now with shy gravity as they stood there. She felt that they were quite alone in the crowd — on a mysterious island where they could not be reached. She had never before experienced this sense of *aloneness* with anybody. She talked with him as with an old friend.

Dominic was taller than Vivian, so slightly built that he gave one the impression of great height. He was so dark, too, that he might have been mistaken for a Spaniard. Charlotte presumed from that deep tan that he had spent much time abroad in the hot sun. His hair, under the barrister's wig, worn for tonight's entertainment, was black as a raven's wing springing back vitally from a broad forehead. His face was lean, a little hatchet-faced, lips repressed, even stern; yet, when he smiled, he looked youthful. But it was his eyes which interested Charlotte. For they were not dark, as one might expect with such colouring, but of a profound purplish blue. Whose eyes had she seen like these before? She asked herself the question but could not answer it. They were very beautiful eyes for a man and full of deep melancholy. What was his history, she wondered.

Suddenly Dominic said:

"You look at me very questioningly, Lady Chase." She blushed. He found enchantment in the way she touched one burning cheek with a lace-mittened hand and apologized.

"It was discourteous of me to stare."

"You were not staring, but I wondered what question you wished to ask me."

"N-nothing," she stammered with a laugh.

"I know," he said, nodding, "you have heard something — but not everything — about my relationship with the Englesbys. You would like to know more? Or do I flatter myself?"

"Indeed, you are exactly right, Mr. Unwin."

"A great many people have been intrigued by the position I hold at Englesby Castle."

"Oh!" exclaimed Charlotte, "it would seem most discourteous to wish to pry into the private life of my guest. I do assure you — "

But Dominic broke in.

"Somehow I feel I should like to talk about myself. A desire," he added, "that very rarely moves me."

"I am honoured."

"Walk with me a little," he said suddenly, "unless you wish to dance."

"No, I would rather walk with you."

"You will not be cold? The night grows cooler."

"I am not at all cold," she said breathlessly.

She took Dominic's arm and strolled with him across the moon-silvered lawn, toward the lake. Other couples walked by them, laughing and chattering. Charlotte felt a strange inner glow for which she could not account. She only knew that she wanted to go on talking to Dominic Unwin, and to hear him talk. What a voice he had! It was the rich golden voice of the born orator.

She remembered hearing Cecil tell her husband of the enormous impression

Dominic had made in the House with his maiden speech. Charlotte could feel that warm humanity of which Lord Marchmond had also told her. Dominic gave her a feeling of confidence which, she could believe, must have led many thousands to return him as their Member.

"Is it a fact that you have never visited Clunes before?" she asked him. "Vivian tells me that in the past your family came here, but you — ?"

"Not I, because there is such a difference of age between Cecil and myself," he said. "He and I seldom have the same friends. You forget that I am getting on for forty."

"I wish *I* were," sighed Charlotte.

"Why?" he asked, smiling down at the beautiful face.

"Because, when one is young, one is always making mistakes," she said before she could restrain herself.

"I find you full of good sense already and, possessed of more learning than most of your contemporaries."

"Thank you," she said, conscious of deep pleasure.

"And before I tell you a little more about myself," he went on, "I would like to know something more about my charming hostess — or would that be insolent?"

"Heavens! You could never be insolent, Mr. Unwin."

"Then tell me. Cecil seems as untutored as myself on the subject, though he has spoken often of your husband and the boyish escapades they shared at Oxford. But never of you."

Charlotte bit her lip.

"I — I have been much in the background," she said, and was conscious of Vivian's constant pressure upon her to say nothing to anybody about her past. But somehow to this grave man with his penetrating gaze she did not wish to lie.

Quietly Dominic said:

"Once I, too, was much in the background, Lady Chase."

They had come to the edge of the large lake which was fringed with delicate birches. The water was like a sheet of silver in the luminous night. Dominic stood still a moment, barely noticing the feather-like pressure of the girl's hand through the curve of his arm, yet feeling her to be very near in spirit. He was disturbed by his own reaction to that light touch. She was a child, but ageless. He could talk to her as he could not talk to many an older woman.

Abruptly, he said:

"I was adopted when a child of ten by the Englesby family, you know."

Even Vivian's threat which hung over her so constantly could not keep her from exclaiming:

"And I, too, was adopted. For my late mother-in-law took me from London to live at Clunes, in the Lodge, when I was twelve."

"I went to Cirencester to become the privileged son by adoption of the kindest of all great people, the Marquess and Marchioness of Englesby," said Dominic.

She looked with fresh interest at the sensitive face of this intriguing man.

"Pray, tell me more," she begged.

"Your history, first," he smiled.

She glanced at the lake. They heard the sudden mournful cry of a half-awakened heron nesting somewhere in the rushes. Charlotte's fingers played with the magnificent necklace about her slender throat.

She whispered, "I never speak of myself. Please keep what I tell you a secret."

"Your confidence shall be very safe with me, as I hope my own will be with you," he said gravely.

So he learned of that night of fog upon the Embankment when the Chase carriage had so nearly run over little Charlotte Goff, and of all that had followed at Clunes. All, that was, save the personal story of her love affair with Vivian. Dominic was no inquisitive boy to probe too deeply into a young girl's secrets. He kept quiet but guessed without being told what had really happened between those two. He said:

"We both have much to be thankful for. I was born in obscurity and might have been nothing. You started in poverty and have become an exalted wife and mother, and mistress of one of the most beautiful homes in England."

"My little daughter is adorable," she admitted.

He noted that she did not include her husband in her rhapsodies. Poor child, he thought, she was not very good at concealing things; but Dominic had drawn his own conclusions about Lord Chase. Little though he had seen, in recent years, of Cecil, he had often heard his adoptive parents begging him to give up this friendship with Vivian, rumours of whose bad reputation had drifted even as far as Cirencester.

"And now for your story," she said.

He told her briefly all that he knew about himself. What delighted her most was to see that he had no snobbery in his nature, none of Vivian's hateful arrogance and pride. Pride, Dominic Unwin might have, but of the right kind. And he loved all people, both of high and low degree. He was unashamed of his beginning, just as she in the depths of her heart had never felt embarrassed by knowledge of hers. Perhaps, she thought, it was his early experiences that had made him so sensitive. Loneliness and pain can enrich as well as embitter a man.

He did not actually know the secret of his parentage for he could remember little except an existence even more poverty-stricken than her own with Aunt Jem — a harsh life in a Charity school. He made light of this but admitted that he had suffered years in this school of bullying, intense cold, and even hunger. But he had soon risen above the heads of the other small boys, being possessed of a remarkable memory and many talents. One of his teachers had taken a strong interest in him (following the pattern of Charlotte's education). He had shown a brilliance of mind and wit, which amazed his teachers and finally caught the attention of the Marquess of Englesby who had, at the time, been a patron of the Charity school. The Marquess was a kindly gentleman, most interested in child welfare and his wife had had no children. So impressed was the Marquess by the intellectual powers of the orphan who knew no name save 'Dick Smith' that he had taken him down to Englesby. Lady Englesby was immediately attracted by his raven hair and sad blue eyes, and she kept him at the Castle. There, he was given a tutor and at the age of fifteen he went to Charterhouse.

His name had been changed to Dominic Unwin. 'Dominic', because it came from the Latin for '*Sunday*' and it was on the Sabbath that the boy first visited Englesby. '*Unwin*' was a family name on the Marchioness's side, and belonged to her favourite brother who had died young.

Dominic had been profoundly happy and it was a happiness that had not been lessened by the totally unexpected birth, at long last, of an heir to the Englesbys. The fifteen-year-old boy became a devoted brother to little Cecil, who, in turn, looked up to and admired his brother by adoption. Dominic had all the brains. Poor Cecil Marchmond possessed few.

Later on, the two boys saw less and less of one another. The young Earl of Marchmond was still at Preparatory school when Dominic got a double first at Oxford where he read Classics and Philosophy. There he became seriously interested for the first time, in politics. His adoptive parents were delighted.

Dominic gave Charlotte this history of himself with but faint, modest emphasis on much that he could have added about his talents. He ended by telling Charlotte that now, as a Member of Parliament, he was fulfilling his chief ambition.

"That is," he added, drily, "as far as worldly desires go. There are times when I feel that they go no way at all, and that true happiness and contentment lie in a man's soul alone."

"Oh, with that I agree!" exclaimed the young girl earnestly. "I, too, discovered that fact."

"You, who are so young, should still be brimming with the joy of life," he said, smiling.

She made no reply. Once again he was struck by the belief that this lovely young girl was not happy; and by an uncomfortable fear that Vivian Chase deserved his reputation as a libertine. Did she love him? She could not. She must already be disillusioned.

He tried to speak lightly.

"*La Jeunesse dorée*," he said. "Golden youth. You have it. Would that it were also mine."

"But you have a wisdom and experience which I envy," she said with a deep sigh.

311

"I am not to be envied for experience. It has, in my case, been a tragic tutor," he said abruptly.

"You have never married," she said.

"No, never, and never shall do."

"Forgive me."

"Good heavens — for what?" he asked.

"For touching on a subject obviously painful to you."

Her sensibility, her sweetness suddenly broke through a crust in Dominic Unwin which had not been penetrated for many a long year. He stood a moment, hands clasped behind his back, staring across the romantic lake. His eyes held pain and sadness.

"I *was* to have married, when I was barely thirty," he said in a low tone. "She — died."

Quick to sympathize with suffering in any form, Charlotte murmured:

"I am so *very* sorry."

He turned to her.

"I have not spoken of this since it happened, not even to my dearest Lady Englesby, whom I regard as my mother. But — somehow you draw my story from me. Perhaps by virtue of the fact that you remind me of *her*. She, too, was only seventeen, very lovely and passionately attached to her books. She spoke somewhat with your voice. When I first heard it, I could have sworn that my poor little Dorothea lived again."

Charlotte stayed silent, intensely aware of what he was saying. After a moment he continued his story.

Eight years ago, he had met Dorothea Palmerston. She was distantly related to the famous statesman of that name. For the first time, Dominic had fallen in love. He had never been one to fritter his time away with pretty girls. When he loved it was deeply, and with his whole being. He described Dorothea as 'an angel of purity and goodness'. Charlotte felt her cheeks grow hot. The bitter thought leaped to her mind:

'*He likens her to me but what would he think if he knew how far I fell from grace before my marriage?*'

Dorothea returned Dominic's love. After a year's engagement they were to be married. Her parents were distinguished people. A grand wedding had been arranged in London. The Englesbys were, at the time, in their London house in Porchester Square. Dominic was with them, the happiest of men. Not only did a fine Parliamentary career stretch before him, but he would have a lovely talented young woman for a bride. Their home was prepared — a house in Richmond, for Dorothea was particularly fond of riding and Richmond Park was a favourite place with her.

The rest of that story was melancholy. On the very eve of the wedding, Dorothea went riding with her sisters in Richmond Park. Her horse was startled by something white which lay on the verge of the road. The animal took the bit between its teeth and bolted. Dorothea was thrown, her back was broken and she died instantly.

"She was buried," said Dominic in a low voice, "in the bridal gown she should have worn for me. Something of me was buried with her on the dreadful day of her funeral. Life continues, Lady Chase, but one never really recovers from such a catastrophe."

They had reached the terrace of Clunes. The gay sounds of a quadrille drifted through the French windows.

Once again they had returned to the glittering atmosphere of the ballroom. The brief interlude of close companionship which they had exchanged was ended. Dominic knew a strange regret. Having unveiled some of the pain in a heart so long concealed from the world, he could not but feel a yearning towards the one who had inspired such confidence.

As for Charlotte, she stood a moment, hands clasped, looking up at him with eyes that were full of tears.

Hastily Dominic said:

"Oh, confound it, I have distressed you and on the night of your ball — how thoughtless of me."

"No, I am deeply honoured because you have told me about Dorothea. I think it is the saddest story I have ever heard, but I am glad you related it. I shall never forget it."

"No, no, you must forget," he said. "It is all so long ago now, and as I have just said — life must go on. Once more — forgive me for striking at your tender heart. I have made you sad."

"*I was already sad,*" she said, and sighed. The sound was torn from the very depths of her being.

"Lady Chase — " began Dominic. But she had gone; run away from him. He watched the hooped, brocaded gown with the ruffled laces vanish in the crowd. He was left with only the faint odour of Charlotte's fragrance, and a memory of those honey-coloured eyes brimming with tears. And most of all a memory of those words:

'*I was already sad*'.

They had shocked him. Poor Charlotte Chase, poor child. He would have given a lot to be able to help and comfort her; whatever her sorrow. Yet, he was still little more than a stranger to her.

Dominic walked into the ballroom. It was hot and full of the perfume of a thousand dying flowers. He looked for Charlotte but could not see her. When finally he did catch sight of her she was accompanied by her husband. She threw Dominic a half smile but turned away at once, almost as though frightened to acknowledge him. He wondered why.

Vivian was drunk, slithering on his crutches, but he had thrown off his gait of beggar and discarded the patch over his eye. His face was inflamed, his fine features blurred by the wine he had been consuming. He looked horrible, Dominic thought, but Charlotte was gallantly trying to hide his condition from the guests, keeping one arm about him, smiling and bowing to their friends, pretending that it was the highly polished floor that caused Vivian to stagger so foolishly.

Dominic looked intently at the couple for a moment then, with a feeling of acute depression, turned and left the room. He went up to his own chamber from which he did not emerge again that night.

18

TWENTY-FOUR hours later, Dominic Unwin, with his brother Lord Marchmond, left Clunes. The young mistress of the house speeded the parting guests. Vivian was not well the morning after the Ball. He stayed in his rooms. No one had seen him but Volpo, who had, in his sardonic fashion, informed Charlotte that his lordship wished to remain undisturbed while his indisposition lasted.

Charlotte was none too happy about that message. Either it meant that Vivian was secretly drinking (aided and abetted by the vicious Portuguese who valeted him) or that he was genuinely sick.

But she had had one glorious morning of golden sunshine, with the brave sight of yellow-trumpeted daffodils as far as the eye could see, colouring the borders along the drive. A morning when she had much to do, starting with the attention she had to give to little Eleanora, then her duties to the guests. But finally, a memorable hour alone with Dominic Unwin. This, while Cecil Marchmond and the other men took horses from Vivian's stables and went riding. The ladies stayed in their rooms.

Dominic did not wish to ride. He lingered in the library with Charlotte who showed him many of the books collected by the late Lady Chase, some of which Charlotte had read and studied.

To Charlotte this was the most precious hour she had ever spent with any human being. So deeply impressed was she by the fine mind of this unusual man twenty years or so older than herself, that she had no consciousness of the difference in their ages. She only knew that she had found the perfect companion. One to whom she could talk and by whom she could be understood. They were agreed on so many matters. She sat down at her piano and played Bach for him. He listened gravely; then came to the piano and complimented her upon her talent. He himself then played for her, while she sat with hands folded in her lap, listening, watching him, and feeling deep peace; a joy which she had seldom experienced in the past except in a milder form when she used to study in this very room with Eleanor Chase.

Dominic was a finer pianist than Charlotte, and she was quick to comment on the fact. As he finished and turned on the stool to face her, he smiled at her youthful flattery.

"Maybe my technique exceeds yours, but of the two of us you would have made the better pianist. And remember that I have made music my hobby and practised for many years. I started before you were born."

Laughing at this, he rose and sauntered across the library. He picked up a slim volume of Keats which she had just shown him. He, too, was a great lover of that sensitive young poet. Charlotte's gaze followed him. She liked him dressed like this, in his grey travelling suit; sombre yet elegant. As he turned the pages of his book she looked at the fine stern profile, the dark springing hair. Was there a hint of grey over the ears? Maybe the sun showed up the silver threads. Remorseless time had already laid a finger upon Dominic Unwin. But she was filled with an emotion tantamount to hero-worship. He was, she thought, a man whom any woman, young or old, might adore. Little wonder the young Dorothea had loved him. And now she knew to her bitterness and cost the utter emptiness of a love based upon the senses alone, a sensuality rooted in dishonour. Now she knew that she had never really loved Vivian Chase at all. The shadow of fatality chilled her very being as she remembered the man who lay upstairs sleeping off the effects of a debauchery. Her little dream of regenerating Vivian, of growing to care for him again, was fast dying; if not already dead. She closed her left hand convulsively, hating the sight of her wedding ring. She thought of the babe which she had just fed and fondled; her own spirit was crushed.

"Alas, my poor babe," she thought, "and alas, for the folly of my passion which has burnt out, and left me only the ashes of despair."

Dominic raised his head. He glanced toward her as he closed the volume of poems.

He, too, had found this morning more than agreeable. It had been a pleasure shared unreservedly with this intelligent, sensitive young girl. Difficult for him this morning to believe her a wife and mother. The showy brocaded dress, the valuable jewels of the Pompadour, had been laid aside. Today Charlotte was a child, her chestnut hair looped simply back, tied with a velvet bow. A child, in her simple lilac-coloured gown with only a gold cross hanging from a chain at her throat.

She looked so defenceless, so sad; the sight pained him.

Then she glanced in his direction. He could see unshed tears in her eyes. Something terrible weighed her mind and spirit down, he thought.

Involuntarily he stepped to her side.

"Lady Chase — Charlotte — let me call you that, for I am old enough to be your father — " he began.

She broke in, struggling for calm.

"Hardly so, Mr. Unwin."

"Nevertheless, much older than you. Could you not think of me as an elder brother, and call me 'Dominic'?"

"I would like to," she whispered.

"I can think of you as a dear young sister," he went on, "for we seem to have shared much in our beginnings. We are, perhaps, two people set apart from the rest of the world."

She liked to be thus linked with him but her head drooped. Her slender fingers twined nervously in her lap.

"I know that I am set apart in a way that I could never explain to you," she said in a choked voice.

His sense of anxiety for her increased.

"Do you need a friend? Is it detestable of me even to suggest that you, Lady Chase, are friendless?"

Now she raised her face. He read such naked pain in her eyes that it struck him to the very quick.

"Good God, I am right!" he exclaimed. "You *have* some secret grief to endure. My poor child, can I not aid you?"

"I know grief, but no one in this world can help me," she said in a strangled voice.

"Are you so sure? Remember I am a Member of Parliament, a man who speaks to persons of both high and low degree; who sees life not only as it is at Clunes or Englesby, but in the raw among the sick and needy. Frequently I must touch below the surface. I am capable of understanding trouble. Who should be more so than I, who have suffered much myself," he added in a low tone. "If it would help to give me your confidence, I would be more than happy. I might even find some solution."

A moment's silence. Charlotte struggled with herself. She had never felt a greater inclination to tell any man all that had happened with Vivian, all that was happening now. But dearly though she wished to talk to Dominic Unwin, she was too loyal. Vivian was her husband and the father of her child. Sometimes she blamed her own existence for the very deterioration in Vivian's character. Whatever it was, she must not complain to a stranger; least of all to a man who appealed so vastly to her as this one. After a moment she whispered:

"Dear Mr. Unwin — Dominic — I have never before encountered any man in whom I would more gladly confide. I thank you for your interest in me, but my sorrows are not my own. To expose them could serve no useful purpose. What has been — has been. What is to be — must be. I pray only for greater strength of will; for a philosophic mind."

Dominic knit his brows. She was so very young, yet so tragic. He longed to pick her up in his arms and comfort her. It did not enter his head at this moment to regard her as a woman to be loved in a sensual way. But he felt an inexpressible tenderness towards her, such tenderness as he had experienced for no human being since Dorothea died.

"Then," at length he said, "I can only trust that you will remember my existence if you should ever have need of me."

Now her face cleared. She gave him a swift smile which he found ravishing. He was sure that the real Charlotte had a sunny disposition and could be capable of brilliance and humour. It was not natural for her to be so depressed.

"Thank you, thank you very much, Mr. Unwin," she said. "Indeed, I shall never forget what you say."

He took a leather wallet from his

pocket, drew a card from it and handed it to her.

"This is my address, my Chambers are in London," he said. "I go only occasionally to Englesby. The greater part of my time is spent in the House; but should you ever need me, you will find me there — " he pointed to the address on the card.

She looked at it:

'*Mr. Dominic Unwin, M.P.,*
Albany, W.1.'

Somehow that little piece of pasteboard became in a single moment her dearest possession, her talisman against danger — and future grief. She clasped it between her hands and in that childlike fashion which he found so touching, smiled at him again.

"I thank you from the bottom of my heart."

"And I reassure you from mine that you will find me a ready listener to any woe which may in the future overwhelm you. I thank you also for our splendid morning together. It is a rare treat being able to exchange ideas and artistic delights as we have done."

"Yes, it was truly wonderful," sighed Charlotte.

As he put his wallet back in his pocket, he thought:

"God knows what is troubling this poor child, who is herself the mother of a child. But I feel that one day she may want to call upon my help. I do not like or trust the man whose name she bears. It is a thousand pities she was ever permitted to marry him."

At that moment the study door broke open. Cecil Marchmond came in, dressed in his riding clothes, his happy countenance reddened by the wind and the sun.

"So there you are, Dom — poring over books with Charlotte. You two melancholy scholars! You should have been riding with me. It is splendid in Vivian's park this morning."

The older man smiled.

"I have spent a far more pleasant morning with my hostess, whose taste in literature and music matches my own," he said.

"Indeed yes," echoed Charlotte, rising.

She felt an inner glow, a sensation that she was no longer quite alone in this bitter world. Her hands still clung lovingly to the card that bore Dominic's name and address.

She could not see the slightest possibility that she could ever make use of it, of the friendship he had offered her. They lived in different worlds. He, engrossed in his career, she, in her own circle. Yet this morning, the confidences they had exchanged had forged a link between her and this unusual man which nothing on earth could break.

"He is utterly to be trusted," she thought.

She did not see him alone again. Luncheon was a formal affair in the big dining-room, after which all the guests departed and she had to go to her infant. But she slipped the little card into her *corsage* and kept it there. With it she kept the memory of Dominic's deep blue eyes looking with such kindness, such piercing sweetness, down into hers as he bade her good-bye.

"All my thanks for this visit," he said

as he bowed low over her hand, "and pray, convey my thanks to my host."

Then the Chase carriage had driven Dominic and the young Earl to Harling Station. From a nursery window Charlotte watched that carriage disappear round a bend in the drive. A little cloud of dust followed.

She thought, with emotion:

"Now the dust settles over my life again! He is gone. He has gone and — *I could have loved him*. I *do* love him, as my one and only true friend, and, though I may never see him again, I shall always remember him."

As the nurse handed Charlotte the infant, the tiny creature put out a hand and clutched her breast. She bent low over the babe, her eyes smarting with the tears that scalded her lids. Desolately she performed her duties as a mother. Then, feeling strangely tired, she walked out of the nursery. She was about to enter her own room, when she heard a voice coming from her husband's wing.

"Charlotte! Charlotte! where the devil are you? Come here at once."

Her heart sank. She hurried towards

Vivian's bedchamber. Volpo was not there. The curtains were still drawn, keeping out the sunlight. The handsome room, for all its spaciousness, was stuffy and offensive to Charlotte's nostrils. In his big, four-poster bed with the red damask curtains half drawn, Vivian Chase lay in one of his satin bed jackets; gold hair rumpled, face puffed and putty coloured, eyes inflamed. He presented an unattractive spectacle. A carafe of wine, half empty, stood on the table beside him. There were wine stains on the embroidered sheets. Stains on the red satin eiderdown. Beside him, on the bed table, stood a pile of uncut yellow-backed French novels.

It seemed to the young girl that after the calm heaven of the morning in the sunlit library, conversing with a man like Dominic Unwin, this was like a sudden plunge into hell. And Vivian had the devil in his eyes as he growled at her:

"Where have you been?"

"Feeding our child," she said gently.

"Have her weaned," he said, "she takes up too much of your time. You pay less and less attention to me."

"But Vivian," she said, shocked. "It is a mother's duty to nurse her infant."

"Duty, *duty*," he broke in, "you are always the little saint. What an unlucky fellow I am! I had to listen for the first part of my life to a psalm-singing mother; now I must listen to a pious wife. But it does not become you to be so, my dear Charlotte. You amused me better when you were more accommodating."

Her heart sank very low indeed. With the departure of their guests it looked as though Vivian had made up his mind to put an end to all pretence of making a fresh start with her.

"I am sorry," she said, "that you think it necessary to be on these poor terms with me again. I thought we had begun to find true happiness once more."

He lowered his lids. His mouth was loose and cruel.

"Lying up with this damned leg made me fanciful. I gave too much time to thoughts of Heaven. But I am not dead yet, nor do I intend to die. To the devil with superstition. I have at last recovered from the hallucinations from which I suffered after my accident. You should be the first to congratulate me on my recovery, my dear wife."

She stood silent, one hand clutching the cross at her throat. He looked her up and down.

"Where did that unbecoming garment come from?"

"You mean my dress," said Charlotte. "It is one made for my trousseau."

"I thought I told you not to wear any more dresses made by that local idiot. I bought you handsome gowns in Monte Carlo. Where are they?"

"In my wardrobe — " she began.

"Then wear them," he broke in, "and your jewellery. You annoy me by your efforts to remain that little *ingénue* imbecile from the Lodge. God knows why I ever married her."

She made no answer. She thought:

"Indeed, God knows."

"Where is everybody?" snapped Vivian.

"Our guests have gone. They sent you farewell messages, Vivian."

"Good riddance," he said, "they bored me, except perhaps Cecil who is not a bad fellow. But as for that solemn dark-faced foster-brother of his, I could not tolerate him."

Charlotte clenched her hands.

"You saw little of Mr. Unwin."

"Enough to convince me that he is an intolerable bore."

She remained silent. She found that with her whole heart she resented the contempt with which he spoke of Dominic.

Vivian continued:

"I'd like to know the history behind that pious prig from Englesby. His hair and skin are as dark as a Spaniard's."

"Maybe he has Spanish blood. He was, like myself, adopted."

Vivian gave a loud, ugly yawn and stretched his arms.

"Confound this leg," he said between his teeth, "Castleby says it will be another five weeks before I walk without crutches, but when I do — " he gave a laugh and looked at her in a manner that drew a blush from Charlotte's cheek; it was so full of licentiousness.

"May I now go, please," she said, "I was very late last night and I want to rest."

"Late doing what — learning politics

from the mouth of Cecil's upstart brother."

"He is no upstart," Charlotte was fired to answer. "Birth and breeding do not necessarily make princes of men, Vivian. No matter where Dominic Unwin originally sprang from, he is a gentleman with the finest instincts and character."

"So!" said Vivian in a drawling voice, and shut one eye as he looked at her. "How eloquently you speak of our Member of Parliament. Has he touched a cord in your romantic heart, my dear?"

She felt the blood rush to her cheeks and recede again; try as she would she could not keep herself from trembling.

"Please, Vivian, may I go now. Since you choose to be so discourteous to me, I would rather not stay."

She turned abruptly as though to leave the room but he shouted at her so violently that she turned back to him, afraid that the servants would hear.

"Vivian, pray do not shout."

"I will not have you speak to me in such a saucy fashion," he snarled. "This damned leg of mine, and your babe, have kept us too long apart. I think it is time you showed your husband a little love and attention. Do you hear? Come to me — "

Every drop of blood in Charlotte's body revolted from what she knew to be at the back of his poisonous mood. Reluctantly she advanced to the bedside, her nose wrinkling with disgust. She longed to throw back the curtains and let the fresh air of the April day into this stuffy room. She said:

"For the love of God, Vivian, let us not start *this* kind of association again. I implore you to return to your other self. The self that permitted you to treat me with the respect due to your wife."

He laughed and snatched at her, pulling her down upon him.

"I am myself now, in this moment. You smell delicious," he said. "You little hypocrite. Let us see the fire and enthusiasm that led to the conception of our daughter. No more of your prudery, Lady Chase. And I would find you more attractive with fewer clothes."

Praying for patience, she shut her eyes. He wrenched at the fastenings of her pretty lilac gown and bared the smooth marble of her shoulders. As he did this, Dominic's card dropped out upon the bed. Charlotte had no time to recover it. Vivian's fingers seized upon it. He held it up to the light of the bedside table, scowling, then gave a long, low laugh. Such a laugh as struck chill at her.

"Well, w-e-l-l," he said, "*Mr. Dominic Unwin* M.P., *Albany, W.1.* Your new hero. How singularly entertaining."

She choked.

"Mr. Unwin thought — if — if we returned to Eaton Square — we might like his address," she stammered.

Vivian tore the pasteboard into tiny pieces and flung them over the bed.

"That much for Dominic Unwin's address. I have no wish whatsoever to visit the gentleman, neither is it a friendship which I shall encourage for my wife. In any case, Cecil's foster-brother is middle-aged. Let him seek the companionship of women older than you. And if he has developed a slight fancy for my beauteous young wife, he will have to forget it."

She had no words. She looked with

despair at the scattered pieces of card. It was symbolic, she thought, for in just such a way had Vivian torn her life to pieces and scattered it to the four winds.

"Oh, you are contemptible," she broke out in her misery, while he tugged at her curls and her clothes.

He laughed and closed her mouth with a violent kiss.

All the passion and pride in her nature rebelled to such an extent that she tried to pull away from him. He fought her and she was bruised in the contest. His arms were strong with desire and she could not escape. But she sobbed wildly.

"Mr. Unwin is a fine man and I know his address by heart. I don't need the card. I know, I tell you, just where to call upon him if I need his friendship."

"You *wanton*!" he said, "you with a babe scarce three months old. You are disgusting."

"I have done no wrong. Mr. Unwin is a stranger who has become a friend," she cried.

"This ends the friendship," said Vivian

and struck her across the mouth.

After that she cried no more, and she lost all hope of future happiness with Vivian. While she lay in his hateful embrace, in dreadful bitterness, she thought:

'It is all over. He will see to it that I never set eyes upon Mr. Unwin again.'

Yet even in that hell and through the black clouds that swirled around her, she could still see the shining tenderness in Dominic's eyes and heard his voice saying, '*My poor child, can I not aid you?*'

He could not. She was beyond aid, she told herself — bound for ever to this unspeakable man who had fathered her child.

In that hour, overwhelmed by Vivian, she touched the lowest depths of a woman's degradation and despair.

Part Two

19

NINE years later.

Charlotte had already been awake for an hour, when Gertrude knocked on the door and carried in the tray with her early morning tea. Gertrude was astonished to see the lamp on the table beside the bed alight and my lady sitting up, reading what must be one of yesterday's newspapers.

It was bitterly cold this November morning. Gertrude clicked her tongue with disapproval as she saw that her young mistress had not even bothered to put a shawl over her shoulders.

"My lady!" she protested. "You will get a chill. Emily must come up at once and light your fire."

Charlotte smiled and a trifle guiltily laid aside the paper which she had been studying so earnestly.

"I am all right, thank you, Gertrude. But it *is* a raw morning, I must admit."

"It was snowing in the early hours, my

lady," the maid informed her. She drew the heavy blue damask curtains, revealing to Charlotte a dismal, yellowish-looking morning. Charlotte caught only a glimpse of leafless branches of the trees in Eaton Square. But she could see that they were powdered with snow. She was glad when Gertrude hastened to wrap a fleecy pale blue shawl about her. Dear Gertrude — always so tender, so careful of her health. Charlotte had been suffering from a cough that had persisted all winter. She preferred to live at Clunes and lead a country life, even in this bitter weather. But Vivian liked to be in Town during the winter. So here she was. Clunes was shut and would only be reopened for Christmas week.

For a moment, Charlotte lay watching the maid move quietly around the big room, folding one or two articles of clothing, tidying the big walnut dressing table with its triple mirror, re-arranging the towels on the washstand. Her efficiency never failed to impress Charlotte. She had grown, too, to feel quite an attachment for this woman during the nine long years that Gertrude had been her personal maid.

Although always formal, and respectful, she had a human side which Charlotte found soothing. She could rely on Gertrude being behind her in all ways — more especially when Vivian chose to be difficult. And Gertrude felt that the excellent woman was in sympathy with her in her dislike of Volpo. He was their mutual enemy. Charlotte knew that Gertrude tried to save her from his continual spying and many other unpleasant moments. So, although in most things Charlotte had to submit to the will of her husband she had, throughout these years, refused to allow him to dismiss Gertrude.

"She is the one being in my household whom I trust and whom I know is attached to *me* and not only to her job. I will not have her taken from me," Charlotte declared, when Vivian, complaining that Gertrude was a 'sour creature', and ugly, suggested getting rid of her. And Vivian shrugged his shoulders and said no more, being only faintly interested.

True, Gertrude had aged and grown

scrawny and angular now that she was in her forties. The frizzed hair under the white cap with its long streamers, was turning grey. She looked down her long thin nose at most people in a derisive fashion. But all the kindliness of which she was capable shone in her small beady eyes when she glanced in Charlotte's direction. To her, my Lady Chase was one of the kindest, sweetest, and most considerate ladies she had ever served. Gertrude said:

"Will you have your breakfast earlier, since you are awake, my lady?"

"When it is ready, thank you, Gertrude."

"Afterwards, shall Mrs. MacDougal come and see you about tonight's meal, my lady?"

"No, Gertrude. I am dining out. Do you not remember?"

"Oh, yes, I beg your pardon, my lady."

Charlotte added:

"Tomorrow his lordship returns. Ask Volpo to make sure his rooms are well cleaned and prepared."

"I will tell him and Mrs. Mac, my lady."

Gertrude withdrew, closing the door quietly behind her. Outside, she sniffed and tossed her head. Oh, yes, my Lord Chase would be returning tomorrow from his trip to India. And there had been peace and quiet in the house for the last three months. Her ladyship had looked altogether different. A pity he had to come home, the servant reflected as she went downstairs. After tomorrow, there would be noise again, with his lordship strutting around, swearing at everybody in one of his vile tempers, or making my lady cry. No one knew better than Gertrude how often my lady shed tears behind closed doors; what a martyrdom her life was with his lordship.

Gertrude called the tweeny, Emily, sent her hurrying for sticks and coal, and told Lucy to follow and light my lady's fire.

In her big double bed, Charlotte watched the two young maids clean the grate and set a fire ablaze. It was growing lighter outside. There was a rift in the clouds. It might be a nice day, after all. And it was certainly going to be a pleasant one for Charlotte. Fleur Marsh, her great friend, was in Town, and lunching with her, and tonight Charlotte was to accompany the Marshes to a Ball held by Lady Farringale, whose husband was in the Foreign Office. The Farringales had a particularly beautiful house in Piccadilly. Algernon Farringale was a nephew of old General Sir Harry Cawder, one-time guardian to Vivian; and although the two men had nothing much in common, the Chases were naturally on the Farringales' visiting list. So, in her husband's absence, Lady Chase had been invited to the Ball. Fleur's father, Sir Harry Roddney, had known the Farringales for years. So Charlotte was to have the rare pleasure of attending a dance with her dearest friends, and without the sinister shadow of Vivian to spoil it.

Nine years of marriage, following Eleanora's birth, had done nothing to improve matters for Charlotte. All the wealth, and the dazzling position which Charlotte now held, could not compensate her for the lack of love, of true companionship, with her husband. Deep down in her heart she was alone, and comfortless.

It was a loneliness that even mother-hood had not been able to alleviate.

Two more children had been born to Charlotte, both girls. With each birth, Charlotte had suffered agonizingly and received little from Vivian save reproaches, because she had not managed to give him a son. The joy of bringing a new babe into the world had been sadly quenched by the unnatural father's sour reception of each addition to his family. He was never done taunting and blaming Charlotte, as though it was her fault, alone.

Two years after Eleanora's birth, the second daughter arrived and was christened Beatrice, the name of Vivian's grandmother. A gap of three years, then Charlotte tried once more, dutifully, to give Lord Chase the son and heir he wanted. Once more, it was a tiny girl, and this time his lordship got into a drunken rage, stormed out of the house and did not return for three days. The poor unwanted infant was christened Victoria, after the Queen. Charlotte yearned over it, hoping to feed it and give it the love denied by its father, for it seemed particularly small and sickly. But she was not even allowed this pleasure. Little Victoria had been born in 1880. Vivian was bored at Clunes. He wished to go aboard the yacht he had recently purchased. He dragged Charlotte away with him, forcing her to wean the infant, and demanding, as he always did nowadays, her complete attention.

However, the third daughter lived and thrived. All three little girls grew up to be strong and healthy. Charlotte loved them devotedly. But she was not allowed to spend as much time in the nursery as she would have wished. She must ever accompany Vivian on his ceaseless round of social engagements. Even though he did not love her, he was proud of her beauty. It was a beauty that had matured with the years. Now, in her twenty-seventh year she was lovelier than she had been as a young girl. And because of her great intelligence and sympathetic nature, she was a favourite with many people who had little liking for young Lord Chase.

Vivian's character had not improved with age, and once he came into complete control of his father's fortune, he tried to dissipate it in the maddest fashion. He could not bear that any banquet or ball given by their friends should be on a more magnificent scale than those given at Clunes, or in his Eaton Square residence. In consequence, Charlotte was plunged into a ceaseless and wearisome effort to join Vivian in snobbish displays of grandeur. Always she must be at her tailors, her dressmakers, her *modiste* or in the hands of hairdressers and beauty experts. After the birth of each child, she must be massaged and groomed, so that her figure and her face should retain their perfection. Her jewels must outshine all others.

At Ascot and at the Opera, Lady Chase must be talked of as the most dazzling of the young matrons. Once Vivian settled down to his marriage, this had become an obsession with him. But for Charlotte it was a nightmare.

So time went on.

This morning, Charlotte looked back on the years and wondered if she could recognize herself as that shy, warm-hearted girl who once sat at the feet of Eleanor, Lady Chase, and lived at the Lodge in such innocent happiness.

Now she was no longer shy or diffident about fulfilling public engagements, or presiding over her grand household. She was complete mistress of herself and of any situation. She was known in London, and in the country, as a brilliant hostess, a provocative conversationalist. She had acquired polish and tact enough to please any husband. Outwardly she was what Vivian had made her. Even he, who did not love her, congratulated her when she achieved some new triumph. At least in this respect, he admitted that his mother had been right; Charlotte made him a dazzling wife.

But in private life, the pair meant nothing to each other. She suffered his embraces when he demanded them, but she could not love him. She knew that he had mistresses and said nothing. She presented a cool, haughty façade to the world in which he forced her to move. Under it, however, she remained the tender-hearted young girl who had once loved him, and whose love had been dragged through the mud.

As time went on, she felt an increasing resentment against the meaningless life she was forced to lead — its utter sterility. She longed to take her three little girls and flee from the gilded prison of the home Vivian provided. But she could not. She was left with her hopeless yearning for affection denied her, except when she was allowed in the nursery, or on the few occasions when she saw her friend, Fleur Marsh.

Vivian suddenly decided to go to India as the guest of a Maharajah who was at Oxford with him. It was a fascinating invitation to shoot tiger and stay in the Maharajah's magnificent palace. For once, he went away for a long time leaving Charlotte behind him. He also left strict instructions as to the way she was to conduct herself.

"You will adhere to your duties as a mother, madam, and no casting of languishing glances at gentlemen in my absence," he had said.

"Vivian, have I ever behaved in any way other than as a loyal wife?" she had begun, hotly protesting. He broke in, fixing her with his cold, stone-blue gaze, and with sneering lips.

"I seem to remember the day when you placed the address of a certain Member of Parliament in your fair bosom, my dear," he said. "Did you not languish in *that* direction — and as many years ago as when Eleanora was born?"

She had blushed crimson and turned away, her heart beating fast with indignation. But she could also attribute that burning colour to a slight sensation of guilt. Dear God, yes, she remembered *him* — his dear memory had remained with her throughout the years, although she had encountered him but once since their first meeting.

20

SHE had met Dominic for the second time soon after she had discovered that she was to bear Vivian a third child. It was June. Beatrice was still only a baby. Charlotte had accompanied her husband to the Opera. He did not care for music, but he liked people to think he did, and besides, it was 'the thing' to go to Covent Garden in the season. On such occasions Charlotte was happy and excited. She adored opera and particularly Wagner.

On this occasion they were hearing *Tristan und Isolda*. While Vivian yawned and nodded behind his wife, the young Lady Chase sat in their box, kid-gloved hands clasped around the posy she carried, rapt gaze on the stage, her ears ravished by the glorious sound of swelling orchestra, and the voices of tenor and prima donna. Now and again Charlotte's great eyes filled with tears. Her heart throbbed with deep emotion — the desire to love and be loved, to know the ecstasy that Wagner's great love-duet suggested, and of which she knew herself to be capable. But a little snore from behind her reminded her of the grossly physical young man whose wife she was, and who gave her only a repulsive passion as love's counterfeit.

She was then only twenty-two; the mother of two children and a new life just beginning in her womb. She was the unhappiest woman among this glittering crowd of bejewelled and be-feathered ladies. Yet many glanced at her box and envied her the priceless emeralds around her throat and wrists. She was cynically aware of the fact. From time to time some infatuated girl also betrayed an envy of Charlotte because she was Vivian's wife. *If they only knew — !*

Suddenly she turned her head and looked across at the opposite box, conscious that someone was gazing in her direction. She saw a man, wearing formal 'white tie and tails', and with a white carnation in his buttonhole, staring at her through his raised opera-glasses.

Just for a second she felt this to

be insulting and drew back into the shadows. Then suddenly her heart leaped and she leaned forward again, this time raising her own small mother-of-pearl glasses. She focused them on the face of the man. At once she recognized him. It was Dominic Unwin. That same thin, brown face with the large expressive eyes, the air of distinction.

All the emotion already conjured up in her by the highly emotional opera overflowed now, as she saw Dominic Unwin again. She went burning red, then very pale. Lowering her glasses, she sat there, tingling from head to foot. The man in the opposite box continued to look at her.

His companion was a stranger to Charlotte. A woman of some beauty, with a touch of silver in her hair, and wearing a black lace dress with a bunch of violets. She was, perhaps, a year or two younger than Dominic who must, Charlotte ruminated, now be in his early forties. She was conscious of an altogether ridiculous pang of jealousy, a wild envy of the beautiful woman.

In any case, what should it matter to

her? she asked herself, drearily. What was she to Dominic Unwin, or he to her?

They met, during the *entracte*, in the foyer. When at last she came face to face with him she wished passionately that this were not the Covent Garden Opera House, but the quiet library at Clunes, where she could talk to him alone, shut away from the rest of the world.

She wished, too, that she were not *enceinte*, did not feel so ill and tired, and wondered if she looked it. But her lips smiled brilliantly at him as he bent over her small hand and greeted her.

"This is an unexpected pleasure, Lady Chase," he murmured.

So close to him now she could see the marks of time on his face. A few more lines; a silvering of the dark, springing hair. But it suited him. He looked very handsome, she thought. His eyes smiled down at her with the old tremendous kindliness. It was as though the sweetness in those marvellous eyes poured over her soul's wounds and soothed them with a strange, magic balm.

"How are you, Unwin," put in Vivian,

in a bored voice. "And where is old Cecil these days?"

"I believe he is at the moment in Paris," said Dominic, and thought that Charlotte's husband looked much older and had put on a lot of weight. The handsome, golden youth had become a flabby, unhealthy-looking man. Then Dominic introduced his companion.

"Mrs. Lyttleton, a cousin of Cecil's and mine, I think you may know her," he said. "Mercia, incidentally, is a harpist of no mean ability. We occasionally go to concerts or opera together. Her husband is often away in America on business."

Charlotte felt a relief almost more absurd than her jealousy when she first saw Dominic's companion. Of course, she knew now, she had heard Cecil Marchmond and Vivian speak of Mercia Lyttleton. A charming woman, a Marchmond by birth, and devoted to her husband, who was an American. Certainly there was not likely to be a sentimental attachment between her and Dominic.

Dominic stood by, inhaling his cigar, and listening to Charlotte talk with

Mercia. When Charlotte had come down the staircase just now on her husband's arm, he had felt the tempo of his own heartbeats increase; a deep, real pleasure at the unexpected meeting. He had thought much about Charlotte Chase during the last five years. He had never been able to forget the pain in her wonderful eyes, the unspoken regret when she looked at him, and his own unusual emotion at leaving her. He knew, of course, that she had had another daughter; Cecil had called his attention to the fact. And going around London in the season, he often heard her name but had never once run into the Chases. He had, however, felt dismayed by the rumours that Vivian Chase was drinking too much and spending his fortune like water; also that everybody seemed to feel sorry for his young wife. It hurt Dominic profoundly to visualize the unhappiness of that young girl who must remain tied to an indifferent brute for the rest of her life.

Now he found her more beautiful than ever; older, a little graver, more self-possessed. She had, he thought, learned to cover up her personal feelings.

For one moment he managed to draw near enough to speak to her in an undertone.

"How is it with you?" he asked her, bending down his head.

Charlotte remembered for long afterwards the wild thrill that shot through her as he asked the question, the upward surge of joy she had never before experienced in her sad, disciplined life.

Her answer came in a low voice.

"I am tolerably well, thank you."

"And your children?"

She raised her eyes now that were glowing with pride in her motherhood, dispelling the intense sadness.

"Eleanora is beautiful and has grown darker, more like my mother-in-law, Beatrice is her father all over again, golden-haired, blue-eyed, and — "

"Difficult," Dominic might have broken in, but dared not. The word was left unsaid.

Once again, his heart ached for her. She read the message in his eyes and quickly raised her posy to her face, hiding it in case he should see that she recognized his pity and responded to it with all her soul.

After that, the conversation became general. Dominic moved away with Mrs. Lyttleton. Vivian and Charlotte strolled in the opposite direction, bowing and smiling to friends who recognized them. In a cold, sneering voice. Vivian said:

"So! Once again we have met your wonderful politician. Come, why are you not simpering with pleasure, my love?"

Her face crimsoned but she threw back her head proudly.

"I do not simper, Vivian. And there is no necessity for you to sneer at Mr. Unwin. He is publicly accepted as a coming man."

"Splendid," Vivian had sniggered, "I am impressed."

★ ★ ★

But on this cold November morning, as she sipped her morning tea and took up her newspaper again, she was able to luxuriate in the thought of Dominic Unwin and his triumphs. Only on occasions had she heard personal news of him through Cecil, whom she and Vivian met sometimes during the Season when they stayed in Eaton Square. She knew, for instance, that Dominic had remained unmarried. But she could and did, as now, re-reading the account of a brilliant speech he had made in the House, follow his career in the papers and rejoice that he was fulfilling his ambitions as a politician.

Charlotte felt a strange personal pride in his success. He had made a profound impact on her life. He remained enshrined in her heart as a being of infinite importance.

After breakfast the nurse brought the three little girls in to say 'Good morning' to their Mama. The woman stood by, primly watching while her charges climbed on to the big bed, and Charlotte covered their fresh pink faces with kisses. Charlotte looked towards the nurse.

"You may leave them with me, Nanna."

"For only a short time then, my lady," said the woman. She had a cold, hard voice and a cold eye. "Eleanora has to start her lessons. Miss Tuft arrives at nine o'clock. Then I shall be taking the younger ones into the park."

"Why did you not bring them to me sooner?" Charlotte asked reproachfully.

"Eleanora was naughty; she would not eat her egg."

"I do not care for eggs, Mama, they make me feel sick," put in the little girl and nestled her cheek against her mother's hand.

Charlotte looked fondly into the big dark eyes that were so like her grandmother's.

"Then perhaps we could find you something that you do like," she said tenderly.

The nurse broke in.

"His lordship has particularly stated that he does not wish Eleanora to be spoiled. She is far too much of a 'madam' about her food."

Charlotte bit her lip. She felt Eleanora grip her fingers and hold them tightly as if for support. She longed to give it. If only she were allowed to bring up her daughters with tolerance, with humour, as she believed children should be reared. Not with this over-strict discipline, this starched attention to detail which the nurses enforced. But Charlotte dared not defy Vivian's wishes. She knew that he and Nanna had an understanding. Vivian saw to it that his daughters had all that money could buy. He spared no expense in their education. But the children seldom had what Charlotte called 'real fun'.

Little Victoria, of course, was still too young for lessons. Towards her, the nurse softened on occasions; that was obvious. And she favoured Beatrice. But she did not like Eleanora and Charlotte knew it and disliked the woman in return. No, not even as a mother was Charlotte allowed happiness. When she had asked permission to dismiss the machine-like nurse, Vivian replied:

"Certainly not. She is most excellent and controls your daughters, which is what they need. Eleanora is very disobedient and far too fanciful."

This morning, looking at her eldest child, Charlotte brooded over the thought that Eleanora was not difficult, only misunderstood. She was imaginative and highly strung, and she was afraid of her father which annoyed him.

Charlotte's delicate fingers played with the little girl's hair. It had grown much darker and was cut with a fringe. She had a solemn beauty. She looked up at her mother beseechingly:

"Could I not stay with you for a treat, instead of going to Miss Tuft this morning, Mama?"

"It would be nice, my darling," murmured Charlotte.

Immediately the nurse intervened.

"His lordship returns tomorrow and he will ask Eleanora to repeat her lessons and show some progress."

"That is so," said Charlotte reluctantly.

Eleanora suddenly burst into tears.

"Oh, Mama, if only Papa were not coming back and I could stay alone with you, my own dear Mama!" she sobbed.

Beatrice, who was standing by the dressing table examining her mother's tortoiseshell and gold toilet set, joined in:

"You are a nasty horrid thing not to want Papa back. *I* want him."

"*I* want him," echoed Victoria, who sat on top of Charlotte's bed cuddling a huge flaxen-haired doll rather like herself.

Charlotte was silent. She hugged the weeping Eleanora with a sad passion, and looked over her head at the nurse. The woman was, she thought, as cold and hard as her starched white apron and cap, her stiff collar and cuffs, her voluminous blue linen skirts. Charlotte fancied that she dropped her eyes and smiled in a secret, malevolent way.

"I shall have to tell his lordship how Eleanora feels," she said.

Fiercely protective, Charlotte exclaimed:

"Nothing of the kind, Nanna. Eleanora meant no harm. She meant only that she wishes to see a little more of me. Is it not natural?"

The nurse continued to smile in her frozen fashion.

"Oh yes, my lady, but unnatural that she should not wish her dear, kind Papa to come home. Maybe she has heard a grown-up express this same sentiment. I must question her."

Charlotte's throat and face flamed.

Cruel, wicked woman. What was she insinuating? Was she going to whisper that she, Lady Chase, had tried to influence her small daughter against Vivian?

A feeling of confidence which she did not always have when Vivian was in the house made Charlotte defy the nurse this morning.

"Take Beatrice and Victoria back to the nursery. I will speak to Eleanora alone," she said.

The woman pursed her lips.

"Miss Tuft will be here, my lady."

"You heard my order!" exclaimed Charlotte.

The nurse hesitated, then took the two young children by the hand and led them out of their mother's bedroom.

Left alone with her eldest and dearest child, Charlotte hugged and kissed her.

"Do not cry, my love, you shall stay with me a moment longer. Look — on my table by the window is a box of bonbons. Untie the ribbon and choose one for yourself and take two for your sisters."

But Eleanora clung to her.

"I do not wish for chocolates, Mama. I wish to stay with you."

"Do you love your Mama so much?"

questioned Charlotte.

"Oh, very much indeed," said the little girl, nodding, and she looked with adoration at her pretty young mother and touched one of the long silken curls escaping from the little linen embroidered cap which Charlotte wore in bed. Then she added with a sigh:

"But Nanna says that it is wicked to adore anybody except God."

"This is so, my darling," said Charlotte with difficulty.

"And Nanna says I must love Papa even more than you, Mama."

Charlotte had a tart reply ready on her lips but restrained it, colouring angrily. She had to force herself to say:

"Of course, you should love your Papa deeply, of course, darling."

"But he does not like me as much as he likes Beatrice and Vicky. And he is cruel to you."

Now Charlotte went quite white.

"Hush, Eleanora. You must not say such things. Who put such an idea into your head?"

"I heard it," said Eleanora, "and I know, for I have seen you crying and heard Papa's voice shouting at you."

Charlotte shut her eyes. She opened them again and tried to smile, even to laugh.

"My little darling has too much imagination. She speaks a lot of nonsense."

"Oh, *Mama*, can we not go away together, you and I?"

Charlotte could barely find words now, for her eyelids were smarting. How deeply she would love to go away with little Eleanora, the one being in the house who gave her true affection and sympathy.

Charlotte was forced now to send the poor child along to the schoolroom where Miss Tuft awaited her. If she did not, Eleanora would be the one to suffer. For, of course, that heartless nurse would tell tales to his lordship, and receive his praise and thanks (and, no doubt, a sovereign) for her pains.

After the little girl had gone, Charlotte lay still, no longer feeling as bright as she had done earlier. Not even Dominic's photo or the account of him in the paper could console her. Nor, really, had she much heart left for the Farringale Ball tonight, even though she would be with her best friends. She had a sinking sensation that accompanied the knowledge that tomorrow Vivian would be back. What kind of reunion would it be? she wondered. Certainly not an agreeable one. He would not come as a friend, or as a lover, anxious to be once more at the side of a beloved wife. His last letter had merely contained a list of the things he wished done for him in London; the appointments she was to make for him. She knew that once he was back, she would never have another moment to herself.

Charlotte thought of little Eleanora who wanted so much for her mama to take her away.

"Oh, God, if only I could," thought Charlotte, "If only I *could* — never to return!"

She turned her face to the pillow. But her eyes were dry. She had wept too long and too often. It was as though there were no more tears to shed.

21

THE Farringale Ball opened. Lady Farringale, a handsome woman of forty-five, had finished receiving her guests. She stood at the foot of the famous carved rosewood staircase, talking a moment to her tall, bearded husband.

Dominic Unwin was the last guest to arrive. He hastened into the hall, smoothing back his hair, and bowed over his hostess's hand. He murmured an apology.

Lady Farringale smiled graciously and begged him not to feel disturbed.

"We all know how hard you work, Mr. Unwin, and that the House has been sitting late," she said. "The rest of your party are, I think, already here. Cecil certainly is. He, as you know, is an indefatigable dancer and a great stand-by for any hostess."

Lord Farringale now said a few words to the late arrival. He, too, had a kindly smile for the tall, dark politician who had recently distinguished himself on so many occasions.

Dominic was here tonight because the Farringales were distantly related to the Englesbys and at this precise moment there were rumours of an attachment between the young Earl of Marchmond and Lydia, the Farringales' youngest daughter. But it had not entered Dominic's head that tonight would mark his third and most important meeting with the one woman in England who held the slightest interest for him.

He was waltzing with his hostess, threading a way in and out of the crowded ballroom in which there were many beautiful women when he suddenly saw *her*. Charlotte's gaze met Dominic's fully. It was as though an electric shock passed through him. He could feel the blood coursing more quickly through his whole body. Mechanically, he continued to guide Lady Farringale, but his gaze focused on that vision of loveliness in the circle of Cecil's arms.

Charlotte wore a dress of pearl grey gauzy material looped at the back into a high bustle and decorated with

371

diamond drops, which also festooned the embroidered edge of her low *décolletage*. Her hair fell in graceful chestnut curls caught behind her neck. She wore a sparkling diamond tiara. As she came closer to him now, guided by Cecil, who had seen his brother, Dominic noted how well Charlotte was looking tonight. Her lips were actually parted in a happy smile which he had never before seen on that usually sad mouth. This was no child now, but a matron and a mother, he reflected.

He had seen the announcement of her third daughter. It had given him a pang; he knew not why. It was, however, a pang that he had swiftly suppressed, just as he had always tried to drive away from him the very memory of Charlotte Chase. He had no right to the sentiments it evoked. Only when he was very tired and alone, he allowed that image to return — first to bewitch — then to frustrate and to sadden him. He knew that he could have no part in her life, nor she in his. But as soon as she entered his world again, as she had done at the Opera four years ago, he became aware once more that she had a vital message for him, a strong subtle, irresistible fascination.

Lady Farringale had seen the approaching pair. She said to Dominic:

"Here comes Cecil with Lady Chase. Do you know her?"

"Yes, we have met."

"She is charming and unusually lovely," said Lady Farringale, and added in a quick, low note, "but I cannot abide her husband. I was delighted when the Peveril Marshes said that they would bring her alone. Chase is on his way home from India."

Dominic felt a surge of excitement. So Vivian had been abroad, and had not yet come home. He could well echo his hostess's words. How little was *he*, indeed, able to 'abide' Lord Chase.

The music stopped. The dancers began to saunter through the ballroom, either to sit out in one of the conservatories, stroll through the portrait gallery, or seek refreshment in the supper room.

Face to face with Charlotte, Dominic spoke calmly:

"How do you do, Lady Chase? I trust I find you very well."

"Very well," she echoed, and gave him a hand, gloved in white kid, which he pressed almost imperceptibly. But as his eyes looked deeply down into hers she felt the colour drain from her face. She knew an intense emotion at seeing him again. It was a delight she had not expected. She reproached herself because she felt so deeply about him. She must not do so — she who was a wife, mother to three little girls. But it was truly wonderful to look up at that dark, strong face again and hear the rich, low voice which had haunted her dreams throughout the years.

Cecil was talking animatedly with Lady Farringale. Inevitably, Dominic offered Charlotte his arm. Her heart beat quite crazily as she walked with him across the polished dance floor towards one of the conservatories at the back of the house.

The violins were beginning to play again; a throbbing waltz. The big crystal chandeliers gleamed with hundreds of candles. The great house, full of *objets d'art*, was warm with firelight, filled with a dazzling company of some of the most distinguished men and beautifully gowned women in England. But as Dominic Unwin and Charlotte Chase moved together into a quiet, dimly-lit conservatory which was perfumed with flowers and moist with green exotic plants, they had eyes and ears only for each other.

"Are you sure you do not wish to dance?" he asked her.

"Sure," she said, seating herself on one of the crimson plush sofas. Her eyes looked up at him with brilliance and feeling. "I would prefer to talk to you, Mr. Unwin."

"Was it not to be 'Dominic'?" he smiled down into those lovely eyes that innocently forced him to betray a lifetime of self-control.

"Dominic," she repeated, with a rise of colour that made her look like a young girl again — it was difficult, he thought, to believe her any older than when they had met last time, at the Opera.

"Tell me what these years have done for you, Charlotte," he said. "Have they been kind?"

Her lids drooped. She toyed with the carved ivory handle of an exquisite painted fan which she carried.

"Let us talk of you, and your work," she parried.

"Oh, I am tired of myself."

"But you have done great things. I read of you frequently. I saw your photograph in *The Times* only yesterday. They speak of you as a politician who, given the opportunity, could do much for our Queen and country," she said.

He was flattered. His own colour rose a trifle. But he laughed.

"Not so."

"But I hear it from all sides," she insisted. "You work hard and long. I would I could hear you speak in the House. They say you are becoming such an orator that you are a shining light in your Party."

"You are more than kind to me," he murmured, bowing low.

She looked up at the strong, dark face.

"You still live in Albany?"

"Still, except when I go abroad for holidays. My adoptive mother, the Marchioness, has been very ill, as perhaps you have heard. I spent last summer at

Englesby with her."

"She is better, I hope."

"But still a very sick woman, alas."

"I grieve for you. I know how attached you and Cecil both are to her. Incidentally, Vivian and I have not seen much of Cecil these last few years."

"Oh, he is here, there and everywhere. He does not settle down as our parents would wish."

"He has neither the brain-power nor the character of his elder brother," smiled Charlotte.

"You are bent on flattering me," said Dominic. He seated himself at her side, one arm resting on the back of the sofa, while his blue strange eyes examined her critically. She knew it and enjoyed being the focus of his criticism.

They discussed their families; she told him of her three little daughters. He listened, interested, but saddened as he had been at their former meeting, by the sure instinct that she had found neither the peace nor happiness she needed to make her a contented woman. She laughed; she talked brilliantly; she looked bewitching. But the shadow of bitterness, of a desperate distaste for the life she led, weighed her down. He was aware of it. She talked only briefly of her husband. Dominic knew of course that Vivian was the real cause of her unhappiness. But her whole face changed and her eyes sparkled as she described her small daughters, especially the eldest.

"She resembles you?" murmured Dominic.

"Her grandmother, the late Lady Chase."

"And the other two?"

"Beatrice is exactly like her father. Little Victoria too."

Silence fell between them then. The constraint was lifted only when Charlotte made an effort to talk about him again rather than about her affairs.

"How do you view our present political position, Dominic?"

"Has the young scholar grown into a thinking and erudite woman who likes to probe into subjects more usually reserved for men?" he asked, smiling.

"I follow my country's politics, I admit — " she said, but she could not add that it was mainly on account of *his* participation in them.

He told her a little of his present work, his hopes and fears.

"It is a bad business. There have been many serious riots this year."

"What is the cure for such festering sores, Dominic?"

"I hesitate to say," was Dominic's answer, his brows knitted. "Like my Leader, I sympathize deeply with the poor and oppressed. I would like to see us adopt a policy that would extend some kind of national service to the wretched people."

Her heart kindled.

"I agree. I am distressed to see and hear of those who have to beg a crust of bread for their starving families, while women like myself are decked with such as this — " she touched the diamond collar about her throat, then the tiara that scintillated in the chestnut masses of her high-piled hair.

Dominic was charmed by her words and the movement of her long slim fingers. He smiled tolerantly.

"Nay — you have a right to your

jewels — they become you. And the problems of the starving unemployed in our country cannot, alas, be solved by the sale of a handful of diamonds — even were you to give your trinkets to the poor and needy."

"Nevertheless, I often feel undeserving of my position."

"It is rare to meet a woman who troubles to philosophize, to probe under the surface, Charlotte."

"I spend a great deal of time in thinking, Dominic."

"You always did — as a child. Although you are still a child to me," he smiled.

"With children of my own," she smiled back and sighed.

"Whatever has befallen you, it has left you curiously untouched," he said.

Now a fresh constraint fell upon them. In silence they regarded one another. Charlotte felt as though a great tidal wave of feeling surged across her very soul and drowned her, rending her unconscious of all human beings on earth save this one who sat at her side. His eyes held remarkable fire, she thought. All England knew of that fire in Dominic Unwin. The

House had felt the heat of it — the magnetism of his personality as well as the mastery of his subjects. He possessed logic, and a shrewd common sense which had gained him the respect of his fellow Members. Yet he could be pungent, bitter, even merciless in his attack upon those who openly opposed his ideas, his idealism.

Charlotte found herself wondering what it would have been like to have loved and been loved by such a man; to be his wife, mother of his children. The sudden comparison with Vivian was so much to the detriment of the man to whom she was, in fact, joined by the bonds of matrimony, that Charlotte felt a spiritual sickness settle upon her. She turned pale and talked no more.

He felt her change of mood. He tried to recapture the light spirit of friendliness and exchange more views with her but failed. He, too, was conscious of a wild regret — that Charlotte must forever remain forbidden to him as a woman to be wooed and won. For the first time since his own dear Dorothea had died and left him alone and unconsolable, he knew the urgent need of a woman's affection; of the home and family which he had long since replaced by the sterner demands of a politician's career. But it was all to no purpose. Dominic told himself to return speedily to a sphere in which Charlotte Chase did not move — could not touch his sentiments.

"Come, you think too much of dull and weighty matters," he said with a gaiety he was far from feeling. "Let us return to the ballroom. I will do my best to show you that I *can* dance, after all. Will you grant me the opportunity?"

She gained her feet, trying to smile.

"If you wish," she said.

He did not wish it; he would rather have stayed here alone with her and delved further into her quick, delicate mind; listened to her, watched the varying expressions across her beautiful, mobile face. But he no longer trusted himself and that was a knowledge that frightened the man who prided himself on being afraid of nothing.

As they emerged from the quiet perfumed conservatory into the noise and crowd of the great ballroom, he put an arm round Charlotte and with a faint pressure of his hand against the small waist, guided her into the circle of waltzers. Then he knew a thrill that must essentially be dangerous, because it was so vastly exciting.

She experienced the same wild thrill, supported by his arm and with one of his hands clasping hers.

She looked up at him as they danced. She had never known a greater urgency. Neither could Dominic tear his fascinated glance from hers. They might have been alone in that crowd of dancers. She seemed to him without shallow coquetry, or false pride; human enough to be incapable of withholding from him, even if she wished, the fact that she was as greatly drawn to him as he to her.

He yielded to a passionate impulse to allow himself an increase of the pressure of his fingers upon hers. A long look passed between them, enriching a moment that was swiftly lost. They went on dancing sedately as dignity and decorum demanded. When the waltz ended, Charlotte was trembling. Dominic passed a cambric handkerchief over a forehead that had grown moist.

They moved away from the ballroom. As they went, a tall, fair, florid-looking man wearing impeccable evening dress, made his way through the crowd and approached them. Dominic stared, then his muscles tightened. He at once recognized Vivian Chase, despite the amount of fat he had put on, and the innovation of long, fair curled moustaches and side-whiskers which were fashionable.

"Lord Chase!" he exclaimed.

Charlotte stood still. Dominic saw every drop of blood drain from her cheeks. Obviously, Vivian's appearance was a complete surprise to her, and a disagreeable one. Her widened gaze turned from Vivian back to Dominic. He read the touch of fear as well as anguish in that glance, a glance that was almost an appeal for help, help which he could not give and which she must not ask.

Vivian stood before them. He gave an unpleasant smile as he greeted Dominic.

"Good evening, Unwin. I did not think to find our busy Member of Parliament at a dance," he said, with a sarcasm that

Dominic found irritating, but he bowed courteously.

"How are you, Lord Chase? I thought you were on your voyage home from India."

"Yes, how come you to be home, Vivian?" put in Charlotte, trying to speak lightly, although her whole heart had sunk at the unexpected sight of her husband.

"We docked early this morning," he said. "I found I could get back to London this evening instead of tomorrow. I was told that you were at the Farringale Ball, my dear, so I followed on. You are, I am sure, pleased to include my name in your dance-programme, are you not?"

His voice retained its biting, sarcastic edge. His cold blue eyes ran up and down Charlotte's beautiful form, taking in every detail, from her tiara to the tips of her small, embroidered shoes.

"Your dress is charming," he added and crooked his arm. As she placed her gloved hand through it, Dominic intercepted the crushing look of misery in her eyes. It made him feel desperately sad for her. But he was impotent to afford her the slightest sympathy. He only knew that Charlotte hated the man who was her husband and the father of her children, and the fact was singularly distressing to him. Poor lovely, warm-hearted young thing; she deserved a better fate than this.

Vivian spoke again, stroking his moustache, narrowing his gaze as he turned it on Dominic.

"Do you not pity me, Unwin? Coming home unexpectedly to find, instead of a sorrowing wife, a truant who wears my diamonds and dances blithely with her admirers in my absence?"

"Really, Viv — " began Charlotte.

Dominic, flushing angrily, broke in:

"I see no cause to pity you, Lord Chase. You have a very beautiful and gracious wife and an engaging family."

"Do you find Charlotte gracious?" drawled Vivian. "You are to be congratulated. I cannot say that I ever see that side of her. She has only surly looks for me."

"*Vivian!*" protested Charlotte again.

Scarlet with shame, she did not meet Dominic's gaze now. This was too sudden a metamorphosis — the arrival of Vivian to spoil her wonderful evening, and in one of his unpleasant moods. He was not drunk, but obviously in a bad temper. She could guess that he was annoyed because he had reached home to find her out, enjoying herself. He begrudged her any pleasures which he did not himself arrange.

Poor Charlotte was all too soon made aware that Vivian's absence from her while he was in India had done nothing to improve their relationship. True, she expected little from him nowadays; yet one sign of genuine emotion, one ray of warmth might have softened her towards him, so starved was she of affection. But she felt that her very soul was being murdered by his insistent efforts to master her.

She was anxious to get him away from Dominic before he could say anything further to humiliate her and embarrass the politician.

"Come, Vivian," she said lightly. "Let us go through to the supper room. I feel sure you would like some refreshment."

The base cruelty that was never long

absent in Vivian Chase made him take her hand now and press it to his lips with a kiss of simulated passion, while his eyes leered over those delicate gloved fingers at the other man. Dominic's face was rigidly set.

"How thoughtful of you, my love," said Vivian in an oily voice. "Is it not delightful for me to be granted one glimpse of the graciousness you just mentioned, Mr. Unwin?"

Dominic could not bring himself to reply. His hands locked behind his back. Never before had he felt a more impassioned dislike of any human being than for Charlotte's husband.

Great heavens, he thought, what an appalling character! And what a nightmare life must be for the young and tender-hearted woman married to him. He could see clearly now how she suffered. The light, the laughter, the joy of living, which had made her look so beautiful tonight, had been blighted for her by Vivian's return. He pitied and loved her, both, as he watched her walk away on Vivian's arm. The diamonds sparkled on her hair. She moved with grace and distinction. Yet every line of that beautiful form suggested pain to him, pain and the rigid necessity to act her part and conceal her feelings.

It would have been better, Dominic Unwin thought, that they had never met and talked again, never experienced the mutual ecstasy of that dance. For, though held apart from him at arm's length as a conventional waltz demanded, his hand had clasped her fingers and touched her waist; and he had breathed in the fragrance of her glorious hair, felt her silent trembling response to his admiration.

This is madness, he thought as he firmly strode through the hall to ask for his hat and cloak. *I must put her out of my mind. She is married to a monster but she has her children. Her life is set apart from mine. My love can do nothing but hurt her.*

That was the hardest knowledge of all for Dominic to bear — that in her tenderness, her grace, her vibrant need of love and warmth she was *doomed*.

22

DOMINIC did not notice where he was going and brushed into a couple who were coming towards him. He stopped to utter his profound apologies.

He was almost too overwrought to see clearly, but the lady to whom he apologized seemed interested in him.

"It is Mr. Unwin, is it not?" she asked. "I think we met at the Chases' ball in Hertfordshire, some years ago. Mr. Unwin, this is my husband, Peveril Marsh."

Dominic bowed, and forcing a smile, murmured the conventional words expected of him.

Then suddenly he became conscious of interest awakening in him; a queer almost psychic intimation that he knew Fleur Marsh very well. With something of a shock he looked down into her large eyes, eyes as deeply blue as his own, and full of ineffable sweetness. Fleur Marsh!

Yes, he had heard Charlotte Chase speak of her as her dearest friend.

Mrs. Marsh was growing old. Her delicate face was deeply lined. Hair, which had once been golden red, fell in silver curls on either side of her lovely face. She wore a black satin ball gown with white camellias on the *corsage* and a black Mantilla over her head. Like the charming-looking man beside her, she stooped a little, leaning on a silver and ebony stick. For the last five years Fleur had shared with her famous painter-husband this painful scourge of rheumatism that was gradually crippling them both.

Dominic knew of Mr. Marsh's work. He particularly admired, and had frequently gone to see, the portrait Peveril had painted of Charlotte, which had been hung in the Academy before the birth of her second daughter.

But it was more than these things which captured Dominic's attention now. It was the extraordinary feeling that he had known Mrs. Marsh not for a year or two, but all his life.

What *was it*? he asked himself, mystified;

and continued to stare at the beautiful old lady. Then he pulled himself together.

"I — I am just on my way home. It has been a wonderful party, has it not? May I bid you 'good night', Mrs. Marsh, and you, sir," Dominic bowed to the old painter.

"Wait — " began Fleur Marsh in a strange voice.

But Dominic had gone and was lost to sight among the other guests who thronged the hall. Peveril Marsh took his wife's hand. He looked anxiously at her.

"What is it, my dearest? Are you ill?"

She passed a hand over her forehead.

"No, no. It is just that — "

"Just what?" he asked.

She was usually so calm; he had not seen her as *emotionée* as this for many years.

She shook her head as a swimmer does, who emerges suddenly from deep water in which he has been drowning.

"I don't know what came over me just now, Peveril; but Dominic Unwin has such an extraordinary face and compelling personality, and when he

392

looked down at me I felt — "

"Felt what, my love?"

"That I knew him, had always known him well."

"He is Mr. Unwin who has lately impressed the House by so many of his fine speeches. And he is a friend of Charlotte's, too, is he not?"

"More than that, perhaps," said Fleur in a low voice. "For many years he has been her *beau ideal*. But what can account for my strange sensation that Mr. Unwin and I have met? Was it perhaps in another life?"

The portrait painter pressed his wife's fragile hand fondly and smiled.

"It is just a fancy of yours, my darling."

"Of course, I realize the fascination he must have for Charlotte," Fleur said almost inaudibly. "His gaze seems to go straight through one."

"Am I to lose my lovely wife even now that she is an old lady?" asked Peveril on a gay note.

"How can you say such a thing?" she exclaimed, her cheeks pink. "No, Peveril, it is something inexplicable that moved me to the depths of my being. Who *is* Dominic Unwin?"

"Related to the Englesbys, is he not?"

"Yes, now it returns to me," nodded Fleur. "He was adopted by the Marquess and was given one of the family names of the Marchioness."

"Really, my dear, you are quite struck by the handsome politician who so unceremoniously bumped into us," smiled Peveril.

Mrs. Marsh did not return his smile. She seemed in truth to be as her husband suggested — quite 'struck'.

She could not stop thinking about Dominic Unwin. His memory remained with her, worrying her strangely, for a long time.

But now she was given something else to think about, for she saw Charlotte hurrying towards her, looking pale and upset.

"I will not be going back with you, dearest Fleur," the girl said as she reached her friend. "Vivian returned twenty-four hours before expected. He has only just arrived, but he wishes to take me back to Eaton Square immediately. I am going to fetch my cloak."

Fleur looked with pity at the young woman whose private unhappiness was all too well known to her.

"I am sorry, my dear," she said, "can we not persuade Vivian to let you remain longer?"

Charlotte gave a twisted smile.

"No. He has already picked a quarrel with me and is in a rage."

"But why?"

"Because he found me dancing with Dominic Unwin," said Charlotte in a low voice.

Mrs. Marsh bit her lip.

"There can be no reason why you should not dance with Mr. Unwin," she murmured.

"Vivian is wildly jealous, Fleur," said Charlotte in a voice intended for her friend's ear alone.

Mr. Marsh moved discreetly away and left the two women alone.

"For what reason?" asked Fleur.

"Oh, do not ask. I do not understand Vivian, save that he is the same tonight, even after our long separation, as he has been since the day we married — happy only when tormenting me. The fact that I admire Dominic is enough to account for his spiteful attitude."

"I saw and spoke to Mr. Unwin just now," said Mrs. Marsh slowly.

"Oh, Fleur, is he not wonderful?" burst out Charlotte, and then turned away, her face working and added: "*I wish I were dead*. Oh, Fleur, I wish that my heart had stopped beating there, in the ballroom tonight, while he danced with me. I am so unhappy!"

The tears sprang to Mrs. Marsh's eyes.

"Would God I could help you, Charlotte. Sometimes I think Lord Chase is out of his mind."

"I have often thought that," said Charlotte.

★ ★ ★

She drove home with Vivian, listening to the clip-clop of the horses' hooves as they moved along Piccadilly and she looked out at the quiet dark streets. It was very cold at this midnight hour. She shivered, but not only with the raw cold; with exhaustion. This was the effect that Vivian always had upon her — to tear her nerves to pieces, to wear her out. She was not yet thirty but she felt that if she lived much longer with Vivian she would soon be an old spent woman.

She dare not even allow herself the comfort of remembering Dominic's face, and the touch of his hand. In one respect she deserved condemnation from her husband — in that she loved Dominic Unwin. But it was a love as pure and innocent as it was hopeless.

A yawning footman let them into their house. Volpo appeared out of the shadows to greet his master and inform him that he had unpacked the luggage, and that all was ready in his lordship's rooms.

"Excellent," said Vivian. "You need wait up for me no longer, my good Volpo."

"Thank you, my lord. Good night, my lord. Good night, my lady," said Volpo and cast a derisive look at Lady Chase out of the corners of his eyes. She moved up the staircase, her face set into rigid lines. It was indeed the end of freedom — coming back here to find not only Vivian in control but the hated valet back again. How she hated the slimy Portuguese spy!

Vivian followed his wife into their bedroom and told her to dismiss Gertrude who was also waiting up. The maid left the room with a pitying glance at her mistress. Charlotte caught the expression and writhed. It was so humiliating being the object of pity to her own servants.

As she sat down in front of her dressing table, Vivian came up behind her, picked up the diamond ear-rings which she had just taken from her ears and tossed them on the palm of his hand. He leered at her reflection in the mirror.

"You wear my jewels with stunning effect, my dear, and your figure is still magnificent, despite your child-bearing. But I would like to remind you that your smile should be reserved for your husband. I am no fool. I watched while you waltzed with Unwin. I saw how you looked at him."

She shut her eyes.

"Did you?"

"Yes I did!" Vivian's voice rose angrily,

"and I will not have it. If I see you look at another man like that I will thrash you *and* the man you favour. *Do you hear me?*"

She turned and gave him a long bitter look from her weary eyes.

Every drop of blood in her body cried out against the wrongs, the injustice of her marriage. In hopeless misery she sat listening to Vivian's taunts and reproaches and then, worse — his demands for passion. But there came a sudden interruption — a repeated knock on the door which sent Vivian, in a violent temper, to unlock it. He shouted:

"Who is it? What the devil do you want?"

Charlotte drew a dressing gown over her shoulders. She was trembling from head to foot. Vivian flung open the door. The children's nurse stood there, her hair in curl papers, her face less stony and self-confident than usual.

"Oh, I beg your pardon, my lord — my lady," she stammered.

"Well, what is it, woman?" demanded Vivian, his puffy face crimson.

"It's Eleanora — " began the nurse.

Charlotte sprang to her feet.

"What's the matter with Eleanora?"

The nurse gave her a slightly resentful look.

"She was not well earlier in the day. I feared she was sickening for something, and sure enough now she has a high temperature and is delirious. I think we should send for the doctor."

"Oh, heavens!" cried Charlotte; "I must go to her at once."

But Vivian's hand shot out and gripped Charlotte's wrist, detaining her.

"Wait," he turned to the nurse. "What is wrong with the child? Is it not some minor ailment that can soon be put right?"

"I think it more serious, your lordship. I cannot quieten her. She keeps calling for her Mama," the woman added in a sulky tone.

Charlotte tried to get away from Vivian's steely fingers.

"Let me go to her, Vivian."

His eyes narrowed. That cruel look which she knew so well came into his eyes.

"No," he said, "you are far too

emotional, my dear. If Eleanora is ill she will need a calming influence or perhaps a little discipline from her Papa. *I* will go to her."

"She calls for *me*, Nanna said so."

"Nevertheless, you will do as I say and stay here," said Vivian in a low venomous voice.

"I am sure his lordship would be of help, and I suggest we send for the doctor at once," put in the nurse. She then hastened away, but not before Charlotte had seen the satisfied smile that curved her lips.

"Let me go to Eleanora, please Vivian, *please*,"

"When I say so and not before," said Vivian. He went out, shutting the door noisily behind him.

For a moment, Charlotte stood breathing fast, her eyes smarting with tears of frustration. This was the final cruelty. Vivian knew exactly what pain he was inflicting upon her by keeping her from her best loved child when she was ill.

In despair, Charlotte sat down on the edge of the bed and waited for her husband to come back. At least he would tell her how the child fared.

He did not come for a long time. Then, after a long wait, she heard footsteps and voices. Later, Charlotte gathered up enough courage to open the door and go out into the corridor. If Vivian had sent for a physician, it must mean that Eleanora was very ill indeed.

Charlotte caught sight of her husband and the doctor as they were coming out of Eleanora's night-nursery. Vivian looked at his wife in a disagreeable way.

"Pray, return to your bedroom, madam," he said. "Dr. Featherstone agrees with me that in these cases a sick child is better with her nurse."

Charlotte, her face drained of colour, caught at the doctor's arm:

"I must go to her. She has been calling for me, Dr. Featherstone. How is she? What is wrong?"

The doctor coughed and glanced somewhat uneasily at Lady Chase. The poor thing looked distraught. Lord Chase had whispered to him when he arrived that she was hysterical and had to be treated firmly, especially where the children were concerned. He said:

"I am not certain, Lady Chase, but I rather think our little patient has typhoid."

"Typhoid!" repeated Charlotte in a shocked voice. "But that is serious."

"It can be, but with care and good nursing I am sure that we will get her well again."

"Dr. Featherstone is sending a day and a night nurse at once, my dear," put in Vivian. "Eleanora will, of course, have to be segregated from the others. In fact, she is to be left here in the care of two hospital nurses. I will remain a day or two to make sure that all is well. You must take Beatrice and Victoria down to Clunes first thing in the morning and keep them out of the way."

"An excellent plan," said Dr. Featherstone.

But after the physician had gone, Charlotte turned to Vivian, the tears running down her face.

"It is her Mama whom Eleanora needs now that she is ill," she pleaded. "You go with the others to Clunes. Permit me to stay here."

"That would be very agreeable for you,

my dear, I am sure. You would be able to see your charming politician and — "

"Vivian, you have no right to suggest any such thing!" she broke in with indignation. "I want only to be with my poor little girl; typhoid can be most serious for one of such tender years."

"Precisely. That is why Eleanora is to be left in the hands of expert nurses. You will do as you are told, madam, and leave London with your other children directly after breakfast."

"But if Ellie asks for me — " began Charlotte, choking.

"If the doctor thinks it necessary, you can be sent for. Meanwhile I do not wish you to expose yourself to the infection."

She gave him a long look of misery and hatred combined.

"If I ask nothing of you ever again, I ask now to be allowed to stay with Eleanora," she sobbed.

But she was defeated. He would not humour her and she knew it. All thoughts of Dominic Unwin were wrenched from her in this new cruel crisis. She was beyond fighting when Vivian's mood swung from anger to desire and dragged her into his arms. Her agony of mind was such that her reason almost forsook her. She lay in that loathed embrace in a state of semi-consciousness.

When morning came, Eleanora was already shut away from Charlotte in the care of the hospital nurses and Vivian saw to it that she did not go near the child's room. Anguished, Charlotte left the house with Nanna and the two younger children. She was driven in the brougham through the bleak foggy London streets towards the station. Away from her sick child. Away from Dominic Unwin. From everything, everybody, poor Charlotte told herself, that she cared for, or who cared for her.

23

CHARLOTTE did not see her beloved child again until Christmas Eve.

For five weeks, the unhappy mother ate her heart out in the country house to which she had been literally banished. For five weeks little Eleanora was seriously ill; too ill, in fact to know or care who sat at her bedside. Dr. Featherstone's diagnosis of the typhoid turned out to be incorrect. Eleanora had developed some strange fever with symptoms understood by none of the specialists called in by Lord Chase. They hummed and hawed. They ordered various treatments and medicines. Perhaps through luck rather than through their ministrations the little girl did not die. She suffered aches and pains and was often in a delirium, during which she called for her mother; but the sadist who was her father, was determined that Charlotte's longing to answer those calls was not to be appeased. He had scene after scene with her, each resulting in her final defeat. It was her duty, he maintained, to stay at Clunes with Beatrice and little Victoria. He would not have her, or the younger children, exposed to whatever infection it was that had attacked Eleanora.

Fortunately for the little invalid, the two hospital nurses in charge of her in the London house were kindly, motherly women who lavished tender care upon her. They found Lord Chase charming and generous, and never had he been more amiable or tolerant with his eldest daughter than while she lay in her sickbed. He seemed to one and all a devoted father. It was Charlotte whom the nurses criticized. It was hinted by his lordship that my lady was too afraid of infection to come near the place. They thought her a selfish cowardly young woman and pitied the handsome husband.

Vivian, meanwhile, enjoyed himself in London and finally joined his wretched wife and added to her misery by his overbearing presence in the home; his continued taunts because she could not seem to bear him a son. She had conceived as a result of that unhappy night of reunion when he returned from India. She lost much of her sparkling beauty and grew pale and listless with scarcely any spirit left with which to fight her husband.

When appearances forced Vivian to bring Eleanora home, that cold afternoon on Christmas Eve, he continued his persecution of the unhappy mother and the little girl.

"Eleanora is still not well and must be kept quiet. No disruption of nursery rules. Nanna will be in charge," Lord Chase announced the moment he came into the house, carrying his eldest daughter in his arms.

Charlotte, who had been awaiting this moment, wild with excitement and relief, held out her arms to Eleanora, her eyes shining at the sight of the beloved little face, the sight of which had been denied her for so many weary weeks.

"Oh, my darling, welcome home!" she exclaimed.

"Mama! Dearest Mama!" cried Eleanora and struggled to get down and go to her mother.

Vivian called to the nurse who came running down the stairs.

"Take Eleanora up to her schoolroom," he said. "Doctor's orders are that she should have plenty of rest and few lessons for the next month or so. And no excitement *downstairs*," he added, with a meaning glance at Charlotte.

The nurse flung my lady one of her withering glances. As Vivian set Eleanora on her feet, she took her by the hand.

"Come, dear — " she began.

But Eleanora broke away and threw herself into her mother's arms.

"I want to stay with Mama. I have not seen my Mama for ages and ages!" she cried.

Charlotte hugged her daughter convulsively, the tears in her eyes. Critically she examined the small pale face, the pretty little figure in the cherry velvet pelisse and bonnet trimmed with fur. She used to love choosing dainty clothes for her daughters, and Eleanora had worn this outfit last winter. Now the pelisse was too short, she reflected, the child had grown thin and lanky, quite an inch taller since her illness.

"We must fatten you up, my darling — " Charlotte began, covering the small face with kisses and looking fondly down into the big dark eyes which looked back at her with her grandmother's sympathy and sweetness.

But Vivian pulled Eleanora away from her.

"Come! Doctor's orders, Eleanora. None of this emotion and excitement. Go quietly upstairs with Nanna and see your sisters."

Charlotte stood by, nervously agitated, but she said no more. She did not wish to have a humiliating scene in front of the servants. She was blinded by tears of frustration and misery as she preceded Vivian into the library where tea had been laid in front of a blazing log fire. It looked so handsome, so cosy in here; for outside it was bitterly cold, and snowing again. All through Clunes, holly and mistletoe festooned the pillars and pictures and there was a festive Christmas atmosphere. But to Charlotte it was like all the other Christmas Eves: a hollow mockery, a mere reminder of the homely happy celebrations that were allowed to take place in other, happier, homes than this one.

This was the unhappiest Christmas of them all. Once a day only, the mother was allowed to see her eldest child. Eleanora got slowly better but fretted against the continual separation from her mother. She was kept virtually a prisoner in her schoolroom, on the pretext that she must be guarded from all possible excitement.

Charlotte waited for the moment when she was allowed to visit Eleanora for her brief half-hour, as allotted by Vivian. She rarely tried to see more of her because, if she did, Vivian curtailed further visits, and Eleanora always looked forward so passionately to seeing her beloved mama.

Charlotte looked long and sadly at the little girl this particular evening. It was a bleak January day. All Christmas decorations had long since been removed from Clunes. This being a Friday, Vivian was expecting some of his particular friends down from London for a shooting house party. None of them appealed to Charlotte. The men drank too much, like

Vivian, and the wives were pretty silly creatures who had little in common with their hostess.

At this precise moment, Vivian was asleep. Charlotte sat with Eleanora on her lap, the child's thin arms around her neck while the sour-faced Nanna looked on; spying for Vivian, of course, the mother reflected bitterly.

Charlotte did not speak for a few moments. She just sat in silence, hugging Eleanora to her, her face puckered with misery while she stroked the little girl's silky brown hair, hair that had grown a trifle scanty since her illness.

"Dearest Mama, why can't you come and see me more often?" Eleanora whispered in her ear, her small hands tightly clenched about her mother's neck. Charlotte answered in a low voice:

"You must stay up here quietly, my darling, until — until the doctor thinks you well enough to come downstairs again."

Eleanora's eyes filled with tears.

"It is Papa who says I must stay with Nanna, is it not? Is it because I have been naughty? Will you not tell him that

I try hard to be good. I have learned my French lessons well this week. Mlle St. Claire, when she was here on Monday, said that I had greatly improved."

Charlotte swallowed hard. There were a thousand loving things she wanted to say to comfort the perplexed and unhappy child but she dared not. Oh, how she hated that stiff, starched woman in her cap and apron who sat there by the window, sewing, listening with both ears to the conversation, enjoying her mistress's embarrassment. Oh, how she wished that she could take Eleanora and fly from this house, never to return, away from Vivian's abominable tyranny and even from her two younger daughters who teased and taunted Eleanora, even as she, Charlotte, was teased and taunted by their father.

This evening Charlotte felt more ill than usual. She was nearly two and a half months advanced in her pregnancy now and never able to enjoy her food, or sleep well, with Vivian snoring off a drunken orgy at her side. She had to force herself to sit at the head of his table during the interminable, over-rich dinners, listening to his noisy joking friends and trying to pretend that she enjoyed it all.

After her half-hour with Eleanora ended, Charlotte left the child trying not to cry and annoy her nurse. Charlotte's own feelings were unspeakable.

"It is killing me. I can bear my own pain but I cannot live and watch my little Eleanora suffer," she thought. "Oh, God, help me!"

She walked unsteadily down the staircase and stopped before a portrait of the late Lady Chase. She looked up at it with hot bitter eyes.

"You whom I loved and who loved me, your devoted pupil, *you* condemned me to this life with your son. Can you not see from your heaven and pity me the hell in which I exist?" she asked aloud.

When, later on, Vivian joined Charlotte in the library, she approached him with a courage that was rooted in sheer desperation.

"Vivian, I must speak to you. I must tell you. I cannot go on like this," she said.

He was standing before the fireplace in the act of lighting a cigar, and as he puffed at it he glanced malevolently at her. She looked less attractive than usual he thought; that dark blue velvet tea gown made her seem dull. She was sallow and there were dark circles under her eyes. No doubt she was suffering from the effects of this new life that was soon to quicken within her. It had better be a son this time, he thought gloomily.

"For heaven's sake, go change your gown for something of a more charming colour, and apply some cosmetic, if you have any, to your greasy face," he said in a loud rude voice. "Your looks are becoming deplorable."

Nervously Charlotte pulled at her lace-edged handkerchief.

"I do not care how my looks strike you, Vivian. I have no wish to be attractive to you. But I do say, here and now, I will not stand for your mean, cruel efforts to keep me apart from Eleanora."

He smiled and glanced at the end of his cigar.

"I shall not argue with you. My orders must be obeyed."

Her face flushed crimson.

"Will you not listen, will you not relent, Vivian, and allow me free access to my child, and her to me? It is so abominable — throwing me your outrageous orders before that nurse who hates me and is glad to see me humiliated. Or before Volpo whom you know I dislike. Vivian, I am not well. I am *enceinte*. You have a crowd coming to Clunes whom I must entertain. I am physically and mentally unable to stand this state of affairs any longer. You *must* listen to me, and treat me, and Eleanora who loves me, with more kindness."

Silence. Charlotte was weeping. The man in the chair stroked his fair, curled moustache, pretended to be bored, although inwardly he was alert, watching her every movement, listening to her every word. He liked it when Charlotte was reduced to tears.

At length he said:

"My dear, you are overwrought. It is, of course, the result of your condition. I am an understanding man and shall excuse you from the party tonight. You may retire and go to your bed which is what you need."

She strove for composure.

"I warn you," she repeated, shaking, "you go too far."

"Do not dare to issue warnings to me. Indeed, what do you think you can do?" He laughed in the way which so often made her believe that he was smitten with insanity.

"I will go to Eleanora, and I will stay with her, or — " she began, then broke off swallowing.

"Or what," Vivian put in.

"*Or I will leave you*," she said in a choked voice.

His eyes widened. He burst out laughing.

"Leave me? *Oh ho*! That is interesting, very interesting, madam. So you have the money to keep yourself? You came to me penniless, a nobody."

"I never forget that, nor do I cease to regret our union," she said wildly. "But that is old history. You know all too well how young, how ill-advised I was ever to be persuaded into tying myself up to you."

"Come, come, would you have had your precious Eleanora born in shame, a bastard?" he taunted her.

The crude word brought the hot colour to Charlotte's face. She retorted:

"Yes, *yes*, I would. If I could go back, I would rather have borne my poor child in sin and shame, than find myself living under the roof of a man as monstrous as yourself."

She stopped, breathing hard, her face ashen, her eyes wild with despair. Vivian flung away his cigar, stood up and came near her.

"Have you finished?" he said, his eyes flaming.

"No, I say more. That even though I starve, I shall leave this house, work for my living as a menial, anything, rather than subject myself any longer to your brutalities." She broke off and hid her face in her hands, sobbing. She had not dared say so much to him ever before. But now it was out, torn from the depths of her suffering heart.

Vivian turned to the mantelpiece. There stood upon it an exquisite Sèvres clock. He found a key and began to wind the clock, as though in complete disregard of what his wife had said. He even whistled under his breath.

Charlotte stared at his unrelenting back. For a moment, her breath coming unevenly, she watched him while he toyed with the clock. His indifference to her sufferings roused her to sudden madness. She went up to him and beat upon his chest with clenched hands.

"Brute, monster, *devil*!" she sobbed. "Did you not hear what I said to you?"

"I heard; and you bore me," he drawled.

The usually gentle and submissive Charlotte became demented. In her blind passion of resentment she seized the valuable clock from his fingers and dashed it on to the fire-place. It shattered into fragments. There came from it a discordance of broken chimes, a whirring; then silence.

Vivian's face went red. He looked first at the broken clock then at Charlotte's frenzied face. He slapped her cheek with his open hand.

"You bitch," he said.

"You will never strike me or call me by such a vile name again!" she said on a high hysterical note. "I have done with you and with enduring your abominable conduct. I shall leave the house."

"So you have threatened. Go — and be damned."

Outside the door, a young footman with his ear to the key-hole grimaced, moved away and motioned to her ladyship's maid, Gertrude, who was passing through the hall.

"Jimmeney — they're at it, the pair of 'em," he sniggered.

Suddenly the drawing-room doors were flung open. Charlotte, her hair dishevelled, her face ghastly, rushed out, crying as she went:

"You shall not take Eleanora from me. *You shall not.* She goes with me, you inhuman creature!"

Gertrude and the footman hastened away and vanished into the shadows at the back of the hall where they cowered, listening, regarding each other in horrified excitement.

Lord Chase came blustering after his wife.

"If you leave my house, Eleanora stays here!" he shouted. "Do you hear me?

I shall teach you who is the master at Clunes."

Charlotte was, however, beyond fear of such threats.

The last thread of her patience had snapped. She picked up her long flowing skirt and ran up the stairs, panting, followed by Vivian who snarled imprecations at her back. She called despairingly:

"Eleanora, Eleanora. Come, come to Mama — !"

Gertrude, faithful, devoted and deeply sorry for her lady, rushed to the foot of the staircase. She, better than anyone in this tragic household, knew what Charlotte put up with. She also knew how ill my lady was at the moment, how unfit to bear such a terrible emotional scene. Gertrude held her breath for fear as she saw his lordship catch up with my lady and clutch her, by one arm.

"You shall not go near your daughter!" he snarled.

"Let me go," said Charlotte, wildly struggling.

He fought with her, finding her grown suddenly strong in this mad rebellious mood. For a moment the maid watched.

She saw Charlotte release one hand and beat at his lordship's face, a face ugly and inflamed. She saw Vivian try to imprison that fluttering hand again. In so doing, he swung Charlotte round so that she stood with her back to the stairs, poised perilously near to the edge.

Then it happened. Charlotte turned her ankle and slipped. With a final mad effort she released herself from Vivian, but only to totter backwards and fall. She slid, rolling down the stairs. Had they not been so well carpeted, she might have struck her head on the marble and that fall might have proved fatal. As it was, the thick pile saved her. She reached the final stair and lay across it, arms outstretched, like a bird shot in flight.

24

VIVIAN came running down the staircase. Gertrude rushed to her mistress and knelt beside her.

"My lady — oh, my lady!" she gasped.

Vivian stood staring at Charlotte's prostrate form. Her hair had loosened and tumbled across her shoulders. A trickle of blood came from the corner of her mouth where he had so cruelly struck her, in the library. For a moment conscience awakened. Memory took him back to an early morning hour in this very house, when he had attacked his young wife, and his mother had seen, and fallen *dead*.

Ashen-faced, he stared at Charlotte. He could not speak, but only breathed heavily.

Gertrude looked up at him.

"My lady is hurt, perhaps dying, your lordship," she stuttered and began to cry.

"No, no — she moves; she opens her

eyes; she is not dead," answered Vivian. He knelt beside his wife and lifted one of her cold inert hands in his. "Charlotte, you have had a dreadful accident. You have fallen. My poor dear wife, speak to me!" he said in a loud voice, so that all could hear, for by now the hall was filling rapidly with members of the staff. The children's nurse had also come running out of the nursery and leaned over the banisters, looking in a frightened way at her ladyship's figure spreadeagled across the stairs.

Charlotte's dazed eyes moved from her husband's face to Gertrude's. She shuddered, conscious suddenly of a searing pain.

"Get — Dr. Castleby — " she whispered. "I — think — the baby — I am — " She got no further, for her eyes closed and she moaned in a way that made Gertrude's blood turn cold.

During the next few minutes all was chaos. The carriage had just brought four of Vivian's guests up to the front door. They arrived to witness this dreadful scene. Servants running hither and thither, Lord Chase carrying his wife's unconscious body up to her bedroom; while a footman was sent posthaste for the Harling physician.

There was to be no weekend party, no long drawn out dinner for Lady Chase that night. And no possibility of a son and heir for this house.

Charlotte, caught in the throes of a physical agony that temporarily superseded her mental misery, fought for her life until dawn. A London specialist was sent for, and arrived in the early hours to aid the local physician who was quite out of his depth in such a serious case. Lady Chase's life was at stake; not so much on account of her miscarriage as her general lowness of health and spirits. Both doctors agreed on that. She did not seem to want to recover.

Two hospital nurses joined the gathering. At dawn in her big bed, Charlotte lay like one from whom all colour, all animation had been drained. Her face was pinched and sharpened. Her chestnut curls were caught up in an embroidered white linen cap. She looked without apparent recognition at any of the people who bent over her. To Vivian's incessant appeals

425

to her to forgive him, she remained
impervious. The visiting physician, his
finger on the feeble pulse, sat by the
bedside in the dimly-lit, magnificent
bedroom full of the scent of hothouse flowers, and looked sternly at
Lord Chase.

"Your wife's condition is poor, sir," he
said abruptly.

"But surely she is not to die,"
whimpered Vivian.

"No. She will live; but it will be many
weeks before she recovers. I do not wish
to intrude, sir, but I must ask you on
account of my patient's extreme weakness
and the misery that seems to overwhelm
her, if you know of anything in particular
that is troubling her inner spirit. Dr.
Castleby and I are of the opinion, sir,
that it is this, rather than the accident,
the loss of the coming child, which has
brought her so low."

Vivian looked away. Several times
during the night, whenever, in fact, he
had leaned over his semi-conscious wife
and spoken her name, she had shrieked
to him to go away. She called him 'brute'
and 'monster'. He knew that the eminent

London doctor, as well as Castleby, had heard it. Sullenly, he reflected that there were limits to what he could do if he were to retain his place in respectable Society; that if he did not conduct himself more as a loving husband should, he would earn himself an unattractive reputation.

He answered the doctor as pleasantly as he could, mumbling excuses for Charlotte's state of mind; she was highly strung and difficult; he had had a poor time with her. But he would, of course, he said, take greatest care of her now, and induce her as soon as possible to accompany him with the children to some mild climate like Madeira, where the sunshine would revive her.

The physician interrupted. He did not believe a word, for he held privately a poor opinion of Lord Chase and felt the deepest pity for his beautiful wife; sentiments obviously shared by their own medical man.

"Lady Chase asks repeatedly that she should see the child who goes by the name of *Eleanora*," he said. "I would suggest to you, Lord Chase, that the little girl be brought to see her mother, and at once."

Vivian began to excuse himself again, mumbling that Eleanora had recently contracted an infectious illness and that he had considered it unwise to expose an expectant mother to any risk. Of course, he added, he would give way immediately to the distinguished gentleman's suggestion. Little Eleanora, wrapped in a shawl, was brought to her Mama's bed and placed beside her. Sleepy, but excited, the child flung herself on the still, pale figure.

"Mama, dearest, *sweetest* Mama!" she cried.

Now the men at the foot of the bed saw Charlotte's eyes open. Glazed with fever and pain, they rested on her eldest child's face. At once, Charlotte flushed pink and embraced the little form passionately.

"Mama, my own dear Mama!" repeated Eleanora and laid her dark curly head beside her mother's on the big embroidered pillow.

A happy smile replaced the tormented expression on Charlotte's mouth. She gave a long sigh of satisfaction.

Within a few moments, mother and daughter, locked in their embrace, were both sleeping peacefully, side by side. The nurse in charge sat by the fire, watching and wondering what had been going on in this grand house. She was soon to be treated to all the gossip and rumours current in the servants' hall.

When another bleak day of wind and snow, that turned to sleet, broke over Clunes, there were many noticeable changes in that house.

Charlotte was still gravely ill and ordered absolute quiet and care. No visitors came to disturb the peace of the house. Vivian gave orders to the servants that her ladyship's merest whims were to be gratified. Eleanora's little bed was moved into her Mama's bedroom, for the invalid could not seem to feel at ease unless she could see the beloved little daughter from whom she had been separated for so long.

The nurse in charge of Beatrice and Victoria took her charges up to the Eaton Square mansion. His lordship followed. This, too, was Charlotte's wish. She could not bear to look at Vivian's florid, deceitful face or hear his hypocritical voice praising her, inquiring after her health, giving her promises that she knew he would not keep, once things settled down again.

Charlotte asked that Fleur should come to her. Mrs. Marsh travelled immediately to Clunes, accompanied by her husband. She was shocked by the sight of the poor young woman who looked so thin, so lifeless, so waxen pale. But from the moment that Fleur came to take charge of her, and with Eleanora at her side, Charlotte soon improved. There followed a period of blissful peace for Charlotte. There came a time when she knew even the comfort and happiness of hearing Dominic Unwin's forbidden name spoken in this house. Vivian was still in London, killing time among his card-playing, dice-throwing, hard-drinking friends.

One morning in March, Charlotte who was well again, was sitting by the fireside with her eldest daughter and her friend. They had been playing a game. Charlotte had regained some weight and a hint of colour, and was looking almost her beautiful self again. Once more there had been music and time for books and laughter in her life. It almost seemed as though her late beloved mother-in-law was back at Clunes and she, the radiant girl, seeking knowledge and gaining it. For Peveril was philosopher as well as artist.

Fleur sent the child out of the room on a small trifling errand, then handed Charlotte a morning paper. She had marked a photograph of Mr. Unwin talking to a friend.

Charlotte dropped the paper, looked round her drawing-room, then out at the garden. Rain veiled trees and bushes. The weather was still cold and bleak, March so far had been severe.

"I would like to go to London and perhaps meet and talk to Dominic Unwin again," she said in a low voice.

"He is a fine man and I do not see why you should not enjoy his friendship, my dear."

Charlotte bit her lip, remembering Vivian's insane jealousy and dislike of Cecil's adopted brother. She told Fleur, frankly, why the friendship could never be.

"It is sad," sighed Fleur.

"For me it is more than that," admitted Charlotte in a low yearning voice.

"My poor dear friend," said Mrs. Marsh pityingly.

Charlotte's eyes filled with tears.

"I have been so happy here, with you and Peveril," she said. "I have enjoyed friendship, and freedom of thought and speech, and the joy of watching my darling devoted little daughter grow happy and strong again. But it must all come to an end. I have received a letter from Vivian by this morning's post. He wishes us all to travel abroad the first week in April."

"Are you not to be permitted to live apart from that insensate bully?" demanded Fleur ever hot in her championship of Charlotte.

Charlotte smiled at the beautiful ageless face of her grey-haired friend.

"Nay, it is not possible. I have suggested a separation but he will not hear of it. He makes things difficult by declaring once again that he will make amends, turn over a new leaf and so on. But it is only because he was frightened by my accident and subsequent illness," she added in a low tone. "Once back with me, he will revert to his former self."

"I know, for Denzil St. Cheviot was just such another," nodded Mrs. Marsh, shuddering at the memory of her former husband.

"I must try, too, to love my other two children more," said Charlotte, her brows puckered. "But somehow they do not seem my own; only *his*. They are such cold, unloving little things, and have been turned against me by that unspeakable woman, their nurse."

"Surely you will insist upon her dismissal," said Fleur indignantly.

Charlotte nodded.

"Yes, when she brings Beatrice and Victoria home, she shall be sent away. I shall make Vivian see that this is essential to my well-being."

"And Volpo?" Fleur looked questioningly at her friend. She knew how acutely poor Charlotte disliked the wily Portuguese.

Charlotte shook her head. Even now, she was sure her husband, though wishing to behave tolerably well, would never dismiss his valet. Volpo was too well trained and useful to him, be it as servant, spy or right-hand man. She would have to accept his presence for as long as Volpo continued to serve Vivian without putting the wrong foot forward.

Eleanora came dancing back into the drawing-room, a tiny bunch of blue scillas in her hand. Her cheeks were red, her eyes shining.

"Mama, Mama, look! The first of the year! Soon it will be spring!"

Charlotte took the tiny bouquet and tucked it in her belt. Mother and daughter smiled into each other's eyes. Charlotte thought:

"She is really happy now. God grant that when Vivian and poor little Beatrice and Victoria return they will not seek to destroy that innocent happiness."

But, alas for Charlotte, that appeal to her Maker was not destined to be granted.

For Vivian was about to spring an iniquitous surprise upon the wife who was seeking to resign herself to a fresh reconciliation, for her children's sake. A surprise suggested by that very man whom Charlotte distrusted and abhorred. It was Volpo, himself, up in Eaton Square, in attendance upon his master after an amusing evening spent by his lordship in the company of his less moral and respectable friends, who whispered in his ear that it was regrettable that after this my lord would be forced to settle down and lead a godly and sober life with his family.

"It will not suit your lordship," Volpo said sadly while he folded Vivian's clothes. "Would my master not prefer his freedom once again?"

"Fool, how can I get it, tagged and nagged at by a lawful wedded wife?" muttered Vivian sourly.

The valet's thin lips smiled.

"I have an idea, but fear to present it to your lordship in case he might think me monstrously impudent."

Vivian blinked at his valet and kicked off a shoe.

"You *are* a monstrously impudent fellow, but you are a loyal servant and know what I like and do not like. What is your idea? Come, tell me before I fall asleep."

"A divorce, my lord, surely would set you free again."

"Divorce?" Vivian echoed the word crossly then snapped: "Fool, how can I divorce a faithful wife? If you cannot think of a better plan than that, shut your mouth."

"But I know more than you think, my lord," Volpo continued, kneeling before Vivian, and starting to remove his master's other shoe. "I fancy I know how her ladyship feels about a certain gentleman as I have taken the liberty, on your lordship's behalf of course, of watching and listening. I know how she preserves certain newspapers which contain this gentleman's photograph and — "

"Hold your peace," interrupted Vivian, his face scarlet. "I, too, know of such things, but I can assure you her ladyship is as pure as a lily — " He laughed coarsely, "And I could find no reason whatsoever to defile her name and rid myself of my domestic chains."

Volpo remained silent. That silence

was pregnant. Suddenly a host of ideas swarmed in Lord Chase's ugly mind, inflaming him further to the idea of release from Charlotte. Since the night of her accident he had been forced to give way to her; but he hated her more than ever for that very fact. To find her out in a falsehood, put her in the wrong, be able to cast her out, and remain righteous in the eyes of Society, that would be a triumph indeed.

He prodded the kneeling valet with his toe. "What plan can you suggest, fool?" he asked. "Spit out your idiot suggestions."

Volpo did not take offence. He knew my Lord Chase too well. He knew, too, that if he could help him to rid himself of a wife who had, from the very start, been a burden to him, he, Volpo, would be remembered — and rewarded.

He stood up and began to talk —

25

TWENTY-FOUR hours later the Marshes reluctantly bade farewell to Charlotte and left Clunes. It had to be, greatly though Fleur disliked having to leave her friend. She and Peveril must return to Pillars and, in any case, Charlotte expected her husband to return to Clunes with the two younger children this week-end.

Somewhat to Charlotte's astonishment, Volpo came down to the country house alone on the Thursday. His lordship had sent him in advance, he explained, and handed her ladyship a note from his master. This was couched in affectionate terms and asked Charlotte if she would spare her personal maid to go up to London and fetch Beatrice and Victoria.

Knowing your dislike of Nanna, I have dismissed her, he wrote. *You can choose a new nurse whom you will prefer and meanwhile you will not be distressed by the presence in the house of one to whom you are hostile. Volpo comes to open up my suite at Clunes and I shall be with you, my love, in the morning. Pray accept this bouquet as a token of my sincere desire to start life afresh as your loving and faithful husband.*

Charlotte read this note with astonishment. It seemed so unlike Vivian. But she accepted it for what it was worth and was only too pleased to send Gertrude to fetch the other children. It was a relief to know she need not look again on the face of that woman who had helped so sadistically to keep her away from Eleanora.

For once, Charlotte tried to smile upon the valet who brought her a magnificent bunch of hothouse carnations from his master. She also tried to reassure herself that his smile was genuine, not the treacherous smirk which sent such shivers of repugnance through her.

She sent Gertrude to the station to catch the afternoon train to London, then drove into Harling to a toy shop to choose two new dolls for Beatrice and

Victoria. Eleanora went with her.

"We must give your darling sisters a real welcome," Charlotte said gaily.

Eleanora tried not to be downcast, but in her tender young heart she wished profoundly that Papa and her sisters need never return to Clunes.

That night, Charlotte dined early. After playing her piano awhile, she took herself off to bed.

How quiet it was in the big house; without Vivian and with none of the usual quota of friends whom he liked to invite here. A delicious quiet. Charlotte was even thankful not to have Gertrude fussing over her but to be alone in her bedroom and look after herself.

She was beginning to feel quite strong again. She glanced at her reflection in the cheval mirror. In her long peignoir of white cashmere with its lace collar and cuffs, she looked tall and thin. Her face was thinner than usual; she no longer seemed so young, but old for her twenty-seven years, with a sad maturity, a gravity of eyes and lips. She had, however, regained much of her beauty and an added dignity born of excessive suffering nobly endured.

Her large eyes gazed back at her; they seemed to her, stranger's eyes. She could hardly believe that she had ever been that Charlotte Goff who had learned so much at Eleanora Chase's knee, and who had once worshipped Vivian as a young god.

She was in bed and half asleep when she heard carriage wheels on the drive and a dog barking.

She was a light sleeper and sat up at once, struck a match and lit the candle in the silver stick beside her. She listened, her pulses racing.

Again the barking dog — then men's voices — then a knock on the front door.

Charlotte frowned. Who could the caller be at such an hour? Her jewelled clock on the mantelpiece showed her that it was nearly eleven.

She got up and put on her peignoir. Tying the girdle, she walked to the door and opened it. She saw a gleam of light and heard voices below. She moved quickly along the corridor. Could it be that Vivian had chosen to return unexpectedly? It would not be unlike him to choose such an unorthodox and inconvenient hour.

Then she heard a voice that sent the blood surging to her face and throat. A man's deep rich voice. It said:

"I wish to see Lady Chase — "

Charlotte gasped under her breath.

"*Dominic — Dominic Unwin*!"

What in heaven's name was *he* doing at Clunes and at such an hour? The last train had reached Harling station at nine o'clock. He asked for *her*. What could have occurred?

Charlotte was thunderstruck. But whatever the explanation of this extraordinary visit, the knowledge that Dominic was here, down in the hall, shook her to the core. She forgot that she was only wearing night-attire and dressing-gown. She ran down the wide staircase and stopped midway as she saw Dominic. He was wearing a cloak, and hat in hand, stood at the foot of the stairs. He was talking to Volpo who had, it seemed, opened the front door to him. Volpo was apologizing for his own night-attire over which he had thrown a coat.

Dominic did not listen to Volpo now. He looked upward at Charlotte, watching her as she came down the stairs. He had never seen her thus; with the glory of her unbound hair curling to her shoulders, she was slender and inexpressibly graceful, he thought, in her white *déshabillé*.

Volpo also looked up at his mistress. He bowed.

"If I have your permission, my lady, I will retire."

She did not answer. She seemed to be incapable of speaking, of looking in any direction save Dominic's. Volpo smiled and slunk away. He left a lamp burning, then closed the baize-covered door that led into the butler's pantry. But once outside, he rubbed his hands together gleefully and stood pondering. So far, so good; his plan was working out. Now for the rest. He must just listen, and wait.

Charlotte reached the bottom stair. She stood before the man whose face was ever before her mind's eye, no matter where she was or what she was doing. She said:

"Mr. Unwin — Dominic — you are

always welcome but why have you come here at this strange hour? I do not understand — ”

He pulled a piece of paper from his pocket.

“I received this, brought to me at the House by messenger this afternoon,” he said.

She stared, noting how tired he looked, almost careworn, as though the terrific work, which he had been doing recently in the House of Commons, had sapped his strength, both mental and physical. But his eyes were still young, as brilliant as ever, and his personality as vital. He made her feel as he always did — that his presence filled the entire house, not merely a small space.

She said:

“What has your note to do with me?”

He stared back at her.

“It was *from* you — ” he said.

“From me?” she repeated. “It cannot possibly be. I have not written to you, Dominic.”

“But — I do not comprehend. Read it, Charlotte,” he said, and his cheeks flushed. He added: “I must confess, it confounded me, but I came when and how you requested. I could not do otherwise."

So warm, so vibrant was his tone, so full of strange meaning his handsome eyes, Charlotte felt as though she was being caught in a whirlpool of mysterious excitement and flung right off her feet.

She was beginning to shiver for it was cold in the big hall at this late hour. She turned from Dominic, the note still unread in her hand.

"Follow me," she said in a low voice, "We cannot stand here. It is too draughty. Let us go into the library. Perhaps the fire will still be burning in there."

He followed her, drawing off his cloak.

"Have you a match?" Charlotte asked him.

"I regret I have not."

She bit her lip and glanced into the library. The curtains were still drawn together and all was darkness save for a red gleam from the grate which showed that the fire still smouldered. She said:

"Then will you bring the lamp from the hall and from that we will light the others."

He went back and fetched the lamp. She bade him set it on the mantelpiece. As he did so, she bent and poked the fire and set up a little blaze.

"I will put on more wood," she began.

"Allow me," he said, and bent to find logs in a copper urn which he saw beside the fireplace. Charlotte, too, bent down. Almost the two heads touched, the dark, silver-streaked one of the man and the bright head of the young woman. Simultaneously, still kneeling, they turned and looked into each other's eyes. Each now felt the rapid warmth of each other's breathing; they were so close together in that dim roseate glow of the awakening fire. It was as though they looked into each other's very heart and soul and, magnetized, were unable to look away again.

There was silence now in the great house of Clunes. A warm rich pregnant silence. For Charlotte the world stood still. For the man, the moment was as a revelation of an emotional storm as wild and impossible as a dream. Usually so reserved, he had believed himself capable of only the lightest, most transient appreciation of a woman's charm and beauty. Because of Dorothea's death, he had thought that his heart had died — at least to *that* kind of emotion.

Yet now tonight, in this crazy moment, so close to Charlotte Chase, alone, not yet knowing who or what had brought him here, he temporarily lost his iron mastery of self. He uttered her name in a shaken whisper:

"*Charlotte!*"

She answered, her gaze still held by his, one hand pressed to her bare throat.

"Dominic," she answered in a strangled voice.

He caught at her and pulled her on to her feet. For a single instant she was no longer Lady Chase, another man's wife, but his own dear Charlotte, all his, melting to his touch. Wordlessly he kissed her on the mouth. Her senses swam. It was a moment full of poignant impassioned feeling for Charlotte. She knew now that she loved him with a love that was born of a new, mad hope, and of an old, anguished despair.

It was her first real kiss of pure

awakening love. She was once more the Charlotte of years ago, the ardent girl who had had so much to give, but who had lost even the desire to give after her terrible marriage. Dominic with her sweetness crushed to him, her lips opening under the pressure of his, was deeply aware that this was the last, most significant passion of his life.

Only a moment could that sweet yet bitter kiss endure. Then, with a gasp, Charlotte broke from him, her hands pressed to her burning cheeks.

"Merciful God, what are we doing?" she whispered.

He put a hand to his head.

"Forgive me, Charlotte, beloved. I had no right."

"But I love you, Dominic."

"I love you, Charlotte."

His simple and direct assertion brought her but brief joy. She gave a low cry and buried her face in her hands.

"It can never be."

"No, never. It is my unhappy fate to have to say so. But I care for you with all my body, heart and soul. I did not really know it until tonight."

"I have loved you from the first day I looked on your face," she said, and, uncovering hers, gazed up at him, her eyes half blinded by tears.

"I knew it *almost* for a fact when I received your letter, for I laid everything aside — my most important work — to come to you."

Now the fire was burning brightly. But the great library was full of shadows for there was still only one small lamp alight. Charlotte shivered. Her hands were cold as ice. She said:

"The letter. Yes. What about this letter that I was supposed to have written?"

"*Supposed*?" he echoed. He looked down at her with a questioning expression. "Where is it? Please read it, Charlotte. I do not know your writing, so I could not judge. Read it and tell me what it means."

In a daze, she looked down. She saw the white notepaper on the crimson carpet. It must have dropped from her fingers when Dominic swept her into his arms. She picked it up and, taking it to the lamp, scanned it. As she did so, her features froze into a look of sheer

449

amazement and fear.

This was what she was supposed to have written:

Dominic,

I believe you to be my dearest, my only man friend. I need your help. I need it urgently and can only ask for you to give it — in secret. It is essential nobody in our circle of friends should know about this. I am alone at Clunes. Vivian is still in London and will be till tomorrow. Please come to me tonight. Take the last train to Harling. It will get you there by nine, but go to an inn — anywhere — only do not approach Clunes until after half past ten. Then drive here — you can get a carriage from the Station Livery Stables — and knock on the front door. One of my servants will admit you. I deplore the fact that I must ask your visit to be so clandestine. Only do not fail me. I will explain all when I see you. Oh, Dominic, do not fail me. Come, I implore you.

Charlotte

Twice she read this amazing missive — the second time aloud. Dominic, his dark face half in shadow from her, his brow furrowed, his eyes watching her, said:

"*Vivian*, I knew that meant — your husband. You see the terms in which this appeal is couched? Coming from you, how could I disregard it? I was flabbergasted — I admit. I could not think what plight had placed you in the position of having to make such an appeal to me. At first I was doubtful whether or not I should do as you asked. Then because of my deep regard for you, I knew I *had* to agree. I was sure you would, as you said, explain all when I got here."

Charlotte shook her head like one utterly confused,

"But I cannot, for I did not write this letter, Dominic."

"You did not?"

"I swear it."

She pointed to the signature.

"*That* is not mine," she went on, "I write my '*C*' with more of a flourish and two *t*'s I cross together, not separately, like this. I tell you, this was not sent by me, nor would I ever have appealed to you in such a manner."

"I must have been off my head to do — as I did just now," he said under his breath.

She did not hear. She was examining the note again.

"I am frightened," she said. "I do not recognize this writing but I am beginning to see that the letter must have been written by someone who *wished* you to come to Clunes tonight."

"But *who*?" he exclaimed.

"Yes, '*who*'?" she muttered. Biting her lip, she stared again at the signature purporting to be hers. *Who*, indeed, could have done such an iniquitous thing — appealed to Dominic Unwin's chivalry and thus brought him down to Clunes at dead of night?

"I am frightened," she said for the second time.

Tenderness welled up in Dominic. He came nearer her.

"My dear, my dearest, do not be afraid. No harm is done. I must just go away again, at once."

Her eyes burned up at him.

"No — wait — this mystery must be solved. It is a dangerous situation. Maybe a trick," she added.

"But who would play such a trick?"

She was silent. Her mind whirled with a dozen crazy ideas. None seemed sensible. The person who had written to Dominic in her name could only be one who knew of her secret friendship with him; and of his feeling toward her. It was no kind friend who had arranged this nocturnal *rendezvous*. It must be an enemy — someone wishing to hurt Dominic and put *her* in the wrong. Now Charlotte's face went deadly white. A sickness stole over her. There could only be one being who would wish to do either of these things. His name leapt before her sight in letters of scarlet. *Vivian*.

It was not Vivian's writing, but he could have induced someone to pen the note for him, and sent it to the House of Commons this morning.

She swayed.

"It may be Vivian himself, who has tricked you here," she said hoarsely.

Dominic stared down at the lovely, blanched face.

"Calm yourself, my dearest; it cannot possibly be."

"It can. You do not know Vivian Chase. He is a fiend, a devil incarnate. This may well be some devilish plot on his part."

"It cannot be," repeated Dominic incredulously.

"I tell you it can. And now I am beginning to understand many things, My personal maid, Gertrude — he has made me send *her* away for the night and Volpo is here!" Her teeth began to chatter. "Volpo is the Portuguese valet who let you in. He is viler than all others. *He* was sent down here in Gertrude's place — to spy on me. No doubt he was up and waiting for you. I tell you, Dominic, this is beginning to manifest itself as a vile and outrageous plot."

"But to do what?" demanded the astonished Dominic.

"To get rid of me and ruin you," she said.

Dominic stared down into her wild beautiful eyes, then gave a short laugh.

"You are distraught, my dearest Charlotte. It is impossible. Why should Vivian Chase behave so despicably towards you, his wife and the mother of his children? Or to me, whom he scarcely knows, and who has done him no harm?"

"You do not know Vivian — or what my life with him has been — or how jealous he is."

"Do not tell me. I could not bear to hear it," said Dominic, his brown rich skin flushing. "Your face — the thought of you has been before me all these long months and years. I have never forgotten you. On the few occasions when we have met and talked, I have felt that strange but imperative sensation that we were very close, that we must have met, and perhaps loved, in another life. I have many times wished with all my soul that you were free, free for me to approach honourably — in love — in marriage."

She gave a deep sigh. Her eyes looked up into his, less strained, softening.

"Praise God that I have at least heard you say those words. The memory of them will comfort me all the rest of my days."

"Oh, my darling, how can it be possible that you love me thus — you who are so young?" he broke out. "I am nearly twice your age, an old, tired man. It is ridiculous."

"To me you are neither old nor tired, but my heart's ideal," she said, clasping her hands.

He seized those hands and pressed long ardent kisses on them.

"Charlotte, Charlotte my love — would to God I had the right to put an end to the tortures at which you hint, and to take care of you for ever."

She withdrew her fingers and looked with frightened gaze towards the hall. She had heard the silver chimes of a clock. It was close on midnight now.

"You must go — at once, Dominic. I am mad to let you stay here, and I only in my night attire. Go — please — immediately."

He picked up his cloak.

"Yes, but matters cannot rest like this. I will not be the recipient of fraudulent letters which are harmful to *you*. The mystery must be solved. We must discover who has done this thing.

I still can scarcely believe that your own husband, Lord Chase, could perform an act so base, so dishonourable," he added, frowning.

"Vivian knows no honour," said Charlotte.

It was at that precise moment that Volpo stole soundlessly into the hall, in answer to a peculiar whistle, as from a night bird, and opened the front door to admit his master.

26

"EVERYTHING has gone according to plan, my lord," Volpo whispered in Vivian's ear outside the library door, beneath which a crack of light was showing in the darkness. "*He* has answered in person the letter which I penned for your lordship. He came hot-haste. I took the liberty of sending his carriage back to the stables in Harling, so he cannot get away, save on foot."

"Excellent," Vivian whispered back.

He was sober tonight. He had kept away from the brandy for he was bent on business, and unpleasant business at that. But he was in a good humour. He considered Volpo's plan the scheme of a genius. It looked to Vivian as though he had Charlotte on a hook, at last. Whether or not he wrecked an innocent man's reputation — a famous, much respected man into the bargain — he did not care. He only knew that he wanted his freedom from Charlotte, from his marriage. He was no longer going to be hounded into playing the amiable husband.

Now the fun was about to begin. It had all been arranged, in detail, between Vivian and his confidential servant. He was about to revenge himself upon Charlotte for the last ten years of bondage, *and* upon his mother's memory, he reflected with fiendish glee. In addition, his vengeance would extend to the unfortunate eldest daughter whom he would remove from Charlotte once and for all.

Suddenly, with a bold stroke, Vivian flung open the library door.

He had chosen an excellent moment, Dominic had just taken both Charlotte's hands in his and was kissing them in farewell.

"A farewell that must be for ever, else there is no honour in the world," he was murmuring to her. She stood, mute, tearless, looking with anguished passion at the bent head of the man who was so dear to her. A man nearly old enough to be her father. But she loved him and would go on doing so until the grave.

Vivian achieved the full theatrical effect

he desired. The pair, discovered by the fireplace in that tender attitude, swung round as they heard the door open and stared open-mouthed at the man who stood on the threshold.

In horror Charlotte regarded her husband.

As Vivian moved towards Charlotte and Dominic, he bowed, first to his wife, then to the astounded Dominic, smiling evilly.

"My compliments," he drawled. "The tenderness of your attitude makes a touching tableau. It is, I presume, the *finale* to a stolen hour of a more than tender passion."

Silence. Then Charlotte gave a low cry:

"God in heaven! My fears were justified. This has been a loathly trick. It was *you*, Vivian, who arranged the whole thing."

He pretended surprise, letting his monocle drop. He began to dangle it on its black ribbon.

"My dear Charlotte! *Arranged* for you to receive your lover in my absence? Come, come, what sort of a husband do you think I am?"

"Wait," Dominic rapped out. He came forward and confronted Vivian. His face was ashen, his large fine eyes narrowed. "I will deal with this."

Vivian bowed again.

"You will be forced to deal with it, my dear fellow, as the co-respondent in the divorce suit which I intend to bring against you and my faithless wife."

"Vivian!" Charlotte cried the name aloud, her hands pressed to her scarlet cheeks.

Dominic rapped out:

"I fail to understand, sir. You are making a grave mistake and one which requires complete explanation."

"No explanation from *me* is necessary," said Vivian.

"On the contrary, sir, you have just made an outrageous accusation which has no basis whatsoever — " began Dominic.

Charlotte interrupted:

"For heaven's sake, Dominic, do not demean yourself by engaging in a dispute with my husband. *He is out of his mind.*"

Vivian turned his gaze on her. She was

convinced, now, of his madness, so red a light gleamed in those usually stony blue eyes. It was a glance of murderous hatred coupled with triumph.

"Adulteress," he hissed. "*You* will soon be out of my house — with your paramour."

She shrank back, the tips of her shaking hands pressed against her white lips. Dominic restrained himself from striking Vivian across the mouth only by a supreme effort. He realized that it was essential for him to keep his temper. When Vivian had first entered the room, Dominic had been slightly taken aback, not only by his appearance, but by the realization that Charlotte's suspicions of foul play were justified. Now, in control of himself, he stepped neatly in between husband and wife, and brought his dark, forceful face close to the other man's.

"You will take back that word with which you have just defiled the ears of the purest woman on earth, or I shall make you answer to me, Lord Chase."

"To you, her partner in guilt?" Vivian stepped back with a sneering laugh, and his hand went into his pocket and closed over the small neat revolver without which he rarely travelled. One never knew when it might be useful.

Dominic said:

"There is no question of guilt, Lord Chase. That you should say so is an outrage and I insist upon an explanation."

"I have the greater right to demand one from *you*, sir; stealing down to my house, believing me to be in London, in order to spend a forbidden night with my wife. Look at her in her *déshabillé*," he added with a wicked glance at Charlotte. She was as white as the gown she wore, and trembled violently.

"This is all too well contrived a scheme. I see it now," said Dominic tersely. "I have been victimized."

"Oh, great God, do not suppose that I am to blame!" cried Charlotte.

"Never! I know full well that this can never be laid at your door," Dominic said gently. "Do not concern yourself. It is now between Lord Chase and me."

"Between the three of us, sir," said Vivian. "Once again, I ask what you are doing in my house?"

"What are *you* doing here, Vivian?" broke in Charlotte hysterically. "How is it possible that chance alone brought you here at this precise hour, when you were not due to come home until morning with our children."

"I was warned of your intention to receive a nocturnal visitor, madam," he said.

"Impossible. I had no such intention."

"A loyal servant will bear witness that such is not the case."

"Of course, that reptile Volpo — " began Charlotte in despair, under her breath.

"You took advantage of the fact that your personal maid was out of the house, and out of your way," went on Vivian.

"It was you who told me to send Gertrude up to London."

"Innocent enough; in order that she should take care of our daughters."

"It is all contrived, I tell you — " she began.

Dominic interrupted.

"I beg of you to let me deal with Lord Chase. He must, indeed, be out of his mind," he added in a low voice.

Vivian stuck the monocle in his eye again and regarded the politician.

"I understand, Mr. Unwin, that you have always been considered a pillar of the Church, a primrose of respectability, as well as a successful Member of Parliament," he sneered. "It will be an astonishment and, no doubt, a disappointment to your constituency to learn that you have stooped to become the lover of another man's wife."

"That is a lie, sir," thundered Dominic. "I have known your wife for many years, as I have done you, yourself. I have seen her but rarely. I have the greatest respect for her. I value her friendship. But to suggest a forbidden intimacy is infamous and unwarranted. I have never even communicated with Lady Chase by letter."

"Never. He was tricked down to Clunes tonight by *you*!" put in Charlotte.

"Who is to believe that?" drawled Vivian.

"You have got to believe it," Charlotte said in a desperate voice.

"I shall leave a judge of the Divorce Court to decide," said Vivian.

Charlotte gasped.

"You cannot do this thing. It is insane."

"Bah," said Vivian. "Do not waste my time with idle abuse. Faithless creature that you are! Devoted, loving in public, and in secret — well, I shall not bother now to ask what you have done. Enough for me to find you in this incriminating position tonight — alone with your lover."

"He has never been my lover — " began Charlotte frenziedly.

"Hush," said Dominic sternly. "I cannot have you dragged into such an abominable *mêlée*. *I*, and I alone, must answer to Lord Chase."

"You will have every chance of doing so. Charlotte will give you the name of my solicitors. Good night, sir," said Vivian and turned on his heel.

"Wait," said Dominic, the colour leaving his cheeks, for he thought of what a public scandal might mean to Charlotte. "The matter cannot be left like this. You have no proof — "

Vivian turned.

"Every proof. My own valet has just

informed me that you and my wife spent an hour together up in her bedroom and that Lady Chase asked for champagne to be sent up, in celebration. He was offered a bribe but he rejected it. He refused to serve the drink, being loyal to his master."

Charlotte gave a choking cry.

"Unspeakable lies!"

Dominic drew a sharp breath. The muscles on his cheeks were working. His patience was strained to the uttermost. He said:

"Great God, that any husband should stoop so to defile his wife and the mother of his children!"

Charlotte held out the letter she was supposed to have written to Dominic.

"*You* composed this and sent it to Mr. Unwin. *You!* — "

Vivian, pretending not to understand, took the letter, read it, then put it in his pocket.

"You are condemned by your own folly, madam. This epistle proves that you did, indeed, send for Mr. Unwin — No doubt to complain of your lot with me."

"I did not write it; it is not in my hand."

"On the contrary, I recognize the small print which you frequently use for diaries and verse," said Vivian with superb impudence.

She gave another gasp but remained speechless. Then Dominic said:

"Lord Chase, I give you my word of honour as a gentleman that I came here tonight because I was asked to come, but only as a friend — to give any help that was needed. But never have I been into your wife's bedchamber; nor, sir, dishonoured this house or you."

Vivian laughed harshly.

"You may tell that to a judge, sir."

"I admit now that I was indiscreet in coming to Clunes so late at night," added Dominic, frowning. "But I was asked to wait until half past ten, and since I imagined it to be a matter of urgency, I did as I *imagined* Lady Chase, herself, had requested."

Vivian, throwing back his head, laughed again.

"Surely a matter for amusement? You stand condemned by your own conduct.

And even as I walked into this room, you were caught in a highly suspicious attitude."

"Such suspicion shall not be allowed to fall on your wife who is pure and undefiled, sir," said Dominic furiously, "I was bidding her good-bye, a permanent good-bye rather than do *you* an injury."

"Then you admit that what you feel for her is more than a passing regard?" said Vivian triumphantly.

Dominic looked at Charlotte, but answered Vivian with quiet dignity:

"I have no wish to lie to you, sir. I admit that had things been different, I might have expressed more than ordinary affection toward Lady Chase. But when I came here it was not to keep a stolen *rendezvous*. I came out of chivalry — as any gentleman might have done — in answer to a letter full of distress, asking for secrecy."

"A letter that I would never have dreamed of sending," put in Charlotte hotly.

"I do not believe either of you," said Vivian.

Charlotte covered her face with her

hands and moaned:

"Alas — that this should happen to you, Dominic — through me — through my insane husband — oh, God, why did I not die before this night!"

Even in the singularly disagreeable position in which he found himself, Dominic Unwin felt not the slightest sense of anger against Charlotte whom he loved. He could see how he had been snared.

"Do not distress yourself, Lady Chase," he said gently. "I, also shall consult my legal advisers. This vile plot shall be brought to light, and Lord Chase shall be made to retract his calumnies."

"The public interest in such an affair will do you both such a lot of good," said Vivian with another fiendish laugh. "I shall greatly enjoy the sight of you squirming on the hook, my dear Unwin."

Dominic, taunted beyond endurance, sprang towards the younger man, fist upraised.

At once Vivian levelled the automatic upon him.

"Move a step nearer me, and I fire in self defence," he snarled. "My valet waits outside the door, and will witness that — if I shoot — it is because my wife's paramour has attacked me."

Dominic hesitated. Charlotte had time to throw herself between him and her husband.

"Do not dare," she said to Vivian, her eyes flashing. "Do not dare use that weapon."

But Dominic put her aside.

"This has gone far enough," he said quietly. "Put your revolver away, Lord Chase. You must be out of your mind."

"He is — *he is*," Charlotte moaned the words to herself.

Vivian turned on her.

"Get out of this house; and take your lover with you," he said.

"Use that word again, Lord Chase, and I shall fight with you whether you try to shoot me or not," said Dominic, his temper rising.

"He is not — and never has been — my lover!" Charlotte screamed the words at Vivian.

Suddenly Dominic changed his attitude. He had an idea that Charlotte's husband was, indeed, demented; not to be reasoned with. A sickness descended on him; a horror of this depraved monster to whom an innocent and long-suffering woman was tied. All thoughts of himself, the danger to his reputation, his social position, receded into the background. He thought now only of the trembling unhappy girl whom he loved. There was no passion, only the deepest tenderness and pity in his heart as he turned from Vivian and took Charlotte by one arm.

"Come," he said. "No good can come of us seeking to impress the truth upon Lord Chase. If I leave this house, you had better leave with me."

"Never — " began Charlotte, but Vivian interrupted. He flung his head back, bellowing with laughter.

"Now you see sense; and doubtless, my dear Unwin, you have no desire to be shot by an outraged husband."

Charlotte moaned:

"Do not heed him, Dominic. Go. Go quickly — out of his way."

"Yes, go quickly, Mr. Unwin," echoed Vivian, "and take my erring wife with you."

Charlotte was trembling so violently that Dominic had to hold her arm in order to support her. She broke out, desperately:

"My children! *Eleanora!*"

"The children stay with me," Vivian said with a sly smirk at her. "You do not expect, do you, madam, that I will hand my innocent daughters over to the mother who has dishonoured them? And her poor husband," he added with a hypocritical sigh.

"You know it is false," panted Charlotte.

"Hush! Do not upset yourself further," Dominic said under his breath and tightened his grip of her. He kept a watchful eye on Vivian who had moved away, but Dominic could see that he still handled the revolver. Dominic was no coward. He deplored the fact that Charlotte was here beside him and that he could not do as every instinct in him urged — throw himself, unarmed, upon Vivian and strike that sneering face. But his hands were tied. He dared not risk the bullet entering *Charlotte*'s heart; neither was it of any use trying to reason with a maniac.

473

For the moment, Vivian's vile plan had succeeded.

"Every allegation you have levelled against your wife and myself has been deliberately concocted, and has not one grain of truth in it," Dominic addressed the madman. "Your valet is obviously in your pay. But my lawyers will communicate with yours, sir, I do assure you."

Vivian gave a sweeping bow. He was enjoying not only the discomfiture of the proud politician but the sight of Charlotte's ghastly face. He said:

"And mine will reply, sir. It will make an entertaining case."

"My poor Eleanora — " began Charlotte, but stopped, choking. The mere thought of her little girl so happily sleeping upstairs, ignorant of the hideous menace that hung over her head, reduced her to an anguish she could hardly control. Tears poured down her cheeks. She gasped:

"Let me take Eleanora with me, Vivian, I beseech you."

"Pray leave this house," he said. "You are no longer entitled to stay under my roof; nor shall you ever see your daughters again."

The malice in his voice appalled Dominic. He was filled with apprehension for Charlotte. He knew what motherhood meant to her.

She was crazy with pain at the thought of Eleanora's horror and despair tomorrow when she would wake and ask for Mama and be told by her spiteful father that her mother had deserted her. Charlotte continued to sob out her appeals to Vivian. Dominic saw the sadistic joy in the other man's eyes and it made him shudder. If he had ever had the smallest doubt that Charlotte's private life was a nightmare, he had none now. He said:

"Charlotte, my poor child, come with me now, I will protect you. I swear it."

"*Oh, God*," she said in a voice of despair and looked wildly at him. She loved him; but now it was only of Eleanora that she was thinking.

Vivian, leaning an arm on the mantelpiece, lit a cigar. He was enjoying himself hugely. He knew perfectly well that he had not one shred of genuine evidence against either of these two. But Volpo's evil plan had been so successful, it intoxicated him. He saw that he could reasonably expect now to rid himself legally of Charlotte and so be free of domestic ties. As for the children — a good nurse and governess could take care of *them* down here at Clunes, whilst he, Vivian, roamed the Continent, the world, as he wished. Not a word would Society be able to breathe against him in the future. But Charlotte and Dominic Unwin would stand condemned forever, ostracized.

The sight of the terrible pain on Charlotte's wet white face, as she walked unsteadily out of the library on Dominic's arm, compensated Vivian for every moment of annoyance that he had suffered on account of his marriage.

He called after Dominic.

"Mr. Unwin, have you forgotten that you dismissed your carriage, thinking no doubt that you could spend the rest of the night here, whilst I was so conveniently away?"

Dominic turned back.

"Sir, I did *not* dismiss my carriage."

"Nevertheless it has gone," said Vivian smiling.

Dominic set his teeth. This was fresh evidence of Lord Chase's vile plot to harm his unhappy wife.

"I do confess," added Vivian, "on account of my outraged feelings, I am disinclined to offer you the use of my own vehicles. You can count yourself lucky, Mr. Unwin, that I have so far controlled my temper as not to put a bullet through the head of the man who betrayed me."

"Oh, Dominic, Dominic, things go from bad to worse," groaned Charlotte.

"It is worse only because you must leave this warm house to walk, on a cold night, which you are not fit for," said Dominic briefly.

Vivian was so pleased now with the turn events had taken, he decided to be magnanimous.

"Let it not be said that I have forced a woman, even so abased as my wife, to take a country stroll in poor weather," he said, chuckling. "Besides, Charlotte has never been much of a walker. I will allow my coachman to drive you both to Harling."

Dominic whispered to the half-fainting Charlotte.

"You understand why I am not engaging in a fight now, this moment, with your husband, do you not, Charlotte? It would be to no purpose. He is mad and, if he shoots, you may be the victim. I cannot see you harmed."

She turned her agonized eyes to him.

"I would gladly die," she said, "but I agree with you — to fight tonight is useless. He is capable of killing you and telling the world that it was a *crime passionel* — in defence of his honour."

"Nevertheless it takes all my strength of will to keep my hands off him," muttered Dominic.

Vivian had pulled the bell. Volpo appeared. For a moment the Portuguese valet's narrow eyes turned to Lady Chase's ghastly face, and gloated an instant. He had been listening outside those doors; he was as delighted as his master at the result of tonight's duplicity. It would be a pleasure, he thought, to confront that ugly bitch Gertrude in the morning and inform her that her precious lady had eloped with her paramour.

Vivian told his valet to waken the coachman and order the brougham.

Charlotte said faintly:

"It is bitterly cold. I would like a wrap — "

"You shall have one, or I will see that every man and woman in this country hears of your husband's unnatural behaviour," said Dominic in a loud clear voice and turned his gaze full upon Lord Chase.

Vivian's eyelids drooped. He shrugged his shoulders and looked at Charlotte.

"You may fetch your coat and a night-bag," he said indifferently. "But do not awaken Eleanora or it will be worst for you and *her*," he added malevolently.

27

WHEN Charlotte drove away with Dominic from Clunes that terrible March night, she was in a fainting condition; beyond speech or thought.

Once alone in the cold and darkness, Dominic put an arm about her. She leaned her head against his shoulder. She wore a warm dress, bonnet and cloak — velvet, fur-trimmed, luxurious — but in the small bag by the coachman's side there was only a change of under-linen and a few requisites for the night. She had taken nothing else. Terrified of Vivian, she had fled from the house that had been her home for ten long years. From her abhorred husband who had taken his revenge upon her; and perforce from Eleanora for whom her heart was breaking.

She could no longer weep. She lay with her face pressed against Dominic's coat. He stroked her hand gently. Whatever the turbulence of his thoughts — and all this had been a shock to him — he showed no sign of it. He remained calm and inexpressibly gentle. He tried all manner of arguments, first to reassure her that justice would be done and that she would soon see her children again, then to promise her his support.

But she would not be comforted. When she was able to speak, she did so with complete despair.

"Vivian is ruthless," she said, "without scruple. And he hates me. He will lie under oath in order to ruin me and take Eleanora from me for ever."

"He shall not," repeated Dominic sternly. Then with sudden curiosity, he added: "Why, though, has he also made *me* the object of vengeance? What harm have I done him?"

"Nothing, save that he must have suspected my admiration for you. You are the only man whose friendship I have ever dared to want — no matter how innocently."

Dominic tightened his hold of her.

"My poor child, to what an appalling end has your sweet friendliness towards me brought you."

"I do not mind for myself. But you are a famous man — in the public eye. Scandal must not be allowed to touch you."

"Lord Chase intends that it shall," said Dominic grimly.

Convulsively, she squeezed his gloved hand in hers.

"The idea terrifies me. Oh, forgive me, I implore you, for being instrumental in this. I did not know. I swear I had no knowledge of the letter that brought you to my side."

"I believe you implicitly. I have only myself to blame, because I came hot-haste, believing you needed me, not pausing to act more prudently. I should have realized how strange it was that you of all pure women should seek a meeting of clandestine nature."

"Oh, Dominic, I am more thankful than you will ever know to have you at my side tonight. I have endured too much pain, alone. To have your hand in mine, to hear your voice, gives me new faith and courage."

The carriage moved on slowly through

the cold black night. Dominic thrilled to the haunting quality, the rich promise of love in Charlotte's voice. Once again he realized how dear she was to him, how completely he was enslaved by her, body, heart and soul. Fears for the future, regrets for the past, were swept away on a rising tide of emotions. He gathered her in a close embrace and pressed his lips to her cold, tear-stained cheek.

"My beloved child, alas, that I am so much too old for you! You are young, much too young to have to bear such anguish. But believe that I love you! I told you so earlier tonight, before we agreed to bid each other farewell. I tell you again. I love you, my darling Charlotte. I shall not leave you while you need me, no matter what befalls us."

The words were spoken, clearly and proudly, and hearing them, Charlotte's flagging spirits revived. The rich colour returned to her cheek and the light to her eyes. She flung her arms around his neck.

"You are not too old for me, dear, *dearest* Dominic, I love you better than life itself. I always have, from the first moment we met, and I always shall."

Dominic was suddenly, strangely at peace in this little world of their own making. He remembered neither his great work nor his previous unhampered, bachelor existence. He knew only that he would never be alone again, but must always belong to this lovely tender-hearted woman who to him was still a child, in years.

At last he said:

"Come what may of tonight's frightfulness, something beautiful and sacred has arisen out of it. We have become dear and necessary to each other."

"I like to hear you say that, but how can I allow you to give me your love or protection?" she said sadly. "I cannot, I shall not let Vivian divorce me and — cite *you*!"

Cite him! How strangely those sinister words fell on his ears. A short while ago they would have made him shudder. Now he only bent his lips to Charlotte's cheek and brushed away the tears.

"Do not let us think too much about *that* just now," he said. "First we must consider what is to be done tonight. It is bitterly cold — " He leaned closer to the window and frowned as he saw the rain pouring down. The coachman was shouting to the horses and obviously finding it increasingly difficult to keep them from slipping. "God forgive that madman for turning you out on such a night." Dominic muttered.

"Where can we go until we can catch the first train to London?" she asked.

"You have no one around here, no friend to whom you could tell your story, and with whom I could leave you?"

"No one," she answered shaking her head, "they are all Vivian's friends. Even if they wished to be kindly disposed toward me, they would not want me with a possible scandal hanging over my head. Most of the families in the district have known the Chases for several generations. Remember that I was but Charlotte Goff and they will be only too ready to sneer."

She drew away from him.

"You must see for yourself, it is imperative that you, too, should have nothing to do with me. You must at least prove to the world that we are not an eloping couple."

The next words he spoke were stirring enough to warm her frightened heart.

"In a moment I shall convince myself that we are. I shall resign my seat in Parliament and take you away and make it my life's business to ensure that you never suffer again."

For a moment she could not speak but sat with her slender fingers laced together, and her throat working convulsively. Then she whispered:

"To hear you say it has wiped out years of pain. But it is out of the question."

"My poor child," he said, "and even my love cannot alleviate your fears for your eldest child. I know that."

She shut her eyes. She dared not allow herself to visualize Eleanora's misery tomorrow.

Now the carriage jolted to a standstill. A footman who sat beside the driver opened the carriage door letting a shower of rain on them.

"Harling Station, sir," he said, crossly, for he had been pulled out of his sleep to make this journey.

"Are the doors of the station open?"

inquired Dominic.

"Nay, sir, shut," said the man and stared at his mistress who covered her face against the cold and rain with a fold of her mantle.

Dominic racked his brains. Impossible to allow a delicate woman to be exposed to these grim weather conditions, so late at night. Harling was wrapped in silence. The inhabitants slept. This carriage would not take them further. The driver had Lord Chase's orders. Even if Dominic woke the livery stables and tried to bribe the owner to get out hired horses and vehicle, where could they go? No hired coachman would risk a long drive. Charlotte's great friends, the Marshes, were twenty miles away. Tomorrow she could go to them, but not now.

Dominic said tersely:

"I have no option, Charlotte, but to take you to the local inn, rouse them and ask them to give you a bed."

"I know them at The Bell," she nodded. "Mr. Swain is the landlord. Vivian has in the past spent money drinking there with some of his friends. I would hate to go to The Bell. The

Swains will gossip and everybody in the district will know."

"Lord Chase will, in any case, see that everybody knows. By this time tomorrow there will be little hope of keeping the thing a secret," said Dominic grimly.

The night-wind tore at Charlotte. She shivered with exhaustion and cold. After a moment, she agreed to Dominic's plan. They drove to the Bell Tavern, a sixteenth-century inn not far from Harling Church. The idea of entering the place was repugnant to her but she was helpless. Only, when Dominic said that he could not remain at The Bell, also, she uttered a protest.

"You cannot stay outside in this bitter cold. It is unthinkable."

"I am not young but I am strong and shall not faint by the wayside," said Dominic with a smile, "I can walk to a neighbouring village, be it five or ten miles, and there seek a room for the night. I shall not further embarrass you by remaining in this district."

She longed to say: '*Oh, my love, do not abandon me*,' but remained silent. She would have died rather than embarrass him further. She had been responsible enough already, although unwittingly, for the load of trouble that had fallen on his innocent shoulders.

Dominic roused the landlord and his wife.

Both the Swains came in answer to the repeated knocking. He, with a rough robe over his nightshirt, his nightcap still on his head; she in similar attire, hair done up in curl papers. They were a scraggy, bad-tempered-looking pair. When they recognized the fine lady who stood clinging to the gentleman's arm, they exchanged astonished glances, then smirks.

Of course, they said, bowing low, they would give her ladyship a bedroom, and the gentleman too, if he so wished. But Dominic refused the hospitality and reluctantly left Charlotte in the care of the unattractive couple.

"I will come for you in the morning and escort you to your friends' home," he told Charlotte.

She refused this.

"It must not be. *I* will hire a carriage and go alone to Pillars. You must stay away from me until our position is clarified," she said.

"It touches me that you should think of my good name in the midst of your own terrible plight," he said.

They were alone, for a moment, in the bar parlour of The Bell. In the dim light of the oil lamp which Mr. Swain had placed on one of the tables, Charlotte's face looked to Dominic so pinched and wan that he hesitated to leave her. She had become, this unforgettable night, dearer than life to him. He caught and held her a moment to his heart.

"Try to sleep, Charlotte. I shall be thankful to hear tomorrow that you are with your friends. I have ever been drawn to Mrs. Marsh who is as wise as she is a most beautiful old lady."

"At least *they* will not scorn me," said Charlotte in a strangled voice.

"Nobody shall scorn you," said Dominic and kissed her hands each in turn. "I will love and serve you to the best of my ability," he added huskily. "I shall see Mr. Glover, my solicitor, tomorrow, and we must act upon his judgment. If, as I fear, he says we ought not to meet again,

I will obey, because my only desire is that you should have your children restored to you."

She trembled and clung to him.

"I thank you from the bottom of my heart, but oh, Dominic, *Dominic*!" she broke off and burst into a flood of anguished weeping.

Not for long. She steadied herself and, smiling through her tears, bade him leave her. She was positive the Swains would be waiting, gloating, watching how long they remained together. Five minutes more and Dominic left The Bell and started his uncomfortable walk through the wild stormy night.

Mrs. Swain showed her ladyship to the best room, where she had already lit a small fire. She had also placed a foot warmer in the big tester bed.

"I would have done more had I expected you, my lady," she began, looking at Charlotte in a sly way which Charlotte found offensive.

"It is no matter," Charlotte made herself reply with as much pride as she could muster. "Thank you — for your services."

Mrs. Swain bobbed and departed. Charlotte sat weakly on the edge of the bed. How cold and uninviting was this shabby room. With low ceilings and poor furniture, it had a musty odour and looked hideous after Charlotte's own beautiful bedroom at Clunes. Nevertheless she did not despise it, for at least she could be alone here. Her terrible husband could not disturb her rest — if there was to be any rest for her.

She covered her face with her hands, trying to control her shuddering. She felt dazed by all that she had been through since Dominic's unexpected arrival at Clunes. On the one hand all seemed lost and desperate; on the other lay the memory of Dominic's embrace and the knowledge that he returned her love. But she was assailed by a dozen fears for Eleanora's well-being.

She unclasped her mantle and let the bonnet fall from her weary head. Then she knelt down by the bed and clasping her hands, uttered a wild prayer for help.

"Do not let this thing happen — oh, God in heaven — do not permit it — for my children's sake, and for Dominic Unwin's," she said the words aloud.

In their room next door, the Swains whispered together.

"We'll have a nice story to tell in the morning," said Mr. Swain, "her ladyship arriving with a strange gentleman at this hour. Well, *well* — !" he smothered a ribald laugh.

"Did you note the languishing glances they gave each other?" said Mrs. Swain. "Who'd have dreamed *she* was that sort. His lordship has turned her out — that's plain to see."

"And her with three children," added Mr. Swain.

But Charlotte did not hear. After her prayers, she seated herself by the fire, and leaning back, fell into an uneasy slumber from which she woke stiff and cold and scarcely able to face the day that lay before her.

With one of those swift changes of mood for which the English climate is famous, the March morning that followed was warm, humid and full of the lush golden promise of spring.

Charlotte (who had reluctantly accepted

money from Dominic — she had no choice, for Vivian never gave her a penny of her own), washed and tidied herself and soon after eight o'clock left The Bell Tavern in a hired vehicle. She was terrified that Vivian would get to hear that she had stayed the night in Harling, and was anxious to get away from the district as fast as possible.

She was conscious of Mr. and Mrs. Swain's leering glances which added a touch of insolence to their gushing civility but she hardly spoke to them. When at length she found herself well out of Harling she felt better.

But her agony of mind was terrible to bear. Try as she would, she could not stop imagining what would be going on at this very moment. Eleanora would run into Mama's bedroom and find Papa there, instead. God grant that Vivian would not be too harsh with his little daughter, thought the poor mother. Gertrude, of course, would return to Clunes this morning with the other two children. She would be not only astonished but deeply upset to find her lady missing. Oh, what would

Vivian do? Dismiss Gertrude and bring back that terrible nurse whom Eleanora disliked? And would he really carry out his threat of implicating an innocent man in a trumped-up divorce case? It was a Charlotte in a sorry state who arrived many hours later at Pillars. They had stopped midway to rest the horses and take some refreshment and reached the Marshes' home by midday.

A bemused and half-fainting Charlotte was helped from the carriage by Fleur and Peveril, who were astonished and alarmed to see her.

"Good heavens, my child, what is wrong?" asked Fleur looking with dismay at her young friend's deathly face.

Charlotte had to be given coffee and brandy before she could tell the dreadful story. Once told, she broke down and wept piteously.

"What will happen to Eleanora?" she kept moaning. "And how can we save Mr. Unwin?"

Fleur and Peveril exchanged horrified glances. Peveril said:

"Of course Vivian Chase cannot be responsible. Our poor Charlotte must defend this case on the grounds that he is insane."

"Insanity has to be proved," sighed Fleur, who was sitting beside the couch stroking Charlotte's hair. "It is a monstrous thing but he seems to hold the trump cards. Not many would be willing to come forward and swear that he is a lunatic. But how terrible that Dominic Unwin should be involved!"

Charlotte turned a wild wet face to her.

"I love him with all my heart, Fleur," she said in a choked voice, "and he loves me. Yet we are innocent and almost strangers. Is it not ironic?"

"It is pitiable for you both," said Fleur and her large violet eyes filled with tears.

The old painter adopted a man's practical attitude.

"Come, my dearest," he said, touching Fleur on the shoulder, "let us see that a room is prepared for our guest, and try to take a more cheerful view. At any rate, our home is hers for as long as she needs it."

Charlotte lifted a handkerchief to her

lips and shook her head.

"You are kind, sir, but I came to you in desperation. I ought not to stay. The whole of England may soon ring with this story. My name will be dragged in the mud and it will be wrong for me to allow the world to criticize you two for befriending me."

They assured her, at once, that they feared no criticism. Charlotte Chase and Dominic Unwin were innocent people, victims of a vile and lunatic hatred. Why should they be ostracized?

"You are too good and only what I expected, but Vivian has done enough harm. I would not wish that harm extended to you," persisted Charlotte.

"Be comforted, dear child, and reassured that we can take care of ourselves," said Peveril gently, and smiled at her.

So Charlotte came to the peace, the beauty, the tranquillity of Pillars, and her kind friends.

★ ★ ★

Meanwhile, in London, Dominic Unwin forsook his usual routine of work and drove to Holborn to visit the offices of his solicitors. There he told Mr. Glover his story.

"The whole thing was an abominable trick," he ended, striding up and down the office, his hands locked behind his back, his face pale and stern. "Lord Chase must not be allowed to succeed."

Mr. Glover who had listened in shocked silence, looked at his distinguished client with dismay.

"Indeed he must not. I have *never* listened to a more terrible story."

Dominic came to a standstill before the desk and leaned a clenched fist upon it.

"I ask you to make it your sacred duty to prevent this fearful slur from falling upon a pure and innocent lady."

Mr. Glover, who was an elderly man, coughed and lowered his lids. A little red in the cheeks, he said:

"Forgive me, Mr. Unwin, if I seem impertinent, but I must ask you a few questions."

"Ask what you will," said Dominic, and passed a hand across his brow with an impatient gesture. He had returned to London by an early train this morning after a sleepless night in a small inn little better than The Bell in Harling. After that trudge through a wet stormy night he was exhausted. He had breakfasted in his rooms at Albany in a state of mind that could rightfully be called chaotic.

He answered Mr. Glover's questions; but when that gentleman suggested, apologetically of course, that his client might have been the dupe of the wife as well as the husband, Dominic became a lion in her defence.

"Do not dare suggest any such thing, Glover!" he said indignantly, "I tell you, Lady Chase is first and foremost a mother. She would not have sent that letter for one reason above all others — that it would risk her losing her children."

Mr. Glover looked uncomfortable and added:

"Your pardon, Mr. Unwin, it is my duty to probe into this case in detail. I — I — there was a chance — ahem — that Lady Chase might have wished for a divorce and used *you* — "

Dominic interrupted again, his face burning.

"Such is not the case and can be ruled out immediately."

Mr. Glover nodded and cleared his throat.

"If you will pardon me saying so, sir, was it not a little unwise of you to have adhered so strictly to the detailed instructions in her letter? Did it not seem to you peculiar that Lady Chase should demand a clandestine meeting in the country, late at night?"

Dominic walked to the window. Hands in his pockets he stared down at the traffic in High Holborn. Vans and carriages, horses and costermongers' barrows, vied with each other for space. He could hear their shouts, the clatter of hooves, the rolling of wheels on the cobbles as he stood up there by the half open dusty window. At length he said:

"I admit that I acted on a foolish impulse. I will also confess to you, in confidence, Glover, that Lady Chase is one of my dearest friends. I have the highest regard for her and I felt that it would be unchivalrous to ignore the appeal that I *presumed* she, herself, made to me."

Mr. Glover made various notes and drew his private conjectures. What a position, he reflected, for the distinguished politician to find himself linked in what the world would call 'an adulterous union' with Lady Chase. It was the last shadow that Mr. Glover had dreamed could ever fall across the brightness of Dominic Unwin's life and threaten his reputation.

When Dominic left his solicitor's office, it was in an unhappy frame of mind. Mr. Glover had somewhat bluntly let him know that if Chase persisted in swearing that the note was in his wife's handwriting and the valet swore under oath that he had actually found Mr. Unwin and her ladyship in *flagrante delicto*, it would be a hard case to defend. But it was suggested that counsel's opinion must be taken and an appointment should be made immediately with Sir Travis Emmerton, Q.C. He was one of the finest barristers in England today.

After that, things moved swiftly. Vivian lost no time in instructing his own lawyers and presenting his case. They, in turn, let it be known to Mr. Glover that

Lord Chase intended to cite Mr. Unwin as a co-respondent in his divorce.

That night, every Club and nearly every house belonging to friends and associates of either the Englesbys or the Chases hummed with the news.

It was whispered from one to the other; spoken of in shocked whispers over dinner-tables; smirked at by ladies in their drawing-rooms.

The beautiful Lady Chase had left her husband and children and run away with Mr. Dominic Unwin, M.P. adopted son of the Englesbys.

Cecil was abroad at the time so the story had yet to reach his ears. But the Marquis of Englesby heard it and sent post-haste for his adopted son, from whom he demanded an explanation.

"The great lady who has been a mother to you since you were a boy lies at death's door. How could you have done such a thing? If it reaches her ears it will kill her," the Marquis said furiously.

Dominic answered him.

"I am not guilty and neither is the lady concerned. I have never lied to you, sir. I beg you to believe me now. This story is a vile fabrication on the part of a madman."

Later, when Dominic left Englesby Castle, his heart was heavy, but he did at least know that his adopted father accepted his word. A worse moment arrived. That next morning, he was sent for by his Leader. The great man, himself, demanded an explanation.

"I am amazed and disappointed in you, Unwin. That *you* should be so indiscreet and with a married woman who has children! Good God, what has come over you, man? I would never have believed it."

Now indeed Dominic Unwin knew what it was for the first time in his life to feel the cold breath of scorn upon him, the knife-edge of a vile suspicion. Yet remembering Charlotte's defencelessness and the love that she bore him, he faced the full blast and stood up to it calmly, reiterating that Lady Chase was blameless.

"Lord Chase is out of his mind. I shall defend the case, sir," he told Lord Salisbury, "and Lady Chase is with friends, not at my side. She and

I are not lovers, nor have ever been. I ask you to take my word on this."

Salisbury looked troubled. He had always admired Unwin and marked him down for something big.

He put a hand on Dominic's shoulder.

"I shall try to take your word and pray that it is the truth, for you know what Her Majesty feels about divorce," he added.

Dominic left him with those words echoing in his ears.

By the time that week came to an end he felt as though he had been through a hurricane. He could not put his mind to his work. In the Members' room, he knew that he was being looked at curiously by his colleagues, and in his own Club, one evening, he was cut dead by a certain peer of the realm who happened to have been at Oxford with Vivian Chase.

That slight had a curious effect upon Dominic. If he had not truly cared for Charlotte it might have made him dislike her. For it was a stinging blow to his pride, his sense of what was right and proper. Then it roused a bitter determination to fight this thing to the end, no matter what it cost him — for Charlotte's sake.

He could no longer restrain his impulse to see her, the woman whose name was linked with his and who had become inadvertently the cause of *his* disaster.

He had not heard from her, but a short note from Fleur Marsh had acquainted him with the fact that she was safely at Pillars. To this, Fleur had added an invitation to Dominic to go down to Pillars and see Charlotte when he wished.

Mr. Glover would of course, thought Dominic, say that it would be most unwise of him to go near Charlotte at this stage of events. But Dominic was conscious now of something stronger than mere wounded vanity or fears for his own name. He experienced a deep longing for Charlotte. His love had become like a fire burning brighter and brighter in his heart and soul.

He decided to travel down to Epping and see Charlotte on the morrow.

28

FLEUR MARSH was busy arranging her flowers when her butler announced: "Mr. Dominic Unwin."

Fleur walked toward the door with outstretched hands. She did not know that Dominic was coming but was not surprised to see him here. She had felt that nothing now would keep him away from Charlotte.

It was another lovely spring day. The gardens were a golden shimmer of daffodils. Fleur had just received a basket of flowers from the head gardener, and was about to decorate her morning room. Peveril was in his studio, painting. Charlotte was in her own room. She was busy with Fleur's dressmaker. The poor girl had come away from Clunes with no clothes and Fleur had insisted that one or two dresses must be made for her immediately. Both the women knew well that Vivian would not show Charlotte the courtesy of sending her even a portion of her wardrobe.

Fleur began:

"I am delighted to see you, Mr. Unwin — "

But she stopped and let her hands fall to her sides. Mr. Unwin, she knew, would be distressed by what had recently taken place, but she could not understand why he looked at *her* so strangely. He stared with a mixture of wonder and amazement, and with a pallor that showed under the warm brown of his skin. Fleur's welcoming smile faded.

"Mr. Unwin! Are you ill?" she began again.

He shook his head but remained dumb. His deeply blue eyes seemed to be drinking in the sight of her. Indeed, he could not stop staring at the delicate, lined face of this beautiful old lady who wore an enchanting dress of forget-me-not blue, with muslin frills at the throat, and a fringed blue lace shawl over her narrow shoulders. At length he managed to speak:

"Mrs. Marsh — I — I — " he stopped, shaking his head as though unable to find further words. He began to move into the sun-lit morning room which was, he thought, like the mistress of the house, dainty, beautiful, dignified. She motioned him to a winged arm-chair. He sat down gratefully.

"You must think me mad," he said in a low husky voice. "Indeed I feel that I *am*."

"Oh, dear," said Fleur anxiously. "It is an indisposition, Mr. Unwin."

"To you I must be Dominic," he said in a queer voice.

"My dear Dominic, has this terrible trouble afflicted you so sorely?"

"You mean Vivian Chase's abominations?"

"Yes."

"No," Dominic shook his head. "I can stand up to them well enough. Up till yesterday evening my thoughts were concerned only with *her*, poor sweet Charlotte."

"And hers have been with you," said Fleur gently, "with you and the children from whom she has been so cruelly wrenched. Shall I call her and let the sight of her face revive you?"

Dominic shook his head. He took a handkerchief from his pocket and wiped his brow. He was obviously labouring under some strong emotion. Fleur wondered for an instant if she should send for her husband — that dear man who for forty-six long years had been her staunch defender from all anxieties.

But Dominic said:

"No — let us remain alone. Dear Mrs. Marsh, I have much to say which may come as a fearful shock to you."

"To me?" The old lady's exquisite face coloured. She flickered lashes that were still long and silken. "How can that be?"

"Pray be seated and let me talk to you," he said.

Fleur hesitated.

"Shall I not send for Charlotte, then?"

"Not for a moment. I want to speak to you alone. You are strong enough to stand what I am going to tell you?" he asked.

"Come!" she protested, "you are too mysterious, Mr. Un — I mean Dominic. What can this thing be which is of such significance to *me*?"

"I grieve to have to take your mind back to a time which must have been singularly distasteful to you," he said, "but I think I am right in recalling that you were married to Lord St. Cheviot in London on the 15th September, 1838."

Now Fleur's Dresden-china figure stiffened. With one hand she caught at the cameo brooch at her throat.

"That is so — but *why* — ?"

"I beg you to let me continue," broke in Dominic.

Her brows drew together.

"I am vastly perplexed, but go ahead."

"In the June following you — gave birth to a son."

Now Fleur changed colour. Both her hands gripped at the arms of the chair in which she was seated.

"Mr. Unwin — Dominic — why are you bringing to light these facts relating to my past? It is my husband's and my wish that that period of my life should remain a closed book. I know that you and Charlotte are going through much pain and difficulty, but it cannot compare with the pain to which I was

510

once subjected. It is too terrible for me to dwell upon."

Dominic leaned towards her. His face was as pale as hers.

"I do assure you I would not wish to cause you an instant's distress. The words I speak are wrung from me, but *must* be spoken."

"Tell me what you have to say. Do not delay a moment longer," she begged.

Then Dominic with an immense effort and lowering his head, said:

"That miserable infant did not die as you believed. *He lived. He lived and I am he*."

Silence followed these words. It was as though Fleur had been struck by lightning. Rooted to her chair, she sat staring at Dominic Unwin. For an instant she thought he must be insane and then knew that he was not. Without further questioning, she believed him. Those eyes, of that particular shade of violet which she, and Harry Roddney, her father had possessed, were set also in *his* head. They could be only the eyes of a Roddney that regarded her now.

He spoke:

"Is this too much for you? I know it must be a terrible shock. Shall I call Mr. Marsh?"

She was loosing some of her frozen immobility but she answered faintly. "No — *wait* — tell me more. In God's name how do you *know* this thing?"

Then he told her.

The astounding revelation had come following the serious events concerning Charlotte Chase. Yesterday, while he was still in the House he received a message that his presence was urgently required at the hospital for old soldiers in Chelsea. There, an old Corporal of the Guards, named William Smith, lay dying and had expressed a wish to see Mr. Unwin. He had something of infinite importance to reveal to him.

Dominic knew this man and went at once to the hospital. He had thought William Smith dead. He had lived for the first few years of his life with Mr. Smith and his wife. At that time, William was a lamplighter. Later he went to the Crimea, was wounded and must now be well over seventy. He had not communicated with Dominic for over thirty years.

"But I must not confuse you by telling you the story in this order. I must begin from the beginning," said Dominic.

"Yes, pray do," said Fleur trembling with agitation, her gaze riveted on Dominic's face.

He referred to the hour of his birth. Dominic had all the facts. He knew now that he had been born with a brown skin and that in consequence Lord St. Cheviot, his own father, had in demoniac fury disowned him. The midwife, terrified of St. Cheviot, announced that the baby had never breathed, and carried it out of the house. She had intended to dispose of the tiny body but, realizing that it was alive, took it with her to her cottage in Monks Risborough. There she put it to the breast of a niece who had just given birth to a still-born child. This woman (Mrs. Smith) fed the little boy and became attached to him. She was not repulsed by his colour. Indeed, as he revived, he seemed to grow lighter in hue, and the Smiths admired the beauty of his strange blue eyes, his delicately fashioned limbs. The midwife was too terrified to utter the name of the infant's real parents.

So her niece took the babe with her to London where her husband had secured a new job as lamplighter. Only on her death-bed did the nurse reveal to William Smith, the true identity of the child. By that time the Baron of Cadlington was dead and Lady St. Cheviot had married again.

"I stayed with these kindly people, the Smiths, until I was ten," Dominic went on. "After which, as I think you already know, I was sent to a Charity school, from which the Englesbys adopted me. But it appears always to have been on William Smith's conscience that I was the rightful heir to Cadlington, and that my name was not Unwin but — St. Cheviot. So troubled was he, that in his dying hours he felt he must reveal the facts. Thus he sent that message to me at the House. He handed me this — "

Now Dominic gave Fleur a fine gold chain which had attached to it a tiny enamel heart bearing the initial 'C', in diamonds. Fleur took it on the palm of her hand. Her fingers shook so that they could scarcely hold the trinket. Her face turned from white to crimson. She stammered:

"Great God in heaven, *then it is true*. For while I was in labour, I handed the midwife this chain with the little heart (the initial was 'C' for Cadlington, as you might imagine). I said that when my child was born, the chain was to be placed around his neck to bring him good luck. It was a mother's whim — no more."

"I was surprised," said Dominic, "that the midwife did not steal it. She must have been an honest woman, in her way. And Smith was a decent fellow and did not sell it despite his poverty."

"The one who was supposed to have buried the infant was the best of my two nurses," said Fleur hoarsely. "She was no murderess and would not want a living child to die. I can see it all now. She knew that the Baron would have tried to exterminate the infant had he dreamed it still drew breath. Oh, heavens. And you are here, today, *my son*, my child — a grown, mature man, Dominic Unwin!"

She broke off. Outside in the garden, she could hear the sound of birds singing, and of a bell ringing from Epping Church. She turned her gaze again to the face of this man, this politician, whom she had once thought little more than a stranger. Terrible, wonderful, *incredible* fact. *He was her son.* Her babe, who forty-six years ago had not died but lived to become a distinguished Member of Parliament.

Now she knew why she had been so curiously drawn to Dominic. She understood many things. She realized why he had shown unusual brilliance when a child, a mere schoolboy. For had not Hélène Roddney, his grandmother, been one of the most erudite and brilliant women of her time? She could see why his manner held so much charm; for just such another spendid and charming person had been his grandfather, Harry Roddney. Thank God, Fleur reflected, he resembled his father not at all. The brutality, the coarseness, the cruelty of St. Cheviot had passed him by. He belonged wholly to *her* side of the family. There was nothing of St. Cheviot about him except, perhaps, the blackness of his hair.

So he had come to Pillars, his mother's

old home. It was the most fantastic, satisfying thing that could ever have happened to any woman in the world, she thought. What did the hue of his skin matter? He was not, by any means the native that St. Cheviot had feared. Dominic's skin was a light brown such as could be seen on thousands of men in the Latin countries. The delicate lips, the straight nose, eyes, were *hers*. And now Fleur began to trace a dozen other endearing resemblances. The chin was her father's, the smile Hélène's. Yes, he was Lady Roddney's grandson with that strange magnetism that would make a woman love him (as Charlotte did) without hope of reward, for love's sake alone.

All the starved years of her repressed motherhood seemed to fall away from Fleur Marsh. It was with a sob of complete fulfilment that she held her arms out to Dominic.

"My son," she said, her voice breaking, "My dear boy — "

Speechlessly he fell at her feet and laid his head against her knee. The strong man was not ashamed of his tears. He kissed one of Fleur's frail delicate hands repeatedly. For the first time uttered that sacred name:

"*My mother!*"

It was a long time before either of them became calm or practical. There was so much to be said. After a while, Dominic sat beside the beautiful old lady and drank in every word she said. He knew nothing of his father or his inheritance. He wanted to hear everything. It was a staggering revelation — the history of Cadlington, with its great Tower, which had been burned down on the day that his grandfather ran Denzil St. Cheviot through the heart, the poignant story of Fleur's own marriage, the dramatic events that had led up to his — Dominic's birth.

After a moment Dominic said:

"You have endured more than most human beings could bear, my poor little mother. You must have had immense courage."

"It was Peveril who helped me through it. It is to him I owe everything."

"Then I, too, am beholden to him, and could want for no finer stepfather."

"How strange that sounds," sighed Fleur. "Only the other day when he heard me sigh, he guessed that it was because I had always missed the little child whom I thought had perished. It is strange, Dominic, but I seem to feel no ill will towards you because you are St. Cheviot's son."

"I pray not," said Dominic and raised his mother's hand to his lips, "for you will from now onward, in unison with Charlotte Chase, become the light of my life. I shall always be fond of the mother who adopted me; ever grateful, also to the Marquess who gave me my chances in life. But blood is thicker than water, and you are truly *mine*."

"My darling," whispered Fleur, her eyes brimming with tears.

Dominic stood up. Walking to the window, he looked out at the grounds. He felt dazed. He had felt so ever since seeing William Smith yesterday. He went on talking to Fleur.

"In time to come, there is much more that I must know. This native blood of mine, I am curious about it. I had always imagined myself Spanish or Italian, perhaps, but *African* — no!"

"Let it not displease you, my dear," said Fleur gently, "your African great-great-grandfather was, so I was told, a fine and noble man. There is no disgrace in your ancestry."

"And my grandmother — Lady Roddney — showed no sign of it?"

"None. Like me she was white-skinned and red-haired, except that she had very dark eyes."

"Strange," muttered Dominic. "So it was I, alone, who reverted to type, after three generations."

Fleur stretched out her hand.

"Do not let that disturb you, Dominic. I remember the poor old doctor who delivered me, telling me one day when we were discussing this question of black blood, that it was not likely ever to happen again. The time is past. *Your* children when you marry should be one hundred per cent European. And, dear Dominic, you do not *look* native — but Spanish, or Italian, or Greek perhaps. With those intensely blue eyes you might be truly an Englishman who has been much in the East."

"If I resemble *you*, it is enough," he said. "I am the most fortunate man on earth to have found such a beautiful, gentle mother."

"Your father — " she began and stopped.

"My father seems to have been an unpleasant fellow," said Dominic with a grim smile.

"In some way he resembled Vivian Chase," she sighed. "Yet Denzil *had* noble blood in him. He was a fine sportsman and a man of tremendous courage. There was only one swordsman in Europe to match him and that was my father, Harry Roddney."

Fleur's heart thrilled. Old and frail though she was, even today the indomitable spirit of Hélène Roddney burned in her blood. She was proud, proud to look at this splendid serious-minded man whom Charlotte loved and know that he was her son.

"Dominic," she said as though she found the word sweet, "*Dominic* — I like that name. *Unwin*, too, has served you well. But you must, in future, bear your rightful title. You will take this story to my family solicitors. The Cadlington estates must be returned to you, as well as the immense fortune which Denzil left and which I as his widow refused to touch. But *you* are Dominic St. Cheviot. Thus the full circle comes around! By some strange chance, yours are the same initials as his. '*D. St. C.*' Once more there is a Baron of Cadlington. The best and noblest of them all," Fleur added softly.

It was at this juncture that Charlotte and Peveril came into the room. They had met in the hall, each on their way to join Fleur for tea.

When Charlotte saw the tall man in grey her heart jolted. All the misery and anxiety of the past few days dropped from her shoulders.

"Dominic," she said in a strangled voice.

He took her hand, looking at her wan sweet face with great tenderness. Now that he saw her again, he knew how much he had wanted this reunion. It did not seem to matter what evil Vivian Chase was scheming, what devil's brew he had in store for them.

Silently they regarded each other. Heart and soul were in that gaze.

Peveril walked to his wife's side. Shocked, he saw that her lashes were wet.

"My dearest, something has happened to upset you — " he began.

She squeezed his hand and interrupted.

"No, but listen, my beloved, for I have astounding news for you — news, that will, I think, thrill you, for my sake. Dominic — " she turned to address her new-found son — "take Charlotte into the garden. It is fine and warm. Walk with her awhile and tell her what you have just told me. I will repeat it all to Peveril."

Still holding hands, Charlotte and Dominic walked out into the sunlight.

29

THE story that Dominic related to Charlotte left her amazed and delighted.

"How *wonderful!*" she exclaimed, "to know you are the son of one who has been such a dear friend to me."

Dominic and Charlotte were sitting in the arbour that faced the ornamental lake; that same arbour in which Dominic's grand-parents had sat hand in hand, fifty years ago.

Dominic played with one of Charlotte's fine long hands. He looked at it thoughtfully.

"Do you find it repellent that four generations back there was African blood in my family?"

"Of course not," she said indignantly, "why should I?"

"There are those who would be put off."

"Not I. We are all God's children — black or white — and, dear Dominic, there are thousands of people who must be ignorant about their origin. Who amongst us can boast of pure unbroken lineage? Besides — I like you as you are. I love the essential man in you. I respected you as Dominic Unwin. I revere you neither more nor less because you have become the Baron of Cadlington."

He kissed her hand fervently.

"That title falls strangely on my ear. I have yet to get accustomed to it."

"In a way it takes you further from me," she said on a sudden note of sadness. For up till now she had been excited and happy, concentrating on his personal news.

"Why so," he asked, "on the contrary you should feel nearer because I am Mrs. Marsh's son."

She bit her lip and did not reply. He saw her shiver as she turned and gazed with melancholy across the sun-gilded lake.

"You are thinking of our invidious position, and of your children," he asked gently.

"Yes," she nodded, "all day, ever since I last saw you, I have been worrying about Eleanora. The days have seemed like years because I have no notion of what is going on at Clunes."

"Poor little Charlotte."

"Do not pity me," she said with a strangled sob, "for I have repeatedly blamed myself that you are tied up with me in this beastliness. Vivian has already made the news public. Yes, we have heard echoes of it down here. London is, I am sure, buzzing with the disgraceful scandal."

"It is," said Dominic grimly.

Charlotte looked at him with eyes full of love and a profound humility.

"Whatever happens, do not hold this against me," she begged. "*I* would have died rather than allow a shadow to fall upon *your* name."

"Hush, child," he said, "I have repeatedly told you that I never blame you; that I am happy to stand by your side in your tribulation."

"But Dominic — " began Charlotte.

"No," he interrupted, "say no more, beloved, for I tell you here and now that if Lord Chase is instrumental in ruining my good name — I shall not let it eat into my heart like a festering sore. That heart is too full now of the thought of you — and my mother. Let it be remembered that I am Baron of Cadlington — a St. Cheviot — and a Roddney. These are powerful names, and I have a new birthright, a proud heritage that will enable me to defeat Vivian Chase. Yes, no matter what he does to me. There remains not only my unflinching desire to retrieve the good reputation of the St. Cheviots that my father lost but my wish to protect you and restore you to your children."

He covered one of her hands between two of his. Tenderly he regarded her. She wore a fringed cashmere shawl borrowed from Fleur, and the tobacco-coloured travelling dress which she had put on before she left Clunes. Sorrow was engraved on her features. The cheek bones jutted out a little. The eyes were enormous and heavily shadowed. Yet there sat upon her still, he thought, that air of innocence, of unworldliness, that made her look so young despite her harrowing experiences.

"My dearest," he said, "the more that

I am with you, the more do I feel that I would like you to drop your defence of the case and let your husband do his worst. Then, when the case is over, we could be married."

The burning colour swept her face.

"You have said that before but I must always answer in the same way. Never, never, can I be instrumental in taking you from the work you love."

"But child, I have grown to love *you* more — far more — than my work."

She bent her head and passionately kissed the firm strong hands imprisoning her own.

"I love you, Dominic, dear, *dear* Dominic. I worship you, but I must be strong and so must you. Emotion might lead you in this crisis to feel that you would gladly abandon your career for me. But there would come a day when you would regret it. It can never be."

The touch of her fresh young lips against his fingers thrilled him and filled him with a strange humility. He took her head between those hands which she kissed and raised it. He looked deeply into her eyes.

"My beloved Charlotte — unselfish to the end. You cannot love me more than I do you. That love has become an integral part of my existence. And ever a wonder and amazement," he added, "for I am an old man compared with you."

"I want no more of other men," she said. "And to me you are young and all that my heart desires. But, oh, Dominic, I can see nothing but separation ahead of us."

"My darling child, how can I ever let you go back to that hell on earth at Clunes?" he muttered, rising to his feet. She too, rose and stood beside him. His arm gathered her close. In silence they looked across the lake and beyond to the fringe of silver birches, so delicately green, bearing the first buds of spring. She said:

"At this moment, I, too, feel that I could not bear to go back. But for my children's sake, particularly for Eleanora's, I must. I have no choice. Besides I do not feel I ought to leave poor little Beatrice and Victoria to grow up with *him*. For he will train them to be as he is — selfish, cold, worldly — "

"If he loses the case, I have no doubt you could plead and prove cruelty, and get a judicial separation."

"Gertrude, my personal maid, would certainly witness what I have been through," she nodded.

"On Monday I shall see my lawyer again and ask him to travel down here and talk with you and hear your side of things," said Dominic. Then he took her into his arms. "Meanwhile, my dearest, know that I love you above all things," he said and kissed her on the mouth.

Her hungry heart responded to that kiss. Her lips clung to his while her two hands clasped his neck. This was the fulfilment of all her dreams. This was love as she had always wanted it; far, far removed from Vivian's gross appetite. But that warm generous heart of hers was near to breaking as she walked with Dominic back to the house. They must not meet in the future, except before the stern eye of their legal adviser. And

Dominic must not come down to Pillars again until the case was heard.

"There is, of course, a chance that Lord Chase will drop it," Dominic said finally.

"I do not think so," said Charlotte in a low voice, "not while he thinks that there is a chance of perpetrating a final act of injustice upon me."

"We shall see," said Dominic gruffly, "little more and I shall seek him and fight it out with him in person, for my blood grows hot at the mere thought of all that he has done to you."

But Charlotte paused and looked up at him with eyes full of fear.

"I implore you not to go near Vivian," she breathed. "There would be a fight. He would try to kill you, as he threatened to do at Clunes, then present himself to the world as the outraged husband. Oh, *no*, Dominic, do not risk that for my sake — or for your *mother*'s."

"What must he not do for my sake?" came from Fleur Marsh gaily. She had heard Charlotte's last words as the couple entered the hall, for she, herself, was coming to look for them and tell them that tea was served.

She looked radiant, and wore a posy of yellow primroses pinned to her dress. Peveril had just picked them for her in the woods where they had walked and talked together of this new and wonderful thing that had come about.

"That word '*mother*' falls very musically upon my ear," she said looking almost shyly at her tall strong son.

Dominic took one of her hands and bending over it, kissed it.

"My dear little mother, you have all my homage," he said huskily.

The old artist, who had joined the group, put his hands in his pockets and stared with some astonishment and curiosity at Dominic Unwin. The even tenor of existence at Pillars had indeed been disturbed by the news that had been brought here this morning. Peveril could scarcely believe it. Yet he, too, could not doubt that this was Fleur's son. For now he saw that it was with her violet-blue eyes that Dominic looked at him. The eyes that Peveril had admired so greatly when, as a youth, he had first grown to love Fleur St. Cheviot.

When she had first broken the shattering news to him, he had reflected how vastly interesting it was to know that her unfortunate babe had not after all perished at birth. A relief to know that Dominic had grown into this fine and noble man. For Peveril could not recall one thing that he had liked about the late Baron of Cadlington. Strange, *strange*, to look now at Dominic's darkly tanned face, the fine resolute features, and even mark the resemblance — (yes it was there) — to Denzil St. Cheviot himself. What a mad fool Denzil had been to disown such a son. As for the hue of his skin, he was by no means negroid — far from it. And had not Lord Salisbury, himself, said that Dominic was 'a shining light in the House'?

Peveril, artist and dreamer, was not one to concern himself with worldly affairs. But he knew well enough the gravity of the present situation. He knew that it would not be good for Dominic's future if Lord Chase was granted his divorce. No matter how much they loved each other, the 'guilty' pair would be outlawed by society. And that would hurt Fleur who was Dominic's mother as well as Charlotte's friend.

Well, it was no good jumping the fence before coming to it, Peveril decided, and held out a hand to Dominic who grasped it warmly.

"I welcome you as a stepson," said Peveril with his delightful smile, "and I must now be permitted to use these old eyes of mine and paint your portrait, before they fail. Incidentally one of the finest full length portraits I painted in my life was of your own father at Cadlington. I remember well the black St. Cheviots. The hair and brows of your ancestors are yours. A pity my painting was burnt with the rest of the treasures."

Dominic smiled and smoothed his greying hair.

"I thank you, sir, for your kindly welcome and for all that you have ever done for my mother."

"She is utterly happy to have her son restored to her so miraculously," said Peveril.

From that hour onward the two men were destined to be great friends. Charlotte's heart was full as she walked beside Fleur into the drawing-room. That night there was a festive dinner party at Pillars. Mother and son appeared radiantly happy in their discovery of each other, and could not stop talking. Peveril had ordered his choicest wine to be served. Toasts were drunk and speeches made. And from the walls of the beautiful, panelled room there smiled the painted faces of Sir Harry Roddney as a boy in hunting attire, and of Fleur's lovely mother in her radiant youth. Looking now at Hélène Roddney's face, Charlotte could trace a very strong resemblance to 'La Belle Hélène's' grandson.

There was much talk about Cadlington and the old title and estates and how Dominic would at once visit his mother's lawyers and set about proving his identity and attending to the legal side of the matter.

It should all have been so splendid, so perfect, Charlotte thought as she listened and, now and again, exchanged long significant glances with Dominic. But, alas, the shadow of the unpredictable future remained to chill the warmth of her own gay spirit. Was she, she wondered, destined never to know peace of mind or respite from suffering?

To her sad question there could be no answer on that unforgettable day.

30

A DARK shadow hung over Clunes. In the great kitchen, sitting at the long scrubbed wooden table which was the pride of her life, Mrs. Snook, the cook, discussed matters in a sombre way with her friend the housekeeper, Mrs. MacDougal. The other servants were busy at their work, for the master was expected home to dinner tonight.

A plump duck was roasting. Vegetables were now being prepared in the adjoining scullery. Volpo, who usually arrived before his master, had just been down to tell the staff to put the best foot forward. His lordship had weighty matters on his mind and needed a good dinner. Tomorrow he would be entertaining a large house party, but tonight he was alone. "Not very well, and going to bed early," Volpo had observed with a sly wink at Mrs. Snook.

The cook sat with her arms crossed, gossiping.

"*Not very well!* H'm! *that* means the drink again," she said with pursed lips.

"Aye, it's been a turrible time since her ladyship flitted," agreed Mrs. MacDougal.

They had discussed Charlotte's disappearance from Clunes *ad nauseam*. All the servants here felt pity for her ladyship. Those who served her had received nothing but kindness from Lady Chase. His lordship's charm was less frequently displayed and then, as a rule, only for the younger and prettier maid servants. He had many times stormed abuse at Mrs. Snook if the meal was not to his liking.

Volpo had told them that her ladyship was a wanton and had gone off with a fine gentleman in politics and that she would never be seen at Clunes again.

The two senior members of the female staff could not believe this possible. But Volpo assured them that he had both *seen* and *heard*, and would be giving evidence for his lordship. Neither Mrs. Snook nor Mrs. MacDougal were happy about it. They were both righteous, God-fearing women who could not approve of infidelity. But her ladyship was angelic.

She could *not* be guilty. They would hand in their notice. They intended to follow Gertrude — poor Gertrude who had already gone — dismissed at a moment's notice.

"I don't like what's going on here," announced Mrs. Snook with a nod and a compression of her lips, "and one person I cannot abide is that hoity-toity Nanna who has come back to torment poor Miss Eleanora."

"Aye," said the Scotswoman and sighed heavily. "That puir wee lassie. I saw her face this morning, all puffed up with crying for her Mam. It isn't Christian to treat her as his lordship is doing. They say he yelled at her and slapped her because she kept greeting for my lady. It's only natural for the bairn to do so."

"I'd like to know the ins and outs of it," said the cook. Leaning forward she whispered over her tea-cup, "Take it from me, Mrs. Mac, that slimy valet knows more than he tells *us*. But you know Emmy, that girl we had as under housemaid — the one who was fetched away by her mother because of her condition? — "

"Aye," said Mrs. MacDougal in a shocked voice. "The puir creature, Emmy, and she only sixteen."

"I warrant from what Volpo said that it was the *master*!" declared Mrs. Snook, sniffing.

"I shall be glad to get away from this place and back to ma native Scotland where there are no such carryings-on," said Mrs. MacDougal.

It was a warm spring evening, with a slight drizzle casting a veil across the beautiful gardens of Clunes. Shortly after six o'clock Vivian Chase, driven from Harling station in his brougham, entered the house. He was in a foul temper, having had several nights of drinking and gambling in London where he would have preferred to remain; but convention ruled that he must return home and be with his children. After all, he was supposed to be the sorrowing husband, left to console the abandoned little ones. He would be judged accordingly if he, too, deserted them.

Until the divorce was over and Charlotte ruined once and for all, he must, he suppose, retain an air of respectability.

But he had arranged for several of his more amusing friends to come down this weekend and liven up what he called 'this tombstone of a house'. As soon as he was free of Charlotte, he intended to shut the place up and go abroad for a long while.

Everything got on his nerves down at Clunes. When Nanna brought the three little girls to bid him good night, he stood in front of the library fireplace, fingers locked behind his back, and looked at them with complete lack of humour or paternal warmth. He was irritated even by his pets, the golden-haired Beatrice and Victoria who kissed him prettily and prattled about their games. His brooding gaze rested on his eldest child. Heavens, what a little sight she had grown since her mother left! According to the nurse, the wretched brat never stopped weeping. Her eyes were swollen, her face was pinched and she had a furtive hang-dog look that destroyed her natural childish charm. She trembled when he spoke to her. In consequence, he bellowed and frightened her still more.

"Smile, damn you! What the devil is

the matter with you? Anybody would think you were ill-treated in this house where you have everything you want, and for which mark you, miss, I pay handsomely."

The nurse stood by looking at his lordship under her drooping lids. She, herself, had lost all patience with Eleanora. At first she had tried to be kind to her because she was sorry for the child, and had stretched a point and allowed her to talk, upstairs, about her mother, which his lordship had strictly forbidden. All Eleanora could do was to beg to be allowed to go to Mama. Gradually the woman lost patience and a great deal of slapping and bullying went on.

Eleanora pressed her fingers to her lips. Her huge weary eyes scrutinized her father with a mixture of terror and defiance. She was so confused by what had happened that she could not attain any degree of peace or understanding. All her security had gone. She had been so happy with Mama. It had given her a hideous jolt when she had run gaily along to the bedroom that fatal morning and found Papa, alone.

Vivian glared at her. Now that he could no longer vent his spite on Charlotte, his ill-temper, inflamed with constant drinking and debauchery, was directed against Charlotte's best-loved daughter.

"Answer me!" he snarled at her, "Why do you not smile at me?"

She shrank back but dared to utter the words that were ever foremost in her bemused little mind.

"I want to see my Mama. When is my Mama coming home?"

The ugly colour rushed to Vivian's flabby face. He raised a hand as though to strike the innocent little girl, then let it fall.

"You will never see your Mama again! Get that into your stubborn mind and learn, also, to be agreeable to your Papa," he said in a furious voice.

Eleanora buried her face in her hands and began to sob in a terrified way. The nurse hustled the three little girls out of the library, and up the stairs.

Vivian pulled the tapestried bell. When the butler appeared, he snapped:

"Bring brandy, then send Volpo to me."

"Yes, my lord. What time would your lordship like to dine?"

"I shall not be dining at home. It depresses me," said Vivian who had in that moment decided that he would go down to Roma Gresham's house and try to find some amusement. He was beginning to pity himself and even foster a belief that he was, indeed, an outraged husband deserving sympathy and consolation. That *bitch*, Charlotte, he thought venomously, no doubt she was with her friends Fleur and Peveril Marsh, if not with her lover. As for *him* Vivian had received through his lawyers an ice-cold but telling missive from Dominic Unwin, suggesting that he intended to fight this case to the bitter end and prove both his own and Charlotte's innocence. He had added that once that was done, he would be glad to meet Lord Chase in person, and fight a duel with whatever weapons Lord Chase cared to choose.

Duel, indeed, Vivian had snorted when he read this letter. He had no intention whatsoever of indulging in a hand to hand combat with Mr. Unwin. A shot in the back was one thing, but a duel in which he, Vivian, might be the loser, was another.

That was last week. Whilst in London and at the Clubs or walking down Piccadilly, Vivian had raised his hat to several distinguished ladies and gentlemen and been put out when they looked the other way. It would seem that a great deal of sympathy was directed towards Charlotte and Mr. Unwin, which was displeasing to Vivian; it was no part of his scheme that *he* should be ostracised, rather than Charlotte and Dominic. And now had come this new excitement over Dominic's real identity — an unpleasant shock for Vivian. Dominic had made inquiries and proved to the hilt the fact that he was no foundling adopted by the Englesbys, risen to fame only through brains and wit. He was lawful son and heir of the late Baron of Cadlington and of *Fleur Marsh*, formerly widow of the Baron. As Dominic St. Cheviot, he owned a great title and vast estates all of which he was claiming.

Whichever way the wind blew, it seemed to Vivian that Charlotte might get the best of it. He had hoped to make an outcast, a divorcée, of her and ruin Mr. Unwin's career. But the career would be of secondary importance now to a gentleman possessed of an older title and bigger fortune than Vivian's own.

These facts had only been disclosed to Vivian last night and so accounted for his ugly humour this evening.

When Volpo came into the library in his stealthy way, Vivian, who had started to drink brandy, snarled at him:

"I wish to get out of my travelling attire. Have the hip bath taken to my dressing-room," he snapped. "And my dinner clothes laid out. I intend to call on an old friend."

Volpo put his tongue in his cheek. So long had he served my Lord Chase now that he knew perfectly well who the 'old friend' was likely to be.

Cook was ranting and carrying on in her kitchen because the splendid meal she had prepared for his lordship was no longer wanted. Volpo, at this moment, felt scarcely more agreeable than Vivian. He had had a 'few words' with his master in London yesterday, for the first time since he had entered his service. Volpo had served his master well by arranging that evening with Mr. Unwin and so helping to get rid of my lady. No other servant would have thought of such a scheme or carried it out with such cunning. And what had been his reward? Nothing so far but a miserly present of five sovereigns. Last night Volpo had suggested that he would like a little more and Vivian had told him to go to the devil.

At this moment Volpo looked moodily at his Lordship, Vivian, stretched in a chair, glowered back at his valet,

"Well — what is it — what are you gaping at me for?"

Volpo cleared his throat.

"Just a slight matter of finance, my lord."

"Finance!" echoed Vivian and then flung back his head and laughed. "I see! Another request for money. You insolent fellow, are you stooping to blackmail? Is that it? Do I not pay you handsomely enough for your meagre services? Get out — run to your duties. I want my bath."

But Volpo stood his ground. He was not afraid of his master. *He knew too much*. His hot Portuguese temper could be aroused as easily as Vivian's.

"Your lordship fails to recall that without my services which he dubs 'meagre', her ladyship would still be here to nag and annoy him. Also that — "

"Get out!" interrupted Vivian, showing his teeth.

"But my lord, I have a right to demand payment for what I have done," began Volpo indignantly. "It was a dangerous action. It still has danger attached to it. Everyone in London says Mr. Unwin is very angry and I shall be called upon to commit perjury on behalf of your lordship when the case is heard."

On normal occasions, Vivian would have seen the truth in this and behaved with more discretion; for after all Volpo was his confederate. But things were not going as he wanted, and, when Vivian was crossed, he lost all powers of reasoning. In maniacal rage he flung the glass of brandy straight at the valet's face. The hunchback ducked but not quite in time. The glass hit his forehead and shattered. The brandy splashed half blinding him. He gave a cry of pain and clapped his hands to his face.

"Get out, reptile!" shouted Vivian. "Do not let me see you again tonight or hear you mention what you have done for me. Remember only what *I* have done for *you*, you insolent Portuguese cripple!"

Silence. Volpo cowered back, whimpering, trying to wipe his eyes with his handkerchief and to staunch a trickle of blood on his forehead. He was hurt but not badly. The true hurt was in his mind. He swung from a servile devotion to his master to burning and implacable hatred. He could see that he was not to be rewarded as he had anticipated, for services rendered to Lord Chase. Very well. Let his lordship rave, and insult him. He would live to regret it.

Vivian had not bargained with the spirited blood that ran in Volpo's veins. The hot blood of a Latin who knows the real meaning of the word *vendetta*.

The hunchback turned on his heel and walked quietly out of the library, the handkerchief held to his face. Vivian did not see him again before he left Clunes and was on his way to Roma Gresham's establishment.

The early drizzle of the day had cleared up and and a glorious night followed with a full moon. After his bath, Vivian felt in a better humour. Seeing that it was so fine, he went on foot to Roma Gresham's house, walking through the grounds of his home, through the orchard and out of the little gate into those very woods wherein he had seduced young Charlotte Goff more than ten years ago.

His mind was far removed from her, however, and concentrating upon the anticipation of an amusing evening *chez* Roma; a new love, a new thrill to while away the night. He did not like to be alone, or to think too much. What little conscience he possessed had a habit of waking when he was by himself. The memory of his dead mother and his living wife returned to trouble and upbraid him. He knew himself infinitely guilty towards both.

In the moonlight, impeccably dressed in the latest fashion, a diamond pin flashing in his cravat, a cigar between his fingers, golden hair pomaded, fair moustache curled, he looked handsome and attractive. Vivian Chase at his best. Almost the romantic boy to whom little Charlotte Goff had given her heart.

He reached the gates of Mrs. Gresham's house and strolled through, unaware of the fact that he had been followed all the way from Clunes by the deformed figure of his man, Volpo. Volpo walked stealthily and silently like a cat. He kept in the shadows until the very moment that Lord Chase reached the front door of Mrs. Gresham's discreet establishment which was heavily shuttered and curtained for the night. Then the hand of vengeance struck. Under cover of the portico, Vivian reached out towards the knocker, but never touched it.

He felt a sharp and terrifying pain between his shoulder blades. He uttered a cry of pain and fear that was stifled in its birth. The cigar dropped from his fingers. He crumpled up in a heap, passing from full pulsating life into an impenetrable blackness, the anguish of sudden and violent death.

Without a backward look at the figure of the man who had called him an insolent Portuguese cripple, Volpo turned and ran out of sight. He made his way back to Clunes as quickly as he had come. Within the next few moments, wearing an apron, he was in the pantry, cleaning his lordship's shoes; making a noise, talking to the other sleepy servants so that they should notice him and be ready to swear if necessary that he had never left the house.

It was Mrs. Gresham herself who found Vivian. She had a Siamese cat which she wished to let out. As she walked out of the house she stumbled over something. With a cry of horror, she saw a man wearing evening dress and an opera cloak lying across the steps. Roma let the cat fly from her arms and set up a scream which brought her servants hurrying out to her. They turned the body over. As Roma Gresham saw the bloodless face, the dishevelled fair hair, the clenched teeth grinning hideously in the moonlight, she shrieked again.

"Oh, God, *it is Lord Chase*!"

She could see that he was dead. This was the last time he would ever come to her house to dine and wine with her 'friends' (and pay handsomely for the pleasure of it!).

How he had died, she knew only when one of the servants lifted his hand and she saw that it was covered with blood. The butler muttered:

"There is a wound in his back. It looks like murder, madam."

At that, Roma Gresham foresaw appalling scandal and herself and her hideaway implicated. She would be ruined. One of the gentlemen who had been dining with her came out to see what was afoot, and was just in time to catch his hostess as she fainted dead away.

31

SOON after nine o'clock next morning, a man on horseback galloped up to the front door of Pillars. He slid from his sweating animal and knocked loudly on the door.

Charlotte heard the knocking. She had been awake for a long time, tormented by her longings both for Eleanora and for Dominic. She, like Mrs. Marsh, usually breakfasted in bed. But on this particular day the countryside looked so beautiful, with an amber sun breaking through the mists, that Charlotte rose and dressed.

She was halfway down the staircase when Fleur's maid way-laid her and told her that Jameson, a stable boy from Clunes, had come with an urgent note for her.

Charlotte's golden eyes widened with astonishment. Her colour heightened.

"I will see him at once," she said.

She had written three days ago to Mrs.

554

MacDougal; a short piteous note begging for news of the children.

Now that Gertrude has left, I must rely on you to help me and to believe me that I am innocent of the accusations directed against me, she had said. *Pity a mother's torn heart and send me news of my daughters. If you have the opportunity, tell Eleanora that her Mama did not desert her. With all my heart I implore you not to betray this confidence to his lordship.*

There was a wild hope in Charlotte's heart that Mrs. Mac had taken pity on her and sent Jameson with a reply.

The tow-headed stable boy looked curiously at his one-time mistress, touched his forehead, and handed her the note. Charlotte's heart began to knock even before she slit open the envelope which was addressed to her in a somewhat illiterate hand.

"Mrs. Mac sent me with this," said Jameson, "I would have come earlier, my lady, but Firefly lost a shoe and I had to stop at the smithy at Epping."

Charlotte did not reply. Scanning Mrs. Mac's letter, her face went ashen. The terrible news made her feel sick. Two lines only:

Come home at once, my lady. His lordship has been murdered.
                    Flora MacDougal.

Charlotte, shaking from head to foot, stared at the stable boy.

"Do you know the contents of this letter?" she gasped.

"Yes, my lady, 'tis a turrible thing."

"But what happened? Tell me all you know."

"I don't know nothing, my lady, save his lordship was found wi' a knife wound in his back."

"A knife wound in his back," repeated Charlotte.

She swayed and had to catch at the lintel of the door by which she was standing.

"*Merciful heavens!*" she whispered.

The boy went on to say that first thing this morning, Mrs. Mac had sent a pantry-boy to rouse him, and bidden him ride his fastest to Epping. Mrs. Mac had received her ladyship's note. She knew where to find her. Last night his lordship had gone out to dine, Jameson volunteered, and the police had brought his dead body back to Clunes just before midnight. When Charlotte questioned him further, she presumed that Dr. Castleby had seen Vivian. He said that the knife had gone straight through the heart. Most of the maid servants were in hysterics. Mr. Volpo, the valet, refused to leave his master's body and had been weeping over it ever since.

Charlotte bade Jameson go through to the servants' quarters and get a meal and a glass of ale. She then rushed upstairs to Mrs. Marsh's bedroom. She threw herself beside Fleur's bed.

"Vivian is dead. He is *dead*," she cried, breathing fast, Mrs. Mac's letter crumpled in her hands.

When Fleur discovered what had happened, she turned as pale as her friend, but in her practical way called for Peveril to fetch brandy, for Charlotte looked ghastly. It had been a terrible shock to her.

"Keep calm, my dearest," begged Mrs. Marsh, "do not give way. Yes, Vivian is dead. Someone whom he has injured, has taken his revenge."

"But who — who could have hated him as much as that?"

"It remains to be seen."

"*I* hated him, but *murder* — the very word fills my soul with horror."

"You must go at once to Clunes, to your children," said Fleur. "I will send a message to my coachman. He shall take you."

Charlotte stood up. Some of the colour returned to her cheeks.

"Yes, I must go to my children," she breathed.

Mingling with the sense of shock and dismay came a sense of overwhelming relief. *Vivian was dead.* She was free. Without divorce, or any act of law, she had been set free from the tyrant who had tried so monstrously to destroy her life's happiness.

She could go back to Clunes — *to Eleanora.* There would be no one to stop her. Unhampered, she could deliver her poor daughter from that dreadful nurse and restore her childish faith. Unhampered, she could seek to control Beatrice and Victoria, too; and, with God's help, mould their little characters into a rightful way of life, as Vivian would never have done. She was free — *free to love Dominic*.

The reaction was almost too much for Charlotte. She flung herself into her friend's arms, and the two women wept together.

Stroking Charlotte's head, Fleur whispered:

"I will write at once to my son and bid him come here to see you. Do what has to be done at Clunes, and after the funeral return to Pillars. Bring your little girls with you. I know a nurse in the village who is kind and devoted and who will look after them."

Charlotte kissed one of Fleur's frail hands. She loved Fleur Marsh more than ever, for was she not Dominic's own mother?

"You can be sure I shall come back as soon as I can for this is more truly my home than Clunes has ever been," she said.

But there was much to be gone through before a new day could obliterate the black night of Charlotte Chase's long martyrdom.

She reached her house on this ironically lovely morning and found the beautiful house that Eleanor, Lady Chase, had loved so much under a sinister shadow. The master of Clunes was laid out in his bedroom, still and rigid under a white sheet. The blinds were down at all the windows. Except for the sound of weeping and whispering as the staff tip-toed around, there was silence. The silence of death.

Charlotte's first action was to fling off her bonnet and coat run straight upstairs to the nurseries.

"Eleanora," she whispered, "*Eleanora*!"

Nurse had gone. According to Mrs. Mac who had taken charge here in her sensible Scots fashion, the woman as soon as she knew his lordship was dead, had abandoned her charges and taken the first train from Harling. A young nursery maid remained in charge of the three little girls.

Eleanora was in bed with a slight fever.

Beatrice and Victoria had gone out with the nursemaid to pick wild flowers.

"Best to get them away from the house, your ladyship," Mrs. Mac observed.

"Thank you," said Charlotte in a strangled voice, "and thank you for all you have done for me. You shall be rewarded."

Mrs. Mac bobbed.

"I am sure we are all pleased to see your ladyship back," she said and dabbed at her eyes.

A cry rose from Eleanora's little bed as she saw the beautiful, pale-faced woman who ran across the big bedroom towards her.

"Mama! Mama!" the child cried in a frenzied voice and held out her arms.

"My darling! Oh, Ellie, my *darling*!" said Charlotte, and gathered the slight white-robed body to her heart. For a long time mother and daughter wept together. At last Eleanora said:

"I have been so miserable. Please, please, dearest Mama, never leave me again."

"Pray God I shall never have to," sighed Charlotte and laid a cool hand on the little girl's hot forehead.

Eleanora echoed the sigh.

"Now I will eat my dinner," she said. "My food kept sticking in my throat at mealtimes, Mama, and made me sick, and Nanna and Papa were cross. But today I will eat lots and lots because my own dear Mama is home again."

Mrs. Mac wiped a corner of her eye again with her frilly apron and went downstairs to tell Mrs. Snook that she had never witnessed a more affecting scene.

"And if my lady is guilty as a wife and mother, I'll eat my hat!" she exclaimed.

The two servants fell to gossiping in their usual way. Rumours were already spreading through the district that his lordship had met his death in a house of ill repute actually down *here*, in Harling.

"Serve him right," they said, "it was what he deserved." "Poor Mr. Volpo," they said. "Nobody liked him, but he seems in a bad way, so upset about his master."

Poor Mr. Volpo, had they but known it, was not so much upset as frightened. He had killed Lord Chase in a mad fit of rage. When the local police first questioned him, he had felt that he carried things off quite smoothly, and that nobody suspected that it was he who had stabbed his master. But there were gentlemen from Scotland Yard on their way down from London to investigate, and of them Volpo was a little more apprehensive.

He had buried the knife with which he had stabbed Vivian in the woods between here and Mrs. Gresham's house. He did not think it possible that he could be convicted but the Portuguese was at heart a coward. He swung from hatred to remorse. Some of the tears which he had shed in his lordship's bedroom by the side of the poor corpse had been genuine. For the most part he remained locked in his bedroom. Servants passing by, heard him alternately moaning and uttering prayers in his native Portuguese.

Came the moment when Charlotte had to stand beside Vivian's bed, which she did, leaning heavily on the arm of Dr. Castleby.

"He is at peace," muttered the old doctor.

At peace, thought Charlotte; yes, he who wrecked the peace in this house for me and for our first child. And God alone knows how many others he hurt.

At peace, foully murdered, yet now, how strangely young he looked! It was almost the Vivian whom she had first married. Thinned and spiritualized by death were those bloated features. The eyes were closed. The lips bore a slightly ironic smile as though Vivian Chase had found at last the answer to the riddle of the universe. He looked handsome and proud in death as a Chase should, Charlotte brooded. One of the women who had laid him out had put a posy of flowers between his folded hands. "*He makes a beautiful corpse,*" they said. But Charlotte saw no beauty in him, neither did his dead body soften her heart or draw from her a single tear. She knew only bitterness and that loathing for him in death that his terrible cruelties had aroused in her while he was alive. She could not forgive him — *yet*. She had put on the black garments and weeds of widowhood. The sunlight was shut out from this house; but Charlotte was no hypocrite. She could not mourn such a husband's passing. Her own torments she might have forgiven, but not Eleanora's.

As Dr. Castleby led her out of the death chamber, he said:

"It is to be hoped that Scotland Yard will find the murderer. It must have been somebody after money, although Lord Chase's wallet was found untouched, which is curious. Presumably the assassin was disturbed at his deed and fled."

Charlotte passed a handkerchief over her lips. She and the doctor were in the library now. On the desk were all the documents which she must hand over and sign, once the family solicitors arrived. She could see that there was much to be done. The doctor inquired anxiously after her health and suggested that she should go to bed; but Charlotte answered that she was well and able to perform her duties. Soon there would be an inspection by the London police who would take over the criminal investigations. Later, the funeral arrangements. No one of Vivian's relatives was left to mourn him except one of his old great aunts who was well over ninety-five and senile.

Dr. Castleby who had seen Charlotte through the births of all her daughters and the many illnesses in this house marvelled now at her coolness and composure.

He said nothing, but in his heart the old doctor was profoundly glad that my Lord Chase had died — even in so violent a manner. Lady Chase, poor pretty young thing, had had more than her share of suffering — and well Castleby knew it.

Late that afternoon Charlotte faced the Chief Inspector from the Criminal Investigation Department of Scotland Yard. He was soon satisfied that Lady Chase had nothing to do with the crime and had been staying at Epping at the time.

"We offer our deepest respect and sympathy, my lady," the chief inspector told her.

Charlotte moved into another wing of the house, taking her three daughters and the nursemaid with her. The little girls were too young to know what had taken place. They played happily in their room, or out in the gardens.

Over Eleanora had come a marked and rapid change. Her temperature fell. She lost her expression of strain and fear, but could scarcely bear to let her darling Mama out of her sight.

Charlotte bade her be good and read her books, or play card-games with her sisters who were behaving with greater friendliness now that Papa was not here to influence them against Eleanora.

Charlotte looked at the faces of the little girls and then away again. Beatrice's eyes were the turquoise blue of *his*. Charlotte reflected, '*I will have to train myself to forget the resemblance, and to love poor Beatrice and Victoria, as I do Eleanora.*'

★ ★ ★

It was some time before suspicion turned upon Vivian's personal servant. Volpo tried to answer the Chief Inspector's repeated questions with nonchalance, and failed. Finally he began to tremble and cry and dropped down in a kind of seizure. They carried him to his room. The detectives, discussing the matter with Lady Chase, suggested that it might well be the hand of a Latin rather than an

Englishman that had plunged the fatal knife between his lordship's shoulder blades. When the *post mortem* was carried out, it became obvious that the wound was caused by a long sharp kind of blade resembling a *stiletto*. The weapon was missing but the police were out with the dogs, continually and carefully examining every step of the pathway that led between Clunes and Mrs. Gresham's house.

Investigations were carried out at Roma Gresham's establishment, but it was decided that nobody there was guilty of the crime. The crime, in the Inspector's opinion, had been committed by one at Clunes who knew his lordship's intentions to visit that house, and had followed him. *Who else but his personal valet*, whose answers were so wild and unsatisfactory?

"Volpo was devoted to my husband — " began Charlotte.

The Inspector interrupted her.

True, Mr. Volpo was devoted but it must also be remembered that her ladyship had, in confidence, told the detectives that Mr. Volpo had plotted with his lordship to give false evidence about her own conduct. Was it not possible if this was a fact, that his lordship and Mr. Volpo might have fallen out over the question of money? Unsuccessful blackmail might, indeed, be the cause of the crime.

Before darkness fell upon Clunes, the Inspector had proved his point.

Charlotte had gone to lie down in a room shared with her beloved eldest child. Exhausted and overcome by the horror of the whole proceedings she tried to sleep and failed.

Vivian's body had been removed from Clunes. That had been a relief to her. This evening the former master of the house lay in a coffin covered with purple velvet drapes in the little church at Harling. She could not stop thinking about it. Of the horror of sudden and violent death. Somehow her mind would keep reverting to that day, years ago, when Vivian had been taken into the same church with a wound in his head, and imagined that he saw his own coffin there. Strange that it should have come to pass just as he visualized it.

Between her hands, Charlotte held a letter which she had received earlier in the day from the man who was now Lord St. Cheviot.

Beloved Charlotte,

Tomorrow, I travel to Pillars in order to be near you if you need me. At last a ray of light shines through the darkness. The hope that when these fearful days are over, you will come to me and allow me to take care of you for ever.

I love and revere you. I am with you in my heart and spirit during your present ordeal.

With my most tender affection,

Your Dominic.

Charlotte kissed this letter and mused about Dominic and his future. She was still too dazed to think clearly about her own. But it was good to know that Dominic with all his chivalry, his idealistic love, awaited her. And, whereas at one time she would have been shocked by the thought of his abandoning his political career as he now firmly declared

570

he would do, she realized that now, as the Baron of Cadlington, there would be other important work for him to do — his own estates in Buckinghamshire to be put in order and a new house to be built out of the ruins of Cadlington Hall, once his ancestral home.

It was six o'clock in the evening when one of the maids knocked on Lady Chase's door and told her that the Chief Inspector wished urgently to see her in the morning-room.

Very pale and spent, she went downstairs where the Inspector stood talking to two policemen in plain clothes. Then Charlotte saw the familiar hunch-backed figure of Vivian's valet. He was crouched in a chair, his head in his hands. His wrists were manacled.

Charlotte uttered a cry. Volpo raised his head. His face was ghastly, yellowish in hue, sweating. His black eyes rolled at her. He fell upon the floor, and grovelled at her feet.

"My lady, my lady, forgive me, intercede for me, do not let them hang me!" he babbled, obviously in a state of wild terror.

Charlotte recoiled as he caught at her black skirts.

"What is this?" she demanded.

The Chief Inspector informed her that they had just arrested Volpo for the murder of her husband. Right from the start, after his first investigation, the detective had suspected the Portuguese. Volpo had not been very clever in his efforts to conceal his crime. Two glaring clues led to his final arrest. A pair of shoes belonging to him, and found in his room, were still damp; with wet leaves similar to those strewing the pathway through the woods, clinging to the soles.

Then, an hour ago, one of the police dogs had picked up the scent and led them to the dagger which the Portuguese had buried in those same woods. On the blade they had found not only traces of blood, but Volpo's initials. It was an Italian-type stiletto. It had been identified as belonging to him. Several of the other manservants at Clunes had often seen it in Volpo's possession.

All was easy after that. At first the valet attempted to make denials, but finally broke down and confessed to the crime.

While the Inspector took down notes, Volpo croaked out the whole story, adding his personal reasons for the murder.

So at last, Charlotte, white and silent, heard of the infamous pact he had made with Vivian to ruin her. The note that Charlotte was supposed to have sent, had been written *by Volpo* himself. She was told the whole sordid story.

"I will confess it to the judge," babbled Volpo, "but do not let them hang me, my lady. You are good and kind. His lordship was out of his mind — stark raving mad. He tortured you. I will swear to it, if you will only ask them to spare my life."

But Charlotte hid her face in her hands and could not answer. It was all too terrible. They took Volpo away. She was left alone and soon a great calm seemed to descend upon her — and Clunes. A sense of thankfulness. The full circle had come round. Not only was she free from Vivian, but Dominic's good name — and her own — would be cleared.

Tomorrow, Volpo would be charged in court with the murder of his master.

His confession would be read. The newspapers would blazen forth the facts, and not a soul in London but would soon know that Lord St. Cheviot and Charlotte Chase were guiltless, victims of a madman's desire for revenge and a servant's treachery.

For a long time after the detectives had left Clunes, Charlotte sat alone in the morning-room, thinking — trying to re-orientate her emotions — to believe that she was indeed freed from evil, liberated from pain.

Beside the fireplace there hung a miniature of Vivian's mother as a girl, with curls falling upon a snowy bosom and large eyes shining. Charlotte gazed at it. Involuntarily, she thought: *"Eleanora will look like that when she is sixteen — "* And she whispered:

"Dearest Lady Chase, the only mother I ever knew, maybe in your spirit world you have already received the soul of your erring son. Maybe your tears, your prayers, will save him from eternal damnation. Who is to know? But this I promise you — that the Clunes which you love shall not be allowed to go to rack and ruin. That your grandchildren shall learn to laugh and dance here. The old title is extinct but *your* graciousness, *your* tenderness, we will all remember. Vivian, poor madman, we must learn to forget! — ”

Somebody knocked on the door. As Charlotte said, "Come in", a little crowd of her servants, headed by Mrs. MacDougal, filed in. They stood there. Mrs. Snook, the cook, looking red and anxious. The butler — Lucy the housemaid — and other familiar faces. They formed a little circle around her. One by one they bowed or bobbed. Then Mrs. MacDougal, with her soft Scots burr, said:

"Begging your pardon, my lady, we have all come to offer our sincere condolences in your ladyship's grief and — *ahem*" — she coughed — "we know now about Mr. Volpo's confession, my lady. We want, one and all, to state our righteous indignation at the undeserved misery which his wickedness caused our kind and gentle mistress."

Mrs. Mac broke off with another cough. The servants nodded at each other and smiled at Charlotte. She sat before them looking very white and shadowy-eyed and a little dazed. All strength, all buoyancy, seemed to have left her. She was obviously so deeply moved that she could not speak for a moment. Two tears gathered in her eyes. In a strangled voice she said:

"I thank you all — from the bottom of my heart."

They tip-toed out of the morning-room again, as though they wished to leave her undisturbed.

"That is one of the nicest things that has ever happened to me," Charlotte whispered to herself.

But that apology from the staff, the awkward but kindly suggestion that all was now understood, and that her name had been completely cleared, was only the beginning of others. Letters of understanding, of condolence, couched in conventional terms and hinting secret sympathy, poured into Clunes from all parts of England. The hand of friendship was rapidly extended to Lord Chase's widow and to the new Lord St. Cheviot. In itself, the discovery of the Baron was one of the most romantic and dramatic events that had taken place for a long time. The full story of the boy whom the Englesbys had adopted, swept like wild-fire through the country.

Within a few short weeks, Dominic St. Cheviot and Charlotte Chase became hero and heroine of a tremendously stirring drama. Those who had not bothered before hastened to call at Clunes, to send flowers, and drop cards, and issue invitations. But Charlotte's one wish was to get away — to hide from the world. There were only a few letters of sympathy and friendship which she really valued. One was from Dominic's adoptive mother, the fine old lady who had not long to live. She wrote to Charlotte immediately after Vivian Chase had been laid to rest in the family crypt at Harling.

I know all from Dominic, and of his high regard for you. You must have suffered very greatly, my poor child. There is not much time left to me — but perhaps if I last awhile longer Dominic will bring you down to Englesby Castle.

I know that he loves you and I would like to look upon your face before I die.

Dominic has been as dear to me in this life as my own son. The affection between us is not changed by the knowledge that his own mother still lives. But the Marquess and I both are glad that his true name and rightful heritage have been restored to him.

Charlotte showed that letter to Dominic about a month after Vivian's funeral. They were sitting together in the drawing-room at Pillars.

Clunes was shut. Charlotte and her children had come to stay with Dominic's mother. Later they intended to take a house at Trouville where the children would get sea-air, and Charlotte a complete change. Fleur and Peveril were going with them — their first holiday away from their beloved Pillars for many long years. Fleur's physician had said that it would do neither of them any harm. They both suffered from a rheumatic condition and it would be beneficial for them to get away from the low-lying Essex country.

Dominic would, of course, go over to France to see them. But most of his time must be spent in Buckinghamshire. There was a number of legal formalities to go through connected with the late Baron's possessions. Dominic was engrossed now in the business side of his inheritance. He had put politics completely behind him.

"All I want," he said, "is to make the new Cadlington a home worthy of you and the three little girls who are to be my stepdaughters."

This morning, as Dominic read his adoptive mother's letter to Charlotte, he felt a pleasurable thrill. The shadows were, indeed, lifting. There seemed no barrier now to the greatest joy of all — his marriage with Charlotte. She stood by one of the tall windows with the sunlight falling upon her, looking a little thinner and older in her black dress which was relieved only by a white frill at her throat and wrists. But there was peace in her eyes, those lovely eyes in which, far too often, he had read fathomless sorrow.

"Shall you come with me to Englesby before you go to Trouville?" he asked her.

She looked up at the fine face of the man whom she worshipped.

"I would like to, Dom."

She often used this foreshortening of his name now. It reminded him, he told her laughingly, of his boyhood. They always called him 'Dom' at Englesby.

She held out both hands to him. He took them fast.

"Sometimes I wake up and ask myself if it is true that life can have changed for me so blissfully," she said. "Am I really that same Charlotte who dared not speak your name — who hardly dared think of you?"

He put his lips against the slender fingers, kissing each one in turn.

"My dearest, try to feel as I do that your past life was a nightmare, and that like all nightmares, it has vanished upon awakening, and will never return."

They stood a moment with their arms about each other. Through the window Charlotte could see her three little girls playing croquet with Gertrude — dear devoted Gertrude who had rushed most willingly back to serve her mistress.

Since Vivian's death, Eleanora had put

on weight. How well she looked, thought the mother. And it was a great joy to her to see, also, that her two younger children were gradually thawing in the sunshine and warmth of the love she extended to them. They were learning not to snap and quarrel or look at life in the cold, self-seeking fashion their Papa and former nurse had encouraged. Today, it was not only Eleanora, but also Beatrice and Victoria who called eagerly for 'Mama' and ran to her loving arms.

Dominic said:

"It is a beautiful day, my dearest. Shall I drive you and the children to the forest for a picnic. Would you like that?"

Charlotte laughed. He liked to hear Charlotte laugh — it was a new and delightful habit she was forming.

"I haven't had a picnic for so very long! I think it's a charming idea," she said.

Fleur opened the drawing-room door and put in her pretty head.

"My dears, Peveril is taking me for a turn down by the lake. Is there anything you want?"

Dominic, still holding Charlotte's hand, turned to her.

"Nothing, Mother, we are planning a picnic with the children because the sun is so warm and it will do them all good to be out."

"Splendid," said Fleur. "I will call Gertrude and tell her."

And the beautiful little old lady went out smiling, well satisfied. She felt that she had never seen a happier and more handsome couple than her wonderful son and his future wife.

Yet again, she thought, fortune was smiling upon Pillars. Here, her own parents Hélène and Harry Roddney had lived and loved. Here, she, Fleur, with her dear Peveril had reached the fulfilment of her dreams. And now the third generation — Dominic, her son — and Charlotte Chase were soon to solve the problem of life together.

"God is good," said Fleur Marsh as she walked slowly out upon the velvety lawn to join the children. They rushed eagerly towards her. Already they were beginning to feel that she was, virtually, their grandmother.

Once Fleur had thought she needed no happiness save that which she had gained with her husband. But now she had her son. And she could see into the not too distant future when she would also have a lovely and devoted daughter-in-law.

"God is good," said Fleur Marsh again, and opened her arms to receive Charlotte's three little girls.

THE END

TO FIGHT THE WILD
Rod Ansell and Rachel Percy

Lost in uncharted Australian bush, Rod Ansell survived by hunting and trapping wild animals, improvising shelter and using all the bushman's skills he knew.

COROMANDEL
Pat Barr

India in the 1830s is a hot, uncomfortable place, where the East India Company still rules. Amelia and her new husband find themselves caught up in the animosities which seethe between the old order and the new.

THE SMALL PARTY
Lillian Beckwith

A frightening journey to safety begins for Ruth and her small party as their island is caught up in the dangers of armed insurrection.

THE WILDERNESS WALK
Sheila Bishop

Stifling unpleasant memories of a misbegotten romance in Cleave with Lord Francis Aubrey, Lavinia goes on holiday there with her sister. The two women are thrust into a romantic intrigue involving none other than Lord Francis.

THE RELUCTANT GUEST
Rosalind Brett

Ann Calvert went to spend a month on a South African farm with Theo Borland and his sister. They both proved to be different from her first idea of them, and there was Storr Peterson — the most disturbing man she had ever met.

ONE ENCHANTED SUMMER
Anne Tedlock Brooks

A tale of mystery and romance and a girl who found both during one enchanted summer.

CLOUD OVER MALVERTON
Nancy Buckingham

Dulcie soon realises that something is seriously wrong at Malverton, and when violence strikes she is horrified to find herself under suspicion of murder.

AFTER THOUGHTS
Max Bygraves

The Cockney entertainer tells stories of his East End childhood, of his RAF days, and his post-war showbusiness successes and friendships with fellow comedians.

MOONLIGHT
AND MARCH ROSES
D. Y. Cameron

Lynn's search to trace a missing girl takes her to Spain, where she meets Clive Hendon. While untangling the situation, she untangles her emotions and decides on her own future.